FORGED IN BATTLE

BOOKS BY MARC ALAN EDELHEIT

GUARDIANS OF THE DARK
Off Midway Station

FANTASY

THE STIGER CHRONICLES
Book One: Stiger's Tigers
Book Two: The Tiger
Book Three: The Tiger's Fate
Book Four: The Tiger's Time
Book Five: The Tiger's Wrath
Book Six: The Tiger's Imperium
Book Seven: The Tiger's Fight
Book Eight: The Tiger's Rage

STIGER: TALES OF THE SEVENTH
Book One: Stiger
Book Two: Fort Covenant
Book Three: A Dark Foretoken

THE KARUS SAGA
Book One: Lost Legio IX
Book Two: Fortress of Radiance
Book Three: The First Compact
Book Four: Rapax Pax

The Eli Chronicles

Book One: Eli

Book Two: By Bow, Daggers & Sword

Book Three: Lutha Nyx

The Way of Legend: With Quincy J. Allen

Book One: Reclaiming Honor

Book Two: Forging Destiny

Book Three: Paladin's Light

The Claimed Realm

Book 1: Legacy's Edge

SCI-FI

Born of Ash

Book One: Fallen Empire

Book Two: Infinity Control

NONFICTION

Every Writer's Dream: The Insider's Path to an Indie Bestseller

FORGED IN BATTLE

MARC ALAN EDELHEIT

SECOND SKY

Published by Second Sky in 2025

An imprint of Storyfire Ltd.
Carmelite House
50 Victoria Embankment
London EC4Y 0DZ

www.secondskybooks.com

The authorised representative in the EEA is Hachette Ireland
8 Castlecourt Centre
Dublin 15 D15 XTP3
Ireland
(email: info@hbgi.ie)

ISBN: 978-1-80550-168-8
eBook ISBN: 978-1-80550-167-1

ONE

"Captain, we are in the designated parking orbit over Tenebris," Lieutenant Connor Hale reported. "Station-keeping protocols engaged—gravitic drive is on cooldown. Atheena is now monitoring."

"I am on it," Atheena, the ship's constructed artificial intelligence, reported. Her calm and steady voice seemed to come from all around them.

"Very good," Captain Jaxon Steele replied, his gaze shifting down to the HTD—the holographic tactical display—that floated before him on one of the many screens located around his command station. Steele studied the shifting icons and faint outlines that represented the ships sharing the orbital space around Illidra V, or as the locals called it, Tenebris. The planet had been named after one of the original settlers.

The display marked out and identified dozens of other vessels, from cargo haulers to mining rigs, freighters and personnel transports, all slotted into their designated positions around the cold, desolate planet. Hundreds of planet-to-orbit shuttles and freight haulers were in motion. That did not include the craft flitting about from one point of Tenebris to another. To many, it would be an impressive display of organization by traffic control, but this planet was a veritable backwater, and the movement on the displays before him was nothing Steele hadn't seen before.

Tenebris was a dwarf planet, situated roughly fifteen astronomical units from Illidran's dying star, a G-type main-sequence sun whose pale light was faint at this distance, casting the planet in a shadowy half-glow. Its dark, barren surface was scarred by ancient craters and dotted with industrial outposts that clung to the landscape like stubborn barnacles. Tenebris was a world of black rock and bitter cold, with an atmosphere so thin it was barely worth mentioning. Its inhabitants could not go outside without specialized breathing equipment and cold-weather survival gear. To do otherwise was to court death.

To Steele, Tenebris seemed a gloomy ball of ice and stone drifting on the edge of a decaying solar system. He could scarcely imagine what kind of life one could eke out on such a forsaken rock—yet, somehow, for centuries, millions of people had called the place home, their cities and habitats built deep underground or within vast, enclosed domes that dotted the surface.

With a quick motion, Steele widened the view on the HTD, allowing the tactical display to expand and encompass the entirety of the Illidran Star System. The display reshaped itself, bringing the system into full view. Five planets orbited the fading star, their trajectories traced out in fine lines of light.

The system's main asteroid belts, known as the Shattered Reach and the Periphery, were dense and crowded with mining operations, resource haulers, speculators, and more—pirates and smugglers, not to mention illegal habitats and settlements.

Illidran was part of the Protectorate, a patch of space seized by the Union after the last war with the Valkorian Hegemony, one of the Union's more disreputable neighbors. Despite claiming the region, which encompassed four settled star systems, the Union had stopped short of fully integrating the Protectorate. The only way that would happen was if the people of the Protectorate voted for it, and Steele could not see them doing that anytime soon. The disparate peoples that called this stretch of space home disliked the Union almost as much as they hated each other.

So, instead, the Protectorate had become a sort of buffer zone between the Union and the Valkorian Hegemony and operated under a complex arrangement of limited autonomy, each system governed by its own elected representatives and local administration but overseen by a Union-appointed governor.

Steele studied the HTD for a long moment. Thousands of starships and smaller intersystem craft crisscrossed the system, arriving and departing from trade hubs, industrial stations, and orbital habitats. Cargo ships ferried goods between the planets and the asteroid belts. The traffic lanes were crowded with vessels of every size and type, from massive freighters and mobile mining and refinery platforms to agile shuttles and various other craft, each with its own purpose, its own destination. The system's space lanes pulsed with activity, as though clinging to life even as the star itself dimmed, slowly succumbing to the ravages of time.

Steele shifted his focus and brought the tactical display back, narrowing his attention to the space immediately around Tenebris. *Ranger*'s systems showed the planet's artificial satellite network—a cluttered web of old and ancient stations, communications relays, orbital habitats, and defensive platforms.

For all its gloom, the world below was a vital part of the system's industrial backbone. Yet, as Steele studied the display, he couldn't shake the feeling that living out here was a precarious existence, one dependent on the Union's largess and military support.

"Captain." Lieutenant Mia Calder turned slightly in her chair to glance back at Steele. Her dark hair was pinned back in a tidy bun, revealing the calm focus in her green eyes. "Traffic control welcomes us and has authorized our shuttle drop directly down to Malborne Industries. A delegation will be waiting for the envoy at the corporation's spaceport."

"Very good," Steele replied, his voice steady as he glanced once more at the HTD, verifying what she'd just told him. He could see the path traffic control had cleared for the shuttle's descent, a narrow corridor between civilian traffic. "Let's get this show on the road. Launch the shuttle. The quicker this business is finished, the sooner we can get moving and be on our way."

"Yes, sir," Calder responded crisply, swiveling back to her station, her voice calm and efficient as she relayed the orders down to the shuttle pilot, along with the flight path they were to follow. Her fingers danced over the console, bringing up the shuttle bay interface. She initiated the launch sequence, coordinating with the flight deck. "Shuttle is prepped and launching."

Ranger's internal sensors registered a brief pulse of energy as the shuttle's engines flared to life, and the HTD updated to show the small craft departing from the ship's ventral hangar bay. On the display, the shuttle appeared as a glowing icon rapidly descending toward Tenebris, following the designated drop path.

Steele watched the icon move steadily downward, a thin thread of data trailing behind it as altitude and trajectory readings updated in real time. His thoughts drifted to Malborne Industries, one of Tenebris's larger industrial firms, one tied closely to the Union's military. He had been briefed on the assignment: transport a diplomatic trade envoy, one Duncan Miller, to discuss commerce agreements and economic assistance within the Illidran Star System and, if need be, to other points within Protectorate space. At least, that was the official assignment.

Unofficially, Steele suspected, there was more at play. Malborne Industries had a reputation for secrecy. The corporation, amongst circles in Fleet, was rumored to be an Intelligence Directorate front. And with the political tensions simmering just below the surface throughout the Protectorate, he couldn't shake the feeling that the true nature of this visit might be more than simple diplomacy. But all that was above his pay grade and purely speculation.

"Shuttle is clear of the ship and on course for Malborne Industries Spaceport," Calder confirmed, glancing briefly over her shoulder at Steele. "Estimated time to arrival is thirty-two minutes."

"Good," Steele said, nodding slightly. "Keep me updated on their status. Send it to my console and make sure the envoy knows to check in once they make contact."

"Yes, sir," Calder replied and turned back to her station.

The bridge settled back into its quiet rhythm, the crew's focus returning to their respective tasks as the shuttle continued its descent, leaving *Ranger* hovering in Tenebris's cold shadow.

Steele let his gaze wander across his command deck, taking in the familiar sights and sounds of the bridge that had become routine over the last few months. The space was a carefully crafted blend of functionality and understated elegance, at least in Steele's opinion, each detail purposeful, each station positioned with the crew's roles in mind. The circular layout created a natural flow of communication and data, with stations recessed slightly into the deck to give the captain an unobstructed view of the main display, his officers, and bridge crew.

Steele's own command station was raised and surrounded by multiple screens, providing him with all the information he needed to manage the ship's systems and coordinate with the crew. Though his station afforded him a panoramic view and rotated as needed, he could feel the energy and focus of his people at their posts.

Hale, stationed at the helm, was seated slightly forward of Steele's command chair. He was tall and lean, with sandy-blond hair and a calm, easy confidence that radiated from him.

To Steele's right, Calder worked at the communications station. She was a petite woman in her early twenties. Her green eyes were bright with concentration, darting between the various displays on her console as she monitored the ship's many communication channels.

Calder's voice was a regular and steady presence on the bridge, issuing orders and relaying reports with a calm clarity that left no room for misinterpretation. With the help of Atheena, the ship's constructed intelligence, she was able to manage a web of incoming and outgoing transmissions without missing a beat. Calder's composure never wavered, even under pressure; she was a grounding presence amidst the chaos of deep-space operations.

Farther back and behind the captain, Lieutenant Zara Ishida was at the tactical station. Ishida was slightly taller than Calder, with a slim build that hinted at years of rigorous physical training and fitness. Her dark hair was braided tightly, resting against the back of her uniform, and her brown eyes moved with deliberate focus across the array of tactical displays in front of her.

The ship's weapon systems, from the maser batteries to the point-defense turrets, were monitored and managed from her station. Ishida exuded a quiet confidence that came from experience—countless drills, live-fire exercises, and combat.

To Steele's left, Ensign Rebekah Quinn manned the sensor and electronic warfare station. The youngest member of the bridge crew, Quinn had an air of enthusiasm that was hard to miss. Her auburn hair was short and slightly tousled, a reflection of her energetic personality. A recent graduate from the Academy and newly assigned to the ship, Quinn was already proving herself to be a competent and valuable member of the team. That said, she was still finding her rhythm, but the potential was undeniable, and so far, Steele was quite pleased with her performance.

Seated beside Steele at her own command station was Commander Evelyn Chase, the ship's executive officer. The XO was composed, her posture upright and her expression calm but alert. Her dark hair was cut short, framing her sharp features in a way that emphasized the steady resolve in her gray eyes. Like Steele's, Chase's station provided her with an array of displays monitoring the ship's status and operations.

There was a quiet authority in the way she held herself, a kind of effortless command presence that reassured the crew and kept them focused on their duties. Over the months since Steele had taken command of *Ranger*, he had come to rely heavily upon her.

As Steele looked over his officers, he took a small measure of satisfaction from what he saw: the quiet competence of professionals. Steele leaned back in his command chair, a subtle relaxation settling over him. He caught Chase's eye as she glanced over at him.

"The envoy took a marine escort, correct?" Steele asked.

"Miller did, sir," Chase replied, "one squad. Is this your first time back in Illidran since the war?" she asked him.

Steele resisted a frown and gave a nod. He did not have good memories of Illidran. He still occasionally suffered nightmares from those days.

"Mine too," Chase said with a far-off look as she tapped at one of her consoles and studied the output on a screen. "I was on the *James Russel.*"

Steele knew that from her record. Both of them had been at the Battle of the Reach, but on separate ships as junior officers.

Chase had also distinguished herself during that action, but the *Russel*, a battlecruiser, had been lost.

Feeling stiff, Steele stretched out his back. He addressed his executive officer. "XO, stand the crew down, with the exception of a watch in each department. We will be on green rotation until further notice. Let's see if we can give everyone a few hours of rest before we break orbit and head deeper in-system. Also send for replacements for the bridge crew."

"At least we won't be here long," Chase replied, her tone carrying a hint of relief. "Miller said he'd be planetside less than nine hours."

"That's what he said," Steele said quietly, stretching out his back again as he spoke. He felt a stab of irritation at the envoy's mission, which had abruptly diverted *Ranger* from a fleet exercise, one Steele had been looking forward to—for it would have truly tested his new ship, stretched her legs and capabilities.

Transporting an envoy was the job of a messenger packet or a light frigate—certainly not a front-line destroyer. Steele glanced back down at the shuttle track and couldn't shake the feeling that the envoy had managed to pull some significant strings to secure a ship like *Ranger* for this assignment. Still, this was the first time Steele effectively had an independent command, without a squadron commander or commodore on hand and looking over his shoulder. He was enjoying the experience.

He rubbed his jaw as he continued to follow the shuttle's track with his eyes. "Let's plan on it being somewhat longer and schedule a departure in, say, twelve hours' time. That will give everyone some time to rest."

"Yes, sir," Chase said, nodding as she made a note on her console. "I'll inform traffic control. Should I ping the other Union ships in-system and let them know we've arrived?"

Stifling a yawn that crept up on him unexpectedly, Steele gave a nod. "By god, I need coffee." He paused and stifled another yawn. "If they're paying attention to the HTD, they'll know we've arrived—but ping them just the same with my compliments. Illidran is a big system after all."

"Yes, sir." Chase began working one of the consoles at her station.

The bridge fell back into its quiet routine, punctuated only by the muted beeps from the consoles and the soft hum of the systems around them. The tactical display continued to project the slow dance of ships drifting through their assigned parking orbits, with some tagged as preparing to depart and others in motion and just arriving, while Tenebris loomed below, the planet's dark, rocky surface a distant shadow beneath them.

A quick manipulation of the HTD confirmed to Steele that three Union warships were currently in-system: the heavy cruiser *Resolute* and two frigates, the *Viper* and *Spear*. Their designations appeared in pale blue icons on the holographic display. All three ships were attached to the system defense and therefore on-station.

"Hmmm."

"What?" Chase asked, glancing over at him.

"I didn't know *Viper* was in-system," Steele said. "Her skipper, Valon, was in my Academy class. Do you know him?"

Chase shook her head. "I do not. I've never had the pleasure, sir."

"A good officer," Steele said as his eyes returned to the plot. None of the Union vessels were nearby, the closest being at least two days distant at cruising speed. Each ship, while older and perhaps past its prime, added some backbone to the Local Defense Force—the LDF—tasked with maintaining order in this remote corner of the Protectorate. The *Resolute* was currently docked at High Ring. Captain Emilia Rourke was designated as commodore, which told him she had command of all Union mobile forces in Illidran. He did not personally know her, but while he was in-system, barring his orders, she was nominally his boss.

"Send word to the *Resolute*," Steele said after some thought. "Commodore Rourke has the flag in-system. Inform her of our mission and that we'll be burning to High Ring to put in at the shipyard for reprovisioning after we drop Miller off at Yarith."

"*Ranger* is the newest ship in the fleet," Chase replied with a sidelong glance at her commanding officer. "They've all likely been stuck on-station for months. Illidran isn't really a prime posting. You know Rourke and her senior officers are going to want tours. We might as well host a proper dinner, get it all done in one evening and then have it out of the way."

"A formal?" Steele felt sour at that. He hated formal dinners and receptions. They took away from his duties and were a distraction. Ever since he'd taken command of *Ranger*, three months before, there had been too many of them.

"Yes, sir, another formal."

After a moment, Steele nodded his agreement. Chase was right; *Ranger* was not only the first of her class, but also the cutting edge of Union ship design—a product of lessons learned, post-war technology, and innovation. With her advanced systems, gravitic drive, and powerful stealth capabilities, *Ranger* represented a new era of starship design, the very zenith of Union shipbuilding technology.

Getting the top job on *Ranger* had ruffled feathers and generated resentment amongst his peers, for Steele had been jumped ahead of others with greater seniority and experience. It was one of the reasons he had worked so hard to stand up his new command... to prove he was worthy. He was determined that no one would find fault with *Ranger*.

Thinking some more of those officers stationed on garrison duty here in-system, he could already imagine the eagerness to inspect *Ranger*'s bridge, her systems and engineering decks, comparing them with their own. "Good thinking, Chase. See to it. Let's make it an official invite for senior officers only. We can set up a buffet in one of the boat bays where there is plenty of room for that sort of thing."

Chase nodded, making a quick notation on her console. "What about the LDF?" she asked, her tone cautious as she glanced back over at him.

"What about them?"

"Do you want to issue an invitation to any of their senior officers? I'm sure they'd be just as interested in seeing what the Union is fielding these days."

Steele considered it for a moment, but the thought of local Protectorate officers probing around his brand-new destroyer didn't sit well, especially after the war, even if it had been a decade before. Many of those officers had fought for the other side, and though they now professed their loyalty to the Union, he, like many in the navy, still had his doubts about their reliability.

The Union's presence in the Protectorate was already delicate, and inviting LDF officers aboard a vessel like *Ranger* could send mixed signals, implying more openness than Fleet Command was comfortable with. There was real danger that the admiralty would frown upon such an invitation.

"No," he said finally. "Union personnel only. With any luck, Duncan will wrap up his business quick and we won't be in Illidran long."

"That's going to upset some," Chase said, arching a brow but keeping her tone neutral.

Steele's lips curled into a half-smile. "I know it."

"Rourke may have questions."

"I understand," Steele said. "I'll handle that if it becomes a problem."

"Aye, sir," Chase replied.

Steele stretched again. He'd been at his station for far too long. He wanted to get in some exercise in the ship's gym, to work out the stiffness and then catch a nap, but he didn't have time for that. He had administrative work to attend to before granting himself any personal time.

"XO, you have the bridge." Steele stood, pulling himself up from his station.

"I have the bridge, sir," Chase responded, settling into command with a practiced confidence. "If it's agreeable, I'll set a four-hour standing bridge watch."

"Good," Steele said. "I will take third watch."

He made his way toward his cabin. As Steele approached the hatch, he noted the armed marine stationed beside it, her stance rigid as she came to attention. Her dark uniform was spotless, and her gaze remained fixed ahead, a model of discipline.

Pausing briefly at the threshold, Steele turned back. "Chase, since we're here for a few hours, pick a local transport that's either arriving or departing. Let's run a snap inspection on her—see if we can catch some contraband slipping through customs. A boarding action will be good practice for our marines."

"Yes, sir," Chase replied, her expression sharpening at the prospect. "I'll alert Lieutenant Knox to get his marines ready and have our assault shuttle prepped."

"Very good." With a brief nod, Steele turned back to his cabin hatch, which hissed open in response to his approach. As he stepped through, the hatch slid shut behind him, sealing him away from the hum and rhythm of the bridge.

Steele's office was a sanctuary amidst the chaos of space, a place where function met a touch of luxury—a rare combination on a warship and a perk of command. The office was spacious for a ship of this class, with walls paneled in a dark, matte finish that absorbed the ambient lighting, giving the compartment a cozy, intimate feel. The space held a quiet elegance, marked by a few personal touches that reflected the character of the man who commanded *Ranger*.

Directly behind his desk hung a framed photograph of his parents. His mother's warm smile and his father's steady gaze seemed to anchor him, a reminder of the life he had left behind, a door that was now forever closed, and the values that had shaped him. Next to it hung a plaque engraved with his Master and Commander Certificate, along with a few others that spoke of his career path and accomplishments since joining the navy, each one earned through years of service and a couple the hard way.

That included his Navy Cross.

The desk itself was a sleek, modern piece of dark metal and composite materials, with a surface that gleamed faintly under the soft lighting. Steele preferred a clear workspace, finding clutter a distraction. Only the essentials remained: a terminal, a few data tablets, and a small collection of neatly arranged physical reports. To the left lay a polished brass paperweight engraved with *Ranger*'s emblem, anchoring a few documents.

To his right, on a low side table, rested a finely crafted model of *Ranger*. The scale replica had been a gift from the shipyard upon the vessel's commissioning, and it was beautifully detailed.

Across from the desk were two padded chairs upholstered in a dark, understated fabric that matched the decor. Positioned in front of the desk, they were ready to seat anyone needing a private word with the captain—from his officers to visiting dignitaries. In the far corner of the office stood a larger table meant for meetings. Four chairs surrounded the table, providing a space where Steele could gather his senior staff for briefings.

Resting on the table was an old-style leather-bound book. *Command Decisions*, by Admiral Stein. He had picked the tome up on his last visit to StarCom One, Fleet Headquarters' library in the Myridorn Star System. The book was pre-Union and several hundred years old, but the premise was still valid, at least in Steele's eyes.

The book was a study on celebrated starship captains of the time and focused on individual tactics they had taken to win or survive difficult situations. Steele was finding it fascinating reading, for he loved strategy. Whenever free time was available, which was rare, he had his nose in a book or a reader.

One day, would others be reading about his tactics, his decisions?

The night before, he'd just finished a chapter about Captain Jabob Thomas. That captain, commanding a destroyer, had found himself ambushed and not only outnumbered, but alone... facing three enemy destroyers in a long-range missile duel.

In a moment of desperation, Thomas had taken the unusual step of ordering his main maser cannons be trained on incoming enemy missiles, something they were not designed to do, let alone track. The tactic had added to his point-defense fire and surprisingly had worked, in the end, saving his ship.

Steele turned away from the table and the book. The hatch to his left led to his cabin. Behind him, the hatch that led to the bridge was a constant reminder that even in the relative privacy of his office, the ship's heartbeat was just a few steps away. The bridge was always present in his mind—a pulse of activity, readiness, and coordination. Steele found a certain comfort in that closeness, knowing he was always near *Ranger*'s core, never far from where he was needed most.

"Atheena, coffee, the usual."

"Coffee, black, two sugars," the construct replied.

A hidden panel on the wall to his left slid aside a heartbeat later, revealing a mug of steaming coffee. Steele stepped over and took it in hand. Moving to his desk, he picked up a tablet, its surface lighting up at his touch. He'd been on duty for more than ten hours for the final approach to Tenebris, for he had turned it into a training exercise for the crew. They had come in under stealth, ghosting past system traffic without anyone being the wiser, essentially sneaking through the detection and defense network. They'd only revealed themselves to traffic control within the last half-hour as they closed in on the planet. He was sure he'd shocked the hell out of the locals: a warship, albeit a friendly one, suddenly appearing out of nowhere.

Stifling another yawn, he took a sip of the steaming coffee and then set the mug down upon the desk. He considered the hatch to his cabin and personal quarters, briefly entertaining the idea of a quick meal and nap, but dismissed it just as quickly. There was much to do, and the thought of unfinished tasks made rest feel somehow impossible.

He thumbed the tablet on, and as expected, several reports awaited his attention. Personnel updates, logistical requests, status reports, and a handful of strategic analyses from Fleet— each one requiring careful review. Balancing his administrative responsibilities, he knew, was the undercurrent of command, essential to the ship's seamless function. It was better to handle them now than let them pile up.

Cracking his neck and preparing to settle in, Steele moved his gaze to the model of *Ranger*. It was a masterpiece of craftsmanship, a precise miniature replica that captured every detail of the real ship in flawless scale. As he studied it, he noted the sleek, angular lines of the hull—the narrow, elongated shape that gave *Ranger* her predatory appearance.

She was a beautiful ship.

Designed for speed and agility, the model's fine, textured finish mimicked the adaptive stealth plating that cloaked the real vessel, allowing it to absorb sensor scans and blend into the darkness of space with a ghostly effectiveness. The rear of the model showcased the four recessed thruster pods that made up the gravitic drive. They were arranged in a tight rectangular formation, a layout that minimized the ship's thermal signature.

Tiny maneuvering thrusters dotted the sides of the hull, all nearly invisible to the naked eye but essential for *Ranger*'s quick course adjustments and fluid handling in the vacuum of space.

The bridge blister was seamlessly integrated into the forward upper hull, heavily armored and shielded behind layers of reinforced hull plating. Along the spine of the model, retractable weapon ports were represented by sleek armored panels. These would slide back to reveal the maser batteries and missile launchers when the ship was ready to unleash her firepower. Just beneath the bridge, the two forward-facing torpedo tubes were subtly recessed, a mark of the ship's lethal capabilities, for torpedoes were typically only carried on larger ships, vessels of the line. Strategically placed across the hull were also retractable point-defense turrets, appearing as minuscule guns on the model but essential to fending off and defeating close-range threats, like enemy missiles or smaller attack craft.

The model also depicted the sensor and electronic warfare arrays, skillfully integrated along the ship's silhouette. In reality, these arrays remained concealed behind stealth panels, extending only when high-sensitivity scans or electronic countermeasures were necessary. Even the orbital dart launcher ports were visible in the model's underside, their housings flush with the hull to maintain the ship's stealth profile.

The engraved plaque on the base read simply, "DD-219 *Ranger*," understated for a vessel with so much hidden power and potential. To Steele, the model wasn't just a technical representation; it embodied the ship's purpose. *Ranger* was a weapon of war, yes, but also a guardian—a shield against the darkness and the barbarians beyond his nation's borders.

Letting out a breath, he returned his focus to the tablet on his desk, where the first item was an engineering report awaiting his review and response. He slid into his chair. He'd delayed long enough. It was time to get some work done.

TWO

A soft chime resonated through the quiet of Steele's office, pulling his attention from the report he'd been reviewing. He glanced up, momentarily disoriented. He'd been buried in administrative paperwork and reports for some time.

"What is it, Atheena?"

"I apologize for the interruption, Captain," Atheena announced in a composed, neutral tone that carried no hint of impatience, let alone urgency. The construct was omnipresent on *Ranger*, a background intelligence that managed and automated countless tasks. "A private call from UNS *Viper Actual* has come in for you over the FTL network. Do you wish to take Captain Valon's call?"

Steele leaned back in his chair, setting the tablet down with a quiet clink. His neck protested as he stretched, the stiffness a reminder of how long he'd been hunched over reports. The one before him was a fitness evaluation penned by Chase, highlighting a crew member she believed was ready for promotion—ready to take the qualification tests, a decision Steele knew would require careful thought.

"What time is it?" he asked, feeling the fatigue of a long day.

"22:46," Atheena replied smoothly, her disembodied presence as efficient as always.

He rubbed at his tired eyes, the weariness settling in as he realized he had been lost in administrative minutiae for over two hours since leaving the bridge. The half-empty mug of coffee on his desk had gone stone-cold.

"The captain of the *Viper* is still waiting. Should I accept the call?"

"Yes, Atheena. Put him through."

The room's ambient lighting dimmed slightly, a visual cue signaling the transition as the call connected. On the opposite wall, a holographic image flickered to life, resolving into the familiar figure of Commander Aric Valon, Steele's Academy mate and, more importantly, an old and good friend.

Standing, Steele walked around his desk before the display, feeling a rush of familiarity. Like his, Valon's office was dimly lit, a reflection of the late hour, but the image was fully illuminated, enhanced by AI.

Valon's short-cropped brown hair had a few more streaks of gray than Steele remembered, and his features seemed even more severe—his hard eyes spoke of countless challenges faced over the years. The right side of his face bore a series of deep scars, the result of exposure to vacuum, a reminder of the dangers inherent in their line of work. Steele also knew his friend had burns across a quarter of his body, a result of the war.

"Jax," Valon greeted him with a grin. "It's been far too long."

"It's been what," Steele said, tilting his head slightly, "five years, maybe a little longer?"

"I think so... Admiral Detan's retirement party on Kalendra is the last time we saw each other," Valon confirmed, a hint of nostalgia breaking through his otherwise hardened demeanor. "I always liked her."

"That was a good party," Steele said, thinking back.

"It was," Valon agreed with a faint smile.

"Time flies. It seems like it happened just yesterday," Steele replied, but his attention was suddenly drawn to the flickering image before him. The holographic transmission wavered, and there was a subtle graininess to the picture—a rare occurrence when it came to communications like this one. He frowned as the distortion grew more pronounced. "I think we have a bad connection."

"It's the solar rejuvenator." Valon's expression soured as the image quality worsened for several seconds. Jagged lines of interference crackled across the projection before stabilizing somewhat, though the image was still grainy. "They're doing something that's messing with communications system-wide. We received a heads-up yesterday that there was a problem, that once again they'd done something they shouldn't or miscalculated... something like that."

"The solar rejuvenator?" Steele repeated, thinking back to what he knew of the system. "What sort of problem? What did they do? Do you know?"

"The idiots running the project have caused some sort of issue," Valon said, frustration plain in his tone. "This isn't the first time either. It's becoming a regular occurrence. Apparently, they've destabilized something in the core, and now the sun's flaring more violently than it should be. It's fried lesser-protected networks and electronics deeper into the system, closer to the star, and dorked with the HTD. To say it's thrown traffic control into chaos is an understatement. We've been dealing with all kinds of disruptions and headaches as a result." He leaned forward, and the holographic distortion wavered again, making his scars seem to pulse with the flickering light. "I'm told it should resolve itself within the next twelve hours, but it's a damn mess right now."

Steele's frown deepened, and he crossed his arms. An issue with the solar rejuvenator project was clearly more than a minor inconvenience. Illidran's star was already unstable, teetering on the edge of a critical phase-shift in its stellar lifecycle.

The rejuvenator was an ambitious and experimental project, backed heavily by Union funding. Colossal in both concept and execution, it sought to counteract the star's decline by using controlled fusion injections. Gigantic magnetic scoops harvested hydrogen and other pertinent gases from Illidran's outer gas giants, funneling the raw material into the core of the star, where it would be compressed under extreme pressure. The hope was to reenergize the star's fusion processes, delaying the onset of further instability and restoring its energy output. At least, that was the idea.

Steele hadn't read extensively about the actual mechanics, but he understood the broad strokes: by carefully managing fusion rates and reinforcing the star's magnetic field, the scientists aimed to dampen dangerous fluctuations. It was a gamble, to say the least, and one that had drawn both skepticism and awe across the scientific community. From the problems he was hearing about, it was clear the science wasn't perfected.

"How's *Viper*?" Steele asked, steering the conversation toward something more familiar. They traded notes a couple of times a year, but beyond that had not spoken much since Detan's party. He'd heard Valon had gotten command of *Viper* over a year ago, but not much more than that.

Valon's face brightened, a proud smile breaking the sternness of his scarred features. "*Viper*'s a good, solid ship," he said, his voice filled with genuine affection. "She's built well and has good bones. Sure, she's older, but she's fast and nimble. We've had to work around some quirks and design issues with some of the upgrades she's received, but I've got a crew that keeps her running at peak performance. In truth, I love the little bitch."

"That's good to hear. I feel the same way about my ship."

"Sometimes I miss being back in Union space," Valon continued, "where things are more predictable, but out here? Every day is different. You never know what exactly you will encounter or have to deal with." His expression turned wistful, the excitement of command shining through. "I tell you, it's—" The image froze, and the audio cut out, leaving a few seconds of static-filled silence.

Steele frowned and waited for the image to solidify again. "I lost you there for a moment."

Valon cursed under his breath. "Damn rejuvenator," he muttered. "It's messing with everything. Anyway, I hear you're putting into High Ring. I might try to meet you there. In fact, I am going to do all I can to make that happen."

"Good, because that's the plan. We should be arriving in about two days, maybe a little longer. We need to reprovision, and I was thinking of giving the crew some shore leave. It's been a long haul for everyone just to get out here and into Protectorate space."

"I think I can convince the commodore to cut our patrol short. If she proves difficult, I may have to come up with some issue for the yard dogs to look at."

"Don't get yourself into trouble on my account," Steele said.

"I can get myself into trouble easily enough and regularly do with the commodore. Oh, and I've got an unopened bottle of Vanderman bourbon I've been saving. A reunion would be the perfect occasion to open it."

Steele's eyebrows shot up. "Vanderman? That stuff's practically a legend, brewed halfway across the galaxy on Old Earth, if I recall correctly."

"You're not wrong."

"Where in the void did you manage to get your hands on a bottle? It probably costs more than your entire annual salary. I've never even tried the stuff. It's too rich for my blood."

Valon's grin widened, a hint of mischief in his eyes. "A few weeks back, we found and neutralized a pirate base hidden in one of the belts," he said with a casual shrug. "During a more detailed sweep and accounting of the contents of the base, I may or may not have 'liberated' it from their leader's personal liquor stash. What can I say—the spoils of war. So, what do you think? Up for a drink and some real catching up? I can't think of a better person to share a bottle of contraband with."

Steele let out a genuine laugh, the weariness of the day momentarily lifting.

"I'll want a tour of that ship of yours," Valon said, a glint of interest in his hard eyes. "Some Vanderman in exchange for a personal tour. How does that sound?"

"I think I can manage that," Steele replied with a nod.

"It's a deal, then," Valon said, but the humor quickly faded from his expression. "So, how's your first command treating you?"

"*Ranger*'s more work than I imagined," he admitted, feeling the strain of the past weeks pressing on his shoulders. "Aric, I tell you, she's something special. I am loving it, truly."

"She's definitely something," Valon agreed. "I've read all about her—at least the unclassified bits. You are one fortunate bastard... you know that, right?"

Steele resisted a scowl. "I don't know about that. It took weeks to work out all the problems, the kind of headaches that come with a new class of ship."

"I do," Valon said confidently. "Only the best of the best are considered for commands like yours, the first real new design out of the yards since the war... Face it, your star is rising, my friend. Everyone can see that."

Steele did not reply. His mentor, Admiral Simms, had told him the same the day he assumed command of *Ranger*. Not everyone in Fleet was as encouraging as his friend. There had been many others who'd been jealous and resentful that a junior officer had got command of such a new and revolutionary ship. Steele keenly understood he had something to prove. It was one of the reasons he worked his crew hard and himself harder.

"You may not have finished first in our class, but back at the Academy, you beat everyone at the strategy games, the ones that mattered. You—" The transmission stuttered, and the image froze, Valon's face caught in a moment of motion before the signal steadied once more. "Damn it. These communication issues are becoming a right pain in my ass. I tried reaching the commodore earlier today, and we managed three words before the line went dead and the transmission was severed. It's really becoming frustrating. Whenever it happens it's giving the pirates and smugglers free rein, because the HTD net goes down over much of the system, especially the closer you get to the star."

"That's not good," Steele said.

"No, it is not." Valon's voice lowered, almost conspiratorially, a seriousness settling in. "Jax, when you get to High Ring, I advise caution about letting your people wander beyond the Union-controlled areas of the station or, for that matter, letting them down to the planet."

Steele's eyes narrowed. He did not like the sound of that. He'd read the security brief Fleet Intel had provided about Illidran but suddenly had the feeling it was not as comprehensive as it could have been. He made a mental note to spend some time reviewing the latest dispatches on the security situation here in-system. "I take it there've been problems?"

"Of late, more than usual." A frown deepened the lines on Valon's face. "The locals are restless, and tensions are boiling over. There've been multiple riots in the last few weeks, nasty stuff all around, all kinds of factions vying for control."

"The Hegemony's work?" Steele asked. "Are they stirring things up?"

Valon gave a shrug. "The latest brief from Fleet Intel thinks it possible, but who knows? They don't have any proof, and if they do, they're not sharing. Bottom line, this system is a powder keg. So many factions are pissed off at each other—half the time it's hard to tell who's on whose side. There are days I wonder why we bothered taking the Protectorate. The place has always been a shithole, the locals no better than animals. But if there's one thing they all agree on, it's hating the Union." Valon paused. "Maybe it is the Valkorian Hegemony. Despite losing serious face when we took the Protectorate, they're still pretty popular here."

"I have no idea why. I mean, why would they want a theocratic overlord back and in power, one that is more of a police state than anything else?" Steele said. "The Hegemony shoves their religion down everyone's throat, at least those they lord over. Hell, the first thing the locals did when we took the Protectorate was murder all the Hegemony priests and those who had converted, along with the collaborators. It took the army weeks to end the hunts, the bloodshed and reprisals."

"It really does not make any sense. But then again, we don't think like the locals."

"Agreed. It doesn't have to make sense to us," Steele said.

"No, it doesn't. There's no doubt the Hegemony want the Protectorate back. Then again, it might just be the locals who just want us out so they can happily murder each other without restraint. When they were in power, the Hegemony never really stopped them from doing that sort of thing. I don't think they cared, as long as the taxes were paid."

"What about the new governor?" Steele asked. "There were hopes back home that, with the recall of the old governor, Tancrest would help mollify the locals, smooth things over, keep a lid on things. I thought she was somewhat popular out here."

"She's trying and she is popular with some of the factions, but the Union's not exactly fashionable at the moment, if you take my meaning. They blame us for all of their problems, especially when it comes to the megacorps that moved in and set up shop after the war."

"I see," Steele said.

"I met Tancrest the other day," Valon said. "We gave her a ride out to an orbital habitat. She's currently touring the system... right now one of the belts, showing the flag to those who still support the Union, shaking hands and kissing babies, assuring them we are here to stay, to guarantee their security. We handed her off to a transport more suited to work in a belt, then moved on to our regular patrol duties."

"What were your impressions?"

"Of the governor?"

Steele gave a nod.

Valon thought for a long moment. "She's the real deal, genuine, smart, passionate. I liked her dog. I just don't know if she can make a difference... Many feel they are being exploited."

"Are they exploited?" Steele asked, curious.

"Honestly, I don't know," Valon said. "And if they are, at least it's to a lesser degree than the Hegemony was exploiting them..." The skipper of the *Viper* paused. "Either way, look out for your crew when you get to High Ring, okay? It can be hard to tell the good guys from the bad."

Steele absorbed the warning, nodding thoughtfully. "Thanks for the heads-up. When we dock, I'll speak to station security to get a better sense of the situation. If it doesn't feel safe, I'll keep my crew shipboard."

Valon's expression was grim. "Regardless of what they say, that might be the wisest course of action. I've not let my people off the ship in weeks."

"Mine won't be happy with that, losing their chance to get off the ship and get in some liberty."

"There have been kidnappings lately. Union personnel

groundside—aid workers, station staff. They disappear and no one has been able to find them. I think—"

The image wavered violently, lines of static crackling across the screen, before freezing entirely. The screen went dark. Steele let go an unhappy breath as he waited for the transmission to reconnect. But the display remained stubbornly blank, a black void.

"Athee—" A sudden, insistent buzzing cut him off. The sound was sharp, garish, and urgent, one reserved strictly for critical situations.

The buzzer sounded again, jarring the relative calm of his office and sending a spike of unexpected tension down his spine. It originated from the bridge.

"Captain here," Steele said, activating the incoming call through his neural implants. His voice was steady, but his senses were now on high alert. "Go ahead."

Commander Chase's voice came through, crisp and direct. "We've received an alert ping from the ground team," she reported and then paused. "We've tried to reach them, but they're not responding. There's some sort of interference. Calder's trying to lock down the source."

"I was just speaking with the captain of the *Viper*," Steele said, relaxing a tad. "He mentioned there are ongoing issues with the solar rejuvenator. It's been messing with communications across the system, extreme solar flares. In fact, we were cut off mid-conversation. Could that be the issue?"

There was another pause before Chase replied, her tone edged with concern. "I think it's more than that, sir. I believe the ground team's comms are being purposely jammed."

The idea of interference was one thing—predictable, even, given the instability caused by the rejuvenator project. But the possibility of deliberate jamming was another matter entirely, one that boded ill. A serious sense of unease washed over him.

"I think there is the strong chance the ground team is in real trouble."

"I'll be right there," he said, his voice tight as he considered what he'd just learned from Valon concerning the situation on the ground. He cut the connection and strode to the hatch, his mind already racing through possible scenarios. If their ground team was in trouble, he'd need to act quickly—and decisively.

THREE

The marine standing by the entrance hatch to his office snapped to attention as Steele emerged and strode onto the bridge. The low hum of the ship's systems filled the air, a familiar background rhythm that he found comforting.

At the back of the bridge, the hatch to the lift hissed open as he made his way to his station, and Lieutenants Hale and Ishida stepped out, both clearly summoned by Chase in response to the escalating situation. Calder and the XO were already at their stations, their focus intense as they worked. Chase looked up as Steele settled into his command chair, the hard lines of her face betraying a growing concern.

"Calder, report," Steele ordered, his voice cutting through the tense atmosphere.

"All incoming comms are down," Calder responded, not looking up as she continued her efforts.

The lift door slid open again, and Ensign Quinn hurried out and onto the bridge, her cheeks flushed, breathing slightly labored. It was clear she had run to get there. Her hair was wet and matted, indicating she'd been caught in the shower when Chase had called her back to the bridge. Without missing a beat, she made her way to her station, dropping into her seat and pulling up the sensor displays.

"I think we are being jammed, sir," Calder added, her voice grim. "We cannot send or receive."

"Think or know?" Steele frowned, leaning forward slightly. "Are you sure it's not an issue on our end?"

Calder glanced back at him, her green eyes resolute. "I am certain the problem is not on our end, sir. This isn't a malfunction on *Ranger*'s part. It's wholly external interference, and it's not coming from the solar rejuvenator either. This is focused."

"I concur, sir," Quinn said.

Steele's frown deepened as he rubbed his jaw, the hard edge of uncertainty troubling him. He didn't even feel the stubble on his chin. The alert from the ground team, the sudden communications blackout—it all felt coordinated, deliberate. What if the problems causing issues to the FTL comm net across the entirety of the system weren't related to the problems with solar flares? What did that mean?

"The HTD is down as well, beyond what we can see locally with our own passive sensors," Chase told him.

"Calder, do we have a source of the interference?" he pressed.

Chase looked up from her display, her tone clipped but steady. "I'm trying to lock it down now, sir."

"I can help with that," Quinn said from her station. "Patching you in now to my console and my sensor suite. It should help localize the interference."

Calder gave a nod of thanks and turned her attention back to her monitors.

"This is damn odd," Steele muttered, his mind racing as he rubbed his jaw again. He could feel the puzzle pieces sliding into place, but the overall picture remained frustratingly incomplete. "Chase, sound the ready alert, let's get the crews to their stations."

"Aye, sir," Chase replied, her fingers moving over her console to initiate the alert. The ship's internal lighting shifted, bathing the bridge in an amber-tinged glow as the ready status activated. The klaxon rang out, echoing through the decks below to alert the crew to report. He could imagine many had been relaxing, sleeping. They were now hopping out of bunks, dressing, and heading toward their duty stations.

"You should know we have the assault shuttle inbound," Chase continued. "They were inspecting a tramp freighter. I recalled them as soon as the ground team's signal cut out. They're approximately ten minutes from the ship."

"Good initiative on that." He rubbed at his jaw again, considering the situation he found himself in. "Quinn, raise defensive screens and charge the shields," Steele commanded. The ship needed to be ready for anything. "Hale, let's get *Ranger* prepared to maneuver. Power up the gravitic drive."

"Aye, aye, sir," Quinn responded, her hands already moving over her console.

"On it, sir," Hale reported as he worked at the helm station.

Steele could feel the gravitic drive come to life with a low, rumbling hum that vibrated through the deck and his station. Like a long-slumbering dragon, *Ranger* was waking up.

"Bringing the gravitic drive online now, sir," Hale confirmed, the controls lighting up. "Engineering reports everything is nominal with the reactors. We are good to go to full power when needed."

"Very good," Steele replied.

"Sir," Calder interjected, turning from her communications station with a look of triumph. "I've located the source of the jamming. It's one of the orbitals. It's radiating interference directly at us, an EW platform."

"An orbital?" Chase was surprised by that.

"Yes, ma'am—part of the planet's defensive grid. The satellite is roughly five thousand klicks off the port beam. They are irradiating us fairly hard with a focused beam."

Steele turned to Chase, their eyes meeting in silent agreement. This wasn't a coincidence. They both now understood that tidy fact.

"What did the alert from the ground team say?" Steele asked.

"It was only a ping, sir," Chase explained, her expression mirroring his unease. "Then it was cut off before we could open a channel to them." She paused, taking a quick look down at the screens, studying the data there. "I don't like this, not one bit."

"Neither do I," Steele agreed, the tension in his gut tightening. "Chase, sound general quarters."

"Yes, sir." Chase's fingers moved swiftly across her console as she keyed in the command. The automated tone that followed rang out, echoing through every compartment of the ship.

"General quarters. All hands, general quarters. This is not a drill. General quarters," the announcement blared, its repetition driving home the gravity of the situation. "General quarters, prepare for action."

"Quinn," Steele called, "raise the shields."

"The emitters are not fully primed, sir." Quinn's hands trembled slightly as she worked. It was clear she was trying to keep herself under control. "Bringing them up now. We will have minimal protection only—that is, until the emitters are fully charged, and that will take twenty-four minutes."

"I understand," Steele said, his voice calm despite the chaos. "Partial shields are better than no shields. Get them up."

He pulled up the HTD, the holographic display showing a condensed view of the local space around *Ranger*. Only the immediate area illuminated—an incomplete map of their surroundings that relied solely on the ship's own passive sensors. Due to the jamming, the link to the system's broader defense network was down, leaving them blind to the larger picture.

Steele studied the display, his mind racing. The satellite jamming them, the ground team's distress ping, the abrupt communications blackout—something was very wrong, and the pieces weren't adding up.

"What's going on here?" Steele muttered to himself before addressing the ensign. "Quinn, go active on sensors, sweep the area thoroughly. I want a more detailed picture of everything around *Ranger*."

"Sir," Chase warned, "that could and likely will damage sensitive systems on nearby orbitals and satellites."

"I know," Steele said and saw Quinn looking at him for confirmation after the exchange. "Do it, Ensign, make it happen. With luck it will take care of the satellite jamming us."

"Aye, sir," she responded. "Going active with sensors."

Almost immediately on the HTD, the space around *Ranger* became more detailed as the ship's systems began filling in holes in what the passive sensors had missed. Data tags flared to life as everything within one hundred thousand klicks was being pinged and swept. Atheena was updating data on the nearest civilian ships, orbitals, platforms, and satellites. Even the smallest particles of space debris were being tagged, along with nonfunctioning and old satellites that no one had taken the trouble to remove.

"Sir," Quinn called out, her voice suddenly tight with urgency, "we're being targeted by the defensive network. One of the platforms is actively painting us."

"What?" Chase asked. "Are they insane? What the hell is going on?"

Steele's jaw clenched. That decided it. "Guns, I want that jamming satellite down and I want it down yesterday. Lock masers and fire when ready."

"Sir, there are people over there manning that satellite," Ishida pointed out, worry coloring her voice, "several dozen at least…"

Steele suddenly found himself hesitating. Ishida was correct. By taking this action, he would be crossing a Rubicon of sorts. He would be killing people over there.

Was he making a mistake?

"What do you want to do?" Chase asked.

Steele did not immediately answer. His gaze went back to the HTD, and his eyes fell upon the jamming satellite. It had a flashing red tag, identifying it as hostile. Should he confirm his order? Should he open fire on it? He rubbed his jaw, considering the situation.

It was damn odd.

What were they doing?

At the same time, Steele's gut told him something was very wrong. He had long since learned to trust his feelings… but opening fire? There was no stepping back from that. Should he?

What if he was wrong?

"Do it," Steele said, hardening his voice. "That's an order."

"Aye, sir," Ishida responded, her tone focused and controlled as she brought the weapon systems to bear. "Preparing a firing solution."

Commander Chase looked over, her expression grave. "Are you certain about this?" she asked, her voice low so that only the two of them could hear. "Active sensors in orbit is one thing, going loud is another, sir. We'll be firing on the LDF. As Ishida said, that platform is likely manned. This may be some sort of mistake or exercise we don't know about."

Before Steele could answer, the ship lurched violently. The deck shuddered, and alarms screamed through the bridge, a discordant cacophony of warning tones.

"Incoming maser fire!" Quinn reported and then paused for

a couple of heartbeats. "Shields took the brunt of it and are at twenty percent and holding. Some energy got through and impacted the hull. We've taken superficial damage to our armor along the port side."

"Nanites are working on the damage," Atheena reported calmly. "No major systems have been affected. Damage, as Ensign Quinn reported, is minimal at best."

"This is no exercise. Those bastards mean business." Steele's eyes flicked to the HTD. Two platforms now blinked red, marked as hostile by the ship's construct. One was clearly a weapons platform, its targeting arrays actively tracking and painting *Ranger*. In that moment, Steele understood his hesitation had been a mistake.

"What the hell's gotten into the LDF?" Chase asked.

"Guns... correction." Steele's voice was like ice, his anger barely contained. "Take those two platforms down. If any others light up as hostile, take them out as well. You don't need to check with me, just do it, understand me?"

"Aye, sir," Ishida said, her jaw set with resolve. "Solution set —firing." *Ranger*'s maser batteries discharged with a pulse of silent energy. A low tone sounded from Steele's console, reporting the outbound weapon's discharge. "Recharging the guns."

The ship rocked again, more alarms blaring as another defensive platform joined the fray, shooting at them. The incoming maser fire hammered against their weakened shields, and Steele gripped the armrests of his command chair, feeling the tension knotting in his gut. It had been over ten years since he'd been under fire. Anger simmered beneath the surface—his ship was under attack, and every instinct screamed to protect her and his people.

"Solid hits," Ishida reported, a touch of relief in her voice. "The jamming and maser platforms are down. Targeting the newest threat, firing." There was a long pause. "Good hit, platform is toast."

"Shields are holding," Quinn reported, though her voice carried a note of worry. "But I'm detecting more activity from the defensive grid. We're being painted by additional platforms—multiple targets."

Steele's jaw tightened. The situation was escalating rapidly, and hesitation could prove deadly. The LDF had already unzipped their fly, but they should have done it all at once, not piecemeal. The incompetent fools had given him a real chance.

"Guns," he ordered, his voice sharp, "weapons free. Use missiles and masers. Take down the entire defensive grid within close range. Quinn, engage ECM and countermeasures. Make us a more difficult target to hit. Spoof their targeting systems if you can."

"Aye, sir," Ishida acknowledged.

"Yes, sir," Quinn responded, her voice trembling slightly but she seemed steady enough as she worked. *Ranger*'s hull emitted a series of controlled bursts as EW drones and decoys were launched, creating false signatures to throw off enemy targeting. They spread out around and away from the ship. Patterns of interference rippled through the void as energy emitters went online.

At such close range, Steele had no idea how effective Quinn's efforts would be. He took in the chaotic scene on the HTD. The defensive grid surrounding Tenebris was lighting up like a swarm of angry hornets; more and more of the thirty-two platforms on their side of the planet were flashing red as they began targeting his ship. He knew that, compared to newer installations in other parts of the system, Tenebris's defensive grid was antiquated at best—a relic from the last war, with hardware long past its prime.

Still, outdated or not, there were enough platforms to pose a serious threat. If *Ranger* hadn't managed to get the shields up in time, the initial maser blasts could have shredded the ship's hull, incapacitating them. The thought sent a cold shiver through him. They had been lucky.

Whatever was happening down on the surface, whether a terrorist act or something even more sinister, it was spilling over into space and had dragged them into the middle of it all.

"Helm, how long until we can maneuver under our own power?" Steele asked, his voice tight with the urgency of the moment.

"Four minutes, twenty-two seconds," Hale replied. "The gravitic drive is spinning up as we speak. If we move any sooner, before a full warm-up is complete, we risk damaging the coils."

"Very good." Steele's eyes stayed fixed on the HTD, where the tactical display showed *Ranger*'s maser batteries firing in synchronized bursts as Ishida worked her guns. Beams of focused energy lanced out into the darkness, targeting the nearest platforms and defense stations within the twenty-thousand-klick effective range of the focused energy beams. The ship's two missile pods launched a volley of twenty Mark Five ship-killers, each arcing away from *Ranger* with deadly purpose, aimed at more distant targets. The HTD tracked the missiles' trajectories as they spread out, glowing icons cutting through space like fiery harbingers. Sensors told him none of the platforms had managed to raise their energy shielding yet. He could not understand why that had not happened. Had this been a spur-of-the-moment thing? He was beginning to suspect it had been. Or was it that the enemy, whoever they were, were simply incompetent? Steele did not know and it didn't matter, not anymore. They had started it, and he would see it finished.

"There is no defensive fire," Ishida reported. "No PDS tracking on our missiles."

"That's some good news," Chase commented.

"Sir," Calder called from her station, her voice urgent, "I've restored communication with the ground team. They're under attack by local forces. The shuttle has been hit and disabled." She was holding a hand to her earpiece. "She's not flying anytime soon. They're pinned down at the spaceport and are requesting immediate assistance and evac."

Steele's jaw clenched. The situation was deteriorating fast. His mind raced, calculating options.

"They're on the other side of the planet, sir," Chase said, her tone grim.

Steele nodded, already making decisions as to what he wanted and needed to do in the coming minutes. "Chase, reroute the assault shuttle to the ground team's location. Helm, as soon as we're able to maneuver, bring us around the other side of the planet and put us into low geosynchronous orbit over their heads."

"Aye, sir," Hale responded, eyes locked on his displays. "Gravity drive coming online now."

Steele turned to Calder. "Comms, broadcast an order to all ships in the vicinity: they are to steer clear of our path, or they will be fired upon."

"Yes, sir," Calder said.

"Good hits on targets," Ishida reported, her voice carrying a note of restrained relief. "The defensive grid in our area of space is down. They are neutralized, sir."

Steele's gaze returned to the HTD. The icons representing hostile defense platforms had been replaced by markers designating navigational hazards—wreckage fields of expanding debris. He knew the destruction they'd just unleashed hadn't come without a human cost. The thought twisted uncomfortably in his gut—how many people had he just ordered killed? Dozens? Hundreds? He pushed the thought aside, knowing he couldn't afford hesitation or regret in this moment. He had a job to do and a ship and crew to think of. More importantly, he had people on the ground, and they were under fire.

"Very good shooting, Guns," Steele said, relaxing a tad. "Start working on the platforms farther out and on the other side of the planet. We know their positions, and as they are in geosynchronous orbit, it should be easy to hit them with missiles."

"Yes, sir," Ishida said firmly.

"Sir," Calder called, turning from her station, her face pale. She looked almost sick, her expression grim and haunted. "I'm receiving a broadcast that's being transmitted planet-wide."

"We're underway, sir," Hale reported from the helm. "The ship is moving."

"Very good," Steele said, glancing down at the plot. The space ahead of his ship was clear and she was starting to accelerate. He turned his attention back to Calder. "Go on. What's the broadcast saying?"

Clearly shaken, Calder swallowed. "The LDF and planetary government are broadcasting that they have declared independence, sir," she said, her voice wavering slightly. "They're saying they're now a free nation and no longer under control of the Union."

The words hit like a physical blow. Chase turned, her eyes narrowing in disbelief. "The planet is rebelling?"

"No, ma'am," Calder corrected, holding a hand to her earpiece as she focused on the incoming message. "They're saying *all* of the Protectorate has declared independence from the Union."

A long moment of silence followed that. Steele sucked in a breath and let it out.

"Shit," Chase muttered.

Calder's face grew even more strained as she continued. "They're also calling for all Union personnel in-system to surrender immediately. Anyone who resists will be met with lethal force, and that, sir, includes Union naval assets."

Every eye on the bridge turned to Steele. He sat there for a moment, absorbing what he'd just been told.

Ishida broke the silence. "Sir, there are two LDF frigates inbound. They are actively burning for us at near maximum power."

"When it rains, it pours," Steele said to himself.

FOUR

Steele's gaze was fixed on the HTD, where the icons of the two incoming frigates glowed ominously. They were burning in from deeper within the system, their gravitic drives pushing hard as they closed the distance. Although still out of weapons range, Steele knew it was only a matter of time until things got hot and dicey. A quick calculation confirmed what the HTD already projected: the frigates would be within extreme weapons range in just over an hour.

"Atheena," Steele said. "Have you identified those two frigates yet?"

"They are patrol frigates, Adzuma Class. Would you like me to pull up their specifications on one of your consoles?"

"Please do."

On a screen to his right, the information popped up. Both ships were a hundred thirty meters from bow to stern, each with a crew of thirty-eight. They each carried two five-magazine pods of ship-killer missiles. That meant each frigate could launch a volley of ten missiles at a time. They were also equipped with six maser cannons and a respectable EW and point-defense capability. He was facing the *Tatsua* and *Kei*, both more than ninety years old, which meant they were well-used ships. There was limited information on their commanding officers, but nothing really useful to him.

Ranger had superior firepower and defenses compared to either of those smaller warships. Yet the frigates still posed a significant threat. Their combined assault, even against *Ranger*'s advanced shielding, EW suite, and point-defense systems, could inflict serious damage. They might even manage to cripple him.

"There's also a battlecruiser incoming," Chase said quietly, her voice cutting through the tense silence that had grown up on the bridge.

Steele's eyes flicked back to the HTD as his XO highlighted the new threat, which *Ranger*'s sensors had just picked up. The icon of the battlecruiser appeared, pulsing in a deep red that seemed to radiate menace. The HTD updated with data on the approaching ship, its trajectory and speed displayed alongside estimates of its weapons capabilities.

"The *Starfish*," Chase added. "She's more than two hours out."

Steele's stomach tightened, and he forced himself to consider the unfolding situation calmly. The two frigates were a threat, yes, but the battlecruiser was a *real* problem. Even as aged as those three ships were, their combined firepower would be overwhelming. The battlecruiser alone packed enough firepower to overcome *Ranger*'s defenses in a sustained engagement. The odds were growing grimmer by the moment. The enemy were already at speed, and he was not. He still had people on the ground to recover before he could break away and make a run for it.

Steele's fingers curled into a fist as he weighed his options. He was confident in his ship and crew, but there was no way *Ranger* could hold its ground against a coordinated assault from three warships.

"Helm, how long until we are over the spaceport?" Steele

demanded, his voice steady despite the tension he keenly felt. For the benefit of his people, he needed to project a sense of calm and control. He could not be seen losing his cool, for that would quickly undermine morale and confidence in his command.

"Six minutes, sir," Hale replied, his focus unwavering as he managed *Ranger*'s course adjustments.

"That's going to put us on the opposite side of the planet from those incoming frigates and the battlecruiser," Chase commented. "With luck, it will give us a slight advantage when it comes time to burn."

Steele wasn't so certain about that. Before he could respond, Quinn's voice cut through the air, tight with urgency. "Missile launch. Incoming from the surface! Time to impact, one minute, forty-five seconds."

Steele's gaze snapped back to the HTD. The display lit up with the trajectories of six surface-to-orbit missiles, each one marked as a ship-killer. They arced through the atmosphere below, streaking up toward *Ranger* with lethal intent. A cold knot of fear tightened in his stomach. Even with their shields partially up, the missiles were powerful enough to do serious damage.

"Activate countermeasures," Steele ordered, forcing calm into his voice. "ECM—Quinn, try to spoof them. Point-defense active as soon as they're in range."

"Aye, sir," Quinn replied, her hands moving rapidly over her console. The pressure of the moment was evident in the set of her jaw. Steele watched as *Ranger*'s electronic warfare systems sprang to life, broadcasting false signatures and scrambling signals to confuse the incoming missiles. Meanwhile, the point-defense turrets rotated into position, ready to intercept any warheads that slipped through the electronic net.

"Calder," Steele said, turning to his communications officer. "Send a message to the local LDF and planetary government on an open transmission. Inform them that if they continue to fire upon us or our ground party, *Ranger* will retaliate and begin striking ground targets."

"Yes, sir," Calder said.

Steele's gaze remained fixed on the HTD, his eyes tracking the icons representing the incoming ship-killer missiles. Three of them veered off their initial course, Quinn's countermeasures successfully confusing their guidance systems and sending them burning harmlessly away. But the other three missiles held steady, slicing through the upper atmosphere and into the blackness of space, closing the distance at an alarming rate.

"Point-defense, firing," Quinn reported.

The HTD displayed the flurry of kinetic rounds *Ranger* spat outward, automated turrets shooting out streams of high-velocity projectiles. Each round arced out in a carefully calculated pattern, designed to intercept and destroy the incoming warheads.

For a few heart-pounding moments, nothing happened. The red icons of the missiles continued to streak toward *Ranger*, and Steele could feel every second stretching into an eternity. Then, with a sudden flicker, one of the missiles vanished from the plot, obliterated by a direct hit. A heartbeat later, a second missile was destroyed, and the third followed a split second after. The bridge erupted with a collective exhale, a clear release of tension.

"Nice job, Quinn," Steele said.

"Thank you, sir," Quinn replied, her voice still taut but tinged with pride. Her hands stayed poised over her console, ready for whatever came next.

Beside him, Chase had turned slightly away, speaking quietly into her comms. Steele caught the edge of her tone—low, hushed, and tense—conveying the gravity of the situation to whoever was on the other end.

Steele's gaze stayed riveted to the HTD, his jaw tightening

as the display flickered with a scene that screamed of panic. The once orderly orbits around the planet had devolved into utter chaos. Dozens of ships—freighters, shuttles, private transports—scrambled and twisted through space, their engines flaring at full burn as they moved away from Tenebris in a disorganized mass exodus. Some ships veered so close to one another that a collision seemed inevitable.

Steele briefly tapped into the local civilian comm net. Voices crackled over comm channels, an overlapping mess of frantic pleas, shouted warnings, and barely coherent screams. A battered freighter well past its prime had lost the ability to maneuver. The ship spiraled dangerously, its stabilizers failing to correct its wild spin as it narrowly avoided a shuttle trying to accelerate out of the gravity well.

There was no coordination, no semblance of order, only sheer, primal desperation. Civilians—families, traders, passengers—were clawing for survival, their only focus on escaping whatever cataclysm was unfolding below. The cold, clinical depiction of thrust vectors and ship IDs did nothing to lessen the sense of overwhelming panic that permeated the scene.

"Missile launch," Quinn reported, her voice urgent. "I have multiple surface-to-space missile launches."

Steele adjusted the HTD's view, his heart sinking as he saw over ten ship-killer missiles rising from the planet's surface. The launches came from two separate sites, and the arcs of the missiles painted a deadly picture on the display as they curved a path toward his ship. He quickly glanced at the shield status—forty-four percent, and climbing with every passing moment. It was an improvement, but nowhere near enough to withstand multiple impacts, let alone one. A direct hit could easily rip through their defenses and cripple the ship, ending this show before it even began.

"Same as before, Quinn," Steele said, keeping his voice

steady and calm. "Do your work and take them out. You've trained for this sort of thing. I have full confidence in your abilities and know you can do it."

"Yes, sir," Quinn responded, her hands already moving rapidly across her console. The ECM systems sprang to life again, broadcasting false signals and deploying countermeasures to mislead the incoming missiles. Her concentration was fierce, her training and instincts taking over.

Steele turned his attention to Ishida at the tactical station. "Guns, those two missile sites—if they're in range of kinetic darts, take them out. I don't want them reloading and sending more volleys our way."

"Calculating solutions." Ishida's face became a mask of focused determination as she worked. Moments later, she spoke again. "Firing—two darts away, track is clean, downward path is good."

Steele watched on the HTD as the kinetic darts, propelled by railguns, shot away from the ship, their paths calculated to deliver maximum destruction when they hit.

"Very good," Steele said.

"Sir," Ishida said, speaking up again, "there are two LDF ground bases in range, along with an airbase. If they can scramble aircraft, it could interfere with our extraction effort. Request permission to engage and neutralize all three."

Steele nodded. "Permission granted. Do it. Use whatever force you deem necessary, especially to immobilize that airbase. We can't afford any interference, understand? I want maximum destruction, but no nukes."

"Aye, sir," Ishida acknowledged. There was a tense pause as she set the firing solutions. "Four darts away," she announced. "Two kinetic and two high-explosive. Targeting the airbase and secondary ground bases."

Steele felt the tension on the bridge, every person keyed into the unfolding battle. The HTD tracked the launched darts, and he knew that, even if this bought them precious moments to safely evacuate the ground party, the situation was still far from under control. There were still those three incoming ships to worry on.

Steele's gaze stayed fixed on the HTD, tracking the incoming missiles as they streaked up from the planet's atmosphere. Five of them had already veered off course, Quinn's countermeasures and drones successfully tricking their guidance systems. But five missiles still held true. They had locked onto *Ranger* and were closing with frightening speed. Though old, these ship-killers were still powerful and capable weapons.

"Point-defense firing," Quinn reported. "Close-in ECM active."

Steele held his breath as the defensive turrets continued to spit kinetic rounds, creating a deadly and carefully calculated barrage in the path of the incoming warheads. The HTD updated in real time: one missile blinked out, destroyed. Another followed, and then a third. But the final two still sped toward them, only twenty seconds from impact. Eyeing the incoming missiles, Steele nearly asked for an update on the shields, but at the last moment chose not to. His crew would pick up on his momentary worry and that wasn't the message he wanted to convey. The ship's point-defense systems continued to fire, rounds tearing through the dark, and at the last possible moment, the two remaining missiles vanished from the plot, obliterated almost simultaneously.

Steele released a breath, tension draining from his shoulders. "Good job, Quinn," he said, his voice full of genuine relief and pride.

"Solid hits," Ishida reported from the tactical station, her tone professional but tinged with satisfaction. "Both missile launch sites are down. They won't be firing at us again. Hell, they won't be launching at anyone, ever again."

Before Steele could respond, Chase spoke up, her focus intense as she scanned the tactical data on her own display. "Ishida, I've pulled up a map of all known defensive facilities on this hemisphere of the planet. There's another missile site that hasn't fired yet. Kindly hit it before it does get around to launching a salvo at us. I've sent the target to your station."

"Yes, ma'am," Ishida replied, already calculating a firing solution. There was a prolonged pause. "Dart away."

"Calder," Steele said, focusing on the HTD as he dialed in to track the descent of the assault shuttle. Its course was steady, but his worry for the ground team gnawed at him. The shuttle was less than five minutes away. "Do we have comms with our people on the ground?"

"We do, sir," Calder confirmed, her hands still working the communications console.

"I was just speaking with them," Chase interjected, her voice clipped but steady. "They're under heavy fire from light infantry. The situation is rough."

Steele's brow furrowed. "Can we do anything to help them from up here?" His voice carried the frustration of a captain bound to the bridge as his people fought for their lives far below on a dismal rock of a world.

Chase shook her head, a trace of resignation in her eyes. "I don't think so, sir. An orbital dart would be overkill, and we risk taking out our own people in the process. It's down to the assault shuttle, which is something it's equipped for, and the two squads of marines we have aboard to handle the enemy on the ground."

Steele exhaled slowly, his scowl deepening. "All right. We've done what we can for the moment."

"Yes, sir," Chase replied. "It's a waiting game now."

Steele's jaw tightened. "Do we know how many casualties they've taken?"

Calder glanced back at him. "Two, sir. Both are ambulatory."

"Alert Doctor Yates that we'll be having wounded incoming shortly," Steele said. This was the first time people under his direct command had been injured in battle, and the reality of it felt like a stone sitting uncomfortably in his stomach. He took a moment to steady himself. "Is Miller one of the casualties?"

"No, sir," Chase answered, reading his unspoken concern. "He is not."

Steele let out a breath, the tension easing just a fraction. He knew he had to stay focused, but the personal impact of those injuries was something he'd never grow accustomed to.

Ishida's voice cut through his thoughts. "The airbase is hit. They won't be launching aircraft anytime soon. Damage estimate is catastrophic."

Steele nodded. "What about the other two bases?"

"They've been hit too, sir," Ishida confirmed. "High-velocity kinetic darts struck both. The database identified each as holding an armored infantry and an air cavalry brigade. They—ah—no longer exist, sir."

Steele acknowledged her with a curt nod. Kinetic darts fired from orbit were a terrifyingly effective weapon. Accelerated to hypersonic velocities by railgun launch systems, these solid tungsten rods carried immense kinetic energy. When they struck a target, the energy release was equivalent to a nuclear detonation, driven purely by the force of impact rather than a fission or fusion reaction.

The devastation was absolute—buildings vaporized, underground bunkers crushed, not to mention anything within a wide radius of the target zone leveled by the shockwaves—yet there was no lingering radiation to contaminate the area.

The strikes had bought them precious breathing room to

pull off the extraction, though the scale of destruction remained chilling. Yet Steele's mind remained on the HTD, where the icons of the incoming LDF frigates crept ever closer.

The extraction would be the easy part, he understood. Getting his people out was only one challenge. To escape the system, he would have to confront those frigates—and perhaps even the battlecruiser coming in hot behind them. Time and the odds were not on his side.

FIVE

"We're directly over the spaceport, sir," Hale reported. "Holding in low geosynchronous orbit."

"Keep us on-station," Steele ordered, leaning forward in his command chair, his eyes focused on the holographic tactical display. He quickly confirmed Hale's statement. His ship was where she was supposed to be. As captain, he was ultimately responsible for anything that happened, even mistakes made by his crew. Steele had long since learned to verify as much as possible, for inevitably errors and miscues happened.

"Yes, sir," Hale replied. "Holding station."

"Quinn, any other immediate threats out there?" Steele asked.

"No, sir," Quinn said, looking up. "The orbital defense grid has been neutralized as far as we are concerned, and there are no surface sites within range that could target us—at least, none that I can detect."

"Ishida?"

"Captain, I concur with that statement," Ishida agreed. "I see no immediate threats on the board."

"The assault shuttle is on scene, sir," Calder reported.

"They've made several strafing runs on enemy positions before putting down. We have armored marines on the ground now. They are working to secure the area."

Beside him, at her own station, Chase keyed in a command, and the forward screen of the bridge flared to life. The top-down view of the spaceport was being streamed from one of the optical cameras aboard *Ranger*, providing a clear and magnified view of what was happening on the ground.

The assault shuttle dominated the scene, a massive attack craft bristling with gun turrets and missile pods. It sat in the center of a runway, looking like a predator crouched and ready to strike. Around it, a squad of armored marines had taken up defensive positions, kneeling, with weapons at the ready. One of the marines aimed and fired a burst at something off camera, while another squad was moving methodically toward the main terminal, rifles raised, their movements efficient and precise as they cleared the way forward.

Chase made an adjustment and the view shifted, drawing back. Parts of the spaceport were ablaze, with thick columns of black smoke billowing up and into the sky, marking where explosions had torn through the facility.

Civilian aircraft, once lined up neatly on the tarmac, now lay wrecked, with several still burning. Debris was scattered across the field. Bodies lay on the cracked pavement, some clad in civilian attire, others in military uniforms. Near the terminal, an armored personnel carrier was on its side, flames licking out from its underside and smoking heavily. The machine's turret, upside down, was several meters away.

Steele's eyes narrowed as he took in the scene, wondering if much of the destruction had been the work of the assault shuttle's strafing runs or the fighting that had preceded it.

"There's our main shuttle," Chase said, pointing at the damaged craft. The once-sleek transport now sat broken in a parking area on the lower left side of the screen. One of its engines was mangled and a significant portion of the left wing blown apart. "It's not going anywhere." She paused and looked over at him. "Should we attempt to use the assault shuttle to recover it? Do we even have time for that? I'd hate to leave it behind for the enemy."

Steele considered the question for a moment, his jaw tightening. The damaged shuttle was a loss, and he judged any attempt to salvage it would delay their departure and put more lives at risk. With the enemy frigates on the way, speed was the order of the day. He turned to his executive officer and shook his head decisively. "No. There's no time for that. We'll be leaving her behind."

"Well, that's unfortunate," Chase said. "We are going to be limited to the assault shuttle and the captain's boat."

"I know. The shuttle's loss might hinder future operations, but there's no helping it." He paused, shifting his attention to the communications station. "Calder," he ordered, his voice firm, "make sure the marines know to scuttle that bird before they pull out. I want nothing of ours that's of value left behind for the enemy. Is that understood?"

"Yes, sir," Calder replied, her fingers moving swiftly over the console. "Message relayed."

Steele turned his gaze back to the forward screen, his focus sharpening as he studied the scene unfolding below. A small group had emerged from the terminal, moving slowly, but with purpose, toward the shuttle. At the front of the procession was Miller, flanked by his marine escort, wearing only light armor and staying close at hand.

The marines were using their rifles to sweep and scan about for threats as they moved. Two of the marines in the party were clearly injured, limping and leaning heavily on their armored comrades for support as they made their way toward the assault shuttle. Someone was being carried on a stretcher.

Eyeing the injured, Steele sucked in an unhappy breath and let it out. That wasn't good.

A marine ran from the assault shuttle to the damaged shuttle. Steele watched the marine as they moved up to the back hatch, which was lowered and opened. The marine pulled a device from their battle harness and threw it inside, then legged it, running back the way they'd come. There was a flash as something exploded inside.

The shuttle began to burn a few moments later.

"Sir," Ishida spoke up from her station, her tone urgent. "I've been studying the HTD. We're still tied into the command network and have access to intelligence throughout the rest of the system. The LDF hasn't gotten around to cutting us out of the feed yet."

"They will get around to it," Chase said, "when someone thinks of it."

Steele frowned. The chaos of the last few minutes had consumed his attention, and he hadn't noticed the still-active data link. He turned his focus back to the HTD and adjusted the view to encompass the entire Illidran System.

"The *Resolute* has been fired upon, sir," Ishida added. "She's a wreck, and much of the shipyard at High Ring looks to have been heavily damaged when they took her out."

Steele dialed in on High Ring Orbital Station, and what he saw confirmed Ishida's assessment. The Union heavy cruiser, *Resolute*, had been hit hard. Her hull was fractured, twisted metal, composites, and debris floating in the black void around her. The damage was severe, a total loss. It appeared as if one of her reactors had detonated, damaging much of the shipyard.

The wreck was surrounded by escape pods. Looming nearby was an LDF battlecruiser, the *Valiant*, hovering menacingly a few thousand kilometers from the devastated starship and shipyard. Steele's gut twisted. The *Resolute* likely had no warning of the betrayal. It was clear to him in an instant it had been a brutal ambush that left no time for anyone aboard to react.

How many had died in that strike?

"This isn't good," Chase said. The destruction of the *Resolute* and the damage to the shipyard painted a dire picture. The balance of power in the system had shifted dramatically—and not in their favor. Then again, the Union presence in-system had not been that large to begin with.

Why hadn't intelligence gotten wind of what was coming?

Ishida's next report came like another blow. "The *Spear* is down too, sir. Destroyed by an LDF cruiser."

"What about the *Viper*?" he asked, clinging to a sliver of hope.

"She's burning at full speed out of the system," Ishida explained. "There are three LDF frigates in pursuit, but she's got a good lead, and I don't think they will overtake her. At her current velocity, I estimate she'll reach the Fringe Zone in ten hours and be able to jump before the enemy can come close to engagement range."

Steele let out a relieved breath. At least Valon would get out. *Viper*'s escape was a small mercy, but it would leave *Ranger* the last active Union warship in Illidran, dangerously exposed and alone in hostile territory. Granted, they were near the edge of the system... but still it was a problem. He had to get his crew —and his people on the ground—out of this mess before it swallowed them whole, and given time, it undoubtedly would.

"There are a bunch of ships headed for the Fringe Zone, sir, several hundred at least," Ishida added. "A lot of people want to get the hell out of Dodge."

"I can imagine," Steele replied, his eyes narrowing as he studied the chaotic dance of traffic across the breadth of the system. The holographic display was a storm of movement, with civilian ships of every class and size burning hard, pushing their drives to maximum limits. Freighters, private transports, and even cruise ships—all were making desperate runs for the Fringe Zone, that vital point beyond the star system's gravity well where they could engage their jump drives and escape into Slipstream space. The urgency was real, each vessel a bright icon on the screen, their vectors angled like streaks of light, moving in all directions, aimed at escape and personal salvation.

LDF ships deeper in the system, now marked in red on the display, moved to intercept clusters of fleeing vessels. They were clearly doing what they could to turn ships back, herding them away from potential escape routes. Judging by the wrecks marked on the screen, they had already fired upon several ships that had not heeded their orders.

Such tactics were brutal, and it wasn't hard to imagine the terror of those aboard the fleeing ships as they were cut off from their chance at freedom. The LDF was doing everything it could to exert control, but it was still a large star system, and many would manage to get out before it was all said and done. Anyone with sense, Steele thought grimly, would be doing everything they could to run for the exit and escape.

"What are we going to do about those two frigates?" Chase asked, her voice low and laced with concern. The question hung heavy in the air between them, a reminder of the threat bearing down on them.

Steele's eyes remained on the HTD, the display awash with red icons tracking the enemy vessels. He switched the view back to the approaching enemy. "We're going to have to fight them," he said simply, his tone calm. His mind had been working overtime, turning over strategies, and assessing options. "I've already got some thoughts on what I want to do."

Chase arched an eyebrow, her curiosity piqued. "Care to share them with me?" she asked, leaning slightly closer.

"Not yet." Steele shook his head. "There are too many variables. I need to see how things unfold first with the extraction. We need to get those people off the surface and to the ship.

Then we worry about the approaching ships." He paused and looked over at her as a thought occurred to him. "Out of all of our torpedoes, we have two with stealth capabilities in the magazine—Mark Nineteens, right?"

"We do," Chase confirmed, though her expression remained wary. "But the enemy is actively pinging with their sensors. They'll detect the torpedoes' drives long before they can get close enough to strike and take them out."

"I know," Steele said as he thought, the idea coalescing in his mind. "Get those stealth torpedoes prepped and in the tubes. I want them ready to fire on my order."

"Yes, sir," Chase replied, turning to relay the command to Ishida. "Guns, load the Mark Nineteen stealth torpedoes in the tubes."

"Aye, ma'am. Loading now."

Steele turned his attention back to the forward screen, his eyes locked on the scene unfolding below. The ground team was in the process of loading the wounded onto the assault shuttle. Each moment stretched out agonizingly, unbearably slow, as he watched the marines work together. He clenched his fists, resisting the urge to demand updates—and get them to speed things up. Waiting had always tested his patience, especially in moments like this where the pressure was on and every second felt like an hour. Still, he understood they were moving as rapidly as they could and would be airborne soon enough. They knew time was an issue.

"Atheena," Steele said, breaking the tense silence, "have some coffee and sandwiches brought up."

"Yes, Captain," the ship's construct replied, her voice smooth. Atheena's presence was a comfort.

"And notify all departments to take advantage of the lull," he added. "Let's get everyone fed while we have the time."

"As you command, Captain," Atheena responded.

The order felt small, almost trivial in the face of what they would have to deal with, but Steele knew better. It was incredibly important. The hours ahead were likely going to be hard and long. Keeping his crew fed and ready, even during a momentary pause in action like this one, was as important as any tactical maneuver. It also was part of the routine and would help settle people down. This calm, this eye of the storm, was a gift, and Steele was unwilling to let it pass without use. That said, he continued to watch the shuttle and ground team below, willing them to move faster.

"Sir," Calder said, "I'm receiving a call from one of the incoming frigates, the LDF *Tatsua*."

Steele glanced over, his eyes narrowing. She gave him a shrug.

"What do they want?" Steele asked, though he had a feeling he already knew.

"Captain Crenice didn't specify," Calder replied. "Just that he wanted to personally speak with you."

Steele's jaw tightened, and Chase's expression mirrored his unease.

"I can imagine what he wants," Chase muttered, "and none of it's good for us."

"Put him on the main screen," Steele ordered, standing from his command station. "Split the view—I want to keep an eye on the assault shuttle while I talk."

Calder nodded, and a moment later, the forward screen split in two. One side, the left, continued to show the ground team, the marines working methodically to load the last of the wounded onto the assault shuttle. The other half now displayed the incoming transmission.

The face and chest of Captain Crenice appeared, his image crisp and clear. The man was older, with neatly trimmed gray hair and a face lined with hard edges. He wore the blue and gold uniform of the LDF, and his appearance was impeccable—tailored and pristine, as though he'd stepped right out of a recruitment poster. The creases in his uniform were sharp to the point of cutting, and the gleaming insignia on his collar spoke of rank and authority.

The other captain's gaze was cold and calculating as he looked back at Steele.

"Captain Steele," Crenice began, his voice smooth but carrying a hint of strength beneath the politeness. "I believe it's time we had a conversation."

"How can I help you, Captain Crenice?" Steele asked, stepping forward with a measured calm, his gaze locked onto the screen.

Crenice's lips curled into a thin, humorless smile. "You will surrender *Ranger* and spare us the trouble of taking you down," he declared, his words colored by a thick accent. English was the common language of the Union, but not the Protectorate, and the difference was evident in his pronunciation.

Steele's eyes narrowed. "That's not going to happen," he replied, his voice cold and resolute. "You will not be taking my ship, not now, not ever."

Crenice's smile vanished, replaced by a hardened expression. "Then I will break her. After I am done and finished, you, your crew, and all that remains of your vessel will be nothing more than debris in the void."

Steele's jaw clenched, but he refused to let the threat rattle him. "That remains to be seen. Besides, you are just LDF and playing at being professionals."

Crenice's face darkened, his displeasure evident in the tightening of his jaw and the hardening of his eyes. "It is three to one. You are outmatched, Captain Steele. I urge you to reconsider and surrender before things escalate beyond simple insults. We are gaining on you. We will catch you and we will kill you."

"I don't think I'm outmatched," Steele countered, his voice steady and unyielding.

Crenice barked out a laugh, as if Steele had said something amusing.

"Keep advancing, and I will engage you, Captain," Steele said. "I warn you now, *Ranger* has teeth and she will bite."

"So do we." Crenice's frustration was becoming evident. "This is madness. Think of your crew. Their lives are in your hands. If you don't heave to and shut down your drive, what happens next will be on your head, not mine."

Steele's eyes hardened. "I *am* thinking of them," he said, his voice laced with defiance. "And I will not let them fall into *your* hands. You keep coming at me, Captain, and I will destroy your ships. That is a promise. *Ranger* out."

With a thought, Steele activated his neural implants and cut the call. The screen flickered and returned to the full view of the assault shuttle, which was still on the ground below. The last of the marines, those who had established a perimeter, had drawn back to the assault shuttle and were hustling aboard.

Steele turned away from the screen as the lift doors slid open with a hiss. Two marines stepped onto the bridge, each carrying large bags. He recognized them immediately—one would be filled with tea and coffee cups, the other loaded with sandwiches, either ham and cheese or something else.

Moving back to his command station, Steele took his seat.

"What do you think?" Steele asked, turning to Chase. His XO's expression was as composed as ever, but he could see the steely resolve in her eyes.

"We're going to have a fight on our hands soon enough."

"Agreed." He knew the battle ahead wouldn't be easy, but he had faith in his crew, who he had trained, and in his ship. The waiting was the hardest part, but soon enough, it would end—and they would face whatever came next.

"Captain," Calder reported, her voice cutting through the bridge's tense atmosphere. "The shuttle is in the air. The pilot is pushing it hard, estimating flight time to *Ranger* at roughly fifteen minutes."

"Very good," Steele replied, nodding. "Helm, as soon as that shuttle is aboard, you punch it. I'll have a course for you shortly."

"Yes, sir." Hale's focus was unwavering as he prepared for the next maneuver. "I'm ready."

"Coffee, sir?" a voice said beside him.

Steele turned to find Max Holden, one of the marines, offering him a cup.

"It's prepared how you like it, sir," Holden added.

"Thank you, Marine." Steele accepted the cup. The warmth seeped through the insulation and into his hand. "What kind of sandwiches do you have?"

"Ham and cheese, sir," Holden replied.

"I'll take one," Steele said.

The marine handed over a wrapped sandwich. Steele ran his gaze around the bridge as the marine moved off. His people looked anxious, tense, their nerves visible in the way they held themselves.

"Everyone," Steele said, raising his voice and drawing their attention, "make sure you get something to eat and drink. It may be a while before we get another chance. Consider that an order."

The marines moved from one person to the next, handing out food and drinks, making sure every crew member was taken care of. Steele set the coffee in its holder and unwrapped his sandwich. His stomach rumbled with hunger. It had been several hours since he'd last eaten. He made a deliberate show of eating slowly, projecting an air of calm he did not feel. Chase, sitting nearby, followed his lead, taking measured bites of her own sandwich. Their act had the desired effect; the bridge crew gradually relaxed, finding a small measure of comfort in the familiar routine of eating.

"Captain Crenice is calling again, sir," Calder reported. "Shall I put him on?"

Steele's eyes flicked to the HTD, where the two enemy frigates were still burning toward their position. The enemy ships hadn't slowed or altered course, and he knew that Crenice's call was likely a last attempt to force their surrender and forestall a fight. "Ignore him. I'll do my talking soon enough."

"With missiles?" Ishida asked, a hint of grim humor in her voice.

That caused an amused chuckle to run around the bridge.

"Exactly," Steele replied, leaning forward. His mind raced with plans and possibilities, piecing together a strategy he hoped would turn the tide in their favor as he ate. He had an idea, but it was a gamble.

Would it work? That was the question on his mind.

SIX

Steele took a slow sip of his coffee, savoring the warmth as it slid down his throat and into his belly. It helped to push back the fog of exhaustion and fatigue. The familiar bitter taste was a small comfort, grounding him in the here and now. He'd been tempted to reach for a stim—a quick and efficient way to keep himself sharp, awake, and alert—but he dismissed the thought.

Stims were effective, but they came with a cost. The crash afterward was brutal, leaving one more exhausted than before, and repeated use only made the side effects worse: tremors, headaches, along with a restless agitation that could cloud judgment. No, he'd save the chemical boost for when he really needed it, when the fatigue threatened to become a critical liability. For now, he'd rely on a simple hot cup of coffee.

He let his gaze drift around the bridge, taking in the low hum of the ship's systems, the soft glow of status lights, and the subtle vibrations thrumming through the deck plating, his people at their stations working, doing the jobs for which they'd been trained.

"Four minutes until the assault shuttle arrives," Calder announced, her voice steady, though the tension was there.

"Lieutenant Lane reports the shuttle should be secured within three minutes after landing, maybe faster, sir."

"Very good." Steele nodded. Lane, the flight deck officer, was known for running a tight operation, and in moments like these, every second counted.

"Is the doctor standing by for the incoming casualties?" Chase asked.

"Yes, ma'am," Calder confirmed. "Doctor Yates and the med team are ready and on the hangar deck."

Steele said nothing, for he had expected as much. His attention was fixed on the HTD. The plot showed the shuttle making its final approach, each second ticking away with excruciating slowness. The ground teams, the wounded, and the Union envoy were all aboard. There was a small victory in that. The Union was losing its grip—no, it had lost its grip on the Protectorate, but at least he'd managed to keep his charge safe.

For now, that was enough.

He took another sip of coffee, the warmth doing little to ease the tension in his gut, then set the cup back in its holder. With a thought, he activated his implants and opened an audio channel to Lieutenant Commander Voss, the ship's chief engineer.

"How's the drive, Chief?" Steele asked.

"Purring like a kitten, sir," Voss replied. The engineer's familiar, gruff tone was a comfort, steady and reassuring. "I show no faults or issues. Consider it a well-oiled machine."

"We're likely going to need full power before long," Steele said, casting another look at the HTD, where the icons of the two incoming frigates, still on the other side of Tenebris, loomed ominously as they burned his way.

"It's that serious?" Voss asked, a hint of concern creeping into his voice.

"It is. The Union's lost Illidran," Steele admitted. "If I need to go to maximum power with the gravitic drive for an extended period of time, can I count on it?"

That had only been done in trials.

Voss didn't hesitate. "I can give you 55g once we're past the gravity well of Tenebris and far enough out. She'll handle it for as long as you need it, Captain."

"That's what I wanted to hear," Steele said. Voss was one of the best, and if he said the drive could take it, Steele trusted him. "Very good, Chief." Steele terminated the channel with a thought thrown to his implants.

"Shuttle is docking," Calder reported. There was a pause. "Lieutenant Lane reports the hangar bay hatches are closed and sealed. He's locking the shuttle down now."

Steele didn't waste a moment. "Hale, full military power on the course I gave you."

"Aye, sir," Hale responded, fingers gliding over the controls. "Coming onto that course now. Warp bubble in place, gravitic drive engaged. Inertial dampeners functioning normally. We're moving and underway, sir."

Steele's eyes shifted to his console, watching as *Ranger* began to pick up speed. The numbers climbed steadily—5g, 8g, 10g, and then 20g. Despite the inertial dampeners, the acceleration pressed subtly at them, though the ship's systems absorbed most of the force. They were pushing hard, but until they moved farther out from Tenebris, the planet's gravity well would continue to limit their acceleration. The gravitic drive strained against the interference, but it was holding, humming with controlled power, and they were steadily moving away from the planet and accelerating with every passing moment.

Steele turned his attention back to the HTD. Their connection to the strategic network had yet to be severed, granting him a comprehensive view of the unfolding situation, not only around his ship, but also across the entire star system. His gaze, however, fell upon the two enemy frigates that were closing in from the far side of the planet.

It was time to act.

Working his controls, he sent a precise targeting plot to Ishida at the tactical station.

"Guns," Steele called, his voice carrying the authority of command as he glanced back at his tactical officer, "I want you to launch both torpedoes on the course I just sent. They're to accelerate at maximum power for thirty seconds, then cut their gravitic drives and engage stealth systems. Do you have any questions?"

Ishida's eyes locked onto the data streaming across her display, her fingers already moving to execute the order.

"No, sir," she replied confidently. "I have no questions—torpedoes launching." She paused for a long moment. "Torpedoes away."

Steele watched the HTD as the torpedoes shot from their launch tubes, streaking away from *Ranger*. Once clear of the ship, their gravitic drives engaged immediately, propelling them out into the darkness at incredible speeds.

"Torpedoes running hot, straight, and normal," Ishida reported.

The torpedoes were sleek and compact devices, outfitted with powerful gravitic drives that made them swift and deadly. The warheads they carried were much more powerful than regular ship-killers. Unlike *Ranger* and without a crew, they required only minimal inertial dampeners, designed purely for efficiency and speed in delivering their payload to target.

Steele observed the tactical display as the two weapons shot away from the destroyer, their acceleration ramping up swiftly and cleanly along the precise course he had plotted. Thirty seconds later, their drives snuffed out as planned, and, slipping into stealth mode, both torpedoes vanished from the HTD and plot. They even severed their telemetry links, becoming silent ghosts, invisible to all but the most sophisticated detection systems.

"Torpedoes are dark and cold, and coasting at speed," Ishida confirmed. "Stealth fields engaged."

"Hale," Steele ordered, his voice calm and decisive, "come to new course. Mark 123.45.160, maximum acceleration."

"Aye, sir," Hale responded, smoothly adjusting *Ranger's* heading. "Coming onto that course now—maximum acceleration."

Steele monitored the HTD as the ship executed the maneuver. *Ranger* banked gracefully, aligning with the new vector. Tenebris continued to slowly recede in their wake. The planet's dark and rocky surface shrank into the distance. With every passing moment, Tenebris's gravity well weakened its grip on the ship as they moved farther and farther away.

Steele knew the enemy frigates would be coming around the planet soon enough, but whether they realized what he had planned—had noticed the two tiny torpedoes being launched— was yet to be seen.

Steele kept his eyes fixed on the HTD, watching as *Ranger's* speed steadily and almost painfully crept upward—27g. Each second brought them farther from Tenebris and its restrictive gravity well, allowing the ship to accelerate more freely. Yet even as they gained distance, the impending confrontation weighed heavily on his mind.

A soft ping alerted him to an incoming call at his station. It was the ship's doctor. Steele opened the audio channel, bracing himself for whatever new complication had arisen. "How can I assist you, Doctor Yates?"

The doctor's voice came through, tense and hurried, underscored by the sounds of movement in the background. It was clear she was on the move. "I need to perform a critical surgery on one of my patients and it needs to be done immediately." He could hear the strain in her voice.

Steele's heart sank. "We'll soon be engaged by the enemy. Can you postpone it?"

"That's what I was afraid of, Captain," Yates replied, frustration plain in her tone. "And no, I cannot postpone the surgery. If I wait, he won't survive. It's a civilian from the surface, sir. One of the people Mr. Miller was meeting with. He was shot in the chest and has lost a lot of blood."

"Doctor, do what you must," Steele said, the words clipped but understanding. "I will do my best to keep things smooth, but I cannot guarantee that."

"Yes, sir, I understand," Yates said, her voice resolute.

"Keep me apprised of the situation," Steele added. A sick feeling twisted in his gut, an unsettling mixture of dread and helplessness. He had to trust that Yates and her team could do their jobs even under trying circumstances. She had trained for situations like this, for performing surgery during maneuvers and battle. "Captain out."

He terminated the call and turned his attention back to the HTD, focusing on the tactical display. The enemy frigates were still blocked from a direct approach by Tenebris, but that would change momentarily. The planet's bulk would only shield them for so long. Soon, those ships would emerge, closing the distance and forcing the confrontation Steele knew was inevitable.

"Guns," Steele called, his gaze shifting between the icons of the two incoming frigates and the battlecruiser coming in behind them on the HTD.

"Yes, sir?" Ishida responded, ready at her station.

"How many Mark Sevens do we have?" Steele asked, referring to the long-range, heavy ship-killer missiles in their arsenal.

"Ten, sir," Ishida answered immediately. "That's all we were able to get our hands on at the last stop."

Steele nodded. He'd thought that was the number. His mind was working through tactical possibilities. Mark Seven long-lance ship-killers were the newest missiles and had only just been introduced to the fleet within the last three months. In truth, Steele knew he was lucky to have them in his inventory. The question was—should he use them?

A preemptive strike at extreme range might just see him get lucky with a hit or two, but then again, it carried the risk of squandering precious ammunition and some of his more advanced ordnance.

Chase leaned over in her chair, clearly sensing his thought process. "Are you considering a long-range strike?" she asked, her tone carefully neutral but laced with caution.

"I was thinking of sending a volley around the planet, to hit them as they break the horizon. But I'm worried it'll be a waste of ammunition, that they will spot the strike long before it arrives. Between the two frigates, their point-defense systems could and likely would take down most, if not all, of the missiles."

Chase's eyes narrowed thoughtfully. "I am thinking your assessment is correct. At this moment it is likely we would just be wasting those missiles. When we make our move, we need to concentrate our firepower, overwhelm their PDS with enough simultaneous threats to break through and hammer them hard."

Steele drummed his fingers lightly on the armrest, acknowledging her point. Their conversation helped to make up his mind. They were up to 38g now and almost at normal cruising speed. That said, the enemy were already at speed, and they were still gaining on him with every passing moment.

"We're within extreme engagement range, sir," Ishida reported.

"Ours or theirs?" Steele asked.

"Ours, sir. We can engage, but their effective range is slightly shorter. I've added the respective ranges to the plot."

"Very good," Steele said, reaching for his coffee. The familiar warmth of the drink steadied him as he took a sip, his eyes never leaving the tactical display. "We're going to hold fire for now."

Chase leaned in slightly, her expression thoughtful. "When they get closer we could do a TOT attack. With the missile upgrades, we can be extremely precise in our attack. We know they don't have that capability."

Steele nodded, appreciating her tactical insight. A time on target strike—where multiple missiles were launched at different times to arrive simultaneously at their target—was a potent capability, a game changer, and one their adversaries were likely not aware of... at least he hoped not.

"I've considered it," Steele admitted.

"A coordinated TOT strike could catch them off guard," Chase said. "The element of surprise would be in our favor, and we'd clearly overwhelm their defenses. We could hit them with forty missiles at once instead of just twenty. But..." She lowered her voice, her eyes narrowing. "What's the problem with doing that?"

"We still have that battlecruiser out there and we may need to deal with her before we can escape the system."

"You want to save it, if we're forced to engage them?" Chase asked. "Is that it?"

"Correct. Once we unzip our fly, there is no zipping it back up."

"We have a lead on the *Starfish*," Chase said, "and they're not likely to catch up."

"Unless our drive is damaged in the coming engagement." Steele glanced back at the HTD, where the enemy frigates were steadily gaining on *Ranger*. "Let's see if my trick with the torpedoes will work first, before we try a TOT attack."

His gut told him that the real test was yet to come, and he was determined to keep as many cards up his sleeve as possible, until the moment he truly needed them, especially if he had to engage the heavy cruiser that was just behind the two frigates.

The lift door slid open, and a sharp gasp from Quinn drew Steele's attention to the back of the bridge. He turned to see

Miller, the envoy, stepping onto the bridge. The man's gray business suit was stained with blood, dark spatters marring the fabric. Dried spots of blood flecked his face and neck. His hair was askew.

Miller was a man in his early fifties, though his salt-and-pepper hair and the lines etched into his face made him appear older. He made a beeline for Steele's station.

"I must speak with you in private, Captain," Miller said insistently.

Steele felt a surge of irritation, his jaw clenching at the interruption. "Now is not a good time, Mr. Miller," he replied, forcing his voice to remain calm. The man was a high-level politico. Steele could not just order him from the bridge and expect no consequences at a later date. The man needed to be treated with kid gloves and respectfully.

Miller took a step closer. "This is important," he pressed, his tone carrying a desperate edge. "Critically so."

"Mr. Miller, it will have to wait," Steele said firmly, his patience thinning.

"It cannot," Miller insisted, his eyes locking onto Steele's.

Steele bit back an angry retort, feeling the heat of frustration boil up within him. He was not used to having his authority questioned, especially in front of his crew and on his own bridge. But he reminded himself that Miller was a civilian—and a high-ranking one, at that. Though he was not in the navy, he was part of the government and had had enough pull to have *Ranger* reassigned for his mission. Steele drew in a breath, ready to respond, when Chase stepped in.

"Mr. Miller," Chase said in a diplomatic tone, drawing the man's attention to her, "you may not be aware, but we are currently being pursued by three enemy warships, two LDF frigates and a battlecruiser. The frigates are within engagement range." She gestured to the main screen, bringing up the HTD display as she spoke. The red icons of the enemy ships were clear and menacing, closing in from the far side of Tenebris. "Though the shooting hasn't started, things are about to start happening, and we need our full attention fixed on what is to come."

Miller turned his gaze to the screen, studying the display in silence for a moment. His face shifted, the urgency in his eyes dimming as he processed the situation. Finally, he gave a small, curt nod, stepping back and away from Steele. "I apologize, Captain," he said, his voice now more subdued. "What I have to say can wait until after you have dealt with the enemy. Do what you need to do."

Steele allowed his frustration to ease. "Thank you."

Miller hesitated, then added, "Might I remain and observe the action from the bridge?"

Steele's eyes narrowed slightly. He was tempted to say no, but he relented. "As long as you stay out of the way." With that, he turned his attention back to the HTD, his gaze and mind immediately refocusing on the enemy ships and the strategy he had crafted.

It was almost time for the shooting to start.

SEVEN

"They've cleared the planet, sir," Ishida reported. "Both frigates have line of sight, and their sensors are pinging away."

Steele's eyes flicked to the HTD. The tactical display was alive with information, showing overlapping circles and spheres that marked the engagement ranges of both sides. The enemy frigates had entered his optimal firing range, while *Ranger* hovered just at the edge of theirs, but that was closing fast, as they had a slight edge on him speed-wise. The two ships were still gaining, carried forward by the momentum of their gravitic drives, while *Ranger* continued to build speed, edging steadily toward her maximum capability, which was beyond theirs.

Steele's jaw clenched as he studied the display. Though his ship was gaining speed and would eventually pull away, the engagement window was a precarious ten minutes and fifty-two seconds—long enough for them to unleash several volleys upon him.

A single well-placed hit could prove catastrophic, crippling his ship or even damaging the gravitic drive. That would leave them vulnerable to the battlecruiser, which would likely have the firepower to be able to mop up.

Steele knew he could not allow that to happen. He needed to hurt them and hurt them quickly before a sustained and prolonged engagement could hurt him. It was time to bring them in closer and end it as rapidly as possible.

"Helm, course change," Steele ordered as he transmitted the new plot to Hale's console.

Hale studied the new trajectory, a flicker of concern crossing his face as he glanced back at his captain. "Sir, turning in that direction will slow us down and extend the time we're within their missile envelope. It will even bring the enemy closer."

Steele nodded, his gaze unwavering. "I know," he said, his tone brooking no argument. "I want them closer, with less time to react to our missile volleys. Do it."

"Aye, sir." Hale's hands moved swiftly over the controls, and *Ranger* began to alter course, her sleek hull angling slightly to follow the new heading. The ship's momentum shifted subtly, a change Steele could almost feel, even with the inertial dampeners compensating for the maneuver.

Steele watched the HTD, satisfaction creeping in as he observed the enemy response a few moments later. The frigates adjusted their courses in turn, mimicking his movement. They were eager, perhaps even desperate, to keep him in range and get closer, where their older weapons would be more effective. That eagerness was something he could use against them. He was now perilously close to being fully within their engagement envelope, but he wasn't ready to show his hand.

Chase turned to him, her brow furrowed. "Why haven't we fired yet?" she asked, her voice low so only the two of them could hear.

"Because I don't want them to know our true—our effective range." Steele kept his voice calm, almost conversational, though the tension in the air was thick. "Our missile envelope is farther out than they'd expect. You and I know our true missile range has been a carefully guarded secret. We have the latest upgrades aboard, and if we reveal that now—well, it might give the store away, one that might serve the fleet well in future engagements when we return to Illidran in strength. I want them to think our effective range is comparable to theirs and that no advancements have been made since the war. For all we know, they are sharing intelligence with our real enemy."

"The Hegemony."

"And they have no reason to think otherwise, especially since the Union provided the LDF with those very ships, along with the weapons they will soon use against us. Also, if we are forced to engage the *Starfish*, I am saving that little surprise for them."

Chase's eyes widened slightly as understanding dawned. "I see. I don't like holding back."

"I don't like it either." Steele's expression remained impassive, though his mind was a whirlwind of calculations and contingency plans. It was a high-stakes gamble, one that could pay off in the long run but, at the same time, put them in a dangerous position. Patience, he reminded himself. Timing was everything, and when the moment came, he would strike with precision and overwhelming force.

"Missile launch," Ishida announced, her voice steady despite the tension that gripped the bridge.

That was what he was waiting for. Steele turned his gaze to the HTD, his eyes narrowing as he saw the threat unfolding. Both enemy frigates had fired a full volley. Ten ship-killer missiles were now streaking through the void, accelerating hard toward *Ranger*. Each missile was more advanced than the ones they'd already faced from Tenebris's defense grid. Those missiles by comparison were ancient.

"Quinn," Steele said, his voice calm but firm, "this is your show. Do what you do."

"Aye, sir." Quinn's hands flew over her console, engaging

the ship's countermeasures. "Two minutes, forty-five seconds," she called out, giving the countdown until impact.

Steele's eyes returned to the plot. The two frigates were flying in tight formation. *Tatsua* was leading by a hair. The two ships were no more than ten thousand kilometers apart from one another. It was a good move, meant to maximize not only their offensive, but also their defensive firepower.

"Guns," Steele commanded, "load Mark Sixes into the tubes. Target the lead frigate, the *Tatsua*. I want a solid lock and a firing solution before you launch. Stagger the pattern of attack."

"Aye, sir," Ishida replied. "Staggered attack. Target painted and locked."

The Mark Sixes were powerful, mid-range ship-killer missiles, designed to evade point-defense fire and punch through shields and hull plating with brutal efficiency.

Steele leaned forward in his chair, his gaze locked on the HTD. His course change, and the enemy's reaction to it, was bringing the two frigates into the area where *Ranger*'s torpedoes had gone dark. The torpedoes were still moving at speed and drifting silently in space, cloaked behind an active stealth field and waiting for the moment to wake up and strike.

"Guns, you know what I want with the torpedoes?" he asked.

"Aye, sir," Ishida replied. "I suspect I do. Once our missiles are in final engagement range, the torpedoes are to go live. Is that right?"

"Correct," Steele confirmed. "Make sure the torpedoes target *Kei*, not *Tatsua*. With luck, the sudden appearance of the torpedoes will throw off their point-defense systems and cause just enough confusion to give our attack an edge, not to mention splitting their fire, allowing a decent portion of the missile volley to slam home against the *Tatsua*."

"I understand, sir. Missiles loaded and awaiting your order."

Steele's jaw clenched, but he kept his demeanor composed. "Guns, flush the missile pods."

"Firing," Ishida responded. "Missiles away. Reloading, forty-five seconds."

The Mark Sixes streaked away, burning hard and cutting through the void, accelerating rapidly toward the enemy. Steele felt a tightening in his stomach, a familiar knot of anticipation as he watched the HTD and plot. The enemy's ship-killer missiles were still inbound, burning toward them at speed. The two volleys flashed past one another.

Quinn was already hard at work. She had activated *Ranger's* full suite of countermeasures, launching electronic warfare drones into space. The drones had already begun broadcasting false signals, attempting to confuse and mislead the enemy's targeting systems. Pulses of jamming energy rippled through the void, and ECM screens flickered around *Ranger*, distorting sensor data and masking their true position as best they could.

"They've launched a second volley," Ishida reported, her voice tense. "Ten more missiles inbound. Time to impact: two minutes, forty seconds."

Steele clenched his jaw, the knot in his gut tightening almost painfully. Like the unescapable passing of time, he watched the missiles continue to close. One relentless tick after another...

"I believe those missiles are Mark Threes," Quinn said, her voice clipped but composed as she analyzed the incoming threat data. "High confidence."

Steele didn't respond; his eyes were glued to the HTD. Mark Threes were older, and he understood his ship's EW systems should prove to be effective against them. But—each incoming missile was still incredibly dangerous. He blew out a slow, calming breath and continued to watch. The missiles were closing in, just fifty thousand klicks away, and so far, *Ranger's* countermeasures had only managed to fool a couple of them, drawing the weapons off and away.

The remainder still burned toward them, locked solidly onto their position. His stomach twisted as he watched the numbers steadily tick down to contact. Then, in swift succession, two more missiles veered off course, their guidance disrupted and spoofed. It was a small victory, but not nearly enough.

A quick check of his console showed a glimmer of hope: *Ranger*'s energy shielding had nearly reached full strength, now hovering close to one hundred percent. It wouldn't make them invulnerable, but it would give them a fighting chance if they received a hit or two. Steele took a steadying breath, forcing himself to remain calm as the missiles continued to bear down upon his ship. They had to hold out, and they had to hit back hard.

The missiles continued to close—thirty thousand klicks. Another missile abruptly veered off course, falling prey to *Ranger*'s countermeasures. But the rest burned onward in their relentless approach, unwavering and deadly.

"Point-defense firing," Quinn reported, her voice taut with focus. The ship's defensive systems roared to life, kinetic rounds and directed energy bursts streaking and lancing outward at the incoming missiles. Unlike the simpler surface-to-orbit variants, these ship-killers were built to evade point-defense fire, essentially to survive as long as possible. Their onboard systems made minute adjustments, maneuvering around the physical countermeasures with chilling precision.

At ten thousand klicks, the point-defense finally found its mark. Two missiles disappeared from the tactical plot with a violent flash. A heartbeat later, a third and then fourth followed, their destruction lighting up the HTD. Two more were taken out in rapid succession, but it wasn't enough.

Steele gripped the armrests tightly as the missiles seemed

to merge with *Ranger*'s tag. He barely had time to brace himself before the last missile struck home, impacting the energy shields and detonating with frightening force. The ship rocked, the deck bucking under his feet. The lights dimmed briefly, and a deep, ominous groan reverberated through *Ranger*'s hull, as if the ship itself was protesting the blow. Steele gritted his teeth. Then the bucking ceased, and things settled.

They had survived.

"Energy shielding down to seventy percent," Quinn reported. "Some of that got through, sir. I'm showing several of my point-defense cannons and energy batteries offline and/or damaged."

Steele forced himself to stay focused, calm, and in control. "Atheena, damage report."

"Still assessing, Captain. However, I can report there seems to be no critical systems affected. There appears to be light to moderate damage to the armored hull. No breaches of the inner pressure hull detected. I have tasked nanites to respond to the affected areas and begin effecting repairs."

Heart pounding in his chest, Steele let out a slow breath. His ship was a little battered but clearly unbroken, not to mention still capable.

"Our missiles are in final approach," Ishida reported, drawing his attention. "None spoofed by the enemy EW, or countermeasures. Our guidance systems are clearly better than theirs, sir. PDS systems on both frigates detected. Activating torpedoes—now."

"Very good," Steele replied, his eyes returning to the HTD. The enemy frigates had adjusted course minutely, maneuvering into positions that allowed them to better concentrate their point-defense systems on *Ranger*'s incoming volley.

The screen flashed as the engagement played out in real time, missiles being intercepted and destroyed. Twenty missiles became eighteen, then seventeen, then ten as the enemy's point-defense systems blazed away.

An icon flared on the HTD as *Ranger*'s two torpedoes dropped their stealth fields and roared back to life. The gravitic drives ignited less than forty thousand klicks from the target.

Wondering what it was like on the enemy's bridge and understanding he already knew, Steele gripped the armrests of his command chair, his knuckles whitening as he watched the final moments unfold. As the missiles closed in, the torpedoes drove home from a completely different attack angle. At first the frigates did not react to the attack, then *Kei*'s point-defense shifted almost sluggishly. In the blink of an eye, one torpedo vanished in a flash of light.

Then the remaining missiles, along with the last surviving torpedo, struck their targets with brutal force. Explosions flared, momentarily outshining the stars, as kinetic energy and warheads tore through energy shielding and into the hulls of the frigates.

"Three good impacts on the *Tatsua*," Ishida reported calmly, her voice almost eerily detached. "Good torpedo hit on *Kei*."

Steele exhaled a breath, his heart still pounding in his chest.

"Point-defense firing," Quinn announced. "Ten seconds…"

Steele's attention snapped back to the HTD, where the last enemy missile volley was on its final approach. Five missiles remained, streaking toward *Ranger*. The rest had been success-fully spoofed, chasing phantom targets. But the remaining five were far from harmless, and Steele felt the dread settle in his gut as he watched them close the distance.

There was nothing he could do but watch.

Once more, the point-defense guns roared to life, kinetic rounds and directed energy pulses streaking out to meet and intercept the incoming threat. The missiles dropped from five to three, then two… but it wasn't enough. The ship shuddered under the impact, rocking violently as the last two missiles hammered home. The deck beneath Steele's feet bucked. *Ranger* groaned as though in pain. The lights flickered and then failed, casting the bridge in momentary darkness before stabilizing and coming back on.

"Two missile impacts," Quinn reported, her voice strained but composed. "Energy shielding is down to twenty percent."

"Captain," Atheena's voice chimed in, calm and efficient even amidst the chaos and groaning... *Ranger* protesting. "Moderate damage to the armored hull on the port upper quarter. There is a pressure hull breach on deck two, section three. There is a fire on deck three, section three. Fire suppression systems are engaged. I project the fire will be contained within the next thirty seconds and extinguished in less than forty. Several systems overloaded due to the energy spike and discharge of energy. Those systems are being rebooted. Emergency protocols have been engaged. No word on casualties. Still assessing systems damage. A full diagnostic report will be available shortly."

Steele took a breath, steadying himself. The damage to his ship was mounting, but they were still alive and *Ranger* seemed to be in one piece. It could have been worse. He glanced down at his status display. There were red warning lights flashing all across the board. *Ranger* had been hurt, but she seemed functional, not to mention capable.

"Hale," he called, "how's the drive doing?"

"Still functioning, sir," Hale responded.

"Very good," Steele replied, forcing himself to remain calm. He turned his gaze back to the plot, his eyes narrowing as he assessed the state of the enemy frigates.

How badly had they been hurt?

Would they back off, or were they still determined to close the distance and continue the fight?

"*Kei* is breaking up," Chase said, her voice filled with a mix of relief and triumph. "She's done for, sir!"

Torpedoes were meant for use against larger ships with much heavier shielding and armor. Steele watched the plot, feeling a fierce stab of exhilaration as he saw *Kei*'s icon flicker and die. The ship, still hurtling forward at high speed, began to fracture. Her hull split apart under the strain, and then her main reactor went critical, erupting in a violent explosion that was fully represented on the display. *Kei*'s tag was replaced with a navigational hazard icon.

"Good shooting, Guns," Steele congratulated.

A cheer erupted on the bridge, cutting through the tension and lifting spirits in a moment of shared triumph.

"How's the other target?" Chase asked.

"I judge the *Tatsua* to be heavily damaged," Ishida reported after a moment. "Sensors are picking up secondary detonations and serious atmospheric leakage. Her gravitic drive is fluctuating badly, and she's begun to decelerate. She's braking hard."

"*Tatsua*'s disengaging," Chase confirmed excitedly, her eyes locked on the HTD. "She's had enough."

Steele's gaze followed the *Tatsua*'s plot as the frigate braked and slowly turned away, with the clear intent of limping from the battlefield. The damage they'd inflicted was near catastrophic, forcing the smaller enemy ship to break off her attack.

Ranger had shown her claws, and they had dug deep, sending a clear message to anyone who dared underestimate them. Yet as he watched the crippled frigate struggle away, Steele hardened his heart. There was no room for pity, let alone forgiveness or mercy, not in a fight like this. They had intended to kill *Ranger* and now, he would finish them.

"Guns, I want another volley on *Tatsua*, five missiles, Mark Sixes," Steele ordered, his voice cold and resolute. "Fire when ready."

"She's out of the fight, sir," Ishida protested, hesitating. Her words carried an unspoken question, as if asking if he really wanted to attack a crippled foe, one who clearly had lost the appetite for a fight.

A sharp stab of irritation flared in Steele's chest. He glanced around the bridge, feeling the weight of every gaze suddenly on him, including Miller's. The burden of command meant making decisions in the heat of the moment that others might shirk from or not understand—decisions that could and would likely haunt him later. He could not afford to be questioned. As captain, his orders were to be followed. It was that simple.

"Listen up, people," Steele said. "I will only say this once. This is war. The Union is at war with the Protectorate. The *Tatsua* is still an enemy combatant and can be brought to a shipyard, repaired, and returned to action. We will finish her, here and now. When our fleet comes to Illidran to reestablish control, this action will translate into saving lives... our comrades' lives. More importantly, it will mean one less asset for the LDF to use." He hardened his tone. "Now, Guns, kindly launch that volley."

"Aye, sir," Ishida replied, her voice quiet but resolute. "Missiles launched and away."

A heavy silence fell over the bridge. Every eye was glued to the HTD as the missiles streaked toward the *Tatsua*. The seconds stretched endlessly, each heartbeat echoing with anticipation and the grim finality of what was to come.

Ishida broke the silence. "Detecting no PDS fire, let alone countermeasures. I think *Tatsua*'s sensors are down. Enemy energy shielding is definitely offline."

Steele felt a familiar, sickening tightening in his gut. The *Tatsua*'s surviving crew would have no warning, no chance to react. Death was closing in, and there would be no escape, not for them, not this day.

The five missiles hit almost simultaneously, punching and

driving deep into the enemy ship's hull before detonating. Steele understood he had just killed the ship. No frigate could survive what he'd just done to the *Tatsua*. He watched, one hand gripping the armrest of his station tightly as explosions ripped through the frigate, rapidly tearing her apart from the inside out.

"*Tatsua* is gone," Ishida said, her voice solemn in the sudden silence. "We've killed them..."

"Yes, we did," Chase breathed.

The bridge remained silent, the moment pressing down on them all. Steele kept his face impassive, hiding any flicker of emotion. The decision to kill the frigate had been a necessary one, but that didn't make it any easier. Between the two enemy ships, Steele had just killed at least seventy-six people.

"I warned you, Crenice," Steele murmured to himself, his voice carrying a note of grim finality. On the HTD, the *Tatsua*'s tag flickered out, replaced by a navigational hazard marker that clearly designated the wreckage left in the barrage's wake. "This is on you, not me."

Steele took a breath, his gaze lingering for a moment longer on the HTD where *Tatsua* had been before shifting his focus back to the larger tactical picture. The fight wasn't over. The *Starfish* was still out there and burning her way toward them.

EIGHT

Steele adjusted the HTD, shifting the display's focus away from the wreckage of the destroyed frigates. His attention homed in on the distant icon of the enemy battlecruiser. *Starfish* was edging closer to clearing the shadow of the planet, but despite her relentless pursuit, she was beginning to slip farther behind.

Ranger's gravitic drive now had them pushing 49g, finally outpacing the battlecruiser, which was straining at 48g. *Starfish* was nearing her maximum capacity with which to manipulate gravity.

Steele rubbed his jaw, releasing a quiet breath of relief. The *Starfish* was powerful, yes, but with *Ranger*'s speed advantage, it was now a futile chase, at least from her perspective. They were steadily, with every passing moment, leaving the battlecruiser in their wake, slipping beyond her reach and edging closer to the relative safety of the Fringe Zone.

He scanned the space ahead, studying the faint blips of civilian ships also fleeing from the Illidran System. Small freighters, shuttles, and a few older transports were burning hard for the Fringe, hoping to escape. None were a threat, and, more importantly, there were no ships or warships in their direct path. *Ranger* would reach the Fringe Zone unchallenged.

"Hale," Steele said, "maintain our heading and bring us up to 50g and hold steady there."

"Aye, sir. Will do," Hale responded, adjusting the controls to push *Ranger* to the next level of speed. "50g and hold steady."

Chase glanced over from her console and then back again. "On our current course, sir, we'll be able to go jump drive active in a little over twenty-two hours. I'd say the enemy's got no chance of catching or intercepting us."

"They won't and they don't," Steele agreed, but his eyes shifted back to the HTD. He could see the *Starfish*, now fully cleared of the planet's gravity shadow and settling in on their tail.

He tapped a few commands on his display and brought up sensor data on the *Starfish*. He studied them for a long moment. From the readings of the battlecruiser's gravitic drive output, it was apparent the ship was pushing her drive to the limits, likely in a last-ditch attempt to close the gap. Steele suspected her engineering crew was squeezing every possible ounce of speed from their aging gravitic drive.

He knew it wouldn't help.

A little curious, he pulled up more detailed data on the ship's specifications. The *Starfish* was an older Warrior Class ship—an obsolescent cast-off from the Union's mothball fleet, dragged out eight years ago and put back into service for the LDF. She was over seventy-nine years old and her service history was quite long.

With a crew complement of seven hundred four, she was antiquated by the Union's standards, but still heavily armed. She boasted six missile pods, each capable of launching five missiles every six and a half minutes, along with a strong complement of close-in maser batteries, thirty-two to be exact, and outdated railguns for close-quarters defensive work. All in all, despite her age, she was still a powerful platform.

But it was her drive that gave *Ranger* the advantage. The *Starfish*'s aging gravitic drive, designed for a maximum output of 50g in her prime, was now struggling to maintain just 48g, let alone meet *Ranger*'s speed. Steele felt a quiet satisfaction knowing that *Ranger*'s own state-of-the-art drive could push beyond that limit if needed. There were few, if any, vessels her size capable of such speeds.

"XO," Steele said, closing the screen and turning to Chase. "I need you to start compiling a full damage report. I'd like to see what systems I can rely upon and what I cannot. Also, I'd like a full diagnostic run on the jump drive."

"I'll get right on it, sir," Chase replied, her voice steady. "Recommend we set Condition Two since action isn't imminent. For the time being, we can stand some of our people down, ease the strain and swap out critical positions."

Steele considered the suggestion for a moment. Condition Two—modified general quarters—was still a state of high readiness that allowed the general crew to remain on alert without the full strain of general quarters, where everyone manned their stations. Essential stations related to weapons, sensors, and damage control would remain manned at all times. Non-critical personnel would rotate and help keep them operational.

"Very well," he agreed, glancing over the bridge before giving Chase a nod to proceed. The tension of the last few hours was plain. His people looked tired, weary, and spent. "Do it."

Chase turned to her console, her fingers moving deftly over the controls. A moment later, an automated voice echoed throughout *Ranger*.

"Now set Condition Two throughout the ship. All stations manned and ready in accordance with Condition Two protocols. Repeat, set Condition Two throughout the ship."

The announcement repeated once more.

Steele leaned back in his command chair, stretching out his arms and easing the tension that had settled in his shoulders, not to mention his back. He groaned slightly. He took another sip of his coffee, then returned the cup to its holder.

From the rear of the bridge, out of the corner of his eye, he noticed Miller taking a single, purposeful step toward him. The message was clear: the envoy wanted a word.

"Right," Steele said, rising from his command chair and pulling himself to his feet. "Chase, you have the bridge."

"I have command, sir," Chase replied. "The ship is mine."

"Mr. Miller." Steele turned and addressed him, his tone firm but polite, and gestured toward his office with an outstretched hand. "Would you kindly join me?"

Steele began walking before the man even replied.

"I would, Captain, thank you." Miller fell into step behind Steele.

As they approached the hatch to his office, the marine on duty snapped to attention, her posture rigid and respectful. With a slight nod, Steele acknowledged her as the hatch slid aside, allowing him and Miller to enter. The sounds of the bridge, the low hum of consoles, the random chimes, and the quiet murmurs of the bridge crew faded as the hatch closed behind them, sealing them in a quieter, more private setting.

Steele moved toward his desk and, without a word, gestured to a chair opposite. He sank into his own seat, adjusting slightly to face Miller, who took the offered chair, settling in with a slight air of tension between them both.

"You're going to want to clean up after this," Steele said, breaking the silence. He gestured at the man's suit. "You're spattered in blood."

Miller glanced down at his stained suit as if noticing the blood for the first time. He blinked for a moment, let go a heavy breath, and then looked back up at Steele, his expression becoming a hard one.

"It got a little frisky down there, Captain," Miller said.

Steele decided that was the understatement of the year. "So, Mr. Miller, what is it you wish to talk about?"

"Captain," Miller began, his tone growing grave, "we cannot leave this system."

Steele blinked, momentarily thrown by the unexpected statement. "What?" he asked, his voice laced with patent disbelief. "You cannot be serious. Surely you understand why we must go…"

"We have to stay," Miller repeated, leaning forward and tapping Steele's desk with a finger, his gaze unwavering. "We cannot leave, not yet. We—"

"Are you crazy?" Steele interrupted the man. He was absolutely incredulous, for it was insanity to stay. "The LDF has seized control of this system, and there's an enemy battlecruiser in our wake. The *Starfish* will likely pursue us all the way to the Fringe Zone just to make certain we leave the system. As old as that ship is, she still outguns us by a wide margin. And you want to stay? Tell me you are not serious."

Miller met his gaze without flinching. "That may be true, but it doesn't change the fact that we cannot leave."

"I can arrange an emergency pod for you, Mr. Miller. I will even happily signal the LDF to arrange a pickup for you. That is, if you wish to remain behind, because I do not."

"That would not be ideal, Captain."

Steele exhaled sharply, his frustration simmering. "And why, exactly, is that? Why do you need me to stay in this shithole of a system?"

"The Valkorians are behind what just happened," Miller said, his voice low and tense. "At least, I have been led to believe so. All evidence points in that direction."

Steele felt his expression darken. He wasn't surprised by that announcement. After all, the systems of the Protectorate had once belonged to the Valkorian Hegemony, and they had made no secret about wanting to take it all back.

"I will need more to go on than just that," Steele said.

"I'm with the Intelligence Directorate, naval branch," Miller continued, his tone frank.

"No shit, really?" Steele shot back, the sarcasm sharp enough to cut. "Tell me it isn't so."

Miller blinked, momentarily taken aback. "You knew? Who told you? Or rather, who briefed you on my mission?"

"No one briefed me, and no one told me," Steele admitted, watching Miller's expression shift from surprise to curiosity.

"Then how did you find out?"

Steele let out a sigh. He was spent. His patience had limits, and he was rapidly reaching them. "Destroyers like *Ranger* aren't typically reassigned for diplomatic runs. Those jobs routinely go to frigates or messenger packets, not recon destroyers. The fact that we're here and not participating in a planned fleet exercise is a clue in and of itself. After you had our orders changed, for a low-level trade envoy, it wasn't hard to figure out something was off with your cover story, that you were more than a basic politico." Steele paused. "I've also had, you could say, extensive experience with the Intelligence Directorate, something I would like to forget."

Miller's gaze softened, a hint of respect showing. "That's perceptive, Captain."

"It's hard to forget the smell of Directorate bullshit," Steele deadpanned.

Miller grinned at him. "I knew I'd chosen right when I selected you and this ship."

"Uh-huh," Steele said. "You knew the shit might hit the fan, didn't you?"

"Though my superiors had their doubts, I suspected it would, but a few weeks in the future." He paused, as if considering his next move. "Atheena, verify to the captain my true identity."

The construct's neutral voice filled the office. "Captain, you are conversing with Lieutenant Commander Dillard Macon of the Union Navy, currently assigned to the Intelligence Directorate."

Steele let go an unhappy breath. "So, how can I help you, Commander Macon?"

"In public and before others," Miller—now Macon—continued, "I'd appreciate it if you continued to refer to me as Miller."

"All right, Miller it is." Steele gave a curt, reluctant nod. He'd never much cared for intelligence operatives; they had a knack for making simple situations worse, not to mention more convoluted than necessary, dragging hidden agendas and layers of secrecy wherever they went. It had complicated his life once before, and judging by the direction of where this conversation was headed, it would do so again, and soon too.

"We cannot leave the system," Miller insisted.

"Because the Valkorian Hegemony is behind the uprising," Steele replied, studying Miller's expression. "But that still doesn't explain why we can't jump out and simply report back to Fleet what is happening. It will become their headache at that point, one I will gladly hand off to someone else."

"*Viper* will be doing that for us, telling Fleet what's happened here."

"I don't even want to know how you know about *Viper*." Steele suspected Atheena was keeping the man informed. That or he had a direct link to *Ranger*'s tactical feed.

Miller's gaze hardened. "The reason we stopped at Tenebris was so that I could meet face-to-face with one of our key contacts in-system. And when I say key, I mean he was an undercover operative, one of our top people."

"At Malborne Industries," Steele interjected, piecing the puzzle together.

"That's correct, Captain." A note of fatigue crept into Miller's voice. "The man currently in surgery, Garrand Misope Argonola. He was my contact." He let go a heavy breath. "Doctor Yates tells me he may not survive. He was shot in the chest and his heart damaged."

Steele felt a pang of sympathy, nodding slowly. "I'm sorry to hear that."

"He was one of our deep operatives in the LDF contract department—a good man, a Union man, one placed there intentionally. I was his handler," Miller added, his voice laced with a mixture of regret and respect as he glanced downward. He fell silent.

Steele also remained quiet, allowing Miller a moment. He knew better than to offer empty platitudes.

"The Valkorians have a fleet in the system, a full task force," Miller said, his tone grim. "They apparently slipped it in, a few ships at a time over the last few weeks to avoid detection. So our man told me before everything went to shit."

Steele sat up straighter in his chair, his mind racing. This wasn't good. "How certain are you of this intel?"

"Me, personally... not very certain," Miller admitted, a note of frustration in his voice. "That's why we need to confirm the information I received, which is why we can't just leave..."

Steele's eyes narrowed as understanding dawned. He slapped a palm down on his desk. "Home Fleet will rush to put down the rebellion in the entirety of the Protectorate. They will send task forces to all four systems with the goal of beating the LDF down and restoring order. A section of the fleet will likely be dispatched here to Illidran, thinking it's just a matter of suppressing an uprising, putting the LDF here in its place."

Miller nodded. "Exactly. And if I'm right, our real enemy will be lying in wait, with a much larger force than our people expect. It could be a devastating ambush, and the start of a new war. The Valkorians mean to strike a blow against the Union, and it will begin here in Illidran."

Steele's mind churned with the implications. A hidden Valkorian fleet, positioned to strike... it was a nightmare scenario, one he did not wish to contemplate. He still had bad dreams from the last war. And yet, if *Ranger* could confirm their presence, they might be able to turn the tables and prevent a catastrophe, at least warn the fleet so that when the navy came, they were prepared for the Valkorians. That's clearly what this man wanted of him.

"The Valkorians apparently assured the Protectorate that they'd support their independence with military might," Miller continued, "and it seems they've made good on that promise. There are reportedly thirty-two enemy combatants hidden within the system, including two fleet carriers and a pair of dreadnaughts, with more on the way."

Steele shook his head, frowning. "That makes no sense. Before we took control, the Hegemony ruled the Protectorate with an iron fist. Brutal measures, forced labor, constant surveillance—the locals can't possibly believe the Valkorians would treat them any better if they regained control, let alone guarantee their independence. If they push us out, the Hegemony will swoop back in and simply take over. They'll lose every freedom they've gained, and life will likely be far worse than before."

Miller gave a slight shrug, his face tinged with frustration. "That's the logical conclusion, yes. But no matter how good they have it now, some people are just plain stupid, Captain. There are factions that pine for the good old days, when the Valkorians had their boots on the necks of the people. Sadly, it seems the LDF and local governments are willing to trade stability for a dream of self-rule, self-determination, regardless of the realities of what will happen after the fact. They've clearly bought into the Valkorian Hegemony's bullshit."

Steele shook his head. He still had difficulty believing what he was hearing. In the years since the Union had assumed control, the Protectorate had thrived. Personal freedoms had expanded, the economy was booming, and though there were still more people than jobs, there was more work available than ever.

Yet, clearly for some, the idea of absolute autonomy was worth risking everything, worth rising up against the Union, even if it meant aligning with a brutal regime, one that had kept them subjugated for more than a century. The irony wasn't lost on him: to escape the Union, they'd joined forces with a dictatorship that would likely crush them the moment the Union was out of the way. Could the governments of the Protectorate really be that stupid?

But something still nagged at him... how had they managed to sneak such a large force in-system and under the nose of the Union? He snapped a finger.

"The solar rejuvenator," Steele mused aloud as understanding dawned. "That's how they snuck the ships in—by periodically bringing down the HTD. Every time they dropped the system-wide detection network, they could slip in a ship or two."

Miller nodded thoughtfully. "It is certainly one possibility."

"And another?" Steele pressed.

"They reconfigured their drive signatures to resemble civilian ships," Miller replied. "The LDF controls the system detection network. They covered for the Hegemony—spoofing the information flow—especially if they staggered the arrivals and made sure Union warships were nowhere nearby when Valkorian warships dropped into the system from Slipstream space."

"But hiding them? That's an entirely different story. I understand Illidran is a large star system, but where would they keep these ships once they arrived, especially a large group of them?"

"The Reach," Miller answered. "That's what I was told by multiple sources."

"Within the asteroid field? Are you serious? It may have escaped your notice, but there are thousands of people living and working out there. Any warship would stick out like a sore thumb. Someone would notice and report it or at least talk about it, and then word would get out. You're in the navy. You know how rumors are... it's even worse on the civilian side..."

Miller's expression was grim. "Not necessarily. The Reach is vast, with dozens of mining stations, processing facilities, and independent contractors, not to mention habitats. If the LDF has effectively silenced key witnesses or threatened anyone with knowledge, it could be feasible."

"I'm still not buying it... they'd be seen by someone. Heck, as I said, at the very least rumors would be floating about."

"Unless..." Miller stopped.

"Unless what?"

"What if they've parked those ships within the Exclusion Zone?" Miller suggested. "What then?"

Steele sucked in a breath, the implications sinking in. "The Exclusion Zone is a graveyard," he replied slowly. "It's the site of the last battle for Illidran—a place where hundreds of ships clashed in a brutal, no-holds-barred fight to the death."

"And to this day few are permitted in because of the dangers," Miller added, his voice steady. "Unexploded mines and ordnance, some of which is still live... are spread all across the zone. There are even sentient weapon systems that activate if disturbed. Only specialized recovery teams and select salvage operators are allowed in there, all of which are controlled by the LDF. It would be the perfect place to park a fleet, a place no one would think to look, a place few dare go. More important... the Exclusion Zone is inside the Reach..."

The implications spiraled through Steele's mind. If the Valkorians had indeed maneuvered ships into the Exclusion Zone under the guise of salvagers or simply hidden them amidst the many wrecks floating out there, it would be nearly impossible to detect them—especially if the LDF was actively covering their movements and spoofing the detection network. Yet the complexity of pulling off such an operation was almost unimaginable.

"It would have taken months of work just to pull something like that off. Why hasn't word leaked out sooner?" Steele asked. "What you are suggesting would require the LDF and the Hegemony to go to extraordinary lengths. And if even one person slipped up... the jig would be up."

Miller held his gaze, unfazed. "I agree, it sounds far-fetched, and to be honest, somehow the Directorate missed it. But now that we know, we need to check it out all the same. Captain, we have to go to the Reach and locate the enemy. If there is a Valkorian force in-system, Fleet needs to know... before they react."

"We could just jump out," Steele said, the words almost a plea. "Return home and pass along what you've learned."

"Suspecting and knowing for certain are two different things. If we have concrete evidence... something that could not be ignored or shuffled aside... you know how the bureaucrats are. My work, my intelligence might be ignored..."

Steele's gaze hardened. "You're talking about risking my ship, and the lives of everyone aboard, to confirm a suspicion."

"It's not a suspicion."

"If you're wrong..."

Miller met his eyes, unwavering. "But if I'm right..."

"It means war." Steele felt a chill sink into his bones. "A second great war," he murmured, the enormity of it settling home, "and it would be worse than the first—since both sides have built up considerably."

Miller nodded. "The next conflict won't be confined to a

handful of contested systems; it will tear through the Protectorate, Union, and Hegemony, engulfing dozens of worlds... You know this to be true. In the fight ahead, we will need every edge, every advantage just to survive..."

Steele closed his eyes for a moment, a deeply unhappy breath escaping him. In his mind, he could still see Admiral Kellenin's battlegroup bombarding Mortain's World, pounding it to little more than ash and memory. The Hegemony admiral was a beast, a true monster come to life. He had mercilessly hammered a defenseless and neutral planet, killing millions in the process.

The admiral had been setting an example for the rest of the star system, showing them what would happen if they resisted the might and power of the Hegemony. It had worked too, for the locals had surrendered soon after, submitting to the Valkorian subjugation.

Steele had been a junior lieutenant aboard a light cruiser, one of a handful of Union ships in the system at the time of the attack. They had been helpless to intervene, and had only been present and in-system to assist with the evacuation efforts of Union personnel. When their own commodore had ordered them to pull out, the Union had left a lot of people behind to the tender mercies of the enemy. That had been in the opening days of the war, before the real killing had begun.

"War," he echoed, feeling a sense of dread.

"I cannot order you to turn around, Captain," Miller said, his tone steady. "I don't outrank you and I'm not in your chain of command. My assignment was simply to meet our contact, along with several others, to verify his information and then return home to report my findings."

"And now you're asking me to investigate, to verify this information for you, to prove beyond a reasonable doubt that the Hegemony has a fleet in-system."

"Correct," Miller admitted without hesitation. "I'm asking you to make a command decision—and to do so voluntarily."

Steele remained silent, his mind racing as he processed the enormity of what Miller was asking. This wasn't a simple reconnaissance or a routine mission. Miller was essentially asking him to evade the pursuing battlecruiser, double back, and dive deep into the Illidran Star System, hunting for Valkorian forces potentially hidden within one of the system's asteroid belts—warships equipped with technology nearly as advanced as *Ranger*'s. That said, if he indulged Miller and found nothing, the admiralty would have questions for him. It might even cost him his command.

Miller's voice softened. "I know *Ranger* is important to you, as is her crew. But this is but one ship." He paused, choosing his words carefully. "This single act could make a real difference. It's a risk, I understand. But if we can verify that the enemy is here, and that they have a significant presence..."

"We could prevent the navy from walking into a potential ambush." Steele fell silent for several heartbeats. "And if we're wrong..."

"If we're wrong, you are simply commanding a destroyer that altered course for an unscheduled reconnaissance into hostile territory. There is no doubt in my mind with this ship's stealth capabilities you can avoid the LDF and the detection grid—then escape. But if I'm right..."

"Fleet will be better prepared when they do come," Steele concluded, letting out a long breath. "Instead of bringing a simple hammer, they'd bring a sledgehammer."

"Exactly," Miller replied, nodding. "If we can get hard intel on the force here in-system—"

"If there's even a force to begin with," Steele interrupted, though he couldn't shake the gnawing certainty in his gut. He had a feeling the Union's real enemy was indeed lurking within

Illidran. The Protectorate's sudden uprising made no sense otherwise; they wouldn't risk rebellion without someone powerful backing them up, offering safeguards against Union retribution.

Miller was right.

The enemy was here.

"*Ranger* was built for a mission like this," Miller pressed. "With her stealth capabilities and powerful sensor suite, she can gather intel without detection. She's the perfect platform for—"

Steele raised his hand, cutting him off. "Save your breath. You've convinced me."

Miller's face registered cautious relief. "Then you'll do it?"

"I will." Steele nodded, feeling a surge of excitement at the prospect. The challenge of sneaking back into the system, right under the detection grid's nose, testing *Ranger*'s full capabilities and his own as her captain, was terribly enticing. This was something he'd been dreaming of doing...

It was a risk, and one that might have serious repercussions if he miscalculated, but if Miller was right, the intelligence gathered would more than justify everything. "I'll do it, Mr. Miller. I'll find this Valkorian fleet for you."

"Then you believe they're here," Miller stated, though it was clear he wasn't asking.

"I do. But to pull this off, my XO will need to be brought in. She will need to know your real identity. She must understand what we're up against, what we are facing. The crew, too, will need some details."

Miller paused, considering. "Very well. You can reveal my identity to Commander Chase, but not to the rest of the crew. As for the mission, share only what you need to... that we're hunting an enemy fleet."

"The crew will guess who you are—or at least what you represent," Steele pointed out. "They are not stupid and there's no avoiding it."

Miller gave a small shrug.

"Right... Atheena," Steele said, "please ask Commander Chase to join me in my office."

NINE

"What are your thoughts?" Steele asked, studying Chase's unusually grave expression closely. They were seated in his office, the quiet hum of the ship surrounding them. Miller had left five minutes earlier, leaving the two of them to consider the gravity of what lay ahead, what the man was asking of *Ranger* and her crew.

Chase leaned back in her chair, her gaze drifting up toward the overhead. She took a deep breath, clearly gathering her thoughts, letting the silence settle between them. Steele didn't rush her; he knew this wasn't a question she'd answer lightly, especially after all they had both learned. Finally, she lowered her eyes to meet his.

"I think you've already made up your mind, Captain," Chase replied, her tone measured. "My opinion is irrelevant at this point."

"That's not what I meant, and you know it," Steele countered.

Chase sighed, her fingers tapping lightly on the arm of the chair. "I don't like what we're about to attempt. I would prefer we jump away—get out of this system—and make our way home. But..." She paused, choosing her words carefully. "The potential gains outweigh the risks. If there's even a chance we could confirm the presence of a Valkorian fleet in Illidran, gather information on them, it would be invaluable intel. I can't help but feel we'd be directly saving lives."

"That's my thinking as well and why I am going along with it," Steele agreed, nodding slowly. He could see the same unease reflected in her eyes that he felt himself. "When the defense grid lit us up, I found myself hesitating. That was a mistake, one I will not make again. If Miller is correct, this means war. The Union needs to know..."

"As I see it, we really don't have much of a choice," Chase said, her tone resigned. "If there's a hostile fleet lurking out there, and I believe it likely, we can pinpoint its location, not to mention gather hard data on its composition..." She trailed off.

"Exactly," Steele replied, nodding. "That last bit alone will be quite valuable to Fleet's planners."

"We still need to break off and lose the *Starfish*." Chase's expression hardened, her tactical mind already spinning through the next steps. "Even though we're already on the edges of the detection net, that won't be easy. They're actively pinging away with sensor sweeps."

"I know." Steele drummed his desk with his fingers.

"But there's another issue. Our stock of missiles is seriously depleted. We're also running low on PDS rounds. I don't much enjoy the idea of heading back in-system with limited strike capability."

"We're going to have to look to the secure depots," Steele said.

"You mean Fleet's prepositioned caches?"

Steele nodded. "Exactly. They have their own defensive systems, and the LDF doesn't have the firepower to breach them. Even attempting to do so would be a wasted effort, for everything inside would be destroyed via self-destruct mechanisms."

Chase looked thoughtful but wary. "The LDF will most likely have eyes on those depots. That'll be a problem for us, especially considering they're all deeper in the system. Even if we approach under stealth, the moment we cross into their perimeter and dock at one of the stations, we'd pop up on their sensors as a red flag, an anomaly that shouldn't be there. They'd send ships after us straight off, and it takes time to load munitions."

"Not necessarily," Steele countered.

Chase's curiosity was piqued. "What do you mean?"

Steele leaned forward. "There are two depots in the system the LDF isn't aware of. They have no idea they exist."

"Really?" Chase's eyes widened, and she straightened in her chair. "How is that possible?"

"Shortly after the war, when it became clear we would be occupying the systems that ultimately became the Protectorate, Fleet placed two depots just beyond the Fringe Zone, far enough out and away from known traffic lanes that they wouldn't draw attention."

"Out in the black?"

Steele nodded. "As you can imagine, information on them has been restricted to command level only, captains and above." Steele allowed himself a small, satisfied smile. "They're completely off the books, hidden and camouflaged for precisely this kind of situation."

Chase let out a low whistle, a hint of relief and excitement in her expression. "So, we can rearm and do it without the LDF knowing."

"Exactly," Steele confirmed. "We can replenish our magazines."

"How close is the nearest one?" Chase asked.

"Three days from our current position at normal cruising speed."

"It will take longer to get there while under stealth, then." Chase's eyes narrowed thoughtfully. "We need to break contact with that battlecruiser first."

"I know." Steele rose from his seat, signaling that he was ready to move. Chase followed suit and came to her feet. He strode toward the bridge, Chase close behind. The hatch slid open, and the marine standing guard outside snapped to attention. Steele gave a quick nod of acknowledgment before stepping through, Chase following him onto the bridge.

Hale was at his station and the only one present. Chase had clearly released the others to get some rest and tend to basic needs. They could be recalled at a moment's notice. In the interim, he was holding down the fort.

"Hale," Steele said as he made his way to his command chair, "I have command."

"You have the bridge, sir," Hale replied, completing the ritual of transferring power.

Steele settled into the chair, adjusting to its familiar contours and settling himself in comfortably. To his right, Chase took her seat, her gaze sweeping over the displays. Steele glanced at the status board to his right. It detailed the health of his ship. He noted several yellow and red indicators—signs of systems still under repair, partially functional or completely offline. He'd yet to go over the full damage report.

Turning to the HTD, he studied their current course and speed, then checked the space around *Ranger*. Everything looked good and as it should be. Then he focused on the enemy. As expected, the battlecruiser was still in pursuit. *Starfish* was keeping pace at barely 49g, but *Ranger*, cruising at 50g, was steadily growing the distance between them.

"Hale," Steele called, "let's show the *Starfish* they've got no chance of catching us. Increase speed to 55g."

"Aye, aye, sir, coming to 55g," Hale replied smoothly. "Accelerating."

Subtle vibrations resonated through the deck, a faint hum growing slightly louder. Only those who knew *Ranger* well would notice the change—a sign of the drive pushing beyond standard limits. It was a reassuring sound, a reminder of the ship's power and capability, one of the things she'd been built for: speed.

Steele watched as the numbers on the HTD climbed—51g, then 52g. It was a satisfying feeling, knowing they were pushing beyond what any other warship out in the wider galaxy could achieve. On her best day, *Starfish* could not hope to match *Ranger*. He allowed himself a small, tight smile, picturing the surprise on the enemy bridge as they realized their quarry was pulling away faster than they could hope to follow.

"Is the damage report compiled and ready for review?" he asked, turning to Chase.

"It is, sir," Chase replied. "Would you like it sent to your console?"

He gave a nod. A moment later, the report flashed onto his display, a steady stream of data outlining the extent of the damage across the breadth of his ship.

"It's important to note we had four casualties during the engagement," Chase added, her tone subdued. "Minor injuries only—limited to bruises, contusions, and lacerations. They were treated in sickbay and released. Only one is on limited duty, a marine."

Steele gave a nod, feeling a pang of relief. They'd come through with minor damage—a fortunate outcome, given the intensity of the fight. He took a long moment to scan the report, noting the important details: systems from power relays to shielding nodes had taken hits, some damaged more seriously than others. Repairs were already underway, with the crew working in teams, and Atheena directing automated nanites that would deal with the hull and armor issues. The breach had already been sealed and pressure restored. None of the issues he saw were catastrophic, though he lingered on the line item regarding two point-defense cannons—both were terminal. They'd need a full replacement, and Steele didn't see that happening anytime soon, at least not until they returned to Union space and a shipyard. They'd been lucky, he thought, taking a moment to appreciate just how well *Ranger* had weathered the storm.

"We are at 55g, sir," Hale reported.

"Very good," Steele replied. "Kindly hold it there."

"Aye, aye, sir—holding."

Satisfied, Steele returned his attention to the damage report, scrolling through details with practiced scrutiny. After a while, he glanced up, catching Chase's eye.

"We could always outrun them and then go to stealth and break contact," Chase said.

"The LDF and the Valkorians would know we're still in-system. They would be more vigilant and watchful for anomalies. We need to convince them we've jumped."

"That would be ideal, sir," Chase replied. "Can we create an energy burst of some kind that mimics a Slipstream jump, gamma rays and all?"

"That would be a neat trick," Steele said as he thought on it some. He could not recall anyone ever trying such a thing, for there had not been a need. You either entered Slipstream space or you didn't.

"The jump drive certainly can't fake it," Chase said.

"What about using one of the torpedoes? When their warheads detonate, they release high levels of gamma rays, right? Could we tweak a detonation to make it look like we jumped away?"

"I am not sure," Chase conceded. She thought for a long moment. "The torpedo's warhead would have to be heavily modified to emit a flash of high-energy gamma radiation upon detonation. That will take time. The radiation burst would need to closely mimic the energy spike that occurs when a ship enters Slipstream space, which releases a brief but intense gamma signature visible at long distances. I'd have to check with engineering."

"It's worth exploring."

"I think it is." Chase's expression tightened as she processed the request. "Still, that's a tall order, sir. The emission won't be a perfect match for a jump. If the *Starfish*'s crew is alert and on the ball, and they decide to analyze the burst, they'll likely spot the discrepancy straight off."

"Perhaps." Steele gave a slight nod as he thought through what she'd just said. "Then again, this is the LDF we're talking about. They are not the best, nor the sharpest."

"There is that," Chase said. "And we've already shown them a speed capability they didn't think possible. They know *Ranger*'s a new design. They might even believe our jump drive operates differently, too. We'll be at range by the time we trigger the torpedo and engage stealth mode. The distance alone might be enough to fool them, especially if they don't look closely."

"You were a weapons officer before becoming my number two," Steele reminded her, his voice steady. "I want you to personally work on that torpedo's warhead with engineering." Working the HTD, Steele estimated their position. "At the current speed, we're roughly eight hours from the Fringe Zone. That's your timeframe. Get to it."

"Yes, sir." Rising from her station, Chase moved swiftly to the lift.

As the hatches closed behind her, Steele leaned back in his command chair, studying the HTD. He rubbed his jaw. They'd finally been cut off from the system's strategic network; all he had now was *Ranger*'s direct readings—active sweeps and passive sensor data. Behind them, the *Starfish* continued her pursuit, a single red icon on the plot.

The *Starfish*'s captain wasn't aiming to catch him, Steele mused, not anymore. The battlecruiser was escorting *Ranger* out of the system, shepherding her onward, likely under orders to ensure he jumped. But that tactic might play directly into his hands, especially if they could convince her captain he had jumped and get him to turn away long before he reached the transition point, where *Ranger* would go into stealth mode.

Could Chase do it? They had eight hours. Once more, Steele found himself waiting.

TEN

"Everything is set, Captain," Chase reported as she sat down at her station. "The torpedo is ready. I believe it will work as intended."

"Very good. Set Condition One," Steele ordered, his gaze fixed on the Fringe Zone countdown clock ticking steadily on his display. It was game time, and all that could be done had been done. The bridge was manned and ready. They had been waiting for this moment for the last half-hour.

"Setting Condition One," Chase confirmed.

An announcement echoed through the ship's corridors, the automated tone stark and urgent: "General quarters. All hands to general quarters. This is not a drill. General quarters, prepare for action." The repetition underscored the seriousness, each word striking with a sense of finality that sent a ripple of heightened focus throughout *Ranger* as the rest of the crew rushed to their action stations.

Steele's eyes swept across the bridge. Every officer was at their post, faces intent and steady, already working away at their stations, preparing for what was to come. Pride surged through him, seeing the calm professionalism that permeated his people.

They knew what was at stake and trusted in his command and the plan they were about to execute. There was no uncertainty in their expressions—just resolve and readiness.

The countdown continued, each second ticking away, narrowing the window between preparation and action. Five minutes passed, then four... The steady rhythm of the clock seemed to sync with the thrum of the ship herself, a silent, collective heartbeat pulsing as *Ranger* geared up for what lay ahead.

"*Starfish* is beginning to brake, Captain," Ishida reported. "She's decelerating."

A flicker of triumph crossed Steele's face. He exchanged a brief, knowing look with Chase, then turned his focus back to the plot. The enemy battlecruiser was still holding her course, decelerating and braking, yes, but not veering off. Steele had hoped she might turn away, show more of a sign of relaxing her pursuit—but no, her captain was merely slowing, keeping a watchful eye, assuming *Ranger* was preparing to jump out of the system. *Starfish* was still ushering them to the exit, confident that her presence was enough to ensure their departure.

"Guns, let's get this show moving," Steele ordered curtly. "Fire the torpedo."

"Torpedo away," Ishida confirmed and then paused. "Torpedo moving ahead of us, with one degree separation. Gravity drive cut; torpedo is now coasting and running silent in our wake, sir." Ishida keyed the prepared command. "Detonating."

On the HTD just behind *Ranger*, a brilliant flash flared outward, quite similar to a Slipstream jump. The energy blast was so close, it cast ripples across the display, distorting the readings.

"Cut the drive," Steele ordered. "Rig for silent running."

"Gravitic drive cut," Hale reported, and almost instantly, the background hum and vibration ramped down as the coils disengaged.

"Rigging for silent running," Quinn reported, her hands flying over the controls. "Powering down all non-essential systems. EM profile minimized. Hull temperature stabilizing within stealth parameters. Heat sinks are active and functioning as expected."

Steele watched as the bridge lights dimmed, systems scaling down to reduce their energy emissions and blend into the cold void. *Ranger* was becoming a ghost, vanishing against the backdrop of space.

He hoped the torpedo's detonation had done its job, masking their transition as they slipped into silent running mode. With luck, *Starfish* would believe *Ranger* had jumped, leaving the system, while Steele and his crew fell quietly into shadow.

No one spoke.

It was as if everyone was holding their breath as the seconds ticked by into minutes. As time seemed to stretch out, no one said anything. Steele watched the readouts flicker as *Ranger*'s systems transitioned fully into low-power mode. One by one, indicators dimmed to standby amber. The bridge lights even grew fainter and more subdued. The familiar hum of the engines softened and then ceased altogether as the gravitic coils finally finished their motion, leaving a thick, tense silence in its place, enveloping the crew in an almost tomblike stillness.

"We're dark, Captain," Quinn said, her voice barely above a whisper, as if even the smallest sound might break their cover.

"Coasting, sir," Hale reported quietly from the helm. The ship's momentum continued to carry them forward, a silent shadow slipping through the darkness of space.

Steele nodded, his gaze on the HTD, checking the empty stretch ahead of the ship. Nothing was out there and in their path. There weren't any civilian ships nearby either. They had reached and passed the Fringe Zone. Anyone making it out this far had already jumped away.

"Maintain course. Passive sensors only. Let's stay invisible and see what they do."

Time slipped by as Steele continued to monitor the HTD, watching the enemy battlecruiser slow further and continue to brake. His tactic seemed to be working, though whether *Starfish* truly believed they'd jumped remained uncertain and a serious worry. Only time would tell.

The silence that had grown on the bridge was taut, thick with the collective tension of the crew. Every eye remained fixed on the HTD console at their station.

"We wait," Steele said quietly to himself. "That's right. We wait."

They sat in silence, eyes glued to their consoles. Time dragged on, each second stretching into an eternity. Then the plot updated, and Steele felt a flicker of tension ripple through him. He sat upright and leaned closer to the screen.

"She's turning to port," Ishida announced, a note of excitement breaking through her usual calm and collected demeanor. "The *Starfish* is turning away. She's turning! She's headed back into the system!"

"We did it," Quinn said, almost in disbelief. "We fooled them."

"Yes, we did," Steele said.

A cheer erupted across the bridge, relief and exhilaration spilling over in the wake of their success.

Chase grinned at Steele. "It worked, sir."

Steele allowed himself a small, satisfied smile in reply. "Nice job with that torpedo, XO, and you too, Guns. Excellent work."

"That's something we might want to speak to research and development about, sir," Ishida said, "a torpedo or some type of device that mimics a jump out of system. Something like that might come in handy again."

"Agreed," Steele said and leaned forward slightly, sitting up straighter at his station. "Let's make a note to write a report on it."

"Aye, sir."

"Atheena, put me on the 1MC," Steele said.

"Yes, Captain, you are now live," Atheena's voice confirmed.

Steele took a deep breath and gathered his thoughts. Then he spoke. "This is the captain speaking. Some of you may be wondering why we didn't jump out of Illidran and into Slip-stream space when we had the chance. We still have a job to do here, and it's a critical one." He paused, letting his words settle, feeling the crew's attention, knowing the rest of the ship was listening just as closely as those on the bridge.

"It has come to my attention that the rebellion within the Protectorate may have been instigated by none other than our old enemy, the Valkorian Hegemony. There's reason to believe the enemy has a fleet hidden somewhere in this system, possibly lying in wait to ambush any force the Union sends to restore order. We believe we have an idea of where that fleet might be hiding. I intend to go find them."

He took a measured breath. "Our mission now is to confirm their presence. *Ranger* is a stealth reconnaissance destroyer—this is precisely the kind of operation she was designed for. We will sneak back into the system, locate the enemy, gather intelligence, and return home to give Fleet the information needed to prepare for what's ahead, whether that be all-out war or not." Steele let the silence fill the space after his words, then closed with a simple, determined, "That is all."

"1MC is off, Captain," Atheena confirmed softly.

The bridge settled into a softer rhythm, the tension having eased. They had a new mission—a daunting one that would push both *Ranger* and her crew to their limits. There was no doubt in his mind about that.

"How long do you want to coast for, sir?" Chase asked, her gaze shifting to meet his.

Steele considered the question, letting the seconds stretch as he weighed the risks. "Several hours at the very least. We need to give *Starfish* time to put more distance between us and them before we fire up the gravitic drive and begin working our way to the depot."

"Yes, sir," Chase replied, a look of understanding crossing her face. "Condition Three?"

He gave a small nod. "Setting Condition Three."

Chase keyed the command into her station, and the automated voice came over the speakers once more.

"Now set Condition Three throughout the ship. Secure from Condition One. Repeat, secure from Condition One. Set Condition Three throughout the ship."

Steele leaned back, a wave of weariness washing over him as he stifled a yawn. He needed more coffee. A quick glance at Chase told him she was feeling the strain too, her posture slightly slouched, as if every muscle had finally relaxed. Her eyes were red-rimmed, and her face was lined heavily with exhaustion.

"XO," Steele said quietly, "get some rest. I'll take first watch. You can have the second."

Chase looked back at him, her face a mixture of gratitude and fatigue. "Thank you, sir." She rose from her seat, casting one last glance over the bridge as if to make certain everything was okay before departing.

"Ishida, Quinn, Calder," Steele called, catching the attention of the tactical and electronic warfare officers. "You're dismissed. Call in your backups and take a break. Get some rest while there's an opportunity. Hale," he added, turning to the helm, "you're stuck with me on this watch."

"Yes, sir," came the chorus of replies.

As Chase headed toward the exit, Steele called after her. "XO?"

She paused, looking over her shoulder.

"Again, excellent work," he said.

She managed a small smile, her exhaustion tempered with pride. "Thank you, sir."

With that, Chase and the others left the bridge, leaving Steele and Hale in the quiet.

"Atheena," Steele said, "have some coffee run up for Hale and myself."

"Yes, Captain."

Steele settled deeper into his chair, eyes on the plot, watching the *Starfish* move farther and farther away as *Ranger* continued to coast in the silence of the void.

Steele shook his head. Today had veered wildly off course from anything he could have anticipated when he'd climbed from his bunk. What had begun as a simple courier mission, a milk run to the Illidran System, had turned into something that had almost claimed his life and those of his crew, along with his ship.

The Protectorate had risen against the Union. The Local Defense Force—armed and trained by the Union, supposed allies—had turned their guns on *Ranger* with the intent to kill. There was nothing more personal than that. And now, his mind turned toward the Valkorian Hegemony—the shadowy force behind it all.

If the Hegemony truly had a force hidden in Illidran—and Steele believed they did—he would find it. He would gather the intelligence Fleet would need and bring it back home where it would make a difference, where it would save lives.

Steele leaned back in his command chair, his eyes sweeping across the nearly empty bridge, settling on the quiet displays and the soft hum of a ship at rest, one that was running silently in the dark. *Ranger* had been blooded today. She had weathered the storm thrown against her and struck back, showing not only her claws, but her teeth.

His ship, though small by Fleet standards, was a formidable platform. She was a predator, fierce and deadly. More importantly, she was his to command, and command her he would.

Whatever lay ahead, he knew one thing with certainty: he would see this mission through, for he had committed to it.

ELEVEN

"I am still not reading anything, sir," Quinn reported. "There's nothing on the scope, nothing at all."

The tension in the bridge was so strong it could almost be cut with a knife. *Ranger* had slowed, the usual background hum barely audible under the muted lighting and reduced power levels of silent running mode. Steele kept his gaze fixed on the HTD, watching the steady readout as Hale continued to bring their speed down as directed, their trajectory shifting as they crawled closer to the remote coordinates he'd pulled from his digital safe.

"I don't see anything out there either, sir, even with optics," Ishida repeated, a hint of frustration in her voice. *Ranger*'s stealth systems masked their emissions almost entirely, making them practically invisible amidst the vast backdrop of space— but the stealth systems also limited what they could detect in return, since they couldn't use active sensors. They were on passives only. "If the station's there, it's a hole in space."

Chase cast Steele a sidelong glance, her brow furrowed. He sensed the silent question hanging between them. She trusted his decision to bring *Ranger* out here, yet he knew that even she was beginning to wonder if this supposed depot might be nothing at all, but something that was once here and had since been removed.

Steele himself was beginning to wonder a bit, too. Often, one part of the navy did something without alerting another. That sort of thing tended to complicate operations, when you did not need more problems.

Quinn spoke. "Perhaps if we used an active sweep... just a single focused ping, sir? It might give us a return, something to work with."

Steele shook his head immediately. "No, a ping won't be necessary." He understood the allure of just one ping, the hope it could reveal what lay ahead, out there and concealed in the vast darkness. But the risk was far too great. One ping, even so far out and beyond the Fringe Zone, could potentially betray their presence to not only the system's detection network, but also enemy forces farther in-system that might be alert and watching. Both were unlikely, but it was a possibility—a chance Steele was unwilling to take.

"I agree, the risk in doing that is just too dangerous," Chase said, her voice firm. "The depot's supposed to be stealthed. If it's here, we'll find it without active scans, as we were meant to."

Quinn fell silent, nodding, and returned her focus to her displays. Steele knew the wait was getting to them all—the uncertainty gnawing at their patience. He continued watching the plot, mentally calculating *Ranger*'s position relative to the coordinates he'd been given.

"Hale," Steele ordered calmly, "that's good enough. Kindly bring us to a complete stop."

"Aye, sir, braking," Hale replied. The ship's speed dropped to near absolute zero relative to the star, the engine hum quieting even further as *Ranger*'s motion eased. "Coming to a full stop."

As they slowed to a near halt, the silence felt thick, oppressive. Every eye on the bridge remained glued to their stations, waiting, ready for any indication that they weren't alone, that the station was out there. Steele watched the plot as *Ranger's* gravity drive continued exerting force, as minimal as possible, in the opposite direction.

"We have come to a full stop, sir," Hale confirmed.

"Very good." Steele tapped a few commands on his console. "Calder, I've just sent you the code and coordinates to the station, the direction to transmit. Use a tight-beam laser. Send it immediately."

She turned to him, brows slightly raised. The tight-beam laser was old-fashioned, almost obsolete technology in an era of FTL communications and encrypted data bursts.

"You have your orders," Steele reaffirmed.

"Aye, sir. Give me a moment to energize and activate the laser communication system."

This narrow beam, aimed precisely, would travel directly toward an intended destination. Once sent, no one outside the beam would be able to pick up the transmission.

A minute ticked by as the system powered up. Then Calder's voice broke the stillness, calm and clear. "Sending transmission now. Sent."

The stillness of the ship, the near silence of the bridge—all of it heightened the anticipation, the feeling that they were on the verge of uncovering something hidden in the cold emptiness of space. No response came.

Steele sucked in a breath. He let it slowly out and forced himself to remain calm and collected. He checked their position again to confirm they were at the correct coordinates and the angle of attack for the laser communication. Everything was correct, including the code he'd given Calder.

Still, nothing happened.

Were they in the right place?

Chase glanced over at him in question. Steele gave a shrug

and turned back to the HTD, studying their position once more. They were in the correct place, weren't they?

Where was it?

Then his communications officer stiffened and leaned forward, her eyes narrowing as she studied a display screen. She glanced back at Steele a moment later, a mixture of disbelief and excitement in her expression. "We've received a reply. It's coded and sent directly to your station, sir. I am not authorized to decrypt the message."

Steele's gaze dropped to his screen, where the message began to decode almost instantly and automatically, lines of text appearing in rapid succession. He leaned in, his attention fully absorbed as he scanned the contents. It wasn't a simple acknowledgment. The message came with a set of precise instructions, coordinates, access protocols, and even a sequence for approaching the depot safely.

Satisfied with the initial read, he forwarded the appropriate instructions to Chase, who gave a quick nod, her eyes flickering with interest as she processed the details.

"An approach lane and parking spot," Chase said, looking over at him. "To say I am intrigued is an understatement."

"Once we are parked," Steele said, "we will be towed into the stealth field and to a docking hardpoint. From there we will be able to board the station and grab what we need, munitions-wise."

Steele then tapped a command to share the message with Hale.

"Lieutenant Hale," Steele said, "you should have the coordinates. Follow the instructions to the letter. Set course and prepare to engage maneuvering thrusters. If you deviate, the station will fire upon us. I would prefer to keep that from happening."

Hale swallowed as he absorbed the contents. "Aye, sir. Inputting course now. We will not be using the gravitic drive as per the instructions, only station-keeping thrusters to nudge us into the correct parking spot."

"I wonder why we can't use the gravitic drive?" Chase said as she looked over at him.

"The gravity drive will likely screw with the stealth field," Steele explained.

"That could be it," Chase said. "I could see that happening."

Without the gravitic drive, their progress was painstakingly slow, each small correction made by the station-keeping thrusters keeping them within the bounds of the approach vector. The bridge was a hush of anticipation as Hale moved *Ranger* closer and closer to the designated spot. Then, abruptly, Hale's voice broke through.

"Parking established. I've brought the ship to a full stop, sir."

"Very good." Steele took a deep breath. This was it—they had arrived. "Calder, send a confirmation ping using the same tight-beam laser—same direction as before." Steele kept his gaze on the HTD, where *Ranger* remained locked in position, still cloaked in a stealth field of her own making and nearly invisible against the backdrop of stars.

"Yes, sir," Calder said. "Confirmation ping sent."

"Quinn, drop stealth field. The station needs to see us to tow us in. Keep heat sinks in place and active. Let's not radiate more than needed."

"Stealth fields dropped. Heat sinks in place and active." She paused as something on the scope caught her attention. "Sir, two small tugs just appeared from nowhere. They're approaching the port side. They are older models, Misty Class boats, unmanned."

Steele's gaze shifted to the HTD, observing the tugs as they carefully adjusted their positions. These were older, automated but rugged vessels, their exteriors likely scuffed, pitted, and worn from heavy use, telling of years of silent service in the shadows.

"Chemical thrusters," Steele murmured to himself, noting the plumes from the tugs' maneuvering jets as they appeared and were cataloged on the HTD. The choice of old propulsion tech made sense; it minimized their electronic footprint, keeping both tugs as inconspicuous as the depot they served. Even their power readings were heavily muted and shielded.

"What now?" Chase asked, her voice low, barely breaking the tense silence.

"We wait and let them do their job," Steele replied simply, eyes fixed on the plot. "They're going to do all the work."

A series of metallic clunks echoed through *Ranger*'s hull as the tugs secured their magnetic locks and firmly attached themselves to the destroyer, hard mating. Then they began nudging *Ranger* gently, their steady, careful movements bringing his ship toward... nothing. At least that's what the passive sensors told him.

But Steele knew better.

"We're being moved, sir," Hale reported. "I no longer have control."

"Understood," Steele said. "Allow the process to continue. Do not hinder or impede it in any way."

"Aye, sir," Hale said and leaned back at his station.

"Sir," Quinn reported, "we are moving through a powerful stealth field. I've never seen anything like it..."

"Wow," Chase breathed, her gaze on her screens.

Steele leaned forward, his gaze intent on the HTD as the station's outline materialized, emerging from the obscurity of the stealth field as they passed through it. The structure was vast, massive, far larger than he'd expected, stretching out in all directions with a lattice of docking bays, dozens of hardpoints, refueling nodes, and storage modules that branched off like the limbs of some industrial colossus.

It was incredible.

The station's surface was dark, almost black, clearly designed to absorb rather than reflect light, making it near invisible until you were right on top of it. There were also powerful defenses, maser batteries and missile launchers, hundreds of them, mounted along the station's hull. Steele had never seen so many in one place. From the passive sensor readings, all of the station's defenses were powered down and inert. He knew that could easily change in an instant.

"Wow," Chase murmured again, her voice barely audible, "that's incredible."

The station's central core was flanked by a series of enormous cargo modules, each one, were it a drydock, would be large enough to house a destroyer on its own. From his vantage on the HTD, Steele could make out cranes, transfer arms, and automated docking points.

"This place could resupply a fleet," Quinn whispered, awe edging her tone.

"It could," Steele agreed, his voice steady, though he too felt a sense of wonder. "And it's going to refill our magazine. The Union doesn't build something like this unless it's meant for serious use."

As the tugs continued to guide *Ranger* toward a docking arm that extended from one of the modules, Steele felt a moment of awe wash over him. He'd expected something smaller, not a station so vast. Clearly, Fleet had expected trouble at some point in Illidran and planned for it. They'd prepositioned the supply for extended operations of either a task force or a small fleet, and that didn't count those depots deeper into Illidran that everyone knew about. This was one of two that had been hidden beyond the Fringe Zone.

"Sir, I am receiving a tight-beam laser communication," Calder said. "It's from the station's construct. It reads: 'Welcome to Depot 662-A-5. Would we like to dock immediately?'"

"Advise the station's construct that we would like to dock immediately," Steele said. "Inform it we need to reprovision and refill our magazines."

"Aye, sir," Calder said. "Message sent and received. The construct acknowledges."

Steele turned to Chase. "Once we're docked, take Guns and head over to the station. Find out what is available in stores. Take what you think will work best for us. I'm certain that Fleet hasn't come to swap out what they originally stored here. Use your best judgment."

"So, we're likely looking at older weapons?" Chase asked.

"Mark Threes and Fours is my guess when it comes to ship-killers," Steele said, "older torpedoes too."

"That's not ideal," Chase said, "but it's better than nothing."

"Correct," Steele agreed with a nod. "We have the latest software updates, so we will be able to tie those missiles directly into our systems. Once done, they should be more capable than what the LDF has, at least marginally." Steele paused as something occurred to him. "The station might require my direct command codes and presence to unlock stores. Let me know if it does and I will join you."

"Will do, sir."

As *Ranger* edged closer to the docking arm, Steele watched the depot's towering structure loom larger on the HTD. Its external framework was dense, and he could see layers of armored plating that suggested it had been built to withstand direct fire—a relic from the last war, a time when stations were designed as fortresses, bulwarks that could take tremendous fire, not to mention return it.

"When it comes to the missiles we'll be getting, what about the Hegemony?" Chase asked, her tone filled with concern. "How will they compare when it comes to them?"

"They're a different matter," Steele admitted, a hint of tension creeping into his voice. "Let's hope we don't have to find out. Still, a full magazine is better than an empty one, even if some of the weapons are older. If it comes down to it, at least we'll have something to shoot back."

"Yes, sir," she replied, acknowledging the truth of his words.

The brief silence was broken by Hale. "Sir, we're being pulled into a docking hardpoint. Final approach complete."

Steele gave a nod and then turned to his communications officer. "Calder, alert the chief of the boat and Lieutenant Knox to prepare for docking. We'll need a guard detail stationed at the appropriate airlock."

"Sir?" Calder's voice held a note of confusion and question. "The station is uninhabited. Do we really need a guard?"

Steele's expression hardened slightly, his gaze meeting hers as she looked back at him. "Lieutenant, we have regulations for a reason. Do you know why?"

Calder's face flushed a deep shade of red as she clearly realized her mistake. "Ah... for the unexpected, sir."

"Precisely," Steele replied, his tone brooking no argument. "Whether the station is manned or unmanned, regulations require us to post a guard at any boarding point. On *this* ship, we follow Fleet regulations. Understand me on this matter?"

"Yes, sir," Calder responded crisply, turning back to her station to relay the orders.

Out of the corner of his eye, Steele noticed Chase watching him, her lips quirking into a subtle smile. There was a mutual understanding there, a silent acknowledgment of the lesson Steele had just imparted to Calder. Both of them had been there, in her place as junior officers. For both of them, that had been a long time ago.

A low hum vibrated through the deck as the station's docking mechanisms engaged. This was followed by a sequence of muted clanks and deep clunks as the magnetic locks latched onto *Ranger*'s hull, locking her in place.

On the display, the station's shadowed silhouette filled the screen—a massive, aging structure with lights casting faint, intermittent illumination across parts of its darkened surface, primarily where there were airlocks or outer hatches. The depot seemed to stretch on endlessly. It was truly impressive, at least Steele thought so.

"Docking complete, sir," Hale confirmed. "Umbilical in place and pressurizing."

"Very good." Steele's eyes settled on the umbilical connecting *Ranger* to the depot, now sealed and in the process of pressurizing with breathable atmosphere. It was a lifeline bridging his warship with the silent expanse of the station, a place that felt both foreboding and oddly welcoming, as if it had been waiting for them all along.

"We are secure, sir," Hale reported, his relief plain now that the docking procedure was finished. "Magnetic locks engaged and good. Everything is green."

"XO, stand the crew down. Set Condition Four."

"Aye, sir, setting Condition Four."

When a ship was docked or in port, it typically operated under Condition Four, also known as peacetime watch. Condition Four was a lower readiness, but security was maintained. Only essential personnel were on watch, with the majority of the crew either off duty, on shore leave, or working regular maintenance and administrative tasks.

"Now, set Condition Four throughout the ship," the automated announcement on the 1MC stated. "Now, set Condition Four throughout the ship."

Steele leaned back in his chair and exhaled slowly. Here, docked and surrounded by the protective embrace of the stealth field, he could afford to relax, if only a fraction. He gave Chase a nod. "XO, this is your operation. See to it."

"Yes, sir," Chase replied crisply, standing from her station. "Guns, you're with me."

"Aye, ma'am."

Within moments, both officers had left the bridge, the lift hatch closing behind them. Steele sat for a moment, glancing in the direction of his quarters. The thought of catching up on some badly needed sleep tempted him more than he cared admit. But no—he shook his head. There was something he needed to do first, a duty he'd not had time to deal with until now.

Standing, Steele stretched slightly before stepping forward. "Hale, you have the bridge. If you need me, I will be in medical."

"Aye, sir," Hale acknowledged, his posture straightening. "I have command."

With that, Steele turned on his heel and made his way to the lift at the back of the bridge. As the hatch closed, cutting off the bridge, the familiar hum of the lift enveloped him. The weariness that tugged at him could wait—there were duties left to fulfill, ones that couldn't be set aside, even now.

"Deck two, medical bay," Steele ordered, and the lift began moving.

TWELVE

Steele stepped out of the lift onto deck two. The air felt cooler here where there was only the medical bay and storage compartments, along with various equipment lockers and machine shops. Much of the deck did not require full life support, for it was automated and run by Atheena.

The corridor was dimly lit, casting a series of shadowed alcoves that lined the bulkhead. Steele's footsteps rang in the quiet, the echo emphasizing the solitude of this stretch of *Ranger* as he started forward toward medical.

With such a small crew, these corridors rarely saw much activity during regular operations, and there was an almost monastic silence that added to the atmosphere here.

It was a lonely place.

As he neared the halfway mark, the med bay door came into view—a solid, reinforced hatch marked with a small blue medical symbol. He reached it and keyed the panel. As the hatch slid open with a soft hiss, Steele nearly collided with Petty Officer Diego Alvarez, who was on his way out. Alvarez, one of the crew assigned to the hangar deck, blinked in surprise before straightening up and snapping to attention. A bandage wrapped around his head was a direct reminder of the recent battle.

"Sorry, sir, I didn't see you."

"At ease," Steele said, eyeing the bandage. He gestured at Alvarez's head. "What happened, sailor?"

Alvarez tapped the side of his head. "When we took that last hit, a piece of equipment came loose from the wall, sir. Rung my bell pretty good, it did, even wearing a helmet," he said with a slight grin. "The doc had me come back to change the dressing and check on the wound. She says it's healing up nicely, sir, and that I shouldn't have much of a scar."

Steele gave him an appraising look. "And where are you off to now?"

"Back to duty, sir. Lieutenant Lane needs help loading munitions from the depot onto the ventral hangar deck. At least, we're preparing to receive the goods, sir. He'll need my help when things start happening, and I should really be going."

"Very well." Steele stepped aside for the man to pass. "Carry on."

"Yes, sir." Alvarez nodded briskly and moved past Steele, his steps quickening as he headed toward the lift at the far end of the corridor.

"Oh, and Alvarez?" Steele called.

"Sir?" The petty officer stopped.

"Way to use your head," Steele said with a straight face.

Alvarez grinned at him. "That's what the lieutenant said, sir."

"At least we both think alike. Next time try to duck."

"I will, sir."

Steele turned away and stepped into the medical bay, the hatch sliding shut with a quiet hiss behind him. Unlike the bridge, the med bay was designed with a soft, almost welcoming atmosphere, an intentional choice to put those who found themselves here for treatment at ease. At least, that was what Steele had always thought.

To his left, a row of diagnostic beds lined the wall, each one separated by a slim privacy partition. The beds were all neatly made, with crisp white sheets, white utilitarian pillows, and a small but visible array of medical tools set beside each one on side tables. All were ready for immediate use. Above the beds, monitors displayed a range of diagnostic information, currently offline but ready to flicker to life at a moment's notice and need.

On the opposite wall, a series of cabinets held neatly organized medical supplies. Each cabinet was clearly labeled, from trauma kits to surgical implements. All, he knew, were arranged with military precision, for Doctor Yates was one of the most organized people Steele had ever met. The air held a faint antiseptic scent—a blend of sterility and recycled oxygen, reminding Steele of the clinical nature of the environment.

At the far end, the glass-walled recovery area caught his attention. Through the frosted glass, he could just make out a figure lying on a bed. The rhythmic beeping of a vitals monitor echoed softly from within, steady and calm, almost like a heartbeat for the room. This was clearly the man they'd pulled from the chaos.

Having just emerged from her office, Doctor Yates was moving across the center of the med bay toward the recovery room. She wore her usual white coat, the fabric crisp and neatly creased, which spoke to her meticulous nature. Her dark hair, streaked with silver, was pulled back in a functional bun, though a few loose strands softened the severity of her appearance. Lines of exhaustion underscored her sharp blue eyes— eyes that, over the years, had seen more than their share of battle wounds and desperate surgeries.

When Yates noticed him, she stopped in her tracks, turned to face him, and approached.

"Captain," she greeted, a hint of warmth behind the usual professionalism. "Checking in or do you need something?"

Steele's gaze briefly drifted to the recovery room before returning his attention to the doctor. She was older than he was, by a decade, and carried herself with the seasoned calm that only years of crises and split-second decisions could instill.

Yates had a sturdy, unshakable presence. Steele had seen her under pressure and been deeply impressed. It was one of the reasons he had requested she be assigned to *Ranger*.

Her eyes were sharp and perceptive, with a depth that suggested an almost endless well of experience. Steele could tell that she missed little; she was always observing, always assessing. Her gaze held a warmth tempered by pragmatism, a reminder that while she cared deeply about those in her care, she would do what was necessary without hesitation.

Steele knew that behind her calm exterior was a doctor who had saved countless lives during the war, sometimes through sheer grit alone. Yates was a fixture on *Ranger*, a steadying force, and as he looked at her, Steele felt the familiar trust he always had for her and the work she did for his people. He knew he was lucky to have her as part of his crew. He also liked Yates and considered her a friend, though as captain he could not openly acknowledge that fact. But they both knew it.

"I came by to check in and see how your patient is doing." Steele waved at the frosted glass. "And how is he doing?"

Yates followed his gaze to the recovery area, her expression guarded but hopeful. "Though he's by no means out of the woods, it looks like Mr. Argonola might live after all. For a moment there, I was not quite certain. It was touch and go, if you take my meaning, sir."

Steele's brow lifted slightly. "Is he conscious?"

"No, not at the moment," Yates replied, a touch of weariness seeping into her voice. "He has lost a lot of blood. I managed to repair most of the internal damage around his heart, but he may need further corrective surgery at some point in the future, surgery that is beyond my current ability." She paused. "You're not the first to come check on him either."

"Miller came by?" Steele surmised.

"He did, several times."

Steele gave a nod. It was not unexpected. He gestured at the recovery room, glancing again toward the frosted glass. "Was he conscious at any point?"

Yates nodded, a faint shadow of concern passing over her face. "Briefly, yes, when he was first brought aboard. He was disoriented, from both blood loss and shock, but he did manage to say a few things."

"Anything useful?" Steele probed.

"That depends upon what you consider useful." Yates hesitated, glancing back at the recovery area, as though she could hear Argonola's wild ravings still echoing through the room. "He kept talking about an enemy fleet. Said they were here, in-system, and that they were lying in wait. He kept repeating that over and over."

Steele's face tightened at her words, an uneasy feeling settling in his chest. He gave a slow, unhappy nod.

"Is that the fleet you're after?" Yates asked, her voice quieter, having grown serious.

"It is, doctor."

Yates seemed to take a moment to process that, her face betraying a flicker of doubt, then a steady resolve. "Well, whatever he believes, it's clear he thinks it's real and the enemy is here in Illidran. And if he's right…"

"If he's right, doctor," Steele said grimly, "we're in deeper than we anticipated, and it likely means a second great war."

There was a long moment of silence. The doctor looked down at the deck and bit her lip.

"Not good," she said. "Miller told me to tell him anything Argonola says—that is, if he wakes—and to send for him immediately." She paused, glancing down at the deck before looking back up at Steele. "Miller's Intelligence Directorate, isn't he?"

Steele gave a curt nod. "He is, and you should keep that to yourself."

"I see. I've never much liked the ID. Trouble seems to surround their operatives. They create all kinds of problems for people like you and me."

Steele did not reply to that but glanced once more at the doctor's unconscious patient, what he could see of the man through the frosted glass.

"Do you need anything, doctor?" Steele asked, his gaze returning to her.

Yates took a steadying breath, a quick glance at her patient revealing the exhaustion hidden behind her calm demeanor. "I used up a significant portion of my blood stores saving him. He is going to need an additional transfusion or two as well. I can synthesize more, but I'll need donors for that. I checked, and you, along with a couple of other people aboard, are of the same blood type."

Without hesitation, Steele nodded. "I'll volunteer. Let's get it done now, while I have the time. I'll also spread the word amongst the crew. I am certain you will have more donors than you can shake a stick at before long. I will see if we can make sure you have all types you need on hand."

A pleased smile softened her usually focused expression. "Excellent. This way, Captain." She led him toward a side room. "How long do you think we'll be docked here at the depot?"

"I am not entirely sure," Steele replied as he followed. "A day at most. I would be surprised if we're here longer than that."

She looked over at him. "And then we'll be out hunting for that enemy fleet?"

Steele offered a nod, meeting her gaze as they reached the room. "That's the plan."

Yates pointed to a reclining chair positioned in the center of the room. The chair's dark upholstery was worn, scuffed in places, an indicator to the many crew members who'd been here before him to have their blood drawn and sampled. The room's lighting was softer than in the main part of the medical bay, casting a soothing glow that seemed designed to relax even the most anxious person.

"Have a seat, Captain, please." Yates gestured toward the chair in question.

Steele settled into the chair, feeling the worn leather beneath him adjust automatically to his weight and size, providing a firm yet comfortable recline. Steele found himself relaxing as he rolled up his right sleeve as Yates sterilized her hands and then prepared a tray of equipment nearby. She moved with the quick, sure confidence of someone who had done this hundreds of times. She deftly pulled a clean syringe from its packaging and attached it to a collection bag. He noticed the small, practiced motions she made as she double-checked the setup, her brow slightly furrowed in concentration as she worked.

"Roll up your right sleeve further," she instructed. Her hands were gentle yet precise as she prepped his arm, pressing her fingers along the inside of his elbow to help locate a vein.

"Yes, ma'am," Steele replied, watching her work.

"This shouldn't take long," she said, giving him a quick, reassuring nod. She swabbed his inner arm with a cool antiseptic pad, the scent sharp and clinical. He felt the pressure of her fingers as she secured a tourniquet around his bicep, then sought out a vein.

"Make a fist," she instructed, calm and steady.

Steele did as asked. Her hands were steady as she inserted the needle with barely a pinch, and he felt a slight warmth as his blood began to flow into the collection tube and then ultimately the bag. She removed the tourniquet, and the bag on the stand slowly filled with a dark red liquid. He found himself staring at his blood, feeling a strange mix of detachment and curiosity. It wasn't the first time he'd donated blood, but under these circumstances, it felt different—a reminder of the toll their mission had already taken. How many had died or been injured by his response to the enemy's actions, his retaliation when *Ranger* struck back in anger? It was something that, in the quiet of the night, would keep him awake.

"Do you think we will see more action?" Yates asked, her voice soft but edged with a weariness Steele could easily understand.

"I hope not. Our plan is to slip back into the system under stealth. With some good fortune, we'll locate the enemy fleet, gather intelligence on them, and be away before they even know we were there." He spoke with a calm he didn't entirely feel, hoping to reassure her. What he was going to attempt with *Ranger* would be incredibly dangerous, risky in the extreme.

"I pray it is so," Yates murmured. She glanced up from the collection bag, her gaze meeting his with a steady, searching look. "How're you feeling?"

"Fine," Steele replied with a faint smile, more for her benefit than his own. He shifted slightly in the chair, feeling the faint pull of exhaustion settling into his muscles. He stifled a yawn. The coffee was beginning to wear off. "Nothing I can't handle."

Yates nodded, her hand steady as she checked the flow of blood, each movement carrying the practiced ease of experience. They sat in a companionable silence, broken only by the gentle hum of the med bay equipment and the rhythmic, reassuring hiss of the air handlers cycling fresh air through the sterile space.

After a few quiet minutes, she spoke again. "Atheena's given me an update on what's been happening... Things are bad, aren't they?"

"In Illidran, yes." Steele's voice dropped a notch, despite

them being alone. "And probably across the entirety of the Protectorate too. The LDF turning on us was only the start. I really don't know how the ID missed it all coming. There had to have been signs." He felt an intense stab of frustration. How many Union Navy personnel had just died as a result?

Yates gave a nod. "There likely were signs. There always are when things like this happen... people get complacent, and that's when things are missed."

"The Protectorate's declared independence, and if the Hegemony really is behind it... things could get worse, much worse."

Yates's expression darkened, a shadow of old memories and fears flickering across her face. "I'd hoped we were done with war." Her voice was so quiet he barely heard it over the medical bay's ambient hum. "Done with the Hegemony, done with killing and maiming."

Steele nodded, understanding the weight of her words. "So did I," he admitted. "I guess we didn't beat them badly enough last time. They might need another lesson."

She gave a quiet nod. "That's what I am afraid of."

"You were on a hospital ship during the last war, right?" Steele asked. He could not think of the ship's name.

"The *Osprey*. Those were difficult days. We were supporting the invasion of Gildarra." She paused, her gaze going distant. "It was bad. The marines in the initial drop took almost seventy percent casualties. The Hegemony troops on the ground did not want to surrender. They had to be dug out of their caves and bunkers one at a time. It was difficult and bloody work."

"That was a hard campaign," Steele agreed with a nod. He'd heard stories from people who had been on the ground. It had been a nightmare.

They sat in silence for several minutes, the only sound the steady hum of med bay machinery and the soft rhythm of

Steele's own breathing. Finally, Yates clamped off the tube, smoothly removing the needle and pressing a clean piece of gauze against his arm.

"Hold that there for a moment," she said and stepped away, before returning. She secured the gauze with a small strip of medical tape. "Stay here; I'll get you some water. Drink a lot over the next couple of hours." She waited a beat, her eyes assessing him with the look of someone who had tended to countless soldiers and sailors.

"I will," Steele affirmed.

Satisfied, she stepped away, her boots making soft taps against the sterile flooring. A moment later, she returned with a bottle of water from a chilled cabinet. The cool condensation beaded on its surface as she handed it to him, her gaze lingering to ensure he drank. He took a long, deep pull from the bottle, the cold water soothing his throat.

"Thanks, doc," Steele said, flexing his hand to get the circulation going again.

Yates gave him a once-over. "Sit for a few minutes. Take a nap if you want. You certainly look tired enough for the both of us, and I already know I am exhausted."

"I will take you up on that," Steele replied, feeling the weight of fatigue settle in as he spoke. The chair was quite comfortable and there were no immediate duties calling him to action. Chase and Guns were on it when it came to refilling the ship's magazines.

"Please do," Yates replied, reaching over to the wall panel. She tapped a control, and the lights dimmed to a softer glow, casting the space in a gentle, restful ambiance. "I'll wake you in thirty minutes, if that works."

"That sounds good, but make it forty-five," Steele murmured, already feeling the pull of sleep as he leaned back in the comfortable chair, his body surrendering to the quiet and tranquility of the medical bay.

"All right, forty-five minutes it is." As she stepped out, Yates pulled the privacy screen closed with a quiet swish, leaving Steele in a cocoon of calm. Her soft footsteps faded as he closed his eyes. In the stillness, sleep claimed him almost immediately, a rare, welcomed escape.

THIRTEEN

Steele's pace was steady and purposeful as he approached the airlock, each step echoing slightly against the corridor's sound-dampening walls. Ahead waited two marines in light armor. Rifles in hand, they watched his approach with sharp, unwavering gazes. The circular hatch of the airlock loomed larger as he neared, a heavy-duty frame bolted into the corridor's bulkhead, exuding both utility and armored resilience.

The hatch's safety markings glowed a muted red. Through the small viewport he could see the reinforced umbilical extending from the airlock, connecting *Ranger* to the station like a lifeline stretching through the emptiness. Dim and sporadic overhead lights illuminated the way along its length.

Both marines, stone-faced, came to attention as he neared, their eyes sharp and alert, embodying the quiet, practiced discipline he expected of *Ranger*'s security detail. Though this was a routine assignment, the atmosphere carried an undercurrent of tension—an awareness that, in space, what was routine could turn critical in a heartbeat.

"At ease."

The two marines relaxed a fraction.

"Captain," one of the marines said. "The XO informed us you were coming. She's waiting for you on the stationside, sir."

"Very good. Open the hatch."

"Yes, sir." The second marine keyed in the airlock sequence. The heavy, hatch loomed in front of Steele, with safety markings glowing faintly along its edges. As the inner hatch slid open with a soft hiss, a gust of cooler, faintly metallic air hit him—different from the filtered, recycled air aboard *Ranger*, sharper and less familiar.

"You're clear to proceed, sir," the second marine said, taking a step aside and standing beside the airlock control panel.

Steele stepped forward, pausing for a moment on the threshold as he took in the scene before him. Through the viewport, the umbilical connecting *Ranger* to the station stretched out through the vacuum.

"Thank you, Corporal," Steele said, stepping through the airlock. The marine triggered the hatch mechanism. As the inner hatch sealed behind him with a heavy, mechanical clunk, Steele felt that familiar sensation of leaving *Ranger*'s controlled and protected atmosphere behind, even if only for a brief walk to the station. It felt like he was leaving his home, which in a way, he was.

Inside the airlock, the low hum of the system was loud, amplified as the pressure equalized and the air hissed almost angrily. He waited patiently for the second door to cycle open. When the outer hatch finally slid aside, it revealed the umbilical in full—its walls heavily reinforced, the overhead lighting casting a soft, wavering, and sporadic light ahead. Beyond, he could just make out the station airlock at the far end, perhaps a hundred meters distant.

He stepped forward, moving purposefully through the dimly lit umbilical. Each step echoed faintly, filling the otherwise silent passage. There were no windows to either side. His gaze remained fixed on the airlock at the end, where he knew

Chase would be waiting. The air was cold, almost frigid. There was a burned scent to it, something that told him it had recently been exposed to the hard vacuum of space. Places like this one always smelled the same to him.

The muffled silence inside the umbilical felt alien compared to *Ranger*'s familiar background hum. Here, the quiet was dense and unsettling, broken only by the subtle creaks and loud pops as metal and composite material expanded and contracted. Each step seemed to echo back at him, the sounds ultimately absorbed in the thick, insulated walls.

As he moved farther along, *Ranger*'s airlock lights faded into the distance behind him, giving way to the dim, utilitarian glow from the umbilical's overhead lighting, half of which did not work and was dark. The airlock ahead looked older, its edges lined with faint scratches and scuff marks, plain hard use. Stopping before it, Steele paused as the station's airlock scanner activated, a faint green beam flickering over him before the outer hatch opened with a low whoosh and heavy hiss of hydraulics. He entered and the hatch closed rapidly behind him. There was a rush of air, and the pressure equalized to the station. His ears popped. Then the inner hatch opened.

Stepping into the station's interior, he felt another immediate drop in temperature, the cold biting subtly through his uniform. The air had a stale, metallic scent, tinged with the faint undertone of recycled systems that lacked the care and precision of *Ranger*'s. Likely this area's life support had only recently been turned on. Overhead lights cast a harsh, sterile glow over the gray walls, creating a clinical ambiance that felt as unwelcoming as the hollow silence surrounding him.

A tablet in hand, Chase waited just beyond the airlock. She was wearing a light jacket. Steele wished in that moment he had thought of bringing a jacket himself, for he should have known life support for the depot would be on the minimal side.

"Captain," she greeted, her tone steady, carrying the usual

undercurrent of respect but with a hint of anticipation. Her breath misted on the air as she spoke.

"XO," Steele responded and glanced around. "Where's Guns?"

"She's checking on the shuttles the station has in stores. One of our pilots, Ensign Cole, is with her. We should be able to replace the shuttle we lost planetside. The question is, do we want a regular shuttle or an assault shuttle?"

"That's good thinking," Steele said and thought for a heart-beat. "I think a regular shuttle will do. *Ranger* is only authorized one assault shuttle. I doubt we will be conducting a serious planetary assault, especially one in force."

"Yes, sir. It was Ishida's idea once we saw them."

Ahead, a short corridor stretched out, lined with old, exposed wiring and conduit panels along the walls. A faint hum of machinery vibrated through the deck, barely noticeable. This station was never meant to be a permanent habitat, but only occasionally used, hence the limited life support. A sign on the wall, with an arrow, indicated the direction of the control center.

"Let's proceed," he said, gesturing forward and down the corridor. "Shall we?"

Steele, not waiting for a reply, started off.

"Yes, sir." Chase fell into step beside him, matching his stride.

The sounds of their footsteps echoed hollowly down the corridor, mingling with the faint buzz of the overhead lighting as they made their way toward the control room. Steele followed the signs and arrows painted along the walls.

"The station's fully stocked, sir," Chase said. "No one's been here for a very long time."

"Did you check the log to confirm that?" Steele asked, glancing over at her.

"I did. It's been about seven years, and that was just a survey crew to confirm the station was still functioning as expected. After that, well, it's like the navy just forgot about it."

"Our good luck, then."

As they continued down the narrow corridor, Steele couldn't shake the feeling of stepping back into the past. The station, though fully operational, bore the marks of its age and long solitude. Dust had gathered in the seams of panels and along the edges of the faded warning labels, hinting at years without human presence. He suspected the station had been towed to Illidran from someplace else, that it had been repurposed.

The lighting cast an industrial glow, harsh and unflattering, emphasizing every scar and scratch on the surfaces. Overhead, pipes and conduits ran the length of the overhead, some covered in a thin layer of grime. Occasionally, they would pass a blinking indicator light or hear the soft whirring of machinery— reminders that, despite its long abandonment, the station's automated systems continued their quiet vigil.

On their journey to the control room, they passed three automated maintenance bots. The spider-like things never failed to send a shiver down Steele's spine. These little machines had no heads, but eight legs. They came in various sizes, from tiny, like an ant, to a medium-sized dog, and performed both internal and external maintenance. Some had internal constructed intelligences. Others were controlled by the depot's construct. Watching them move past, he was thankful *Ranger* had no need of such bots, for they were alien in the extreme.

At several points, they were forced to halt. Heavily reinforced hatches barred the way. Each time, Chase entered her code. They were scanned, and then the blast hatches slid open with a low, metallic hiss, revealing another section of the station.

"As far as I can tell, nothing has ever been taken, requisitioned. The inventory is exactly as it was when the station was first installed. We will be the first to really use this place, other than for a checkup visit. You know, it feels like this depot is frozen in time. It's eerie but... reassuring in a manner of speaking. Like it's been waiting... just for us."

"I've not seen anything like this place since the war," Steele said.

Chase looked over at him in question.

"Though this station's larger, it's very similar to a mobile depot. Did you ever see one of those beasts?"

Chase shook her head. "No. I wish I had though."

"They're just as impressive but are able to move under their own power... sort of like a large supply and ministerial ship but able to accommodate multiple ships of the line simultaneously."

"That would be something to see."

They continued onward, the ambient hum growing subtly louder as they approached the control room and center of the station. The air felt colder, almost biting, and Steele could smell faint traces of lubricants and coolants, preserved in the closed-off environment. They paused at the final blast hatch. Chase input her code and a heartbeat later it slid open, revealing the control room.

As they stepped inside, Steele's gaze was immediately drawn to the expansive windows at the far end. Through the thick composite glass, he could see the depot's main storage bay, a cavernous expanse filled with rows of munitions, fuel pods, and supply crates of all kinds and sizes.

Dim lights cast an amber glow over the inventory. The sheer scale of the resources stored here, the vastness of it all, was impressive in the extreme. From their vantage point, it was clear that this depot wasn't just a simple supply stop; it was a logistical powerhouse, capable of sustaining a small fleet for months on end.

Massive crates containing everything from ammunition and PDS rounds to ship-killer missiles and torpedo casings were stacked in careful arrangements. Steele could even make out the distinctive cylindrical shapes of spare parts for gravitic drives, coils, and stealth modules lined up and attached to one side of the depot's walls. In the shadows near the far end sat several rows of assault shuttles, dormant, silent, yet ready to be outfitted and put to work if needed.

The control room had an almost ghostly air, as if it had been forgotten by time. Each console and panel bore a thin layer of dust, as did the deck. Steele noticed faint dust-covered finger-prints on some of the screens—evidence of whoever had been here last, years past. Each screen was dark, waiting for a touch that would bring it to life.

Chase stepped up to the main console by the observation windows. She reached a hand to the screen, which obediently flared to life. She paused a moment for the system to load, then tapped in a command on the virtual keyboard. Rows of data filled the display, and Chase pulled up an extensive inventory list, glancing at him with a hint of satisfaction.

"As you can see, Captain," she said, gesturing at the display, "this depot is stocked beyond what we'd need. There's enough here to rearm *Ranger* fully—and then some."

Ignoring the monitor, Steele stepped closer to the windows. He looked over all that had been prepositioned here. He turned and looked downward several stories and saw even more—crates and containers stacked in vast, orderly rows. Racks of missiles, pallets of supplies, and armored containers lined the depot's massive decks, not to mention the walls and overhead, all methodically organized and clearly categorized.

Seeing the extent of supplies here, he realized the Union's logistical prowess ran deep, something he'd already known, but here it became more real, more tangible—and this was just one depot in a vast network spanning more than a dozen star systems.

"Quite impressive," he said, his tone filled with understated awe as he took in the view. His gaze roamed over the supplies, the enormous reserve of armaments, fuel, and critical provisions. In moments like these, the navy's reach and capability seemed almost boundless, but he knew there were limits.

"Guns and I have compiled a detailed list of what we need. Do you want to see it?"

"I do," Steele said, turning back to Chase.

She handed him the tablet and he studied it, cycling through it one line item at a time until he reached the end. After a moment, he looked up. "Gravitic mines? You want to bring aboard mines?"

"We were never issued with any." Chase gave a shrug of her shoulders. "It is, or was, peacetime after all. But I thought we might be able to use them, if the opportunity arises. I mean, no one's used mines since the war, right? The ones I want are older models, but they have stealth capability and they are small and easily overlooked. They're also some probes I want to take a look at."

"Probes?"

"Yes, sir, they've been modified and have stealth generators. They may come in useful. The manifest says they've been upgraded from standard recon units. They might be able to detect stealthed vessels too."

"Interesting... all right," Steele said with a shrug. He did not see the downside to taking them aboard. If they found a use for the mines and probes, great. If not... no real loss. "Are you ready to initiate the loading process?"

"We just need your authorization, sir," Chase said and gestured at the display in the control room. "Only a command-level officer can authorize the transfer, and it must be from this control room. We cannot do it remotely."

"Which is why you called me over," Steele surmised.

"Yes, sir."

"Right." He stepped over and tapped on the screen, pulling

up the correct menu. He spent a moment accessing and filling out the supply release authorization form. It was needlessly detailed, clearly the work of some faceless supply officer.

"Command code required," an automated voice said, and in response another form popped up. It blinked, waiting for him to input his command code. Steele keyed it in. There was a slight hesitation and then an automated voice spoke. "Authorization granted, Captain Steele. You have full access to the depot."

"All right," Steele said, turning to his executive officer, "let's get this show on the road."

Chase gave a sharp nod. She spent a moment working her tablet, sending the required list to the depot's construct. The tablet beeped. "The depot has accepted our request." With that, she stepped forward and immediately activated the loading sequence on the console Steele had just used.

The hum of machinery reverberated faintly through the walls as the entire system out in the depot seemed to come to life, conveyors and robotic arms swinging into motion in the storage bay, all visible through the large observation windows.

From his vantage point, Steele watched as a pallet of ship-killer missiles was carefully lifted from the one of racks along the left wall, transferred toward the deck, and placed upon a conveyor belt. The pallet rapidly moved away.

"Everything's automated down there?" he asked, glancing back at Chase.

"Completely, sir. No personnel from our end are required for a standard resupply, at least until it arrives in *Ranger*'s hangar. Then, the rest is on us. The station's construct manages everything on this end, though I'll be overseeing it from here. With luck, we'll be done within a few hours, sir, say ten at most."

"What about the shuttle?" Steele asked.

"Unfortunately, that's not automated. Once the craft is

ready and certified, one of our pilots will need to fly it over to *Ranger*."

Steele nodded and glanced back at the storage bay and the activity within, impressed by the seamless efficiency.

"Good work," he said after a moment.

"Thank you, sir." Chase's attention shifted back to the display as various supplies were marked "in transfer." She tapped in a few more commands and then joined him at the observation window.

Together they stood in silence, watching the munitions begin to move, where they would be ultimately transferred to *Ranger* and taken aboard. Steele took a deep breath, tasting the faint, metallic tang in the air. He glanced over at Chase.

"You need sleep," Steele said.

"After this is all done," Chase said firmly, "I will get some and not before. I've already taken a stim and will be up for the duration." She paused and looked at him closely, her eyes narrowing. "Have you gotten any, sir?"

"Sleep? Only a short nap," Steele admitted, thinking back to the forty-five minutes he'd snatched in sickbay. It seemed like forever since he'd gotten a full night's sleep.

"Then might I make a recommendation? Go get some shut-eye, real sleep, sir, at least eight hours' worth."

Steele found himself hesitant. It seemed somehow unfair.

"Since I've already taken a stim, you can make it up to me when this is all said and done, the transfer is complete, and our magazines replenished," Chase said. "There will be plenty of time as we slow-boat our way deeper in-system."

"All right," Steele said after a long moment. "It's a deal, but should you have any issues, you call straight away."

"There won't be any issues that will require your personal attention, sir. That, I will see to personally."

Steele grinned at her. He liked her approach to issues like

this one. It took some of the burden off him, for he could rely upon her to do a job right. "All right, XO, this is your show."

"Thank you, sir. Now, might I suggest you kindly get moving and find your bed?"

"Right, I will leave you to it, then." With that, he turned and left, returning the way he'd come, the thought of his bed and sleep beckoning seductively.

FOURTEEN

Steele sat in his command chair on the bridge, his gaze fixed on the HTD filling the center console with a quiet glow, detailing the immediate space around *Ranger*. The stealth fields were fully engaged, wrapping the ship in an anti-detection cloak designed to blend in against the star-studded void. At a steady 7g, *Ranger* was cutting silently through space, creeping ever deeper into the Illidran System.

Chase was not currently on the bridge. She was working with Guns and the chief engineer. That left only himself, Hale, Calder, and Quinn on watch. The HTD's image was a ghostly representation of the nearby celestial bodies and objects, each one outlined and tagged accordingly. The intensity of the light of each tagged target was an indicator of the confidence level. Steele studied the display, his eyes flicking over the known and potential contacts—some faintly visible as blips farther out, what were called artifacts of the passive sensors. Artifacts were not fully identified targets.

They couldn't risk using active sweeps to confirm what was really out there—not without breaking cover. And doing that was unthinkable, for they were a shadow in the darkness, driving deeper into the system, hiding in plain view from enemy scanners and the system detection network.

A faint and steady vibration thrummed through the deck as *Ranger* held her course, the gravitic drive up and spinning at a slower pace, each tick pulling them farther from the relative safety of the Fringe Zone and closer to the system's beating heart. As he stared at the HTD, he found it strange being cut off from the system's detection network and knowing so very little. They had trained for this sort of thing, but reality was altogether different.

Steele rubbed his jaw thoughtfully, his gaze lingering on the faint outlines of the nearby traffic lanes. Typically bustling with the ceaseless movement of transports, cargo haulers, and privately flagged vessels, they were now, from what the ship could detect, eerily silent and empty. The channels that usually buzzed with encrypted IFF pings and cordial exchanges from passing civilian ships were practically silent.

With a heavy breath, Steele looked away and reached for his coffee. He took a sip. It had long grown cold. He did not much mind. After a second pull at the drink, he replaced the cup back in its holder, then tapped on the news feed and brought up the local broadcast net, an open entertainment stream that reached every corner of the system. Even amidst the chaos of revolution and potential war it was still broadcasting.

Could he learn anything from it?

"Atheena," Steele said, "what are the newscasts mainly focusing on?"

"Captain, current broadcasts are focused on events occurring within the Protectorate," Atheena reported, her tone as neutral as ever. "Topics include the ongoing unrest in the system, what the locals are calling their independence movement. There are numerous stories concerning the fighting amongst Union loyalists, Union forces, and the consolidation of power, along with the progress of the Congress of the Four Systems and the formation of a temporary governing council."

"Congress of the Four Systems? What's that?"

"The Congress of the Four Systems is a body of representatives that is in the process of forming to help chart the future of what we know as the Protectorate, at least according to the news broadcasts."

Steele's fingers scrolled through the available news channels, each thumbnail displaying anchors with grim or triumphant expressions, depending on the station's allegiance or political bent. There was a brief text description underneath every thumbnail. After a moment, he settled on one feed and tapped it.

One of the side screens at his station flickered to life. A local Illidran news broadcast filled the display, the emblem of the LDF prominently shown in the corner of the frame. There was also a flag he'd never seen before, four stars set against a blue background, behind the anchor.

A stern-looking woman was staring into the camera, her short, slicked-back hair lending a certain severity and hardness to her features. She wore a crisp, dark suit, clearly chosen to convey a sense of control and professionalism.

"Good evening and welcome to *The Nightly News* with Mara Kaveen, reporting from Newburg City on Gildarra." Her voice was steady but with a thin layer of intensity. "LDF forces on Silicara have secured a significant victory today. Following a series of coordinated and precision directed strikes, along with some difficult fighting, Liberation Defense Force, under the command of General Arvin Kole, have successfully forced the Union garrison at Jefferson's Landing to lay down their arms and surrender."

Steele felt himself scowl. This certainly wasn't good news. It was also not unexpected, for the Union presence in the system had never been that large to begin with, even the ground-pounders. The military's mission was mainly to show the flag. The Union primarily relied upon the Local Defense Forces to help keep order. In hindsight, arming and training the locals, those who had professed loyalty, had clearly been a colossal mistake, one made by the bureaucrats, the politicos that ran the Union. They thought they understood how the world worked, but were frequently wrong. And when they were wrong, it was people like Steele who ended up on the firing line, not the politicians.

Steele rubbed his jaw as he considered what he was learning. He found it interesting how the LDF had changed their name. The screen cut to rapid, shaky, on-the-ground footage, mixed in with shots from airborne drones. These showed smoke rising in thick plumes over a ruined and heavily damaged cityscape. Though Steele had never been there, he assumed the shot was from Jefferson's Landing. When the scene shifted again, flashes of gunfire illuminated the ruins of a wrecked street, with some buildings shells of their former selves or entirely collapsed.

The scene shifted once more, this time showing LDF soldiers methodically moving through the streets, their armored vehicles rumbling along, strange banners and flags flapping and snapping in the wind. As the anchor continued to speak, the camera zoomed in on a group of weary Union soldiers, a dozen marines, hands above their heads, being led away by LDF forces into captivity.

"Just moments ago, we received confirmation that General Elias Harker of the Union Marine Corps has formally surrendered and ordered the rest of his command to lay down their arms. This marks a critical juncture and turning point in our fight for independence."

A pre-recorded clip of General Arvin Kole replaced the live footage, his face hard and resolute, standing before a hastily erected blue flag with the four stars, flying over what looked like a government building. The general's name appeared at the bottom of the image.

"Today," the general declared, "we have proven that the people of the Protectorate will no longer be shackled by a distant, dictatorial, and corrupt power. Our victory is not only a military one, a clear and decisive achievement of arms—it is a stand for our sovereignty and the future of our children. Today we struck a hard blow against the imperial fascism of the Union."

The feed returned to the news anchor, her expression filled with plain satisfaction.

"The surrender of General Harker is expected to be the first of several to come, especially since the LDF now has complete control of the high orbitals," she continued, her eyes fairly gleaming as she spoke. "The path to freedom burns brighter with every passing hour. We here on *The Nightly News* commend the bravery of General Kole and all LDF forces who have risked their lives for the cause."

Steele's jaw tightened as he watched. The broadcast faded into images of the blue flag waving triumphantly over the smoke-filled horizon, underscored by the reporter's closing words.

"Stay with us as we continue to bring you exclusive, up-to-the-minute coverage on our journey to independence and self-determination. Together, we stand strong. Together, we *are* strong."

With a tap and a swipe on the screen, Steele terminated the broadcast and keyed another feed, bringing up the next newscast. This time, a male anchor filled the screen from a different network, his appearance sharply polished, hair carefully styled to appear trustworthy and nonthreatening. He sat against a backdrop of an emblem crossed with banners representing each of the Four Systems, which were spelled out—Illidran, Yarith,

Everale, and Fethis. The tone was celebratory, bordering on triumphant.

"In historic news, the Congress of the Four Systems is set to convene in just three weeks' time," the anchor announced, his voice resonating with pride. "This congress, representing the former Protectorate, marks the first step toward forming a new and independent government for our people."

The screen shifted to footage of a cheering and jubilant crowd, people waving banners with symbols of each planet in the Four Systems. The energy was powerful, electric, and clearly contagious as people gathered to celebrate their newfound liberation from Union control.

"The congress will host representatives from each of our worlds, elected by their respective local populations," the anchor continued. "Together, they will work to draft a constitution that ensures the values and freedoms we've long fought and struggled for. In the meantime, the Council of Four, an interim governing body, has been established to oversee our new nation during this critical phase of transition. Leading this council is Doctor Jacob Lamb, who was, as of this morning, appointed as president."

At the mention of Lamb's name, Steele's brow furrowed. He knew the name well—Lamb had been a notorious revolutionary leader, a terrorist, and a butcher of innocents. His organization was responsible for multiple attacks on Union facilities and the deaths of hundreds upon hundreds of people. Captured several years back, he had been sentenced to life in prison without the possibility for parole. The man was a firebrand and trouble. Instead of executing the bastard and making him a martyr, they'd simply stuck him in a Union prison and left him to rot, only he'd been freed. Steele felt his blood boil. The politicians could be so stupid, so short-sighted, so budget-focused. Demobilization after the last war, steadily cutting the garrisons of the Protectorate down to unsafe levels, then... this shit.

"Securing the release of Doctor Lamb was nothing short of monumental, involving a daring commando action by LDF forces. A political prisoner for his unyielding stance and struggle to free our people, Lamb has emerged from incarceration to be welcomed by cheering crowds," the anchor said, his eyes alight with barely hidden admiration. "Today, he stands as a direct symbol of our resilience, our unwavering commitment to independence, and the freedom we deserve."

Footage of Lamb appeared, a tall, lean man with iron-gray hair and a hard, unforgiving face. His eyes were piercing. Standing atop a platform, he was addressing a huge crowd, though his words could not be heard. His fist pumped in defiance. The crowd screamed their approval, their chants thundering forth as if powered by years of pent-up frustration and anticipation of this very moment.

"With Lamb at the helm, the Council of Four has vowed to uphold self-governance, support the congress, and work toward building a government by and for the people of the Four Systems. Doctor Lamb promises a future free from the Union's heavy yoke, a future where each of our worlds stands united in strength and autonomy. In fact, just today we received word that the Valkorian Hegemony's consulate in Illidran has recognized the council as the legitimate ruling body of the Four Systems."

Feeling terribly unhappy, Steele watched as the report wrapped up, the anchor's face unwavering in his prideful expression. To the people of the Protectorate, Lamb was a hero —an icon of resistance and newfound sovereignty. But to Steele, the man was a monster, a reminder of the hard-edged reality he now faced. This wasn't just a rebellion; it was a revolution with deep roots and clear momentum that seemed to be growing with every passing hour. Even without the Hegemony's interference, the Union would clearly have a difficult time restoring order.

"This is a fucking mess," he hissed to himself. The Union's

political leadership had clearly made a grave miscalculation. The Protectorate should have had a larger garrison, a more substantial Fleet presence, not just three ships. "Should have, could have, would have... it's all now spilled milk."

If the Union wanted their buffer zone back—and Steele knew they would—they'd have to fight for it. The navy would be the ones doing the initial fighting and dying.

Steele shifted uneasily in his seat as he selected another feed. The screen changed to reveal a woman with an intense expression, her tone coldly triumphant. Behind her, the flag he was coming to recognize as that of the new government filled the backdrop, four stars over a blue background.

"In further developments, Union Governor Annalise Tancrest, once the highest Union authority in Illidran, is reportedly on the run and in hiding. Sources suggest she, along with her family, have sought refuge amongst scattered pro-Union holdouts, traitors to our people. Other sources claim she may be sheltering with the remaining Union military forces who have not yet come to terms with the inevitable, that they have already lost."

The anchor's words carried a biting edge, clearly reveling in the Union's loss of control. She turned slightly, gesturing to the side as the view shifted to the front of a courthouse in Illidran's capital. The scene was chaotic: hundreds of protestors filled the steps and the street before it, some waving signs with hastily scrawled slogans calling for Tancrest's capture, while others chanted, their voices blending into a frenzied call for justice.

The anchor's voice cut back in, a thin smile on her lips. "We now go live to our correspondent outside the courthouse, where Governor Tancrest has just been indicted in absentia for crimes against the Four Systems and its people. Though Tancrest herself is nowhere to be found, these proceedings mark an official rejection of her authority and an end to Union oppression."

The view zoomed in on a man holding a microphone in

front of the courthouse, straining to speak over the roar of the crowd. Behind him, the angry and agitated protestors held signs emblazoned with harsh demands and slogans: *Try Her for Treason!*, *No Mercy for Union Bitches!*, *Tancrest Must Pay!* A few voices rose above the rest, chanting, "Try her and then shoot her! Death to the Union!"

The reporter nodded grimly as he faced the camera. "That's right, the charges against Annalise Tancrest include abuse of power, brutally oppressing the people of Illidran, and numerous other allegations of gross misconduct and malfeasance. Citizens are demanding swift and severe punishment should she be found or turned over to civil authorities."

The view cut briefly to an image of Tancrest, her stern expression frozen in a public appearance from sometime before the uprising. Her face, once the symbol of Union authority, now appeared alongside words like *traitor*, *criminal*, and *wanted* splashed across the screen.

Steele's gaze hardened as he took in the scene. It wasn't just an indictment; it was a public condemnation—an entire star system casting aside Union rule, fanning the flames of revolution with the image of Tancrest as its chief villain.

The intensity of the people was clear, and he could readily see the zeal in their eyes, as if they could will her capture into existence. For them, Tancrest's downfall would be a powerful symbol, one of the final nails in the coffin of Union influence over the Protectorate.

"Not a good situation, is it?"

Steele turned in his chair, surprised to find Miller standing quietly beside him. The man had approached so silently Steele hadn't even registered his arrival on the bridge. He suppressed a brief flicker of irritation, reminding himself that Miller, for all his quiet presence and civilian attire, was a naval officer, one who was working directly for the Intelligence Directorate.

Miller had cleaned up since their last encounter, now

dressed in a sharply pressed suit, his expression unreadable as he studied the HTD with a practiced eye.

"It certainly isn't ideal," Steele replied, carefully neutral.

Miller's gaze shifted to one of the screens, where he gestured faintly toward the news net, the images of protest and revolt flickering across its surface. "I've been following the broadcasts for the last several hours," he said, his voice low. "From what I can gather, the garrison on Forgeheart is holding, at least for the moment. That may be where the governor and her family have gone. But they want her blood, and badly. God help her if she falls into their power." He glanced toward Steele's office, his brow furrowed with thought. "Still, there's much to be learned from these broadcasts—reading between the lines, trying to pick facts from fiction, where the local factions don't align or agree. It's like a puzzle in pieces just waiting to be assembled."

"That's one way to look at it."

Miller cast another look toward Steele's office, the expression in his eyes clearly a prompt.

"You want to talk in private?"

Miller gave a curt nod.

Steele let out a controlled breath, resigning himself to what was to come before rising and pulling himself to his feet. "Hale, you have the bridge. The ship is yours."

"Aye, sir, I have the bridge," Hale responded with a crisp nod.

"Mr. Miller, this way, please." Steele gestured, and the two of them moved across the bridge. The marine stationed by Steele's office snapped to attention as they passed. Steele gave the marine a quick nod before stepping into his office. The hatch slid shut with a soft hiss, insulating them from the steady hum of the bridge beyond.

Inside, the office was dimly lit, the soft overhead lights casting a focused glow over the desk and chairs, leaving the corners of the office in shadow. The air here was subtly differ-ent, quieter, still and peaceful. Steele moved to his desk, settling into his chair with practiced ease, gesturing Miller to sit across from him.

Miller lowered himself into the chair. His gaze held the same intensity, a clear sign he was ready to address serious matters. Steele leaned forward, bracing himself.

"Captain," Miller began before Steele could speak, his voice grave, "I'm receiving information from across the system—assets sending messages to encrypted arrays, updates on what's happening in their neck of the woods. As you can imagine, none of it is good." He paused, holding up a hand as if anticipating Steele's next question. "And before you ask, I haven't replied to any of them, nor will I, not without your direct approval or direction. I will not give away *Ranger*'s position."

"Thank you for that." Steele took a moment to consider Miller's words. Even through the man's calm demeanor, he could see a shadow in his expression—a glimmer of the strain that months and years of intelligence operations and complex allegiances could leave on a person, especially when you had people in harm's way. Steele rested his elbows on his desk. He understood without a doubt that Miller had people hanging in the wind, men and women he knew and likely cared about.

Steele was quiet for a long moment. "I understand the posi-tion you are in. That said, I want to make this plain. There's really nothing we can do for any of them. I am certain you can appreciate our circumstances. We are the last Union warship in-system. If the enemy learns of our presence here, they will do everything within their power to hunt us down. *Ranger* may be powerful and fast, but she is only one ship. Surely you can see that."

Steele leaned back, letting the silence hang for a moment.

Miller's gaze dropped, his shoulders dipping ever so slightly. "I know we cannot help them," he replied, his voice threaded with resignation. He hesitated, as if the enormity of the Union's loss had suddenly hit him, then looked up, meeting Steele's gaze with a sad, understanding look. "I know it. I don't have to like it, but I know it..."

"The best we can do is find the Hegemony fleet, gather as much detail as possible, and report back."

Miller nodded in agreement, his jaw tightening as he returned Steele's determined look. In that moment, they both understood the significance of their mission. It was not a rescue operation, but a dangerous and necessary hunt.

"How long until we arrive at the Reach?" Miller asked.

"At our current speed, three days. From there, another day to the Exclusion Zone, and that's where we'll begin our search in earnest. I don't want to go faster. There is risk with that."

"Greater emissions from the drive," Miller said.

"Correct. It's more energy that the stealth systems need to overcome, for the heat sinks to absorb and to disperse in a pattern that will not be easily detectable."

"But you could still move faster if you wish and remain virtually invisible."

"Don't ask that of me."

"I won't," Miller said, then paused. "Captain, are you planning on entering the Exclusion Zone?"

"If I can help it, not a chance," Steele said firmly. "I judge it simply too dangerous. The mines laced throughout the zone are enough of a worry on their own, not to mention any active remnants from the last war, intelligent weapon systems and such. That's a risk I'm unwilling to take, even in the area that's been cleared and certified as safe."

Miller's expression softened, curious but cautious. "Then how do you intend to hunt down the enemy? How will you find them?"

Steele's lips curved in a subtle, knowing smile. "At the depot, we picked up a cache of survey probes. I figured they might come in handy, so we took them. Chase and my chief engineer are working on them now."

"Survey probes?" Miller's skepticism was evident as he raised an eyebrow. "What exactly were these probes designed for?"

"Originally, they were meant for deep-space mineral surveys—finding rare and hard-to-get stuff. But after the last war, someone apparently had the bright idea to retrofit several dozen. The probes are equipped with advanced detection systems and have been programmed to search for hidden vessels, those cloaked in stealth fields. Now, whether they will work as advertised or not, I simply do not know."

"What do you mean? Why wouldn't they work, and why would you rely upon them if you were unsure?"

"These probes are someone's experiment, one the navy decided not to adopt on a wider scale. They're old, too, and, as such, may not be able to penetrate current Hegemony stealth tech. But—I have ideas on how to hedge our bets, how to use them to find the Hegemony fleet. With luck, we will find out soon enough."

Miller looked at him, intrigued but still wary. "So, they're designed to detect ships lying in wait?"

Steele nodded. "That's what the specs say. These probes apparently can pick up on subtle disturbances—gravitic fluctuations, slight heat signatures that have been suppressed and dispersed by heat sinks, not to mention minor background electromagnetic fields created by stealth systems—fields that standard scans would overlook. In addition, each probe has its own limited construct, so they are smart to a degree, more intelligent than our ship-killer missiles."

"They sound very promising," Miller said.

"I think they could be our best chance to locate anything the Hegemony might have hiding out there without putting us directly in a difficult position, one where the enemy will have no trouble locating us."

"I see." The skepticism in Miller's eyes was plain. "If they are as good as you make them sound then why weren't they fully adopted by the navy? I am not sold on this..."

"Neither am I," Steele admitted. "And trust me, I'm well aware that they may not work as well as I hope, or at all. But I'm not taking *Ranger* into the Exclusion Zone unless I must. And—we have to keep in mind—your information on a Hegemony fleet being in-system might not be accurate. They might have nothing here."

"All right, fair enough," Miller said, his gaze thoughtful but cautious. "Do you think these probes will work as advertised?"

Steele remained guarded. "As I said, I'm unsure. But it's the best option we have right now, and"—he gave a slight shrug—"I intend to find out." He decided to shift the conversation. "What about the messages coming in from ID's assets across the system? Have you learned anything useful, something that can help us?"

Miller leaned back in his chair, crossing his arms as he let out a breath. "Some," he admitted, glancing away with a frustrated look before looking back. "Unfortunately, most of the message traffic is little more than pleas for extraction, demands for help, that sort of thing. Most of my operatives are isolated, scattered, and right now more concerned with their own safety than gathering information. I have several that are on the run and being actively hunted. There have already been reprisals, murders in the streets of Union civilians or suspected collaborators, sympathizers, ugly stuff."

Steele noted the flicker of frustration that crossed Miller's face. He'd seen it before—the fine line between empathy and exasperation, not to mention outright frustration. "Nothing more concrete, then?"

Miller hesitated, glancing down at his hands, which had

unconsciously balled into fists in his lap. He shook his head. "Nothing of value to you." Miller met his eyes, resolve hardening in his expression. "If I catch anything truly important—you'll be the first to know."

"Excellent, that is what I expect," Steele said, then paused for a heartbeat. "I heard Argonola regained consciousness a short while ago and that you've been to check on him. Have you spoken to him yet? Have you learned anything useful from the man?"

"I have spoken with him, and I did learn something useful." Miller retrieved a small tablet from the inner pocket of his suit jacket. He leaned forward and placed the device on Steele's desk. He slid the tablet across the smooth surface toward the captain. "It's why I've come. This"—he pointed at the tablet—"is where he reports the enemy fleet is located and holding station. He said he was pretty sure on it, that his information was rock-solid."

"Rock-solid?" Steele asked, feeling skepticism.

"He went there," Miller said, "and boarded a Hegemony battleship for a meeting."

That got Steele's attention. "Really?"

"My man is one of the cell leaders for Lamb's organization. He's pretty high up in the food chain and has been undercover for more than five years. I wasn't going to pull him out, but he signaled his information was too important, critical even. He needed immediate pull-out."

"Why didn't he just transmit his information? That would have made it simpler." Steele snapped his fingers as the answer struck him. "He didn't want to be burned by ID. He passes along that information, we act upon it, and after the fact, the finger gets pointed at him by Lamb."

"Correct," Miller said. "Very perceptive, Captain. He demanded extraction before passing along his information."

"And that's why you requisitioned *Ranger*."

"Also correct," Miller said.

"I was once approached by ID," Steele said, "just after graduation from the Academy. I turned them down."

"I'm aware."

Meeting Miller's gaze, Steele sucked in a breath and let it out. He picked up the tablet and activated the screen. An image appeared, displaying a specific sector of the Exclusion Zone within the Reach. The Exclusion Zone was a vast expanse of mostly wreckage and debris, the remains of starships and stations, not to mention asteroids both large and small. However, the area detailed on the tablet was a small section of it, barely a hundred thousand kilometers across. It was one of the areas that had almost been completely cleared by the LDF but was still listed as unsafe. Steele's eyes narrowed as he studied the coordinates and the data on this portion of the zone.

"It's the perfect place to conceal a Hegemony fleet," Miller added. "And I'd bet my next month's shitty salary that the entire area has been cleaned out by the LDF and is safe."

"How certain are *you* of this information?" Steele asked, his gaze cutting back to Miller.

"I trust my man." Miller's expression didn't waver.

"Like he trusts you and the ID?"

"I'd bet my career on it and him."

"How about betting your life on this information?" Steele asked. "Are you ready to do that?"

"I already have." Miller met his stare, unflinching. "I'm betting yours and your crew's, too."

Steele gave a slow nod, absorbing Miller's words. His gaze dropped back to the tablet. "All right, that's where we'll head to have a look then, but with what I have in mind, this may be a one-shot kind of thing. Miller, let's hope your intel is solid, because once I unzip my fly it will be time to run."

"It is, and thank you for doing this, Captain," Miller said, a note of gratitude in his voice, which Steele suspected was a rare thing. "I appreciate it."

"I am not doing this for you. I'm doing this because the intelligence we gather may ultimately save lives."

Miller's gaze softened, the faintest hint of respect breaking through. "I do my job for the same reason. I think we are very much alike."

Steele wasn't so certain about that.

A buzzer sounded, and Steele's attention sharpened. He activated the channel with a quick command to his implants. "What is it?"

"You should come to the bridge, sir," Hale's voice came through the speakers in the office. "Sensors are detecting LDF activity near our destination."

Steele's jaw set. "Alert the XO and have her meet me on the bridge."

"Aye, sir," Hale responded.

"I'll be right there," he said, before terminating the channel.

"The enemy's there," Miller reaffirmed, gesturing at the tablet, "where my man said they will be."

"We're going to find that out." Steele stood and moved around his desk and toward the bridge.

FIFTEEN

Steele swept onto the bridge. A step behind him, Miller followed. Steele rapidly crossed to his command station, feeling the eyes of the bridge crew momentarily flicker in his direction before resuming their tasks. Hale, Calder, Quinn, and Ishida were present and at their stations.

"I have the bridge," Steele announced as he settled into his chair, feeling the familiar, steady vibration of *Ranger*'s systems humming through the seat—the pulse of the ship herself. He brought the screens at his station online with a touch to the main display and they instantly flickered to life. He studied the ship's course and speed. Nothing had changed. *Ranger*'s vitals looked good, too.

"The ship is yours, sir," Hale acknowledged. "You have command."

Satisfied everything was as it should be, he glanced up just as Chase entered the bridge, stepping off the lift. She moved to her station and slid into her seat with her usual composure, immediately activating her screens to assess the situation like Steele had just done.

"Hale, report," Steele ordered a moment later, eyes moving

to his helmsman, who turned toward him with a focused expression.

"Sir," Hale began, "Lieutenant Ishida has detected multiple LDF mobile assets moving into the Reach. They appear to be burning toward a location near our approximate arrival coordinates. It's uncomfortably close to the Exclusion Zone."

"Lieutenant Ishida?" Steele prompted, turning his attention to the tactical officer. "What are you seeing?"

Ishida's hands moved across her console, and a second later, the HTD plot sprang to life on the main screen. She gestured with a hand to it. "We've tagged their signals and trajectories. So far, we're tracking what I believe to be two destroyers and three frigates, sir. Confidence on ship types is high based upon their drive signatures. There is possibly a fourth frigate in motion, farther out, but I am not certain on that. She could easily be a civilian transport based on her drive readings. I've marked her as a potential hostile. As you can see, there is one group comprising a destroyer and two frigates, and another, a destroyer and a frigate. They are coming in from different directions and are aiming for the same focal point, converging on it."

Steele examined the tagged enemy vessels on the display. Red flashing icons marked the five LDF ships, as well as the possible sixth. The two groups were also moving along established traffic lanes, which *Ranger* was not. *Ranger* was far off the beaten path.

Beside him, Chase's expression was equally intense as she analyzed the data, taking a closer look at her own station displays, her gaze darting from one screen to the next as she worked. The light from the screens illuminated her face, highlighting the creases of concentration as she considered the enemy's intent. "They're not just out for a routine patrol," she noted, "that much is certain. You don't burn the gravitic coils that hard unless you have a reason."

"Agreed," Steele replied, his voice low as he continued to

study the tactical display himself. "They are after something important."

"But what?" Ishida asked.

"That's the question. Stealth field status?" Steele asked, glancing toward Quinn.

"Fully engaged, Captain, and functioning within normal parameters. Our current profile and signature are minimal. I am monitoring our heat sinks closely." Quinn paused to take a quick breath. "If one of those ships gets close enough, sir, and their active sensors sweep us, even a slight shift could give us away."

"If they keep to their current course," Ishida said, "they won't come that close."

Steele examined the HTD and the plot. He zoomed out, watching the positions of the five tagged ships, each one flashing red on the screen. Their paths were converging, and they were clearly moving with purpose toward something specific.

But what were they after?

The tactical readouts showed each ship's speed, burning at an impressive 48g—enough power output to light up *Ranger*'s passive sensors without issue. Heck, half of the entire Illidran Star System could likely see those ships without the detection network. It was clear they were driving hard, gravity drives radiating energy in all directions, leaving no doubt the LDF was responding to a serious threat or concern of some kind.

Miller stood next to Steele's station, arms crossed, his face grim as he stared at the data feed.

Ishida's calm voice broke the silence. "They're all headed deeper into the Reach."

"Any idea on their destination?" Steele asked.

"Yes, sir. Though they're on different traffic lanes, I've done some calculations, and it appears like they're making a straight-line burn for a place called Meecham's Station. It's a bit out of the way and they will have to do some maneuvering as they close the final stretch, but they're basically all zeroed in on the place, Captain."

An icon and tag flashed blue on the HTD. Ishida had added Meecham's Station to the overview. Steele's brow furrowed, and he quickly pulled up the data tag on the targeted location from *Ranger*'s library. "Meecham's Station..." He glanced over at Chase. "It's a refinery. They process various types of rock and ice there, with a permanent population of roughly six hundred civilians. There is no military presence, no garrison of any kind, but a small police force." He rubbed his jaw, trying to piece together the reasoning behind such a show of force, not to mention urgency.

After a long moment, Chase spoke. "That place is remote, isolated, and as far as I can tell, there should be nothing of strategic value there. And I don't see anything on the HTD that would warrant such a response, at least from what we can observe with passive sensors."

"Agreed," Steele said.

"It is a puzzle," Miller said. "Everything is a puzzle."

Steele looked over at the man and felt himself frown. "I could do with one less puzzle today."

Chase's gaze flicked from Steele to Miller. "What could they possibly want with a refinery? What's out there that's worth sending five ships?"

"Good question," Steele replied, unease creeping into his tone.

"No obvious military value," Miller said, "unless the station or someone there is hiding something the LDF wants to protect or... silence. There's a lot of ugly business going on right now."

"Five ships seems like overkill for something like that," Steele said. "One of those ships would be able to easily handle the station."

"It does seem like overkill," Miller agreed, "and that's why it is a puzzle worth solving."

"They're not quite headed for our section of the Reach," Chase noted, her gaze still fixed on the display. "But they'll come uncomfortably close and be in our vicinity... easy response range if we somehow get spotted and identified."

Steele nodded, eyes narrowing as he examined the tactical display. "Close enough to be a concern, but I judge not close enough to breach our stealth field. At least they shouldn't be able to overcome it."

"Our mission is to locate an enemy fleet, if it's there," Chase said, with a glance at Miller. "A handful of LDF ships diverting to some remote refinery station is a distraction at best."

"That is, if they stay far enough out. They will bear watching." Steele tapped the armrest of his chair with his finger. He did not like this... not now. "Still, it's odd. They're deploying five warships for a remote refinery. Surely the LDF has bigger fish to fry as they consolidate their hold on the system." Steele shook his head. "It's damn odd," he repeated.

"Yes, it is," Miller said.

Steele tapped his console to pull up more data on Meecham's Station. "It's a small industrial hub—a few processing centers and storage facilities. As far as defenses go, there's nothing substantial listed here, just enough to keep the lone pirate away, a couple of maser batteries, and three old particle cannons... shields and defensive screens are minimal at best."

"Could be other vessels are present, sir," Ishida suggested. "If they're running silent, or simply sitting off the station with stealth fields engaged, we wouldn't pick them up—that is, unless their drives go hot and they light off somewhere in a hurry."

"I suppose that's possible, but if there was a ship or ships there, I think they would have already made a run for it. We'd be seeing them too, as they burned away."

"As I said, this is a puzzle," Miller murmured, almost to himself, his gaze steady on the screen.

"Sir," Ishida said, "I've got a sixth ship in motion—a cruiser, Atheena's pegged her as the *Latan*. We just picked her up. She's farther out and burning hard at 47g."

On the plot, the cruiser's icon flared to life, marked by a red flashing tag. Like the rest, her projected destination was aimed for Meecham's Station. Feeling intense frustration, Steele rubbed his jaw. Clearly it had been a terrible mistake to provide the LDF with such powerful mobile assets, to entrust them with the policing of their own systems, while at the same time steadily drawing down Union military assets. Now, it had come back to bite them... trusting the locals. Would the politicians ever learn from their mistakes? He found himself doubting that. In his experience, they and the bureaucrats never learned. No... they made the same mistakes over and over again, ones even a blind man could readily see coming.

Steele leaned in, studying the plot. The LDF was adding a significant asset to this gathering force, which only deepened the mystery. The cruiser's signal pulsed in sync with its high-energy output—a signature clear enough to register even on *Ranger*'s passive sensors.

What was really going on here?

"At their current rate, the first group of ships, the destroyer and frigate, will reach the target area in about eighteen hours, sir, the second in nineteen," Ishida said. "The *Latan* in thirty hours."

"Whatever they're after, it's important," Chase said, her voice carrying a hint of unease. She shared a brief look with Steele. "They'd not commit so many assets were it not."

"I think so too," Steele replied, "but this may be one mystery we're better off not bothering to get involved with. Right now, it doesn't concern us directly. Our mission is straightforward. We find the enemy fleet, learn what we can, bug out, and go home, hopefully without any further difficulty."

"Sir," Ishida said, "once they reach the station, they'll likely go silent as their drives cycle down and drop off our sensors. We'll lose them from the plot. After that, if they are operating at low power levels and reduced emissions, there's no telling what they will do or where they will go."

Steele looked to Hale. "Helm, ease us back to 5g. Let's slow down a bit and lower our signature some, make it more difficult to be detected. We'll keep our profile as low as possible as we approach the Exclusion Zone."

"Aye, sir," Hale confirmed, hands moving over his controls, "reducing to 5g." The slight shift in thrust was barely perceptible, but Steele felt the tension ease, the vibration running through his ship reduce a small measure, as *Ranger* began slowing. "Braking."

"Hale, estimated arrival at our target destination at currently set speed?" Steele asked, leaning slightly toward the HTD display.

"At five gravities, sir, we're looking at just over forty-eight hours," Hale replied.

"Captain, I understand tamping back the drive, but why the slower approach, the reduction in speed? *Ranger* is a veritable ghost. We could simply coast in." Miller's gaze shifted from Steele to the main screen and the markers on the HTD showing the LDF ships converging on the small and isolated station.

"Mr. Miller," Steele said, gesturing at the plotted trajectories on the main screen, "it has to do with the warp bubble set for 7g. There is less of an energy requirement to maintain it at 5g. We'll fade into the black easier." Steele paused and waved a hand at the main screen. "I also want to see what happens when they get to the station. They're putting an awful lot of resources into this for a reason. Whatever they're up to, it should all be over within a few hours, and maybe when they are finished, they will burn away to put out the next fire. That will make things easier for us."

"I see." Miller nodded. "Is there anything I can do to help?"

"Perhaps there's some way to learn what they're up to. Maybe message traffic on the"—Steele glanced around his bridge crew—"civilian side. What do you think about that? The news services might be talking about this commitment of force."

Miller straightened, clearly catching the hint in Steele's words. "I understand, Captain," he said, a glimmer of intrigue in his eyes. "I'll get right on it and do what I can to help by scanning through the news reports and the civilian comms traffic in-system. There are bound to be ships, freighters, and transports talking about this on open channels..." His voice was lower now, almost conspiratorial, as he gave a brief, respectful nod. "I'll see if I can get any useful information flowing our way."

"Calder," Steele said, turning to his comms officer, "scan the civilian channels as well. See if you can learn anything that might shed some light on what the LDF is doing."

"Aye, sir."

"I will let you know if I learn anything, Captain," Miller said and started for the lift. Steele watched as Miller exited the bridge.

Chase glanced back toward the lift door, her brow furrowing slightly before she looked back at Steele. "What did Miller want? Why was he on the bridge?"

"To talk," Steele replied. "We will speak on it later."

She gave a nod.

"How's the probe reconfiguration coming along?"

"Quicker than expected," Chase said, shifting her attention back to him. "Ishida and I have done all we can with the software upgrades to the probe constructs. Engineering is working on them now. They should be ready to go within twelve hours, maybe sooner..."

"Good."

"I don't think anyone's tried this before," Chase continued. "I'm curious to see how it all works out."

"I am too. But first we need to get to the Reach and the edge of the Exclusion Zone without incident." He paused and sucked in a breath before letting it out. "I don't like this show of force the LDF is putting on. It spells trouble."

"We're definitely in hostile territory," Chase said.

"That we are, XO, and we best not forget it." Steele turned his attention back to the HTD. The display flickered softly as the enemy ships continued their high-speed beeline approach to Meecham's Station. The two of them fell into a contemplative silence, lost in their own thoughts, both watching the LDF ship marked by small, glowing icons.

The Reach's shadowy depths lay ahead of *Ranger*, dense outer patches of asteroid fields and debris-choked passages offering no easy route to their destination. They could not take the normal traffic lanes for obvious reasons. The course Steele had ordered plotted avoided the sensor buoys and arrays of the detection network.

Doing that had added significant time on their journey. Steele did not mind that, for when they entered the Reach, should it prove necessary, there would be places to hide amongst the fields of rock and ice chunks... Besides, at the moment, stealth was more important than speed.

His gaze tracked back to the enemy ships. With some luck, they'd not prove to be a complication in what was to come. Between the Hegemony and the LDF, Steele had an uncomfortable feeling he might have bitten off more than he could chew.

SIXTEEN

Steele's grip on the armrest of his command chair tightened as an asteroid the size of a city block drifted past *Ranger*'s hull, missing by what felt like the breadth of a fingernail. The navigation alarms beeped and chirped their irritating warnings, but there was no real danger thanks to Hale's skill at the helm. Still, Steele's stomach churned at the near miss. The damn thing had come too close, something that normally would be avoided at all costs.

He turned his attention from the plot and HTD to the opticals. The asteroid's surface was pockmarked with craters, a history of countless collisions etched into its rocky face. Jagged spires jutted outward, glinting faintly under the ambient light of Illidran's distant sun, as if the asteroid itself were a bristling beast, a veritable monster stalking angrily through the void.

The Reach sprawled out around them, a chaotic expanse of tumbling rocks and dust clouds stretching for millions of kilometers in all directions. It wasn't a singular belt but an intricate, sprawling maze of overlapping regions, each with its own density and unique quirks.

Some areas were sparse and relatively open, where sunlight

gleamed and glinted off iron-rich fragments no larger than a grain of sand, shimmering like distant constellations in the night sky. Others were dense with looming giants, like the one that was now firmly in their wake—enormous asteroids dozens of kilometers long and wide that lumbered through the darkness with deceptive slowness.

Amidst the chaos, there was motion everywhere. Smaller rocks collided and shattered, sending sharp fragments spiraling outward in glittering arcs along new and dangerous trajectories. Clouds of fine particulate matter swirled in gravitational eddies. Occasionally, bursts of reflected light hinted at metallic veins within the rocks themselves, precious ores long sought by miners who routinely braved this hazardous expanse in the search for wealth and fortune.

Rogue asteroids passed in unpredictable arcs, their trajectories altered by unseen forces—gravitational nudges from nearby clusters, or the long, lingering effects of Illidran's sun. Some were barren and dull, while others glimmered with deposits of rare metals or carried deep, ancient scars that hinted at catastrophic events from millennia past.

The deeper they ventured into the Reach, the more the asteroid field revealed itself as a graveyard of human ambition. Wreckage occasionally surfaced amidst the rocks or flew by *Ranger*—twisted girders, shattered and broken hulls of old mining ships, and the skeletal remains of long-abandoned platforms.

Through the thick of it, *Ranger* maneuvered delicately, her gravitic drive ensuring a smooth passage even as her sensors worked overtime to map the shifting debris immediately around the ship. The Reach wasn't just an asteroid field; it was a labyrinth of constant motion and danger. Only the brave, desperate, or foolish ventured out here willingly, and Steele found himself wondering which of those categories he fit into as they pressed farther into the chaotic expanse.

The area known as the Graveyard, or as most simply called it, the Exclusion Zone, comprised a small but lethally hazardous fraction of the massive asteroid field. It stood as a memorial to one of the final and fiercest battles of the last great war. Strewn with the wreckage of countless ships—some shattered, twisted, and broken beyond recognition, others eerily intact, thoroughly devoid of life—the zone spoke directly to the human cost of war. Hazardous mines, sentient defense systems, and unexploded ordnance haunted the region, making it a no-man's-land for all but the most desperate or reckless.

In the chaotic and resource-rich expanse beyond the Exclusion Zone, the asteroids were a patchwork of geological diversity, each bearing the scars and compositions of its tumultuous origins. In many areas, the Reach was renowned for its abundance of mineral-rich asteroids, where dense clusters of iron, nickel, and titanium drew mining corporations and prospectors like moths to a flame. These metals were the lifeblood of industrial production, feeding shipyards and construction hubs throughout the system. Alongside these staples, rarer treasures like platinum, palladium, and even iridium were extracted.

Rare metals like these fueled fierce competition amongst mining interests, and the remnants of once-booming operations dotted the Reach. Some were still active, with automated drones tirelessly excavating and refining ore, while others were abandoned—victims of economic downturns or the ever-present hazards of operating in the belt.

Other sectors of the Reach held asteroids rich in carbonaceous chondrite and water ice, making them invaluable for sustaining life and fueling spacecraft. Modest water-harvesting facilities were scattered throughout these regions, as they extracted ice and converted it into hydrogen for fuel, oxygen for life support, and water for drinking. The conversion plants were often semi-autonomous, with crews monitoring their operation from remote stations and habitats nestled safely within defended asteroid clusters.

Large swaths of the outer Reach were dominated by silicate asteroids, composed mainly of magnesium, iron, and silicon minerals. These regions were less coveted for their immediate value but held long-term promise. Geological survey teams favored these zones for their relative stability and structural integrity, scouting out potential sites for future bases or refueling stations. The larger silicate asteroids formed semi-stable orbits, creating natural gathering points for explorers, surveyors, and people looking to hide, homestead, or simply escape from their problems.

These silicate giants often carried fewer navigational risks, as their orbits tended to be more predictable and the debris fields around them less dense, making it easier to navigate. Over time, some had become makeshift hubs for survey vessels and prospecting crews, with temporary outposts and beacon buoys marking them as safe havens, refueling and reprovision stops in an otherwise treacherous expanse.

Despite its dangers, the Reach was a paradox of opportunity and peril. The potential wealth locked within its chaotic expanse was immense, but accessing it came at a cost and serious risk. The region was unforgiving, and more than a few mining operations had vanished without a trace, victims of disasters, equipment failures, or worse, pirates.

Some of the larger asteroids in the Reach concealed dense metallic cores, remnants of ancient planetesimals—once the building blocks of planets, now shattered into fragments during the violent formation of the Illidran Star System.

These metallic asteroids—rich in iron, nickel, and other heavy elements—were treasure troves for mining operations, their gleaming cores telling stories of a chaotic past. Their density and irregular shapes created gravitational quirks that made navigation a real nightmare.

Over the last two days of travel, Steele had immersed himself in all the data he could access about the Reach. Geological surveys, navigation reports, and mining records formed a mosaic of knowledge that painted the asteroid field as both an opportunity and a deathtrap. While he had operated in asteroid belts before, none had compared to the sprawling, chaotic expanse he was now taking *Ranger* into. The Reach wasn't just an average belt—it was a labyrinth of hazards, teeming with potential discovery but fraught with dangers that could obliterate even the most prepared crew.

Their current approach vector was a calculated path, weaving through the less densely packed and populated outer regions of the Reach. This route had been deliberately chosen to avoid, wherever possible, civilian traffic and known habitats scattered throughout the belt—outposts, mining hubs, and water-harvesting stations that might detect them. Even so, the risk of discovery loomed large. All it would take was a stray sensor sweep that originated too close or an unexpected encounter to shatter their stealth and alert the system to their presence.

The vector itself was no less perilous. The Reach's gravitational micro-fields, created by the constant motion and interaction of countless asteroids, could subtly shift a ship's trajectory, which was something Hale was actively watching for and guarding against. Even with *Ranger*'s advanced navigational systems, Steele knew they were only a few missteps away from a catastrophic collision.

It was not a comfortable feeling.

Each asteroid they passed carried its own unique risk: jagged edges capable of tearing through a ship's hull like tinfoil, magnetic anomalies that could scramble sensors, and loose debris fields that moved like invisible currents.

Still, *Ranger* was uniquely equipped for this kind of mission. Her advanced sensor suite and precise thrusters provided a slim margin for error, and Steele trusted his crew to adapt to the shifting challenges of this belt. Trust, however, didn't ease the tension that had settled over the bridge. Every officer and crew member felt the weight of the mission, their focus sharpened by the stakes.

Steele's gaze shifted to the navigation plot. The vast, three-dimensional map of the Reach filled the HTD, displaying a tangle of asteroid clusters and hazard zones marked about his ship. He noted how their route threaded cautiously through the outer edge of a dense cluster of rock.

As they edged deeper into the Reach, Steele couldn't shake the thought that, despite all precautions and efforts, they were threading the needle in a storm of knives. Every decision—every small course adjustment—could be the difference between success and catastrophic failure.

A couple of hours ago, they'd had a close call, skirting within a hundred thousand kilometers of an unregistered habitat. The off-the-books installation had been cleverly nestled within a large asteroid, its dense metallic core providing both shielding and camouflage. Quinn had detected faint power signatures radiating outward—evidence of multiple systems operating within, including life support and possibly mining equipment. Whoever lived there had taken great care to remain unnoticed. Steele seriously doubted civilian ships would have detected the low-power emissions.

His tension had eased only slightly when Quinn confirmed there were no active scans coming from the habitat. Still, the encounter was a reminder of how many eyes could potentially be watching, even in the farthest reaches and remotest stretches of the system.

The people calling that hidden habitat home were almost certainly off-the-grid miners. Steele imagined them eking out a living by harvesting the asteroid's rich veins of ore and metal. These were isolationists, no doubt, who wanted as little to do with the Union—or anyone else—as possible. Their hope was likely simple: if they ignored the wider universe, it would ignore them in return.

Just to be safe, he'd ordered an immediate course change. It wasn't the only adjustment he'd made since entering the belt. Twice now, he'd had *Ranger* alter her course after detecting faint active scans from deeper within the belt. The scans were weak, amateurish, and far from military-grade, but they carried the unmistakable flavor of trouble.

Out here, with the Illidran System in the throes of rebellion, even the most innocuous signal could belong to someone willing to sell their information to the highest bidder—or worse, someone ideologically aligned against the Union. Isolationists, pirates, smugglers, or newly emboldened locals—none of them could be trusted. Steele, his crew, and *Ranger* were alone out here.

Steele rubbed his jaw, his mind racing as he replayed the incidents in his mind. It was unlikely they would have been able to penetrate *Ranger*'s stealth field, but Steele was unwilling to take that risk. If they were discovered, all it would take was one comms burst—one panicked cry of "Union destroyer sighted in the Reach!"—along with their coordinates, and they would be compromised and forced to make a run for it.

As *Ranger* pressed on, Steele couldn't shake the growing sense of unease. Each decision felt heavier than the last, the stakes higher with every passing hour. Trust was a luxury he couldn't afford, and vigilance and training were the only things keeping his crew—and their mission—alive.

Scratching an itch on his neck, Steele kept his gaze riveted to the plot. The tactical display glowed softly on his console, a representation of the swirling chaos just beyond the hull.

Ranger was holding steady at 1g, creeping through the hazards on maneuvering thrusters alone. Hale was at the helm, his hands steady on the controls as he deftly followed the plotted course and made changes as he saw fit. Each minor adjustment expended precious propellant, the kind they couldn't easily replace, adding a quiet weight to every maneuver.

Beside him, Chase was seated at her station, her attention laser-focused on her own screens. The faint glow of her console reflected on her face, making her expression unreadable. Though she didn't show it, Steele knew she was as keyed up as he was, scrutinizing the data for any anomaly Hale, Quinn, or Ishida might have missed. The ship's passive sensors worked tirelessly, painting a good but incomplete picture of their immediate surroundings. Every passive sweep, every new ping of debris sighted, every energy signature detected out in the darkness added another thread of tension to those on the bridge.

The six LDF ships they'd tracked two days earlier—two destroyers and four frigates—had reached Meecham's Station. The questionable target had turned out to be a fourth frigate. Then they'd gone dark. Steele felt his jaw tighten as he thought about them. No drives lit up on the plot, no comms traffic from them since, nothing. They'd completely disappeared. It was as though the ships had been swallowed whole by the Reach.

Even Miller's network of contacts had failed to report on them, a silence that gnawed at Steele's nerves. He'd made it clear to the ID officer that no outgoing transmissions were to be sent, not while those ships lurked nearby. The risk of detection was simply too great.

The civilian channels were quiet, or relatively so, depending upon your point of view. Someone was always saying something... with no mention of LDF activity at Meecham's Station. It left Steele in a frustrating bind, unable to discern whether the ships had moved on at speeds too low for passive detection or were lying in wait, hidden and biding their time. But for what? Their silence only amplified the feeling of operating blind, along with his sense of unease.

Meecham's Station sat a mere ten million kilometers away—a stone's throw, in the grand scale of space—but it may as well have been on the other side of the star system. Steele leaned back slightly in his chair, his mind spinning through contingencies.

He found a small measure of reassurance in one fact: if *Ranger* were discovered, the Reach itself would hinder any pursuit. The LDF ships wouldn't be able to burn directly toward them at the highest speed possible. They'd have to navigate through the same chaotic asteroid field, a slow and deliberate process. That delay would buy Steele and his crew time—time to react, to potentially escape, or to strike, if it came to that.

Still, that comfort was cold and thin. The Reach was as much a trap as it was a shield. Every moment they remained undetected was a victory, but also a gamble. And Steele was all too aware of how quickly his good fortune could run out in this game of silent maneuvering.

"Sir, we are approximately seven million klicks from the edge of the Exclusion Zone," Hale reported.

Absently, Steele nodded, keeping his eyes on the HTD, where the nearest hazards were marked with glowing amber and red tags. Their target was still far off, but each kilometer felt like an eternity under the conditions they faced.

"At our current speed, that's thirty-six days," Chase said, her tone pragmatic as she analyzed the situation. Her sharp eyes flicked between her screens. "However, if need be, we are within extreme range from which we can launch the probes."

Steele leaned forward, considering her assessment. "And how long will it take the probes to reach the target area if we launch now at below normal cruising speed?" The plan was to get much closer before launching, but he understood that could change in a heartbeat.

"Even at reduced speed to account for the debris field, approximately eighteen hours, sir," Chase replied. The faint glow of her console cast her face in an austere light as she worked through calculations. "We can adjust their flight paths to avoid the densest clusters. They're also construct-guided and will be able to make adjustments as they go, but still, we'd likely lose a few before they reach the target. That will reduce our chances at success."

"Sir," Ishida interrupted, her voice carrying a slight edge. "I have what appears to be another unregistered habitat on an asteroid three hundred thousand kilometers off the forward port quarter. I've marked it on the plot. No active sweeps detected." Her tone suggested she wasn't ruling out the potential for trouble.

Steele shifted his attention to the plot, his jaw tightening as he spotted the tag Ishida had added. The habitat was nestled within an asteroid larger than most in the area, its location cleverly hidden in a larger crater. "How certain are we it's unregistered?"

"There's no beacon or registration code," Ishida said. "And it's giving off minimal energy signatures. From the size of the structure and its positioning, I'd say it's off the books, sir. From optics alone, I can see a docking gantry for larger ships, but none currently there."

Chase shook her head, her brow furrowing. "I have a feeling the deeper we go, the more habitats and illegal operations we're going to encounter. People drawn to the Reach aren't exactly known for playing by the rules."

"Agreed," Steele said, rubbing his chin as he considered their options. "Keep an eye on it. If we detect any movement or active sweeps, I want to know immediately."

The bridge settled into a tense quiet, each officer focused on their tasks. Beyond the hull, the asteroid belt loomed like a cosmic minefield, and Steele knew Chase was right; the closer they got to the Exclusion Zone, and the deeper into the Reach they went, the more dangerous this would become.

Steele fixed his gaze on the habitat marked on the HTD. His eyes lingered on the sparse data the passive scanners had managed to glean. Like the last habitat they'd encountered, the core was embedded deep within a sizable asteroid, its structure barely distinguishable from the surrounding rock and probably stealth coated. The limited power readings suggested a small, self-contained operation—likely miners or scavengers eking out a living far from prying eyes. It didn't appear to be a threat, but Steele wasn't taking any chances.

As far as he could tell, the inhabitants had no idea *Ranger* was out here, ghosting through the belt. And with luck, it would stay that way. Still, a persistent tension coiled in his gut. They were deep in hostile territory now, with LDF mobile units prowling nearby and the possibility of an enemy fleet lurking in the shadows ahead.

"Sir," Ishida said, breaking his thoughts. "The asteroid field increases in density just ahead."

Steele's eyes shifted to the plot, where the field grew more chaotic with smaller objects and particles. The faint glow of marked hazards and shifting debris painted a picture of an increasingly treacherous route.

"I'm on it," Hale said from the helm, his hands steady on the controls. His voice was calm, but there was a subtle undertone of focus there. Hale was a man who thrived on challenges, a consummate professional and expert at his craft. Piloting a ship as large as a destroyer through an asteroid belt was no small feat.

"Helm, do you need to decelerate further?" Chase asked, her tone carrying a thread of concern. Her gaze flicked between Hale and the plot.

"No, ma'am, I do not," Hale replied. He glanced back at her, his expression resolute. "I can handle it. I'm certain."

Steele watched Hale for a moment, reading the confidence in his posture and the focus in his eyes. Hale had proven himself time and again as a helmsman, and Steele trusted him.

"Very well," Steele said. "Keep us steady and avoid drawing any unwanted attention. I remember that incident with the shuttle over Kalendra. Traffic control wasn't too happy about that. I had some hard questions put to me. No showboating, Mr. Hale, not today."

"No, sir, and yes, sir," Hale said, his cheeks coloring as he returned his attention to the controls.

Steele leaned back slightly, his fingers tapping the armrest of his chair. The stakes were rising with every passing kilometer, and he knew the margin for error was razor-thin. For now, all they could do was move forward, one careful step at a time.

As best he could, he sat motionless in his command chair, his gaze fixed on the HTD as *Ranger* inched her way forward. The quiet hum of the bridge provided a faint backdrop to the charged atmosphere that had settled over the crew. The tension was so thick it felt like it might snap under its own weight. Despite this, Steele projected an air of calm, his expression steady and unreadable. It was a calculated and crafted demeanor, one meant to reassure his people that their captain had everything under control and was confident in their abilities.

Steele watched as his helmsman deftly guided the ship through the chaotic maze of rock and debris. At times, the field seemed to close in around them from every corner, massive asteroid fragments tumbling lazily through space. Some rocks bore the telltale signs of mining operations—sheared edges, faint scorch marks, and embedded equipment long since abandoned to the void. Time and again, Hale got them through it all.

Through the hull, the ship's maneuvering thrusters could occasionally be heard, hissing and groaning in faint protest as Hale adjusted their trajectory with minute precision.

Steele felt the tension in his crew like a live wire strung taut across the bridge. Chase's eyes darted between her displays and the HTD, her fingers tapping a silent rhythm against the edge of her console. Ishida, like Quinn, was utterly focused, her brow furrowed in concentration as she monitored the passive scanner feed and what was around them. No one spoke unless absolutely necessary. No distractions could be allowed.

Over the next hour, their path brought them past four more unregistered habitats. The HTD flagged each one as they came into range—dim power readings emanating from structures embedded deep within massive asteroids. Some appeared to be remnants of old mining operations, the faint energy signatures suggesting automated systems left running, perhaps to maintain life support or processing equipment. Whether there were people inside, Steele couldn't say, and he wasn't about to take any unnecessary risks to find out.

"Another habitat," Ishida reported quietly, her voice barely above a whisper, as though speaking too loudly might disturb the delicate balance they maintained. "Energy readings consistent with life support. No active scans detected."

Steele gave a small nod but said nothing. Each habitat they passed was another potential threat—another set of eyes that might notice them and sound the alarm. The inhabitants of these off-the-grid settlements were often fiercely isolationist, but that didn't mean they wouldn't sell out a Union destroyer.

A flicker on the HTD drew Steele's attention.

"I have a ship on the scope," Ishida reported.

"What do we have?" Steele asked.

"A small craft, sir. Fifty thousand kilometers off our port bow. Passive scans and drive signature suggest a tramp transport, Morcomi Class... she's moving away from us. Speed is low... less than a g and likely navigating the field with great care. I'm guessing she's a smuggler, for her emissions are tamped down, but out here... who knows?"

Steele leaned forward, studying the faint blip on the display. The craft was far enough away to pose no immediate threat, but her presence was a reminder of just how crowded this lawless stretch of space could be. "Keep an eye on her," he said. "Let's make sure she keeps moving in the other direction."

"Aye, sir," Ishida acknowledged.

And so, the routine resumed, *Ranger* plodding steadily onward, moving through the shifting chaos of the asteroid field, steadily leaving the tramp behind. The faint hum of the ship's systems provided a constant backdrop, blending with the occasional hiss of maneuvering thrusters as Hale adjusted their trajectory.

"Coffee, sir?"

Steele glanced up to find Ensign Peter Singh standing a few steps away. In one hand, Singh held a carrying tray with several steaming cups, while the other held a sealed cup of coffee, which he extended toward Steele. Quartermaster Sara Nivens was handing a tea to Chase with a polite nod.

"Thank you, Ensign," Steele said, accepting the coffee. He felt its warmth radiating through the insulated cup, a small but welcome comfort in the midst of the cold, calculated environment of the bridge.

Singh gave a crisp nod before moving on to the next station. Steele lifted the cup to his lips, taking a careful sip. The coffee was fresh and near scalding hot—and prepared exactly how he liked it. The bitter, rich aroma filled his senses, momentarily cutting through the sterile scent of the ship's recycled air. He let the taste linger for a moment before placing the cup in the built-in holder at his station, leaving it to cool slightly.

Chase, seated at her own console, accepted her tea from Nivens. "Thank you, Chief."

Steele allowed himself the faintest of smiles. "A little caffeine never hurt anyone."

"No, it doesn't." Chase raised her cup in a silent toast before taking a sip, her focus quickly returning to the plot before her, the momentary distraction giving way once more to intense focus. The ship continued her careful crawl through the field, every meter forward a small victory in their quest to close on the Exclusion Zone undetected.

"Sir," Ishida said, her voice taut with unease. "I'm detecting weapons fire near Meecham's Station."

"Weapons fire?" Chase turned sharply, her focus snapping to Ishida.

"Aye, ma'am," Ishida confirmed. "Detonations consistent with ship-killers—masers and missile bursts. It appears three ships are engaged in shooting at one another. There's significant distortion and interference from the field. The dust and density are wreaking havoc on our passive sensors. It's hard to get a clear picture of exactly what's happening... but it doesn't look like they're targeting the station itself."

Chase frowned. "The LDF is shooting at each other?"

"If I had to guess, that's what it looks like, ma'am." Ishida's brow furrowed as she stared at her readouts.

Steele leaned forward, his expression unreadable but his voice carrying a trace of irony. "So, they're not one big happy family after all. I find that... just shocking."

"The firing is intensifying," Ishida reported. "I think more ships are joining the fight... hard to tell. The energy signatures are fluctuating, but I can't get a clear count. It's maddening not being able to see through all this interference."

"At least they're happily killing each other instead of shooting at us," Chase remarked dryly.

"There is that, XO," Steele said, his tone wry but his gaze sharp.

He pulled up the data on his own display, the fuzzy sensor readings and erratic energy spikes painting an incomplete and frustratingly vague picture. The HTD showed brief and violent flashes—powerful energy discharges, heat blooms, and the tell-tale trails of missile propulsion—before the signals were swallowed by the Reach's distortive environment.

Steele rubbed his jaw, scanning the chaotic data for

anything useful. "It's a mess," he admitted, his voice low. "We're too far out, and the field's doing its job to hide whatever's happening out there."

Chase shot him a glance. "It's strange, though, isn't it? Meecham's Station doesn't seem to be the target. So, what's their objective? Or their grievance?"

"Good question," Steele said. "Maybe a disagreement about the spoils of war... or perhaps the rebellion isn't as unified as they'd like us to believe. The loyalists might still have a say in what's going down."

"Whatever it is, it's to our advantage," Chase said.

Steele gave a curt nod but kept his eyes on the HTD. He didn't like mysteries, especially not in the middle of hostile territory. Whatever was happening out there could be an opportunity—or a complication waiting to happen.

"It's over," Ishida announced after a few tense minutes of silence. Her voice was measured, but there was an undercurrent of relief. "Whatever happened, it's done. The fighting's wrapped up."

Steele let out a slow breath and shifted his focus back to the HTD, recalibrating the display to the plot ahead. The chaos near Meecham's Station was indeed over but their mission wasn't. He still had a job to do and he meant to do it right.

Steele returned to watching as Hale's steady hand on the helm guided *Ranger* through the hazardous terrain with skill. The low-powered defensive screens of his ship shimmered faintly on the display, pushing and deflecting much of the smaller debris away from *Ranger*—dust, fragments, and loose particles that swirled like a chaotic snowstorm in the void. Occasionally, a dull, resonant *thump* reverberated solidly through the hull, signaling the impact of a larger chunk of rock, ice, or some type of debris. Steele tightened his jaw at each sound, knowing full well what it meant.

Running under stealth mode, *Ranger* couldn't fully activate her shields without lighting up the passive or active sensors of anyone nearby. Instead, they relied on the ship's armored hull to absorb the impacts—that and the defensive screens. The low-grade battering wasn't ideal. Minor abrasions and microfractures formed on the shell with each hit, but Atheena was on it, deploying repair nanites to address the damage as it occurred.

Steele knew this wasn't sustainable. The constant impacts were like a slow bleed, and while *Ranger* was sturdy and built tough with a heavily reinforced outer hull, this environment wasn't kind to any vessel, in stealth mode or not. Yet there was no alternative.

Steele leaned back slightly in his chair, though his eyes never left the plot. The bridge remained quiet, save for the subtle hum of the ship's systems and the occasional muted impact against the hull. The charged atmosphere mirrored the precariousness of their journey. Then, the soft *hiss* of the hatch to the bridge opening cut through the stillness. Steele turned his head and immediately spotted Miller stepping onto the bridge.

Miller's expression was hard and grim. Steele's eyes narrowed slightly, a sense of foreboding settling in his chest. The man was carrying a tablet, clutching it tightly as he approached.

Whatever news he carried, it wasn't good.

Miller made his way across the bridge and stopped beside Steele's station, glancing down briefly at the HTD, studying it for a long moment before looking him directly in the eye. Without a word, he held out the tablet, his lips pressed into a thin line.

Steele accepted it, his fingers curling around the device. "What is it, Miller?"

Miller didn't respond immediately. Instead, he leaned closer, lowering his voice as he spoke. "Captain, we've got a problem, a real problem."

"Mr. Miller, this is not a good time," Chase said sharply, her voice clipped as she spotted the man from ID standing by her captain's station.

Miller didn't break stride or relent, his expression set and urgent. "Captain, this is important," he said, brushing past Chase's remark.

Steele hesitated for a fraction of a second. His gaze flicked to Chase, who was watching Miller with a mixture of suspicion and annoyance, before he thumbed the tablet on. The screen illuminated. He scanned the message, his jaw tightening as he absorbed its import. His heart began to pound.

"Where did you get this information?" Steele's eyes locked back onto Miller, probing for answers.

"There are still Union broadcasting satellites positioned around Illidran," Miller explained, his tone matter-of-fact but edged with tension. "Some of them haven't been destroyed or compromised by the LDF yet. We also have a few stealth communication platforms out there—ones they don't even know exist." He pointed at the tablet. "This encrypted message was sent to one of those platforms and then broadcast broad-spectrum across the system."

Steele glanced back at the tablet, rereading the contents again with a growing sense of unease. His gut tightened as he processed the implications. Without a word, he handed the device over to Chase.

Her eyes widened as she read the message, her usual composure faltering for a brief moment. She looked up sharply at Miller. "This is correct?"

"I'm afraid it is," Miller replied, his voice grim.

"That's why the LDF went to Meecham," Chase breathed. "That's why they bloody went to that godforsaken place..."

"But they're no longer there," Steele said, his tone dark. "That much is clear now. They didn't find what they wanted and moved on. Perhaps that's why they were shooting at one another?"

"They were?" Miller asked, surprise plain. "I find that interesting..."

Steele turned his gaze to Chase and gestured at the tablet. "How far are those coordinates from our current position?" he asked, already considering their next move. He shifted his focus back to Miller. "You know they'll start hunting them soon enough. They've probably already started."

"I know it, Captain," Miller said, his jaw tightening. "That's why we need to move quickly."

Chase tapped a few keys on her console, pulling up the relevant coordinates. "Sir, the place in question is six and a half hours away at 1g," she reported, turning to meet Steele's gaze.

Steele nodded, his mind racing. The pieces were falling into place, but the picture they painted wasn't a hopeful one. Time was not on their side, not anymore, and they were now in more danger than ever.

Steele rubbed his jaw, weighing his options. Should he continue toward the Exclusion Zone as planned or break off now and follow the new lead, the one he knew in his heart they couldn't ignore? The stakes were high no matter what course he chose.

He turned toward Ishida. "Guns, if we launched the probes now, how long would it take them at cruising speed to reach the Exclusion Zone, a step up from what we'd planned?"

"Sixteen hours and fifteen minutes, sir," Ishida replied crisply.

"You're thinking of launching early?" Chase interjected, her tone tinged with concern. "I don't advise that, Captain. The closer we get, the better the probes' chances for success. The field will undoubtedly take some of them."

"Ma'am," Ishida said, glancing at her console, "the onboard guidance systems are designed to navigate around much of the debris. They shouldn't have much of a problem doing it. They also have shields. But... at those speeds, we will still likely lose a few."

Steele sucked in a breath, his fingers drumming lightly against his chair. The clock was ticking, and every decision carried a risk. He gave a final glance at the plot, the Exclusion Zone looming like a dark specter. He made his decision.

"Guns," Steele said firmly, "begin launching the probes, max cruising speed. Helm, prepare for a course change. XO, send those coordinates to Hale."

"Aye, aye, sir," Ishida said. "Launching probes."

"Hale, stand by for the new destination," Chase ordered, inputting commands at her station.

"First wave of probes is away, sir," Ishida reported. "Thirty-two successful launches. Reloading for the second wave, stand by."

"New destination received, sir," Hale said, "course plotted and ready."

Steele nodded. "Wait until the second and final set of probes are away. Then execute the course change and bring us up to 2g."

"That's going to be dangerous, sir," Chase said, her expression hardening. "If the enemy is actively out there and hunting, or any habitats we pass have operational sensors, there is an increased chance they could spot us."

"I know it," Steele said, his voice resolute. "I don't see that we have much choice in the matter. Speed is now the order of the day."

"Second wave away," Ishida called out. "Helm, you are clear for the course change."

"With your permission, Captain?" Hale asked.

"Permission granted," Steele said. "Execute course change."

"Decelerating," Hale said, his voice steady. The ship shuddered slightly as the maneuvering thrusters fired, rapidly realigning *Ranger*'s trajectory. "Maneuvering thruster pods engaged. Coming onto the new course. Prepare for gravitic acceleration."

Steele glanced toward Miller, who stood watching quietly. Steele handed the tablet back to the man. "You realize this could be a trap," Steele said, his tone heavy with warning. "It could be a setup to flush out any hidden Union assets still in the system."

"It's not, Captain," Miller said, meeting Steele's gaze with conviction.

"Are you certain about that?" Chase asked, her skepticism evident.

"I am," Miller replied without hesitation. "I know who sent the message. They were aware I was in the system, and it was directed to me. This is important."

Steele looked at him for a long moment, then gave a single nod. "We're going to find out one way or the other."

"That's what worries me," Chase muttered, her fingers tapping absently at her console.

"Thank you, Captain," Miller said.

"Mr. Miller," Steele said, his expression a grim one, "thank me after we're safely away from Illidran."

SEVENTEEN

"We are at a full stop, sir," Hale reported, his voice steady but tinged with the weariness shared by the entire bridge crew.

It had taken over twelve grueling hours to reach the coordinates provided by Miller. This region of the Reach was a treacherously dense cluster of asteroids and debris fields, both large and small. Steele's gaze swept over the HTD, which displayed a chaotic map of their immediate surroundings. It was crowded with overlapping hazard markers, highlighting the pure density of the immediate space around them and the absolute danger it contained.

The ship's progress had been painstakingly slow, creeping forward at just barely half a g as they closed the final leg. Steele had felt compelled to order such a reduction in speed, the third since setting out, to keep damaging collisions to a minimum. Even at that cautious speed, the field had taken its toll on *Ranger*. The faint hum of the defensive screens was a constant presence on the bridge now, a low vibration that resonated through the hull and signaled their ongoing struggle against the smaller rocks, dust, and other debris ricocheting off the ship's protective field. Larger impacts caused occasional sharp thuds that reverberated loudly through the hull, each one a reminder of how vulnerable *Ranger* was in this environment.

"Report on the damage to the screens," Steele said, breaking the silence.

"Screens holding at sixty-eight percent efficiency," Chase replied, not looking up from her console. "They've taken a beating, sir. Multiple strain fractures across the forward grid. Outer armored hull is damaged. Atheena is tending to that as we speak. No major issues to report."

Steele grimaced but nodded. It wasn't unexpected. Defensive screens were designed to divert minor impacts, not take a sustained and relentless physical battering. The emitters alone had to be stressed beyond critical levels. *Ranger*'s armored hull, reinforced for combat, had fared better but was not unscathed. With every passing moment, his ship was taking some level of damage.

How much could she take? How much was too much?

Steele's real concern, however, was their dwindling supply of maneuvering propellant. A screen at his station displayed the troubling figure: forty-one percent remaining. Each thruster adjustment had drained their reserves further. The ship still had enough to navigate out of the Reach when the time came, but that didn't leave much room for error.

Steele stared intently at the HTD, its three-dimensional display rendering the surrounding space in eerie, holographic detail. They were parked less than five kilometers off an unremarkable iron-nickel asteroid, its surface a mottled patchwork of craters and jagged ridges. Despite its bland appearance, the asteroid's sheer size made it a point of interest. Nearly a small planetoid, it hung in the void like a dark and silent sentinel, reflecting just enough sunlight to reveal its ominous contours.

The HTD tagged the asteroid with basic data: composition, estimated mass, rotational speed, and trajectory. Nothing seemed out of the ordinary. Its most remarkable feature, Steele mused, was the dense cluster of smaller debris that orbited it like a chaotic halo, likely a result of the minute gravitational field it exerted. The debris, shifting unpredictably, made even approaching the asteroid a nightmare, let alone attempting to mine it. The danger had likely kept this rock untouched, a forgotten and isolated giant in the hazardous expanse of the Reach.

He glanced over at Quinn, who was hunched over her console, her face lit by the soft glow of her screens. "Have you gotten any readings from that rock?"

Quinn straightened slightly and shook her head. "No, sir. I've been running scans using optics and passives. There's no indication that this place has ever been touched by machinery, let alone human hands. I can find no thermal signatures, no metallic anomalies outside of its natural composition. There's nothing special about it... at least that I can detect using passive sensors."

Steele let out a slow breath, his fingers tapping lightly on the edge of his station. The asteroid was as lifeless as it looked, yet its isolation and sheer size made it an ideal hiding spot—or an ideal trap.

To his left, Miller stood quietly, a silent observer. After snatching some sleep, the man from ID had returned to the bridge a short time before, as inscrutable as ever. He held a tablet in one hand, his attention fixed on the main screen at the front of the bridge. The screen displayed the asteroid in stark detail, a massive, almost oppressive presence against the dark backdrop of space. The play of faint sunlight and shadow on its surface lent it an air of quiet menace.

"Guns?" Steele's voice broke the silence. His gaze remained fixed on the HTD, its display offering no answers, just the cold indifference of data. "Are you seeing anything out of the ordinary?"

"Nothing, sir," Ishida replied, her tone as steady as the hum of the ship's background systems. "I hate to say it. There's nothing out of the ordinary out there..."

"I don't like this," Chase said, her brow furrowed as she glanced at Steele. "We should be able to detect *something*—energy emissions, structural work on this asteroid, *anything*. Maybe if we reposition and move around to the far side, we'll get a better view on what's over there."

"No," Steele said firmly. "We've already burned through too much propellant. Until we know more, we're staying put." His eyes shifted to Miller. The man's expression was unreadable. "Well? We're here. Where are they?"

Miller stepped forward with quiet purpose, crossing the bridge to Calder's station. He handed her the tablet he carried.

"Lieutenant," Miller said, his tone brisk, "kindly transmit this message as written, exactly as it reads, to these coordinates using a tight-beam laser."

Calder glanced down at the tablet, her brows knitting together as she read. Her lips moved silently, forming the peculiar words of the message. "*The bear is in the hall?*" she asked, skepticism laced through her voice as she looked back at Miller in question.

"It's code, Lieutenant," Miller replied, his tone betraying no amusement. "Kindly send it as is."

Calder hesitated, her gaze flicking to Steele for confirmation. He gave her a curt nod.

"Do it," Steele said, leaving no room for debate. "Get it done."

"Yes, sir." Calder bent over her console, her fingers moving across the interface as she input the transmission. The quiet beeping of her station punctuated the tense silence on the bridge.

The oppressive stillness hung in the air, broken only by the faint whir of air handlers and ventilation systems and the occasional rustle as someone shifted at their station. Calder finally straightened, her hands falling to her sides.

"Message sent," she reported.

Steele nodded, his expression unchanging, but the tautness in his shoulders betrayed his concern for anyone who really knew how to look. Chase was likely one of those few. Everyone on the bridge held their collective breath, waiting for a response—or something—to break the mounting tension. The asteroid on the main screen loomed larger than life, inscrutable, as if mocking their presence with its silence.

"I guess now we wait," Chase said quietly, her voice pitched low enough that only Steele could hear. Her eyes on the main screen, Chase's unease was palpable. "Hopefully someone is listening."

Steele gave a small nod. His gaze remained locked on the asteroid displayed before them, its lifeless iron-nickel surface pocked with craters and shadowed crevices. The silence on the bridge was oppressive, each second dragging out longer than the last. Minutes dragged by, one after another.

"Do you want me to retransmit the message?" Calder asked.

"No," Miller said. He moved to stand beside Steele's station, his posture calm but his expression unreadable. "They've received the message. There's no need to send it again."

"You're certain about this?" Steele asked, his voice low and deliberate, the words weighted with skepticism as he looked over at Miller. "You are sure this is the place?"

"I am quite certain, Captain," Miller replied without hesitation, his tone unwavering. "We just need to give them time."

Turning his attention back to the main screen, Steele waited a few more tense moments, watching the unmoving asteroid as if willing it to react. He opened his mouth to speak but was interrupted by Calder's sudden movement. She sat bolt upright at her station, her fingers freezing mid-gesture as her eyes widened.

"I don't believe it," Calder breathed, her voice a mixture of disbelief and awe. "I really don't believe it."

"What is it?" Steele asked, his tone sharpening, the bridge crew now fully alert.

"We're receiving a reply," Calder said, hands hovering over her controls. "It's coming in on a tight-beam laser—a live feed. Permission to put it on the main screen, sir?"

Steele's eyes flicked to Chase, then back to Calder. "Do it."

With a quick nod, Calder executed the command. The asteroid on the main screen flickered and dissolved, replaced by the image of a Union marine captain with a flight badge standing in a dimly lit command space. Behind him, two other marines stood, their faces partially shadowed by the room's subdued lighting. The command space itself was cramped but functional, with walls lined by outdated control panels that hummed and flickered with light in the background.

The marine captain was a stark figure, his closely cropped hair and sharp jawline giving him a hard-edged appearance. Fatigue lined his face, his sunken eyes betraying exhaustion and a wary skepticism. As if struggling to process what he was seeing, the man blinked and stared into the camera, his expression a careful mix of guarded hope and suspicion.

He glanced over his shoulder at one of the marines, a lieutenant by the insignia on her uniform. She gave him a shrug before he turned back to the screen.

Steele leaned forward slightly, his hands gripping the edge of his console. For a moment, neither man spoke, the tension thick as the marine studied the bridge crew of *Ranger* through the feed, measuring them.

"I am Captain Steele of the UNS *Ranger*. With whom am I speaking?" Steele's voice was steady, though his sharp gaze was assessing the other man on the screen.

"Captain Smith, Union Marine Corps," the man replied, his shoulders easing slightly, the tension in his posture dissipating just a fraction. A faint flicker of relief passed over his face. "I am so very glad to see you, Captain. You have no idea how much it pleases me that you're here."

Steele caught a slight shift in Miller's stance beside him, the ID officer's sharp eyes narrowing as he took in every detail of the exchange. Still, the man said nothing. It was clear he was content to allow Steele to handle things.

"It's my understanding you're looking for a ride," Steele said with calm authority as he leaned upon the armrest of his command station. "For you and your people?"

"We are, sir," Smith confirmed, a note of heavy weariness in his voice. "Our transport burned through all its propellant just getting us here to the safe house."

"And where is *here* exactly?" Steele asked, leaning forward slightly. He glanced down at one of the screens on his station to confirm his next words. "We're showing no emissions whatsoever from the rock you're on, let alone transmitting from."

Smith gave a tight nod, his expression flickering with what seemed like both frustration and resignation. "It's a listening post—or at least it was. As I understand matters, the Union emplaced it here during the last war. After the fighting ended, the post was sealed up and shut down. When things went balls up, we were already in transit. We hit Meecham's Station first to tank up, but after that..." He gestured vaguely around him, the weight of the decision apparent. "We made our way here to hole up and hide. There was no safe haven open to us."

Steele's eyes narrowed slightly, his thoughts turning over what Smith had just revealed. The safe house's location made sense for a listening post, tucked deep in the treacherous field where few would dare to ever venture. He glanced briefly at Chase, who was already working at her station, pulling up data on old Union installations in the area. She looked back over at him and shook her head after a moment.

"It is an ID installation," Miller said quietly. "This listening post is not recorded in Fleet records, let alone databases. My counterpart over there would have access to the information."

"Captain Smith, how many do you have with you?" Steele's voice was firm, cutting through the tension on the bridge.

"Forty-three souls." Smith's weariness was evident, but he stood tall despite it. Steele could respect the man's strength.

Before Steele could respond, Ishida's voice interrupted, urgency tightening her tone. "Sir, I'm picking up active scans emanating from somewhere at least two hundred thousand klicks out."

Steele's gaze snapped to his tactical officer. "Details?"

"The scans appear to be military-grade... I'm fairly certain of that," Ishida said, her fingers working her console. Her brow furrowed as more data streamed in. "They're powerful. I'd wager it's one of the starships that was at Meecham's Station. They're hunting..." She trailed off, her gaze shifting to the main screen where Captain Smith's worn expression stared back. The man's expression tightened.

"They're hunting us, sir," Smith said.

"We're going to have to get this show on the road," Steele said, turning back to the marine officer. His tone was clipped, decisive. "Captain Smith, you said you have forty-three souls over there? That is correct—no more, no less?"

"Yes, sir," Smith replied with a firm nod. "Forty-three souls... and a dog."

Steele blinked, surprised. "A dog? Really?"

"Yes, sir," Smith said, his expression unchanging. "A good dog, really. She is... a good dog."

For a moment, Steele considered the absurdity of it—forty-three human lives at risk, and yet they'd made room for a dog. But he didn't have time to dwell on it. A faint chuckle from Chase broke the tension briefly, though her focus quickly returned to her console.

Steele turned to Chase, who gave him a curt nod, her

expression steady but focused. "It'll be tight, sir, but we can handle that many. We'll make it work, hot bunking and all. Life support will handle it as well." She shifted her attention to the screen. "Captain Smith, is your transport capable of making a run over to us, shuttling your people over? We're sitting five kilometers off this rock you're currently calling home."

Smith shook his head, the exhaustion in his eyes tempered by determination. "No, ma'am. She's docked in the base's hangar, and we just barely managed that. Her tanks are dry. My pilot doesn't even want to attempt it... and I'm the pilot."

Chase frowned, exchanging a glance with Steele. "Is there room for one of our shuttles in the docking bay? If there is, we could send one of ours."

"Unfortunately, no." Smith's voice carried the weight of his frustration. "The transport took serious damage just getting here. She's not flight-worthy. I doubt I could even power her back up safely... but there is a hardpoint to mate with—an airlock system. I'll send you the coordinates."

"We're going to have to drop stealth systems to dock," Chase said, turning back to Steele with a grim expression. "I don't like that idea. We'll be more visible."

Steele rubbed his temple, the tension rolling off him in waves. "I don't see that we have any choice," he said as he looked back over at her. "If we're going to get those people out of there, we're going to have to do this the old-fashioned way... and that's by docking."

Chase let out a long breath, shaking her head. "It's always something, isn't it?"

"The enemy is far enough off; they likely won't see us," Ishida said. "At least, not in the short term. I'd say it's a long shot at best."

Steele turned his attention to her, his expression sharp. "Have you picked up the ship yet? Or is it just her scans you are detecting? Can you identify her and the class?"

"Just the actives, sir," Ishida replied with a shake of her head, her eyes fixed on the tactical display. "And they're powerful. If I had to guess, I'd say they're systematically scanning each large asteroid in the area, searching for a hidden base."

"That's not good," Chase said.

Steele's jaw tightened. The enemy wasn't just searching blindly—they were on the hunt.

"Captain," Calder interjected, breaking the tension. "I have the coordinates for a hardpoint dock. It's located on the far side of the asteroid."

"Kindly send the coordinates to helm," Steele ordered, nodding briskly. Then, turning back to the main screen where Captain Smith still stood, he added, "Captain, get your people ready to move and board *Ranger*. I want to be on our way as soon as humanly possible. Understand me on this, there can be no delays. The enemy is out there, and they're hunting for you."

Smith straightened, his exhaustion momentarily overshadowed by resolve. "Understood, sir. I'll have them ready."

"And don't forget the dog," Chase added. "I've always been fond of dogs."

Smith grinned at her. "We won't forget Maggie, ma'am. You can count on that."

"Very good," Steele said. "We'll be seeing you shortly."

"Yes, sir." Smith's image flickered, then disappeared as the screen went dark, leaving the bridge silent for a moment.

Steele turned back to Chase. "Make sure docking prep is prioritized. I want a rapid in-and-out. We'll need to be ready for anything."

Chase gave a short nod, already at her station. "Understood, sir."

The pressure was mounting, and every second counted. They were walking a tightrope, deep in enemy territory, with time and luck as their only allies, if they could even be considered as such.

"I have the coordinates and specs for the hardpoint," Hale reported. "It's going to be a little tricky, sir, what with all the debris. In addition to that, this rock was never designed to accommodate a warship the size of *Ranger*—it's built for smaller ships. We'll need to use our umbilical to bring them aboard."

Steele gave a curt nod. "Understood. Make it happen. Bring us around the asteroid to mate with the hardpoint."

"Aye, sir. Maneuvering now," Hale replied. "I estimate thirty-eight minutes to get us into position and extend the umbilical."

"Very good." Steele turned toward Calder. "Lieutenant, notify the chief of the boat and Lieutenant Knox that we're about to have guests. Everyone coming aboard is to be thoroughly screened. No one—and I mean no one—comes aboard armed. I don't care who they are. This is my ship, and I make the rules. Is that clear?"

"Aye, aye, sir," Calder acknowledged, her fingers already flying across her console to relay the orders.

Steele shifted his gaze back to the HTD, manipulating the display to focus on the area Ishida had flagged. A small blip marked the origin of the active scans, and Steele stared at it for a long moment, his expression grim. There was an enemy ship out there and they were steadily approaching his position.

"Guns," Steele called, his tone sharp as he noticed something odd, "those scans seem... quite deliberate, as if they've stepped them up a notch."

"I agree, sir." Ishida's eyes were locked on the tactical readouts. "They're systematically scanning every nook and cranny, searching for any possible hiding places. And their trajectory suggests they're moving in our direction at 1g."

"I concur as well, sir," Quinn added, her voice edged with tension. "They're being very methodical. This is no random search."

Steele's frown deepened. "What about the possibility of

additional ships? Those scans seem a little too powerful for one..."

Ishida hesitated, her brow furrowed as she scrutinized the data. "Now that you mention it, sir, I believe there is another ship farther out, also conducting active scans, but it might just be a sensor echo. I can't confirm at this range."

Steele understood. It was another ship, and that one too was likely headed in their direction.

"This just keeps getting better and better," Chase muttered as she leaned back in her chair, her eyes never leaving her console.

Steele straightened as he studied the situation unfolding on the plot. They were walking a razor's edge. That much was certain.

"Let's focus on getting those people aboard," Steele said finally, his voice steady. "And make damn sure we're ready if the situation changes or something unexpected happens."

"Yes, sir," Chase said.

Steele nodded, his lips pressed into a thin line, but he remained silent as he shifted his focus back to the plot. The ship's holographic display illuminated the slow progress as Hale carefully maneuvered *Ranger* around the massive asteroid. *Ranger*'s movement was excruciatingly deliberate, their speed reduced to a crawl as they inched closer to the hardpoint. Every adjustment burned precious propellant, a fact Steele tried to push from his mind, though the thought gnawed at him like an open wound.

The hull reverberated with a heavy *thump* as a piece of debris struck home hard. Steele winced, his hand tightening into a fist. It wasn't just his ship—it was his responsibility, a tangible extension of his command. The sound felt like a blow to his own body, but he kept his expression neutral, unwilling to show his unease to the bridge crew. He had to be the rock upon which they rested and trusted.

Finally, after what felt like an eternity, they reached their destination. The external optical arrays zeroed in on the hard-point, cleverly camouflaged against the asteroid's rugged surface. Even spotting it took effort, and Hale had to make several minor course corrections to align the ship properly.

"We're on-station, sir," Hale said with no little amount of relief. A sheen of sweat beaded his brow.

"The chief of the boat is extending the umbilical now," Chase reported from her station. "He estimates we'll be mated in just under ten minutes. Once the seal is confirmed, we'll have sufficient atmosphere in the umbilical to begin the transfer of personnel."

Steele's gaze flicked toward the bridge hatch as it slid open and then closed. Miller had quietly left. Letting out a weary sigh, Steele rubbed his eyes, the strain of the hours pressing heavily on him. Fatigue clung to him like a second skin; the stolen moments of sleep he'd managed to stitch together weren't nearly enough. He glanced briefly at his cabin hatch, the temptation of a shower and shave tugging at him powerfully, not to mention a few hours of shut-eye. But he dismissed the thought almost immediately—there was work to be done.

"XO, I'm going to go down to greet our guests and welcome them aboard," he said finally as he pulled himself from his command station and stood. He took a moment to stretch out his back. "While I'm gone, plot a course to the Fringe Zone, least time," he added, looking toward Chase. "The moment they're aboard, I want us decoupled and moving away from this place. Is that understood?"

"Yes, sir," Chase replied, already working at her console.

"You have the bridge, XO," Steele said, straightening.

"I have command, sir," Chase confirmed, her voice steady and professional, all that he'd come to expect in his executive officer. Like him, she was a rock for the crew.

Steele turned and made his way to the lift hatch, his steps

purposeful despite the exhaustion pressing down on him. The hatch slid open before him. He stopped, his thoughts turning to the people he was about to bring aboard—forty-three souls and a dog, each carrying their own story of desperation and survival amidst the chaos that had fallen over the Illidran Star System. His duty was to get them safely off this rock, out of the Reach, and hopefully back to the Union.

Could he do it? Could he manage that?

Steele glanced back over the bridge and his people working there, their professionalism plain to his keen eye. He felt a fierce stab of pride at not only his crew, whom he had trained personally, but his ship.

Ranger would not fail them.

Steele would not fail them. He resolved to get everyone home. With that, he turned away and entered the lift. The door slid shut.

"Deck four," he said, and the lift began to move.

EIGHTEEN

The lift hatch slid open with a soft hiss. Steele stepped out and immediately found himself confronted by Lieutenant Commander Morgan Voss, his chief engineer. The corridor—leading left toward main engineering and right toward the primary boarding port, where the umbilical was currently being extended—was empty save for Voss himself. It was clear the man had been waiting, likely anticipating Steele's arrival.

"Sir," Voss said with a casual familiarity that working together over the last few months had seen built between them. "Atheena told me you were on your way down."

"Did she now?" Steele raised an eyebrow. "So, you decided to ambush me? Is that it?"

"Not quite, sir, but close enough to the mark." Voss shrugged, the movement loose and unbothered. Despite the neatness of his uniform, there was always something inherently unkempt about the man—like a tightly wound spring just shy of unwinding. In his thirties, Voss was stocky and square-jawed, his black hair defying the regulation cut with its perpetual unruliness.

Voss's hands were always stained by some oil, grease, or

solvent from his constant tinkering. His dark eyes were in a perpetual squint, as if years of peering at intricate mechanisms and displays had left them permanently narrowed.

"I just thought a face-to-face would be better than the bloody comms. Too much nuance gets lost over a channel, if you know what I mean, sir."

Steele glanced down the corridor, its sterile lighting reflecting off the bulkhead in sharp, clean lines. The subtle hum of the ship's systems pulsed beneath his feet. Here, near main engineering, they were close to the gravitic coils, which were spinning in idle mode. Steele could feel the deep vibration of the coil movement through his boots. He turned his attention back to the engineer. "So, let's talk, then. How can I help you?"

Voss crossed his arms, his square jaw tightening just enough to show his frustration. "It's real simple. Get my ship out of this damned asteroid field, sir. That's how you can help. She doesn't belong here, taking continual hits from debris and errant rocks, like some glorified target drone. It's cruel and unusual treatment, hard on my girl, it is..."

Steele let out a slow breath, nodding as he absorbed the engineer's concern. He knew he should have anticipated this conversation. "You have no idea how much I want to do just that, Voss. Trust me. I don't want to be here either."

"I'm sure you already know this, sir," Voss continued, his tone taking on a sharper edge, "but the longer we linger without shields active and engaged, the more damage *Ranger* will take. Atheena's pushing and burning through nanites faster than they can be produced on my end, and that doesn't even take into account the propellant we're using for maneuvers and station-keeping..."

Steele raised an eyebrow as his concern grew. "What's the status on the repair nanites?"

"We are making more," Voss said, his squint deepening, "but it's not fast enough to keep up with the rate they're being consumed. At the current pace, if we stay put, we'll burn through the last of them in eight hours. That's if Atheena doesn't have to deploy more to deal with a major strike—one that causes significant damage. Without nanites, we'll have real problems. We will be on borrowed time at that point—and that doesn't count taking the ship back into battle."

Steele folded his arms, considering the situation. "And if we raised the shields?"

"You'd save the hull and me some trouble," Voss admitted.

"We'd also light up like a beacon on the darkest of nights. Every active scanner within a hundred thousand klicks would see us, not to mention the detection grid. So, it's not exactly an option, at least not now." Steele paced a few steps, rubbing his jaw. "What's the next best course of action?"

"Move," Voss said firmly. "Find a less dense sector of this bloody belt—something with less particulate matter hammering at the defensive screens and armored hull. It'll give Atheena some breathing room, and it'll stretch what nanites we've got left... also give us time to manufacture more and replenish our stores."

"How much more time would that buy us?"

Voss scratched his temple in thought. "Hard to say exactly, but double or even triple what we've got now. It won't solve the propellant issue, though."

"Noted," Steele said, turning his gaze for a moment down the corridor toward the boarding port and umbilical. "How much do you know about what's going on?"

"Atheena's kept me updated on some of it, what she's permitted to say," Voss replied. "I know we're docking with an off-the-books station to pick up some Union VIPs. I have no idea who they are, other than they're important to someone and that coming here is complicating my life greatly."

"They are important."

"If you say so, sir."

"I do say so," Steele said in a hard tone, feeling his irritation rise. There were limits to his patience and Voss was now testing them.

"Okay, sir."

"We really don't have a choice. I had to bring *Ranger* to pick them up."

"There's always a choice," Voss countered, his words carrying the weight of a man who had spent his career solving mechanical problems and engineering issues no one else could manage. Steele knew Voss cared more about the machine than people. He was crazy gifted when it came to starship systems, but not so much personal interactions. That was just how the man was wired, and most times it suited Steele just fine, for it was to *Ranger*'s benefit.

"Not in this instance," Steele said and then held up a hand before Voss could reply. "I can tell you this: as soon as those people are aboard, my main goal will be to get us out of the Reach. From that point we're headed out of this system and into Slipstream space."

"Back to the Union?" Voss asked, his voice carrying a note of hope.

"That's correct," Steele affirmed. "I have no desire to linger here, especially with the enemy on the hunt, and the LDF is hunting these people. They want them something bad."

Voss glanced in the direction of the boarding port, which was out of view, farther down the corridor and around a bend. He looked back at Steele. "So, as soon as they are aboard, we're leaving?"

"That is the plan."

"Good," Voss said, his relief evident. "Because you've stressed my baby something fierce, Captain. *Ranger*'s going to need prolonged time in a shipyard. I'm talking several weeks' worth of work. I can only imagine what the yard dogs are going to find wrong when they get their hands on her."

Steele grimaced and resisted a groan. "It's that bad?" He already knew the admiralty would have hard questions for him upon their return. A major repair effort would only add fuel to the fire of the inquisition that would be waiting. "The damage control reports haven't made it seem all that serious."

Voss folded his arms, his jaw tightening. A slight look of disappointment crossed the engineer's face. "That's because we haven't had the time or ability to properly assess the outer hull. It's too dangerous to go outside. Once we're out of this mess and can get an external look—eyeball her properly—I expect we'll find significant damage—microfractures in the armor plating, holing, pitting, deep scoring... the kind of wear and tear nanites can't fully patch, let alone fix on their own. I am thinking"—he paused to scratch an itch on his cheek—"that she'll need a full reskin after the beating she's taken."

Steele's stomach sank at that bit of news. Voss understood *Ranger* better than anyone. If he said it was so, then it was likely true. Worse, the cost and time of such repairs would not go unnoticed. The admiralty would be demanding explanations for *Ranger*'s hard use, and there was no doubt Steele had used her hard, on his own initiative. When they returned, his actions would be under a microscope, and he'd be forced to defend himself.

That was, if they managed to get back.

Steele thought on what he'd just been told for a long moment. With a heavy breath, he nodded. "I understand. Trust me, *Ranger* is as much my baby as she is yours. It pains me to see her take this kind of abuse."

Voss's expression softened slightly. The man knew that Steele loved the ship just as he did. Apparently satisfied he'd made his point, the chief engineer stepped aside for Steele to continue on his way. "I know, sir. I just had to voice it, to say what's on my mind. She's still holding together, and we'll keep her that way for you. Do what you need to do to get your job done and I will do mine."

"Right, we'll talk some more later, when there's time, all right?"

"Yes, sir. That's a promise."

Steele clapped Voss on the shoulder as he moved past. "We'll see her through this. *Ranger* might be battered, but she is far from broken."

"Aye, aye, sir. Truer words were never said."

Steele made his way from the engineering section toward the ship's main docking port, moving rapidly down the corridor. As Steele turned the bend, his gaze settled on a group of armed marines waiting just ahead. They were outfitted with rifles and light body armor. Their presence added a layer of gravitas to the situation. The marines snapped to attention as Steele approached, shifting aside to clear a path for their captain to pass.

Just beyond, Knox and Master Chief Petty Officer Lucas Brant stood by the main airlock hatch, their postures straightening instinctively when Steele drew near. Knox, always sharp and disciplined, had his sidearm holstered on his hip, the glint of its polished surface catching the light faintly. He wore only shipboard fatigues and boots, along with his service cap, no light body armor like his men.

Beside Knox, Brant exuded a calm but firm demeanor, his weathered features and gray hair betraying a lifetime of service to the Union. He also wore a sidearm and Steele knew the man could use it, too, for during the last war Brant had personally led an effort at successfully repelling a boarding action. He'd won the Navy Cross for that and almost died doing it.

Miller lingered a few paces behind them, leaning casually against the bulkhead. His silence spoke volumes; his sharp gaze and the faint tap of his fingers against his thigh betrayed his inner tension. Though he was wearing civilian clothing and was out of uniform, there was no mistaking the calculating presence of the intelligence officer. Steele knew that after today, there would be no doubt amongst the crew the man was an ID operative. Chase had told him there were numerous rumors flying around about that already. There was simply no helping it, not now.

Steele slowed his steps as he neared the group and came to a stop. His eyes swept over the marines, Knox, and Brant, noting their alertness and the subtle tension in their postures.

"Gentlemen," Steele greeted. The main airlock remained sealed, while the red and amber light above it pulsed steadily, indicating the pressurization process was still underway.

"We've got a good connection and lock with the umbilical, sir. We're about to open the hatch," Brant said, his grizzled and raspy voice steady. "We're just waiting on the umbilical to pressurize. It should be done momentarily, and then we can start the transfer—moving people over a few at a time."

"I wish we had a bigger airlock," Knox muttered. "Get this process moving faster."

"I thought you marines liked to hurry up and wait," Brant commented.

"Isn't that everyone's job at one time or another in the military?" Knox asked. "Waiting on someone else to do their job so you can do yours?"

Brant simply grunted at that. It was an old argument, one Steele had heard many times before. He well understood the sentiment and the frustration at having to wait.

Still, what they were doing was incredibly dangerous. Operating in the cold, hard vacuum of space meant precautions were paramount, critical even, and at times like these there was no rushing things. Both the listening post and *Ranger* would keep their respective airlocks sealed until the umbilical pressurization was complete and confirmed.

And then, only one side could open at a time, a cautious

safeguard against the catastrophic risks of explosive decompression, which was an especially real possibility in the midst of an asteroid belt like the one *Ranger* was currently operating in. The umbilical might be heavily armored to guard against such an event, but it was far from completely safe.

"We estimate about forty minutes to get everyone aboard," Brant continued. "It's not ideal, sir, but we'll do it as quickly as we can."

"I know you will, Chief." Steele's gaze flicked to the sealed hatch. The rhythmic red and amber flashes from the overhead light added a sense of urgency to the proceedings, as if even the airlock hatch wanted to get things moving along at a faster pace.

"We've prepared for any trouble, sir." Knox gestured at his marines. "As ordered, no one comes aboard armed. We will disarm everyone, including the security detail if there is one. Any weapons will go to the armory for storage and accounting."

"Excellent," Steele said, well pleased. His thoughts shifted. "We're going to have to find quarters for everyone. Have you started working toward that effort?"

"The XO and I have already got people working on that, sir," Brant assured him. "We're setting up a temporary staging area, with privacy partitions on one of the hangar decks. We'll also need to hot bunk some... but that should not be a real problem, at least on our side. Some of those coming aboard might resent such accommodations."

Steele frowned slightly but nodded, recognizing the unavoidable logistics. "And if we need that hangar deck operational?"

"We clear it quick as we can, sir, and do what we must," Brant said with a matter-of-fact tone. "As you know, *Ranger*'s not a large ship, and we're about to double our crew complement. People are going to be tripping over one another until we can offload them at some safe haven... God only knows when that will be."

Resigned to the inevitable, Steele let out a slow, unhappy sigh. "There's simply no way around it."

"No, sir," Brant said, his expression serious. "There's not."

"For the time being, we will just have to make do," Steele admitted, his gaze lingering on the flashing red light above the airlock. The thought of his carefully managed ship packed with additional people—many of whom were likely to be civilians unused to military protocol—was far from comforting. There would be problems and headaches that he would need to deal with. He had no doubt about that.

"On the bright side, I hear there's a dog coming aboard, sir," Brant said.

"There is," Steele confirmed with a nod.

"I like dogs," Brant replied, a trace of fondness in his voice. "About time *Ranger* had one aboard. That, or maybe a cat."

Steele shot him a sour look, his tone wry. "I've never been much of a cat person myself."

Knox grinned as he chimed in. "I'm with the captain on this one. Dogs are better than cats, smarter too."

"Either way, it's good for morale," Brant said, folding his arms across his chest. "A ship's pet might not be regulation, but the admiralty's always tolerated them and it does wonders for the crew's spirits. You should think about it, sir, consider allowing the crew to adopt a pet."

Steele let out an exasperated breath, shooting Brant a sideways glance. "Enough said. I'll leave that in your capable hands, Chief."

"Really, sir?" Brant's eyebrows rose in genuine surprise. "You'd let *Ranger* take aboard a new crew member, one without a serial number?"

Steele gave an absent nod, his focus drifting to the airlock where the red light was finally starting to blink its transition. "When we get back home, you can handle it."

A faint ping sounded as the airlock's status indicator shifted from red to amber and then to green. The hiss of venting gas followed as the seals within the hatch worked to equalize.

Brant's grin widened. "You won't regret it, sir. I'll take care of everything. It won't be no bother."

"Just make sure that whatever pet you pick, it doesn't become a nuisance or get in the way," Steele warned, pointing a finger and wagging it at the chief of the boat for emphasis. "And one more thing—no parrots. I've served on ships with birds before, and I'll tell you now plain off, we're not bloody pirates. Understand me on this?" He turned his gaze impatiently back to the airlock. "They also shit everywhere. At least dogs and cats can be trained."

"I understand, sir." Brant nodded, his expression mock-serious. "Dog or cat it is... I'll even take a vote from the crew."

"Very good," Steele said with a nod. "Now, let's focus on getting these people aboard. We've got bigger concerns than a ship mascot."

"Aye, sir," Brant said.

There was a heavy clunk from the airlock, followed by a ping that echoed faintly in the confined space. The green light had gone firm and was holding solid.

"She's pressurized," Brant announced, stepping forward to the control panel beside the airlock. His hands moved quickly over the controls, first keying in his security code, then authorizing the operation of the hatch. With a hiss of escaping air, the inner hatch slid open, revealing several figures standing within.

At the forefront was a woman close to Steele's age. She was striking, pretty even, with shoulder-length brown hair tied neatly back into a single braid, though it was clear she'd seen better days. The dark circles beneath her eyes and the tension etched into her features spoke of sleepless nights and hard decisions.

She wore a tailored dark gray suit that looked rumpled, like she'd worn it for several days in a row, which he considered quite possible, yet somehow she managed to maintain an air of authority and dignity. Steele found himself not only impressed, but intrigued, for she had a presence about her that spoke of inner strength.

In her left hand, she held the leash of a golden retriever, the animal's tail wagging enthusiastically as she glanced at those on the ship and in the corridor beyond with bright, curious eyes. The juxtaposition of the dog's carefree demeanor against the grim determination and hardness of the woman was almost jarring.

Behind her, two armed Union marines flanked the airlock. Rifles at the ready, their eyes scanned the corridor beyond with quick, practiced movements. The woman signaled to them, and after a moment, they relaxed and pointed the muzzles up at the overhead. Despite their protective stance, Steele noted the faint lines of weariness on their faces as well. These were soldiers who had been pushed to their limits.

The last occupant in the airlock was a nondescript man in a dark business suit. He stepped up beside the woman, his eyes flicking across the corridor and its occupants, including Knox's marines. He carried himself with the restrained tension of someone unaccustomed to being this far from the safety of a boardroom or, Steele thought, the safety of a government office. There was that sort of look about him. He spotted Miller, and Steele read recognition in his eyes. The man in the suit gave Miller a curt nod, which was quietly returned.

The woman exchanged a glance with him, then stepped forward, her gaze locking onto Steele. Her eyes traveled rapidly over his uniform, as if sizing him up, pausing briefly on the insignia at his neck denoting his command rank, and then shifted to the Union flag mounted on the bulkhead opposite the airlock. Her expression didn't soften; if anything, the exhaustion in her eyes seemed to only deepen. Steele thought he saw deep relief there within her gaze as she shifted her attention back to him.

"Permission to come aboard, Captain?" she asked.

"Granted." Steele straightened to his full height, adopting the formality that the occasion demanded. "Governor Tancrest, I am Captain Steele. Welcome aboard the UNS *Ranger*."

The governor nodded, her expression suddenly unreadable. Beside her, the golden retriever gave an enthusiastic bark, her tail wagging even faster. Out of the corner of his eye, he saw Brant grin slightly.

"Hush, Maggie," the governor said, and the dog stilled, but the tail still wagged.

Tancrest held out her hand to Steele. He took it and shook, finding her grip warm and firm.

"You have no idea just how happy we are that you managed to find us, Captain," Tancrest said.

"I understand, ma'am," Steele said.

Brant stepped forward, his demeanor turning all business. "Governor, we'll need to process your people before moving everyone to temporary quarters. That's going to take some time. With all due respect, pleasantries and protocol can wait. We've got to get the transfer started."

"He's right," Steele said with a glance at Brant, "the LDF is actively hunting for you and there is a ship headed our way. We need to get this show moving."

"Of course," Tancrest replied curtly. "Do what you need to do. Don't let me or any of my people get in the way. That's an order, Captain."

"Where is the governor being put up?" Steele asked Brant, turning his attention to his chief. "Guest quarters?"

"Yes, sir," Brant said. "Suite 1B."

"We have injured," Tancrest said suddenly, as if it had just occurred to her.

"Once they're brought aboard, Chief Brant will see your

wounded are transported directly to the medical bay," Steele said. "We will take good care of them. We have a first-rate doctor." Steele paused and gestured back down the corridor. "Ma'am, if you would follow me, I will escort you personally to your quarters and see you settled."

"Thank you, Captain, lead on."

"Chief, carry on."

"Aye, aye, sir."

"Governor, if you please, this way..." Steele gestured down the corridor.

NINETEEN

The lift hatch sealed with a soft hiss, enclosing them in the confined space of the elevator. The air inside was immediately filled with the faint hum of the lift's mechanisms and a subtle vibration. However, it was another sensation that dominated Steele's awareness—a sharp tang of body odor emanating from the governor and the man who had come aboard with her. It was clear neither had seen a proper shower in days, their weary appearance underscoring the toll their ordeal had taken.

The golden retriever at the governor's side shifted slightly, her leash taut in Tancrest's hand. The dog's tail lightly thumped against the lift's wall as she looked up at him.

"Deck five," Steele ordered curtly, his voice cutting through the silence like a blade. He watched as the lift's control panel lit up in response and began its smooth descent. The motion was so refined that, save for the slight pull on his internal sense of balance, he could almost forget the lift was moving at all.

Steele kept his stance firm, his hands clasped loosely behind his back as his eyes flicked between his guests. Miller stood stiffly to his right, his usual air of self-assuredness tempered by the unspoken gravity of the situation. The man in the suit—

someone Steele didn't yet know—fidgeted with an almost nervous energy.

The governor herself, Annalise Tancrest, was another matter entirely. Despite her rumpled appearance, she radiated a weary dignity. Her shoulders were square, her gaze steely and unflinching, though the lines etched into her face betrayed sleepless nights and countless burdens. The faint creases on her suit and the dirt smudges on her cuffs told a story of escape, desperation, and survival.

The dog, seemingly oblivious to the tension in the lift, sat obediently at the governor's side, her warm brown eyes on Steele as if silently judging him or begging for a pet, perhaps even wanting to play. Steele resisted the temptation. The dog's presence added an odd sense of normalcy to an otherwise grim scenario.

Perhaps the chief was right? A ship's dog might not be such a bad thing.

Steele turned his gaze forward, letting the hum of the lift fill the silence. He stared at the hatch and simply waited. Though he kept his expression neutral, his mind was working furiously, weighing the risks of bringing these people aboard, calculating what lay ahead as they made a break for the Fringe Zone. What complications would this excursion, no matter how necessary, bring? At the same time, despite protocol requirements, he knew he had precious little time to waste here. His place was on the bridge.

"This is a shit situation," Tancrest muttered, her irritation cutting like a blade. Her tone was sharp, her frustration barely restrained.

"It is certainly not ideal," Miller replied, his voice calm, though his guarded tone suggested he was carefully choosing his words.

"No, it is not," Tancrest fumed, her eyes narrowing. "I've only just arrived, three weeks ago, and everything goes crazy, and to shit at that." She let go an exasperated breath. "I had such high hopes, but no time to accomplish anything of substance. This all blew up in my face..."

Steele glanced at her, his expression steady. "I don't think there was anything you could have done," he said plainly. "What was going to happen was going to occur whether you were here in charge or not. ID simply missed it." Steele looked over at Miller and then the other man. "Their gaze was simply elsewhere."

The governor's eyes snapped to the man in the suit, her expression hard to the point of being accusatory. Her lips pressed into a thin line before she shifted her attention back to Steele.

"This took real planning, work to pull off," Steele continued, his tone deliberate and calm. "Coordination. Operational security. Nearly the entire Protectorate rose up as one, across all four systems. That sort of thing doesn't just happen overnight. They had help, aid, and planning."

"And speaking of assistance," Miller interjected, his voice cutting through the tension like a scalpel, "you should know there is a Hegemony fleet in-system."

Tancrest stiffened, her eyes snapping to Miller, then to Steele. The man in the suit visibly paled. He tilted his head slightly to the side as he regarded Miller, as if in disbelief. "The Hegemony has a fleet here?"

"They're behind this... this revolution," Miller continued, his tone unyielding in its intensity. "The Hegemony is working from the shadows, pulling the strings like a puppet master, and as Captain Steele said, our gaze was elsewhere. We didn't see this coming."

The lift doors hissed open, revealing deck five's corridor. The sterile lighting bathed the passageway in a pale glow, and the faint hum of the ship's systems reverberated through the walls and decking. But Tancrest didn't move. Her shoulders were rigid, her feet planted as if she'd grown roots.

For a moment, the only sound was the soft panting of her dog, Maggie's warm brown eyes glancing up at her, sensing the sudden shift in mood. Steele studied Tancrest, waiting, giving her the time she needed to process the implications of what had just been said.

When Tancrest finally spoke, her voice was softer but no less firm. "Hegemony," she repeated, as if tasting the bitter word, her anger now tempered by grim understanding. "That explains a great deal, and if true, it means war, another great war."

"It does," Steele said. "But now we know who we're really up against."

Nodding, Tancrest finally took several steps forward, her dog falling into stride beside her, and the group moved out of the lift.

"How certain are you of this information?" the man in the suit asked, stopping in the corridor. His voice was tight with skepticism as his eyes bored into Miller.

"Captain," Miller said, a faint sigh escaping him as he gestured to the suited man, "allow me to introduce you to Jack Zeldin."

"Captain," Zeldin said, inclining his head respectfully, though his expression remained guarded.

"I take it you're Directorate as well?" Steele asked with just enough edge to communicate his discontent.

"I am Intelligence Directorate," Zeldin confirmed as the lift hatch slid closed behind them with a soft hiss. Zeldin gestured subtly toward the governor. "In fact, I am her direct liaison. Illidran was to be my post."

Steele studied the man with a critical eye, his disapproval barely masked. "You people really dropped the ball here. You do realize that, right?"

"That," Miller interjected, "is the understatement of the century. After this, there will be hard questions, such as how it could even happen. And all under our noses? It is really a colossal failure. I expect heads to roll."

"Yes, indeed, and mine will likely be one of them, despite having only just arrived with the governor," Zeldin said tersely, his gaze flicking between Steele and Miller. He turned back to Steele, his tone now tinged with defensiveness. "So, how certain? I've heard nothing—not even a hint of a whisper about a supposed fleet, nothing in the bulletins... only the usual rumors—Hegemony agents stirring up trouble, dissent, working behind our backs to foment instability. So, tell me, how certain are you of this?"

"Fairly damn certain," Miller said with conviction. "Argonola came in."

Zeldin stiffened, his posture suddenly taut. "He did what?"

"He wouldn't pass along his information until he'd been extracted," Miller explained, his tone sharp and matter-of-fact. He gestured toward Steele. "That's how I got here. He sent me a message. I pulled some strings and requisitioned a destroyer, the newest ship in the fleet, one that was reliable and fast." His shoulders rose in a casual shrug, but his eyes were locked on Zeldin, clearly searching for a reaction, as if enjoying the moment. Steele found himself wondering on the two men's shared history, for there was clearly something there. Tension... a rivalry perhaps? What complications would this bring for him? Who of the two was senior? He had so many questions.

"You took a big gamble," Zeldin said, his tone sharp with disbelief. "If the intel Argonola had was wrong..."

"I'd say it worked out just fine for you," Miller countered, a faint smirk playing at his lips as he glanced pointedly between the governor and Zeldin.

"I cannot deny that," Zeldin admitted almost reluctantly,

though his eyes narrowed slightly. "Still, Miller, what you did takes balls, pulling *Ranger* all the way out here. You should have sent word, and we'd have picked him up."

"Our man didn't trust our people here in-system, and judging by what's happened, I'd say he was correct not to," Miller said. "Oh, and he's aboard."

"Argonola is here on *Ranger*?" Zeldin's surprise sounded genuine as he leaned slightly forward toward the other man.

"He is," Miller confirmed, his expression neutral. "He's in medical, recovering from being shot. He took a round to the chest, but he's made it through surgery and is lucid enough to talk if you wish to speak with him."

"Did you shoot him? I seem to recall hearing something about you shooting the man once."

"No. It wasn't me... at least not this time."

"I do want to speak with him," Zeldin said firmly, his tone brooking no argument.

Miller gave a curt nod. "I'll arrange that. He might be laid up, but he can talk. Just don't expect him to be in peak form."

Zeldin nodded, glancing down at the deck, his expression thoughtful. After a few heartbeats he looked back up. "I need to understand exactly what he knows. If he's confirmed what you're claiming, then this could change everything." Zeldin shook his head. "No, it will change everything."

"What about this enemy fleet in the system?" Tancrest demanded, eyes narrowing as she turned toward Steele. "Where are they hiding?"

"We think they're in the Exclusion Zone," Steele replied evenly. "Apparently, they snuck into the system under the cover of the solar rejuvenator blocking and interfering with comms traffic or through someone messing with the detection grid. We're not sure. Either way, they are here..."

"The Exclusion Zone?" Tancrest echoed, her voice tinged with disbelief. Her gaze hardened. "You *think* they're there?"

She looked between Miller and Steele. "You don't even *know* where they are, do you?"

Steele met her sharp look with a calm one of his own. "We think we have an idea on where they are hiding," he admitted, glancing toward Miller, "but we should know for certain soon enough. And if they are there, I intend to get that intelligence back to Fleet where it can do real good and make a difference in what is to come."

Zeldin's brows knit together as he studied Steele, a flicker of alarm crossing his expression. "Don't tell me we're going to the Graveyard?"

"Not a chance," Steele said firmly, cutting through the tension in the corridor. "Under no circumstances will I be taking *Ranger* there. As soon as your people are aboard, Governor, we're bugging out and heading for the Fringe Zone."

Zeldin's shoulders relaxed slightly, though his expression remained uneasy. "Good," he said quietly. "That place is a deathtrap."

"It's not just a deathtrap," Tancrest interjected, her voice icy. "It's a reminder of the worst this system has endured, a near defeat by the Union. With just bare luck, we snatched victory from the jaws of defeat. If the enemy is there... and hiding..." She trailed off, her lips pressing into a thin line. "This really does mean war." She paused, growing silent. "The only reason to hide is to wait... on the Home Fleet."

"That is a distinct possibility, one we considered, one I think a very real threat," Steele admitted.

"It's an ambush," Miller said plainly.

"But even so," Zeldin pressed, "Argonola's intelligence hasn't been verified. That's why you're in the Reach, isn't it?" His sharp eyes studied Steele carefully and then flicked to Miller. "You could have taken what our agent provided, the information in trade, and run for the hills. Instead, you're here, risking it all, to verify the enemy is actually in Illidran."

"Correct," Steele replied. "If you are going to do a job, you might as well do it right."

Zeldin's gaze narrowed. "So, if you're not going to the Exclusion Zone, how exactly do you plan to confirm whether this enemy fleet is here or not?"

"We've launched a number of sophisticated probes," Steele explained. "I have high hopes they will work."

"Probes?" Zeldin raised a skeptical brow. "That's it? That's all? That's your plan?"

Steele's lips twitched into the faintest of smirks. "Probes with a kick," he said confidently. "I don't think our enemy will be expecting them, and with some good fortune it will get us what we need, confirmation-wise, without too much risk."

"And if it doesn't work?" Zeldin asked.

"Then we go home and report what we know." Steele looked down the corridor lined with identical hatches, each leading to a compact crew quarters or shared berth. It was time to move things along. Deck five was primarily dedicated to crew accommodations, a utilitarian space, clean and functional, though lacking in much comfort. *Ranger* was, after all, a ship of war.

Steele turned to Tancrest and gestured farther down the corridor. "Governor, I'd like to get you settled. You need rest and time to recover."

Tancrest studied him for a moment. Her dog sat patiently by her side, tail swishing lazily against the deck. "You have a ship to run," she surmised, her tone tinged with resignation. "Is that it?"

Steele gave a brief nod, his expression unreadable. "That's exactly right. My crew and I have work to do, and the situation out there is far from stable. We're operating off the grid, with no access to the local detection network. There are enemy out there actively hunting you, and not far off at that. We still need to make our way out of the system and hopefully without being spotted. *Ranger*'s already shown her teeth and engaged not only a planetary defense network but two frigates. Just getting here to pick you up has taken a serious toll on her. I'd prefer to just sneak out and not get noticed again."

Tancrest sighed, her exhaustion evident. Her understanding was also clear as she nodded. "Very well, Captain. Lead the way. I would very much like to clean up."

Steele led them down the gently curving corridor, their boots echoing faintly against the polished metal deck. The ship's utilitarian design was evident in the clean, unadorned walls and overhead, punctuated by occasional lighting panels and softly glowing directional indicators.

A pair of crew members rounded the corner ahead, their uniforms crisp despite the ship's constant activity. They stepped aside respectfully, pressing their backs to the wall as Steele and his party passed in the narrow corridor. The governor barely acknowledged them, her focus inward as she absently adjusted her grip on the dog's leash to keep the animal moving with her.

The group continued down the corridor, the curvature of *Ranger*'s hull subtly visible in the narrowing perspective. At the end of the passage, two reinforced hatches stood opposite one another. These were the guest quarters, typically reserved for visiting officers, dignitaries, or VIPs. Steele stopped in front of one and gestured for the others to halt.

Using his implants, he transmitted the command to unlock the hatch. It opened with a faint hiss, sliding aside and revealing a compact but tidy cabin. Steele stepped over, gesturing Tancrest forward.

"Here we are, Governor." His tone was professional, but there was a touch of empathy in his eyes. "It's not much—a bunk, couch, table, and private toilet with a shower—but it's the best accommodations available at the moment and more than most of my crew have."

Tancrest stepped forward, her gaze sweeping the interior.

The cabin was spartan but clean, its design prioritizing function over luxury. The bunk was narrow but well-padded, set against the wall beneath a small viewport that offered a simulated and ultimately unrealistic view of the swirling asteroid field outside. A fold-down table and a single chair occupied one corner, while a compact shower stall and toilet were tucked discreetly into an alcove. Released from the lead, the dog padded inside, sniffing the unfamiliar space before settling on the deck with a satisfied huff.

Steele hesitated. "I'd offer you my cabin, which is next to the bridge," he added, his voice softer, "but we're in an active combat zone. Regulations prohibit me from doing so. I apologize for that, Governor, for I need to be available at a moment's notice to my bridge crew."

"I understand," Tancrest said, her voice weary but sincere. She stepped fully into the cabin and turned to look at him. "After the last few days, this will be more than adequate, Captain. Thank you for your kindness."

Steele gave a short nod. "If you need anything, use the cabin's comm panel to contact the bridge or the ship's construct, Atheena. Someone will assist you."

"Noted," she said, glancing at the small shower. "Besides showering, I am looking forward to getting some uninterrupted sleep... something that has eluded me over the last few days."

"It's been a little rough," Zeldin admitted, his voice heavy with exhaustion. "We were on a goodwill tour of the outer Reach settlements when the balloon went up. We barely managed to get the governor away and to safety."

"The bastards blew up the transport ship we were using." Tancrest's voice was sharp with lingering rage. "The *Salusant* was tethered to the station's docking ring. It nearly took out half the station we were at and killed thousands of civilians. Had it not been for my security contingent and some local loyalists, I'd either be dead or rotting in an LDF cell, and even then, they almost got us... persistent bastards."

Steele drew in a slow, measured breath, letting it out through his nose as he considered her words. "I'm glad we found you, ma'am. I'll do all I can to get you and your people home safely. Now, all you need to do is sit back, relax, and enjoy the ride. With some good fortune, we'll handle the rest and it will be uneventful."

Tancrest's expression softened, and she placed a hand lightly on his forearm. "I appreciate that, Captain. I really do. Thank you for everything you've already done."

Steele nodded, his expression earnest. "When there's time, we'll talk more. For now, duty calls. I need to return to the bridge."

"Of course," Tancrest said, stepping back and releasing his arm. "I won't keep you any longer. See to your duties."

Steele turned his attention to Zeldin and then to Miller. "You'll find him a place?"

Miller inclined his head. "He can bunk in my cabin. There's a couch in there that pulls out. I am sure he will find it preferable to the hangar deck."

"I think so, too," Zeldin said with a faint smile. "Besides, he and I have a lot of catching up to do, and I want to hear what Argonola has to say."

Steele's gaze lingered on them for a moment before he nodded. "Good."

He turned back to Tancrest, offering her a respectful nod, then pivoted sharply on his heel. Retracing his steps down the corridor, his boots struck a steady rhythm against the deck plates. As he made his way back toward the lift, Steele felt the pressure of responsibility settle on him. That and the unknown. He'd been away from the bridge long enough. It was time to return to the command center of his ship and ensure they stayed one step ahead of the enemy.

TWENTY

"I have the bridge," Steele said as he settled into his command chair, its worn, sturdy contours immediately conforming to his frame with practiced familiarity.

"You have the bridge, sir," Chase replied. "Command of *Ranger* is yours."

Steele tapped the central display embedded in his console. The screens flared to life, bathing his station in a faint blue-white glow. Streams of data scrolled across the displays, detailing the operational metrics of *Ranger*.

His gaze methodically swept over the status board, where a cascade of readouts provided a living picture of the ship's health: reactor and drive output holding steady, defensive systems on standby, and life support cycling within optimal ranges, amongst many other critical and noncritical systems.

Satisfied that everything was within nominal parameters, he turned his attention to the HTD. The holographic tactical display hovered just above the console, a meticulously crafted three-dimensional map of their immediate surroundings. Glowing markers represented asteroids, debris fields, and the unregistered habitats they'd detected earlier, while a soft pulse marked the ship's current position along with enemy combatants that the ship had identified throughout the system.

Steele's sharp eyes scanned the HTD, taking in every detail with the practiced ease of a seasoned captain. Satisfied with what he saw, he leaned back slightly and glanced around the bridge. The muted hum of machinery and the occasional soft beep of an interface filled the air. The space was alive with quiet and trained efficiency. Each member of the bridge crew was at their station, heads bent in concentration as they worked.

Steele turned his attention to his executive officer. "Report."

"We're still taking on people from the listening post," Chase replied, her voice steady but edged with tension. "The chief of the boat reports six wounded amongst them. Those were the first brought aboard. Injuries include gunshot wounds, concussive trauma, and burns. The wounded are currently in sickbay and under Doctor Yates's care. She reports no life-threatening cases at this time."

Steele's brow furrowed slightly as he absorbed the report. "What's the estimate to conclude embarkation operations? How much longer do we have?"

"Less than fifteen minutes, sir," Chase said. Then, as if anticipating his next question, she added, "We've also detected two additional contacts out in the field. Both appear to be moving generally in our direction."

Steele's gaze sharpened, and his attention snapped to Ishida at the tactical station. "Guns, put known contacts up on the main screen."

"Aye, sir," Ishida replied. With a few deft taps, the main screen shifted from an external view of the tethered listening post to the HTD, displaying a detailed overlay of the surrounding space.

The bridge fell into a tense silence as Steele studied the screen. The holographic display was centered on *Ranger* as a steady, glowing green marker tethered to the asteroid-based station by a thin line representing the umbilical. Beyond and farther out in the field, two new red icons pulsed ominously.

Both contacts were less than one hundred fifty thousand kilometers away. He could see the active sensor sweeps and pings pulsing outward from the two ships. They were hunting, and it was evident they were working together as a team, their search patterns overlapping as they swept the area carefully.

Steele leaned forward in his chair, pulling up additional data on the contacts through his console. His eyes narrowed as Atheena supplied detailed tags: current course plots, mass readings, energy signatures, the passive intelligence gathered by *Ranger*'s systems.

"A frigate and a destroyer," Steele muttered, his tone grim as he rubbed his jaw. On the HTD, the destroyer's icon flickered, her energy signature more prominent than the frigate's.

"Aye, sir," Ishida reported, her voice steady but tinged with urgency. "Based on their drive signatures, that's what we've identified them as—a frigate and a destroyer. Oh, and they've increased their speed in the last hour. Their shields are running at nearly full power."

Steele gave a measured nod, his gaze locked on the HTD as he absorbed the information. The enemy ships were tearing through the field at a dangerous clip, moving at 3.5g. Such velocity in this dense portion of the asteroid belt was near reckless, their shields likely taking a punishing beating as they barreled through the debris.

"They're actively scanning the larger asteroids, sir," Chase added. "From what we're seeing, they're targeting anything big enough to hide a base or habitat. My guess? They've figured out the governor's transport has limited range and are systematically checking places where it might have holed up."

"All the larger asteroids," Ishida chimed in grimly, "which means it's only a matter of time before they get to ours."

Steele suppressed a sigh. It was a grim but logical deduction. Their asteroid would inevitably fall under scrutiny—it was large enough to warrant investigation, especially with the tight search pattern the enemy was employing. He let that truth settle over him, his mind racing for a solution. They needed to escape, but the enemy's speed and persistence were complicating matters.

"Their approach is methodical," Chase said, her eyes narrowed at her station. "They're sweeping section by section, but they're moving fast. When we push away, their sensors might pick up our trail in the debris field. Even passive sensors could spot such an anomaly."

Steele nodded again, his expression grim. It was a gamble. *Ranger*'s stealth systems were excellent, but stealth didn't equate to invisibility—especially not when navigating a field as chaotic as the Reach. Their movement would disturb the surrounding debris, leaving a telltale signature for any attentive scanner operator.

"That said," Chase added, "they're LDF. Their tech isn't exactly top-tier, and their crews aren't the most experienced. There's a chance they won't pick up on the trail..."

A small but not insignificant chance, Steele thought. He wasn't inclined to bet the survival of *Ranger*, let alone his crew, on underestimating the enemy. He would not make that mistake.

He studied the HTD for another moment, his gaze narrowing on the approaching contacts. He needed to change the dynamic, to force the enemy to react rather than continue to methodically sweep their way closer and stumble upon *Ranger*'s presence or her trail. He needed them distracted...

But how?

What options did he have?

Steele's voice broke the tense silence. "Guns. What do we know about their shield strength? I assume they're taking hits from the debris field..."

"Yes, sir, they are," Ishida confirmed. "Their shields are active, but even at full power, the field is surely putting stress on their systems. The frigate's emissions are fluctuating slightly—might be a weak generator or just simple prolonged wear and tear. There's no way to really tell."

Steele rubbed his jaw again, an idea beginning to form. Perhaps he could misdirect the enemy, lure them into overextending and then get them to break off their pursuit and hunt before it had even really begun.

He turned back to Chase. "How are we doing with the transfer?"

"Almost finished, sir. The last few personnel are coming aboard now."

"Is Smith still on the station?" Steele asked.

"The marine aviator?"

Steele gave a curt nod. "That's the man I want."

"I believe he's still over there, sir. He's the senior military officer and is coordinating directly with the chief of the boat to ensure his people get transferred safely onto *Ranger*."

Steele's gaze shifted toward the communications station. "Calder, get Smith on comms."

"Yes, sir," Calder replied, immediately working her console. A few moments later, the channel opened, and Smith's voice came through, slightly strained but clear.

"Smith here."

"Smith, this is Captain Steele. I have a task for you before you can embark."

"And what's that, Captain?" There was a subtle tension in Smith's voice, his exhaustion evident. "I was just about to take my turn to board your ship, sir. I'm one of the last ones left over here, along with my crew chief."

"The transport you used to reach the listening post," Steele began, "can you power her up while she's still in the hangar?"

"Power her up?" Smith echoed, the confusion clear in his

voice. "Why would I want to do that? She's no longer flight-worthy, sir."

"I'm aware of her condition," Steele said. "But we've got two enemy ships closing in on our position. They're systematically scanning the larger asteroids for signs of life. The listening post, even powered up as it is, shows no indication of internal energy sources. That station you're on is too well-shielded. She was designed that way. I need bleed-over and something for them to fixate their attention on, something they can get excited about."

There was a brief pause before Smith responded. "So, you want them to find the base here, sir? Use it as bait?"

"Exactly," Steele confirmed. "Can you handle that?"

"Yes, sir, I can," Smith said, his tone sharpening with resolve. "Might I make a suggestion, though?"

"Go ahead." Steele leaned forward slightly in his chair. "I'm listening."

"The hangar doors for this facility are heavily reinforced and designed to minimize emissions. After powering up the transport, we could leave one of the hangar doors partially open, just a crack, sir. That would make the bleed-off more noticeable, like we were rushed or sloppy or there was a mechanical break-down, something like that."

Steele's lips curved into a small, approving smile. "More emissions bleed-over, creating a stronger signal for them to lock onto. Good thinking, son. Make it happen."

"Yes, sir. I'll get right on it."

The comm line closed with a sharp click.

Steele leaned back in his chair, rubbing his jaw as he consid-ered the unfolding plan. What he wanted to do was a gamble—baiting the enemy to focus on the asteroid while *Ranger* made her escape.

"Helm," Steele said, turning to Hale, "prepare to disengage the umbilical as soon as the last personnel are aboard. I want us moving the moment we're ready."

"Aye, sir," Hale responded, his hands already flying over his console.

"Chase, monitor those incoming contacts closely," Steele added. "The second they shift focus, or accelerate, I want to know about it."

"Understood, sir," Chase said.

"Guns," Steele said, swiveling in his command chair to address Ishida. His tone was calm and cold. It was time to put the plan into motion. "I want those mines we picked up at the depot deployed around the listening post. Position them in the most likely path of those approaching ships and set them to auto-proximity activation when the enemy closes to engagement range."

"The mines, sir?" Ishida's eyebrows shot up for a moment, but then a grin spread across her face as understanding dawned. "Oh, I see what you're doing."

"The mines are to arm as soon as we're clear of the listening post," Steele clarified. "Make sure they remain in stealth until the enemy comes."

Space mines were notoriously tricky to use in combat. Unlike terrestrial or naval mines, they couldn't rely on natural bottlenecks or predictable pathways. In the vast expanse of space, the enemy could approach from virtually any vector. This inherent challenge was one of the reasons the Valkorian Hegemony had chosen the Reach as the site for their final stand in Illidran during the last war. Their strategy had forced the Union Navy into a grueling engagement, one that had turned that portion of the asteroid belt into a deadly killing ground.

"So, the LDF will detect the transport's emissions and think they've stumbled onto something worth investigating, and when they close, the last thing they will expect are stealth mines lying in wait," Chase said, glancing at Steele. "That's the plan?"

"That's what I'm hoping for," Steele replied, his voice steady. He turned his attention back to Ishida. "Guns, deploy those mines as soon as possible. I want them in position and cloaked before we begin pulling back."

"Already on it, sir," Ishida said. The tactical display on the HTD shifted, showing the plotted positions of the mines as they were readied for deployment.

Steele leaned back slightly in his chair, his eyes fixed on the display. The mines were older tech, focused compression warheads, mixed with pulsed pressed x-ray lasers. In the dense particulate environment of the Reach, once detonated, they'd create a deadly storm of shrapnel, enough to cripple or perhaps destroy even well-armored and shielded ships.

"We're running a bit of a gamble here," Steele admitted. "But if this works, it'll give us the time we need to slip away from them."

"Understood, sir," Chase said, her tone resolute. "I'll make sure helm is ready to disengage the umbilical and maneuver as soon as you give the order."

"Very good," Steele said, leaning back into his chair. For the moment, he'd done all he could. Now it was a waiting game—a tense, calculated pause in which every second mattered. Smith needed to finish his task and get back to the umbilical to board *Ranger*. Only then could they untether from the station, push back, and begin their escape.

Steele's gaze shifted to Chase, catching her eye. "Voss cornered me down below. He's concerned about our nanite supply and propellant reserves."

"To be honest, I am too, sir," Chase admitted, her tone edged with unease. "We've been running *Ranger* hard over the last few days. She's taken quite a beating."

Steele gave a small, understanding nod. "We have. Plot a least-time course from here to the Fringe Zone. We'll try to keep as much of it in stealth as possible... minimize maneuvers wherever we can. The fewer corrections, the less propellant we burn."

"I've already been working on that with Hale, sir," Chase said. "Want me to send you what we've come up with so far?"

"I do." Steele was pleased with their initiative.

A moment later, the plotted course populated Steele's main display, a series of glowing waypoints threaded like beads through the asteroid field and beyond. He leaned forward, studying the course with a critical eye. The early waypoints hugged safer corridors of passage within the Reach, steering *Ranger* clear of high-density asteroid clusters and minimizing exposure to active scanning areas. Once outside the asteroid field, the plotted path became significantly more complex. The waypoints multiplied almost exponentially, creating a serpentine route designed to slip past the system's detection grid and avoid civilian traffic lanes.

The sheer number of maneuvers required beyond the Reach gave him pause and some serious concern. Each waypoint represented an expenditure of propellant and a potential point of failure. He frowned slightly and scrolled through the notes attached to the plan, each detailing why a particular waypoint had been chosen.

"Propellant-wise... we're looking at hitting the Fringe Zone with about eighteen to twenty percent of our supply remaining," Chase said.

Steele rubbed his jaw, his gaze flicking between the plotted course and the HTD. "Eighteen percent isn't much, but it's manageable," he said after a moment, thinking they'd likely use up more of their supply. "If we stick to this plan, how much do we lose if we have to adjust for unexpected contacts?"

"Depends on how drastic the adjustments are, sir," Chase replied. "A minor course correction shouldn't hurt us too much, but anything major, say a full-on engagement with another warship, could easily cut that reserve in half—or worse, completely deplete what we have remaining. You know how it could go..."

Steele gave a slow nod, his eyes narrowing as he continued to study the data on his display. The plotted course was precise, each waypoint meticulously calculated to navigate the complex dangers of the Reach and beyond. Chase and Hale's attention to detail was plain, and despite his scrutiny, Steele could find no fault in their work.

Still, unease prickled at the back of his mind. He zoomed out the plotted course to view it in the broader context of the star system as a whole. The screen shifted, revealing the Illidran System with her sprawling asteroid belts, planets, moons, and the distant Fringe Zone, marked by a red border that represented escape and freedom.

His fingers moved deftly over the controls as he examined the route from different angles, rotating the star map to get a better sense of the risks. One sector in particular drew his attention—a stretch of their course that skirted uncomfortably close to Tenebris. The dark, barren world loomed like an unhappy shadow in the system.

"Tenebris," he muttered under his breath, his tone grim. The planet itself wasn't much of a threat—not anymore. It was little more than a frozen, airless rock. But its proximity to their route presented a potential danger. If the LDF had stationed assets nearby, even a momentary lapse in stealth could lead to an intercept. And in their current state, with limited propellant and nanites running low, an engagement was the last thing Steele needed.

"Sir," Quinn said, breaking the tense quiet on the bridge, "I'm detecting energy readings coming from the listening post. The transport's reactor is ramping up and running hot."

"Thank you," Steele replied, his voice steady as he processed the report. Smith was doing his job. The old transport's reactor, now running at an exaggerated output, would bleed enough emissions to draw attention. If the enemy's sensor officer was even halfway competent, they'd spot the power signature immediately as they closed to within fifty thousand kilometers. With any luck, they'd assume the transport was idling in preparation to run—though Steele knew full well that running from a destroyer or frigate at close range was a futile endeavor. It was a ruse, plain and simple.

Would the enemy fall for it?

"Launching mines now, sir," Ishida said as the missile pod indicator beeped sharply in confirmation. "I'm deploying all of them, sir—holding nothing back."

"Understood. Proceed as directed." Steele turned his gaze toward the tactical display, watching intently as the mines were ejected from *Ranger*'s two missile pods in rapid sequence. On the screen, the sleek devices disappeared almost immediately, their stealth fields engaging as they accelerated away and into the dark expanse of the asteroid field. Each mine followed a preprogrammed course, moving slowly toward its designated position.

For a moment, the bridge was silent except for the faint hum of background systems at work. Steele leaned forward slightly, eyes narrowed as he studied the real-time data feed. His attention shifted to the incoming ships on the HTD. The tactical plot showed the two enemy contacts—a frigate and a destroyer—still burning toward their position at 3.5g, shields up, and scanning aggressively. A third was farther away and moving off from them. It was no threat and likely would not become one.

The asteroid and the listening post sat directly between *Ranger* and the approaching LDF ships, an unremarkable lump of nickel and iron surrounded by the debris and particulate matter that defined so much of the Reach. It was an ideal buffer, and Ishida was using it well. Steele watched as she positioned the mines along the far side of the asteroid, directly in the path the enemy ships were likely to take.

"Everything looks solid," Chase said after a long pause. The plotted tracks and final positions of each stealth mine glowed faintly on the display, forming a deadly net that would remain invisible until it was too late for the enemy to react. At least that's how Steele hoped it would be. The battle space had been prepared.

"I see no need to alter your deployment plan, Ishida. Excellent work," Steele added.

"Thank you, sir. The mines will maintain their stealth fields until the enemy closes to engagement range. At that point, they'll go active and target anything within their proximity."

"Smith is in the umbilical, sir," Chase reported. "He's the last one to leave the station. The listening post is now completely vacated."

Steele gave a sharp nod, his gaze fixed on the HTD. "Once he's aboard, unlatch from the station and retract the umbilical. As soon as it's stowed, we'll push back and away from this rock. We've lingered here long enough."

"Aye, sir." Chase turned to the helm. "Helm, prepare for movement and navigation on the plotted course."

"Aye, ma'am," Hale replied, his hands poised over the controls. "Standing by for orders."

Steele felt his heart begin to beat a little faster. They were finally about to get underway. The enemy ships were still closing, and every second now felt excruciatingly slow. He clenched his jaw, forcing himself to exude calm, though inside he felt like a coiled spring, one ready to snap. The Reach, with its hidden dangers, had been their cage. Now, freedom was within sight—if they could only seize it.

"Smith is aboard," Chase reported, breaking the tension. "We are now untethered. The umbilical is retracting, sir. Two minutes until the process is complete."

Steele said nothing, his eyes locked on the plot. Each second seemed to drag, his internal clock ticking in agonizingly slow intervals. He resisted the urge to get up and pace, instead forcing himself to remain seated and composed. Around him, the bridge crew worked with quiet efficiency, but the charged atmosphere was powerfully strong.

"Umbilical fully retracted, sir," Chase finally reported, her voice cutting through the stillness.

Steele exhaled, the tightness in his chest easing slightly. "Helm, how are we? Report."

"We're free and clear to navigate, sir," Hale replied, his tone steady.

"Very good." Steele leaned forward, his voice firm and deliberate. "Helm, execute plotted course."

"Executing," Hale confirmed. His hands moved across the controls. A heartbeat later, a subtle shift could be felt as *Ranger*'s thrusters came to life, nudging the ship into motion.

On the HTD, Steele watched as *Ranger* began to ease off from the asteroid. The plotted course shimmered on the display, a carefully calculated path that would take them away from the listening post and deeper into the belt before ultimately breaking free of the Reach entirely.

The asteroid that had been the governor's temporary refuge rapidly grew smaller on the main screen, its jagged surface fading into the backdrop of the Reach. The enemy was out there and still closing, but *Ranger* was moving, slipping away like a shadow into the gathering darkness.

"Steady as she goes," Steele said quietly, more to himself than anyone else. His mind was already racing ahead, thinking of what lay beyond the Reach, of the Fringe Zone and the unknown challenges that awaited them there. But first, they had to survive this moment, this delicate escape.

The bridge settled into a focused rhythm, the tension easing but not dissipating entirely. Around him, Steele's crew worked.

"Let's hope the enemy takes the bait," Chase said softly, her eyes on the plot.

Steele didn't reply. He simply nodded, his expression

unreadable as *Ranger* slipped further into the depths of the asteroid field, her course set for the freedom of open space.

Steele could feel the faint vibration of the gravitic drive through his chair, a low hum that resonated with the ship's hull as the coils began to spin faster and faster. It was a tangible reminder of the immense power propelling *Ranger* forward, power that was at his fingertips. Despite the tension, it was a heady feeling, one that spoke to the raw capability of the advanced propulsion systems.

"Coming onto plotted course, gravitic drive engaged," Hale reported. "We are moving and underway at point 25g."

Steele's gaze shifted to the HTD, studying the data streaming in from their passive sensors. The enemy ships remained on course, their active scans sweeping through the asteroid field like probing fingers searching.

A sudden, heavy thump reverberated through the hull, jolting Steele slightly in his seat. His jaw tightened at the sound, a grimace flashing across his face. Something sizable had struck *Ranger*'s armored exterior. Even though the defensive screens were doing their job, the dense asteroid field was merciless and unforgiving.

Another impact, louder and more forceful, shook the ship. Steele gripped the armrests of his command chair, instinctively glancing upward at the overhead as if he could see through it to the debris hammering at them.

How much more of this could *Ranger* take?

"Increasing speed to 0.5g," Hale reported.

"Very good," Steele replied, his voice calm despite the lingering unease in his chest. His eyes flicked to Chase, seated at her station. He could see the faint lines of fatigue etched into her face, though her focus remained sharp. They both knew this was a waiting game now—there wasn't much more for her to do here in the moment. Only one of them needed to be present and on the bridge.

"XO," Steele said after a beat, "why don't you get some rest? I'll cover things here for a while."

Chase turned her head, fixing him with a direct look. "I just stimmed not long ago, sir. Rest isn't happening for me... at least anytime soon." She paused, her tone softening slightly as she regarded him. "How long has it been since you got some shut-eye?"

Steele blinked, genuinely trying to recall. "I don't know... maybe fourteen hours? Possibly more."

"Then you should go," Chase said firmly. "I'll handle things here and rotate the bridge crew. You're no good to us if you run yourself into the ground."

Steele hesitated, but the logic was sound, and Chase wasn't wrong. Letting out a reluctant breath, he nodded, suddenly feeling a wave of exhaustion wash over him. "All right. You have the ship, XO."

"I have command," Chase confirmed, her posture straightening as she assumed the weight of responsibility for the ship. "I'll make sure the crew gets rotated and some rest as well."

"Very good," Steele said, his voice carrying a note of trust and gratitude. Rising from his station, he gave one last glance at the HTD, then turned toward his quarters.

Steele's boots echoed faintly against the deck plating as he crossed the bridge. The marine stationed outside his quarters snapped to attention as he approached. Without a word, Steele nodded, and the hatch slid open with a quiet hiss. He stepped through and into the small sanctuary that served as both his office and personal retreat. The hatch closed behind him, sealing him off from the bridge.

For a moment, he stood there, letting the silence press against him. The hum of *Ranger*'s systems seemed distant now, almost muted, but was still a reminder of the ship's ceaseless operations. Steele remained frozen in place, his gaze unfocused. His thoughts churned. His hand rose almost involuntarily to his jaw, brushing against the rough stubble that had grown over the last few days. His fingers trembled faintly, an unbidden sign of the strain he'd been under.

Between the destruction of Tenebris's defense grid, the strikes he'd ordered on the ground, and the two frigates they had engaged... how many lives had he taken? How many people had died because of his commands? The weight of it suddenly bore down on him like a physical force. It wasn't just the numbers; it was the faces he would never see, the stories he would never know.

Killer. Murderer.

The words surfaced in his mind unbidden, cutting deep.

This was what it meant to command a ship of war.

His chest tightened as he struggled against the dark tide of guilt that threatened to rise within. Steele sucked in a deep breath, holding it for a moment before exhaling slowly through his nose. He straightened his shoulders, pushing it all back down, forcing it into the recesses of his mind where it couldn't paralyze him.

"This is not on me," he said aloud, his voice firm but edged with pain. "I didn't bring this fight. The enemy did..."

The words echoed softly in the stillness, as if seeking to convince not just the room, but himself. He shook his head and turned his gaze toward the desk in the corner. The neat surface belied the storm of tasks awaiting him. He would have to sit down at some point—sooner rather than later—and begin compiling the detailed report that Fleet would demand. Every decision, every action, every order would need to be accounted for. Justifying his actions to an admiralty board back home was a certainty, and he knew the questions would be pointed, hard, and merciless.

But not now.

Now was not the time for exhaustive reports or self-recrimination. The job wasn't finished. The mission remained. *Ranger* was still deep in hostile territory, and their escape from Illidran was far from guaranteed. He had to focus, to keep his wits sharp and his resolve steady.

Steele turned toward his cabin, his decision made. Rest was a necessity, not a luxury. He needed to be fresh for the hours ahead. The danger to his ship and crew wasn't over, and exhaustion would only dull his edge. A shower, a shave, and some sleep —if only for a few precious hours. The sequence played in his mind like a mantra as he crossed the short space to his private quarters.

The hatch to his cabin slid open, revealing the modest yet functional space within. Steele stepped inside, feeling a faint pang of longing for the peace he knew would only come after the mission was done, and maybe not even then. For now, he would settle for the simple comforts of hot water, a razor, and a chance to close his eyes, not necessarily in that order.

TWENTY-ONE

Steele stepped onto the bridge, freshly showered and shaved, a marked improvement from the weariness and exhaustion he'd carried just hours before. The faint scent of soap still lingered on him. He'd managed several hours of sleep and a quick meal—nothing glamorous, just a ham and cheese sandwich and some chips—but together it was enough to clear his head and sharpen his focus.

His uniform was crisp, and though his mind was weighted with the responsibilities of command, he carried himself with a quiet confidence as he relieved Chase. The bridge itself was a contrast of energy and calm. The ever-present hum of the ship's systems filled the background, a steady reminder of *Ranger*'s readiness, but the atmosphere was subdued.

Most of the crew had been rotated off duty for rest, leaving the skeleton crew to manage operations. Ensign Derrick Cole manned the helm, his youthful features taut with concentration, while Ishida monitored tactical displays, her fingers moving deftly over her console. Their professionalism reassured Steele as he settled into his command chair.

"Anything to report?" Steele asked Chase as she stood from her station.

"Quiet so far," Chase replied. "We're making good time. The field is finally thinning out, and we're holding at 5g. I've had the shields charged and raised to five percent. It's low enough to avoid easy detection but enough to help manage impacts. Nanite losses have stabilized, and we're now manufacturing more than we're expending."

"That's good news," Steele said, nodding his approval. "Go get some rest."

"Yes, sir."

He watched her leave the bridge before turning his attention to the HTD. The display dominated the central console. The screen projected *Ranger*'s course through the remnants of the asteroid field, which, just as Chase had said, had clearly grown less dense over the last several hours. They were finally making real progress, their speed increased to 5g, a respectable pace given the risks they had been taking. Small fragments still occasionally pinged off the hull and shields, but the lighter debris field meant fewer impacts and less strain on their defensive screens. Steele took a small sip of his coffee, savoring the warmth as he reviewed their position.

"Status on the shields?" Steele asked, glancing at Ishida.

"Holding steady at five percent, no degradation or fluctuation in power levels," Ishida replied without looking up from her console. "Minimal energy bleed. We're balancing protection against detectability as best we can."

Steele gave a nod of acknowledgment. The decision to activate the shields had been a calculated risk. Raising them even slightly increased the ship's energy signature, making them marginally easier to detect. But even with the debris field thinning, he wasn't willing to let *Ranger*'s hull continue taking hits unnecessarily, especially as they increased their speed.

"We're nearly two hours from clearing the Reach," Cole

reported from the helm. His voice held the faintest trace of optimism.

Steele's gaze lingered on the HTD. The worst of the asteroid field was behind them, but the relief wasn't complete. They still had to slip past the detection grid and any LDF assets they could not see between them and the Fringe Zone. He leaned back slightly in his chair, his fingers tapping lightly against the armrest as he considered the journey ahead.

"Keep a close eye on those passive sensors," Steele said after a moment. "We're not out of the woods yet."

"Yes, sir," Ishida replied, her tone sharp and focused.

The bridge returned to its subdued quiet, with only the occasional soft ping of consoles breaking the silence. Steele allowed himself a rare moment of reflection as he sipped his coffee. Commanding a starship often meant enduring these long stretches of calm, where the tension wasn't in action but in waiting.

Seeking a more comfortable position, Steele shifted in his command chair, the soft hum of the gravitic drive a faint undertone to the bridge's quiet. He took another sip from his coffee, the bitter warmth grounding him for a moment, before placing the cup back into its holder. His eyes returned to the status displays, methodically scanning the readouts. The reactors were running smoothly, their outputs steady. The shield emitters were performing within expected limits, maintaining their delicate balance of protection and stealth. The gravitic drive, the heart of *Ranger*'s propulsion, thrummed steadily at 5g.

His gaze shifted to the life support systems. With nearly twice the ship's standard crew capacity now aboard—courtesy of the rescued personnel—the system was operating under considerable strain. Redundant circuits were engaged, and reserves were being tapped into more heavily than usual. While still stable, the display showed subtle signs of the increased demand: elevated CO_2 scrubber cycles, higher water recycling rates, and power usage creeping closer to the maximum threshold. It wasn't critical yet, but it was something he'd need to monitor and likely address.

Steele's attention moved to the HTD. He zoomed out, scanning the surrounding space. Beyond a smattering of smaller asteroids, the immediate area was effectively clear. The passive sensors weren't picking up any contacts. On one hand, the absence of enemy signatures was comforting. On the other, it wasn't. A ship running under stealth could easily be lurking nearby, lying in wait for the unwary.

Steele couldn't dismiss the thought entirely, though he reminded himself that such an encounter was unlikely. The Illidran LDF didn't possess an overwhelming fleet presence. The Union had kept it that way on purpose. The LDF had two battlecruisers, a pair of cruisers, ten patrol frigates—down to eight now, thanks to *Ranger*—twelve corvettes, and six system defense cruisers. Adding to the list were five customs cutters and a couple of logistics vessels.

The LDF's ships were a patchwork of older, mostly outdated models. Many likely suffered from limited maintenance and resource constraints. Even with a full complement, most couldn't maintain an extensive stealth presence. Only a handful of their ships were maintained at the highest levels, and that likely included the two battlecruisers.

Still, there was the *Starfish*. The battlecruiser had turned back toward Tenebris during their earlier maneuvers. After *Ranger* had faked a jump and gone dark, they'd lost track of her entirely. Whether she was lingering in the planet's orbit, lying doggo herself, or actively hunting, Steele didn't know. She might have even moved on. He certainly hoped she had.

But that uncertainty gnawed at him. He continued to watch the HTD as well as the other screens that detailed *Ranger*'s health.

"Captain," Ishida said, breaking the quiet after more than

an hour had passed, "passive close-range scans are still negative. No emissions, no movement beyond basic background noise."

"Thank you." Steele gave a slight nod but said nothing else. The absence of threats didn't ease his vigilance. A quiet sector could change in an instant, and he wasn't about to let his guard down—not with the stakes as high as they were.

The edge of the Reach and open space beckoned, but between them and safety lay Tenebris. The *Starfish* might be there, along with any number of other LDF assets that had arrived after the fight. Steele exhaled quietly, his jaw tightening as his gaze settled back on the HTD.

No, he wouldn't let his guard down. Not yet.

More time trickled by, the steady rhythm of the ship's systems forming a soothing backdrop to the stillness of the bridge. Steele sat in his command chair, the glow of his station's display casting a faint light across his features. The low hum of the gravitic drive and the occasional quiet chatter between stations or call to the bridge served as a reminder that, while calm, *Ranger* was far from dormant.

A pair of marines entered the bridge carrying trays of food and fresh coffee, their boots clicking softly on the deck plating. Steele barely looked up as they moved to distribute the offerings. A fresh cup of steaming coffee was placed by his elbow in its holder, the old one removed, and he gave a slight nod of thanks before returning his attention to the task at hand.

The minutes bled into an hour. Then another.

Nothing untoward occurred. The HTD remained static, the field of asteroids thinning further as they approached the edge of the Reach. No unexpected contacts had materialized.

Steele leaned forward, his elbows resting on the console, as he began addressing the stack of administrative tasks that had accumulated over the past few days. Reports from his department heads scrolled across his screen. Engineering updates from Voss outlined the continued manufacturing of nanites and the current state of the propellant reserves. Medical logs detailed the conditions of the wounded brought aboard, noting their stabilization under Yates's expert care.

Supply requisitions, personnel assessments, and status updates filled his queue. Steele tackled them methodically, pausing occasionally to rub his eyes or take a sip of his coffee, now cold but still welcome.

The reports painted a picture of a ship stretched but resilient. *Ranger* had endured a grueling few days, yet her crew remained professional and focused. Their diligence gave Steele a small measure of comfort. They weren't out of the woods yet, but *Ranger* and her people had proven time and again they were capable of meeting the challenges that came their way.

"Captain," Ishida said softly, breaking the stillness, "no changes to report on the HTD. Enemy vessels are holding their current search pattern, and there are no new contacts of note."

Steele gave her a slight nod, his gaze flicking to the tactical display. "Understood, Guns. Continue to keep me updated."

Returning to his tasks, he pushed down the nagging sense of unease that lingered at the edges of his thoughts. Quiet moments like these were rare and precious, but they were also when complacency could creep in. Steele wouldn't let that happen. Not on his watch. It was one of the reasons he required continual updates that others might consider a waste of time.

"Sir," Ishida's voice broke the steady hum of the bridge. "The survey probes have reached the target area and are dispersing according to plan, using maneuvering jets and propellant only. No communication has been established yet—this is just a time update, marking when they were expected to arrive."

Steele shifted slightly in his command chair, his eyes narrowing as he focused on the HTD display. "Understood. So, we can't confirm how many made it to their positions, how many survived?"

"Not until I send the activation sequence," Ishida replied.

"How long until they're all in position?" Steele asked, his tone carrying the weight of the unknown.

"Approximately twenty-five minutes, sir." Ishida paused for a moment. "But to be absolutely certain, I'd recommend giving it thirty-five minutes. It's a dense field, and some of the probes may need additional time to navigate around obstacles to reach the correct coordinates and settle down."

Steele nodded, his expression thoughtful as he processed the information. "Thirty-five minutes, then. Let's not take any chances. Ping the XO five minutes before activation. She'll want to be here for this."

"Yes, sir," Ishida confirmed, her focus unwavering.

Steele reached for his coffee and took a sip, noting the near-emptiness of the cup. He considered calling for a fresh one but decided against it for now. The hiss of the bridge hatch drew his attention. Turning in his chair, he saw Governor Tancrest standing just inside the lift, her posture hesitant, as if unsure whether to proceed.

"It's all right, Governor," Steele said. He took in her appearance. She'd cleaned up and changed into a borrowed ship's suit, its lines fitting her well enough. Her hair was neatly tied back into a single braid, and though her face still bore traces of the stress she had endured, the exhaustion had largely faded. A few hours of rest and recovery had done her some real good. "Welcome to the bridge."

Tancrest stepped forward, the hatch hissing shut behind her. Her gaze swept the small space, taking in the quiet hum of activity as the crew worked at their stations. For a moment, she stood silently, absorbing the controlled atmosphere, then made her way toward Steele's station.

"How are you holding up?" Steele asked, turning slightly to face her.

"Better," she admitted. "A shower and some real sleep helped."

"Did you eat?" Steele's tone carried the quiet authority of someone accustomed to ensuring his people were looked after.

She nodded. "I did. Thank you. Has anything happened?"

"Nothing significant yet. But we should have some developments soon. Our probes have reached the target area."

"Where you believe the Hegemony fleet might be?" she asked with curiosity and unease.

"Exactly," Steele confirmed with a nod. He gestured toward the empty executive officer's chair. "You're welcome to sit there if you like."

"Thank you, Captain." Moving with a touch more confidence now, Tancrest crossed the bridge and settled into Chase's station. Her hands brushed over the controls, and she tapped a screen to bring up a display. For a moment, she studied it in silence, then gave a faint smile. "This reminds me of my time in service."

Steele raised an eyebrow. "You served?"

"Yes," she said, her gaze distant for a moment, lost in memory. "A long time ago I was a bridge officer. Nothing glamorous. But sitting at a station like this feels... familiar."

"Well, feel free to stay and observe. Just don't push any buttons. Chase won't be happy if anything goes wrong with her console settings."

Tancrest gave a quiet laugh, the sound easing some of the tension that lingered on the bridge. "Noted, Captain. I'll try to restrain myself."

"So, you were in the navy?" Steele asked, his curiosity piqued as he glanced over at Tancrest.

"During the great war," Tancrest said, her voice carrying a note of pride and nostalgia. "I served as a lieutenant aboard the *Ordinai*, a light cruiser."

"What Academy class?" Steele inquired, leaning slightly toward her.

"Sixty-nine. You?"

"Sixty-eight," Steele replied with a faint smile of recognition. "Just missed each other, then."

"Apparently."

"Why'd you leave service?" Steele pressed, intrigued.

Tancrest exhaled softly, her gaze drifting for a moment. "My father was in the diplomatic corps at the time. After the war ended, Fleet demobilized. I was looking at a long stretch in grade before any real chance of promotion. The opportunities in the diplomatic corps were more immediate... and promising, especially with the aftermath of our victory."

Steele gave a slow nod, understanding her reasoning all too well. After the war, a lot of people had mustered out of the service. Promotion in a peacetime navy was notoriously slow. He himself had spent longer than he cared to remember waiting for his turn to advance. First to executive officer, then finally to command a light frigate.

"It was a difficult time for a lot of us who chose to stay," Steele admitted quietly. Memories of long years of grinding bureaucracy and scarce opportunities came unbidden, tempered only by his commitment to his duty and service to the Union.

"You seem to have done all right for yourself." Tancrest looked around the bridge, taking in the sleek, efficient design of *Ranger*. "This is quite the ship, Captain."

"She is," Steele said, a note of pride slipping into his voice. His hand rested on the armrest of his command chair, fingers tapping lightly against the worn padding. "At the moment, she's a bit battered and worse for wear, but she's a good ship. Strong, reliable."

Tancrest offered a faint smile, her gaze meeting Steele's. "I'm sure she is."

"Sir," Ishida spoke up. "I'm detecting increased scan emissions near the listening post. If I had to guess, one of the ships picked up the energy spike from the transport in the hangar bay."

"Very good." Steele's eyes snapped to the HTD. He studied the faint blip representing the distant LDF ship. "Do you have a lock on her?"

"Vaguely, sir," Ishida said, her fingers moving over her console. "I can't determine the class from this distance—we've traveled too far and there is a lot of interference from the field."

"Is there any danger to us?" Tancrest asked, leaning slightly forward in her borrowed seat, her expression taut as she studied the HTD herself.

"Not to *Ranger*," Steele said, his gaze steady on the screen. "They're too far away to pose an immediate threat."

Ishida nodded, her attention returning to her displays. The HTD flashed suddenly, drawing all eyes back to the plot.

"Energy spike and discharge," Ishida reported, her tone clipped. "They've struck one of the mines. It looks like a direct hit."

"Mines?" Tancrest turned to Steele with a mixture of surprise and curiosity. "You deployed mines?"

"I left them a few surprises," Steele said, a wry grin touching his lips.

"I didn't realize active-duty ships carried mines during peacetime," she said with disbelief.

"They don't." Steele's grin faded, replaced by a grim seriousness. "And this is no longer peacetime."

The HTD flashed again, this time with a more violent intensity, followed by another burst a fraction of a second later.

"Two more good hits," Ishida reported with a note of satisfaction. "The rest of the mines are likely in motion."

Steele remained silent, his gaze fixed on the screen as another flash lit up the display.

"I'm detecting heightened scan emissions," Ishida continued. "Looks like point-defense fire. They're engaging the mines."

The bridge seemed to hold its collective breath as a series of energy bursts lit up the HTD, each corresponding to mines being struck down. But even as the enemy's PDS cleared some of the mines, others detonated in rapid succession. The flashes came in blinding waves, their intensity briefly overwhelming the sensors.

"Multiple detonations," Ishida reported, her voice now tight with focus. "Their shields are taking the brunt of it. That can't be good for them."

The HTD flashed again with another detonation.

"It's a destroyer, sir," Ishida said with an undercurrent of excitement. "I've got a solid reading on her drive signature. She's trying to break free of the trap—detecting significant acceleration."

The hatch to the bridge hissed open, drawing Steele's attention briefly as Chase and Quinn entered. Chase stopped midstride, her gaze locking onto the main screen. The HTD display dominated the room, focused on the listening post and the chaotic engagement unfolding there.

"I see one of the LDF destroyers found the party favors we left for them," Chase said with dry humor.

She moved toward them. Tancrest looked up and immediately stood from Chase's station, stepping aside with a polite nod.

"Thank you, Governor Tancrest," Chase said as she settled into her seat, her hands moving instinctively to her controls.

The bridge hatch opened again, this time admitting Hale, who crossed the deck swiftly to his station. Cole rose from the helm before stepping off the bridge. Hale slid into place.

The HTD flashed violently, its brightness catching everyone's attention.

"Shields have failed on the destroyer," Ishida reported. "I'm reading secondary explosions—her hull integrity is compromised. She's hurt bad."

Steele leaned forward, his grip tightening on the armrest of his command chair as he watched the plot. A brilliant burst of light erupted on the HTD, momentarily washing out the area where the LDF destroyer was on the plot.

"Massive energy release—reactor breach," Ishida called out.

As the display resolved, the destroyer was no longer there. In its place was a navigational hazard tag, marking the wreckage and expanding cloud of debris.

"She's gone," Ishida confirmed, her voice carrying a note of triumph. "One of her reactors breached containment."

For a brief moment, silence filled the bridge, broken only by the faint hum of the ship's systems. Steele felt an intense wave of satisfaction course through him, though he kept his expression measured. *Ranger* had struck deep, proving once again that she was a force to be reckoned with, even alone, battered, and outnumbered.

"Well done," Chase said quietly, her eyes scanning the HTD. "One less enemy to worry about."

"Sir," Quinn said, "I'm picking up a significant increase in activity. Multiple ships are in the area now. They're lighting up and I'm reading intensive scans from at least three of the vessels in the proximity of the downed destroyer. They've raised their shields to maximum power."

The bridge hatch hissed open once more, and Calder stepped through with purposeful strides, heading directly to her station.

"Of course they have," Steele said with grim satisfaction. "They've just watched one of their destroyers turn into scrap. Caution would be the natural response—they won't want to share her fate. With luck, their hesitation will give us the window we need to slip away unnoticed."

"Sir," Ishida said, "the probes should be in position by now."

Chase turned toward Steele, her brow furrowed with anticipation. "Should we send the signal now or wait? What are your thoughts, sir?"

Steele leaned back slightly. The decision wasn't without danger—activating the probes with a transmission risked giving away their presence and position. But with the enemy preoccupied by their loss and scanning for potential threats, the moment seemed right.

After a pause, he gave a decisive nod. "Do it."

"Comms," Chase ordered, "send the activation signal to the probes. One pulse only—make it quick."

"Aye, aye, sir," Calder replied.

Steele bent forward, keying a command on his HTD to shift the display's focus toward the Exclusion Zone, where the probes had been concentrated. Ishida mirrored the action on the main screen, adjusting the plot to highlight the sector. Steele's gaze locked onto the map.

"Transmission sent," Calder announced crisply. "One pulse only. Powering down the array now."

His eyes remained glued to the HTD, where the Exclusion Zone shimmered faintly under the plot's overlay.

"All right," Steele said, his tone steady. "Now we wait."

The bridge fell silent as every crew member watched their screens, waiting for the probes to respond and reveal what secrets lay hidden in the graveyard of ships... if there were any. Every second felt like an eternity, the quiet punctuated only by the soft hum of the ship and the faint tap of fingers on consoles.

Silence reigned on the bridge, heavy and unbroken save for the faint hum of the ship's systems. Every officer's attention was locked on their screens as the seconds ticked by with excruciating slowness.

Ishida's voice broke the quiet. "I'm reading multiple detonations in the target zone."

Bright flares appeared on the display, sharp and unmistakable—high-yield detonations erupting in the blackness of space where nothing should have been. The probes had done their work, their compression torpedo warheads detonating in calculated succession, ripping through the void and sending their explosive fury outward in radiating waves.

"Five... six... seven detonations, sir," Ishida continued, her voice rising slightly as more flashes illuminated the darkness. A brief pause followed as she scanned her displays. "Ten... twelve detonations. I can't tell yet if they've struck anything directly or if these are even near misses."

"I know." Steele's tone was measured and calm, though his grip on the armrest tightened. "That's not what I'm after."

Tancrest turned toward him. A mix of shock and curiosity was etched across her face as her eyes darted between Steele and the main screen. "What have you done?" The HTD displayed the unfolding chaos in the Exclusion Zone—energy discharges, shockwaves spreading through the debris field like ripples on a pond. "Based on those energy signatures, you've armed probes with torpedo warheads. Why? Why go to all that trouble?"

Steele didn't immediately answer, his gaze fixed on the HTD. His silence was pointed, deliberate, as if weighing whether to address the question at all.

"I don't understand," Tancrest pressed. "What could you possibly hope to achieve with this?"

"Second set of probes should be going live... now," Ishida reported.

The bridge remained tense as Steele waited, the seconds dragging on like hours.

Tancrest stepped closer to the main screen, her arms crossed, eyes narrowing as if willing the HTD to give her answers faster.

"Telemetry incoming," Ishida announced, cutting through the silence like a blade.

A single data tag appeared on the HTD, its faint blue glow standing out against the vast blackness of space. It blinked for a moment, neutral and unassuming, before rapidly shifting to a vivid red, pulsing with urgency and plain warning.

"She's a big one," Ishida reported. "Atheena has tentatively identified her as a Koenigsberg Class heavy cruiser. Her shields are going up, and one of the detonations was close enough to scorch her hull."

Steele's eyes narrowed as another tag appeared, followed quickly by yet another. Both transitioned to red in rapid succession, the enemy's presence solidifying before them. Then, like floodgates opening, a dozen more tags lit up the display in quick order, flashing red as more ships dropped their stealth fields and raised shields.

"Holy shit," Chase breathed, her voice barely above a whisper as even more tags flared into existence, painting the HTD like a macabre constellation of red.

The hatch to the bridge hissed open, drawing Steele's attention for a fleeting moment. Both Miller and Zeldin stepped in, their expressions darkening as their eyes locked onto the screen. Without waiting for an invitation, they moved forward, stopping near Steele's station.

"Well, Mr. Miller," Steele said, gesturing at the main screen, his voice laced with a fierce satisfaction, "it looks like we've found your fleet."

Miller's gaze was fixed on the display, his jaw tightening. "I can see that," he said grimly. "The Valkorian Hegemony..."

"War," Steele said plainly, feeling his gut tighten. He had another flash of the bombardment of Mortain. "Once more, the Union is in a fight with the Hegemony."

There was a long moment of silence.

"This really means war," Tancrest said quietly. Her horror was plain.

"Sir," Ishida interjected with urgency, "they're firing on our probes. We're going to lose signal shortly."

Steele gave a slight nod, his focus unwavering. "I understand. Do you have a count on what's out there?"

"I do, sir," she said after a moment. "Atheena has classified six as battle wagons, twelve heavy cruisers, at least two carriers, four assault transports, and thirty-two smaller vessels of destroyer and frigate class." She hesitated briefly. "There are likely more out there that we didn't unmask."

"That's still a powerful force," Chase said. "Almost too powerful."

"Yes," Steele agreed, leaning back in his chair. The tension in his posture didn't ease, though, as his mind churned through the implications. "Illidran is now clearly held by our enemy and it will take a serious effort to unseat them, especially with a force like that entrenched here. There's no doubt in my mind more will come or, for that matter, are already on the way."

The bridge fell silent again. The sheer size and strength of the Valkorian Hegemony's fleet was undeniable—and terrifying. *Ranger* had uncovered the truth.

An alarm blared sharply from Quinn's station. Steele's gaze snapped toward Quinn, whose head had already swiveled to the flashing indicator on her screen.

"Active scans, Captain!" Quinn reported, her voice tight. "They're powerful, high intensity. We've been spotted!"

"Which means they're close," Steele surmised, his tone hardening. "Chase, battle stations. Quinn, raise shields. Helm, bring the gravitic drive to full military power."

"Aye, aye, sir," Chase responded as the alert klaxons blared to life throughout the ship. The bridge lights dimmed, bathing the crew in the sharp glow of their displays as *Ranger* shifted to full combat readiness.

"Sir," Ishida's voice cut in sharply. "I'm reading a battle-cruiser off our port quarter, less than fifty thousand kilometers out. She's just dropped her stealth field and is raising shields." There was a pause. "It's the *Starfish*!"

Steele's jaw clenched at the name. If anything, that battle-cruiser should be near Tenebris. "The *Starfish*? What the bloody hell is she doing all the way out here?"

"She must have detected our transmission," Chase said. "I'd wager the LDF stationed her on the far side of the Reach, part of a net to intercept any potential escape attempts—likely the governor's transport if it had made a break for open space."

"She's targeting us, sir!" Ishida reported with an urgent edge as her display flashed with new readings.

Steele's mind raced. The *Starfish* was one of the better-equipped ships in Illidran's defense fleet. If she had dropped stealth and locked onto *Ranger*, there was little doubt about her intentions.

They were in deep shit.

This wasn't going to be about running—it was going to be about surviving.

TWENTY-TWO

"Guns!" Steele barked, his eyes locked on the plot. "I want a targeting solution on the *Starfish*—yesterday. Charge maser cannons and load the missile batteries."

"Working on it," Ishida replied, her hands flying over her console, the tactical displays lighting up in rapid succession.

"Quinn," Steele snapped, "electronic warfare now! Start jamming her targeting systems. Spin up the PDS—get it ready to fire."

"Aye, aye, sir!" Quinn responded, already rerouting power to the countermeasure suite and activating the point-defense system. The hum of energy coursing through the ship was almost physical as she ramped up to full power.

Steele turned his attention back to the HTD, studying the *Starfish*'s position. She was far too close for comfort, her gravity drive and power levels glowing on the HTD as she powered up, shields climbing steadily. His mind raced as he adjusted the ship's tactical position and began working on a new plot and course.

"We need separation," Chase said urgently, her voice taut with tension. "They're too close for comfort."

"Helm, new course. I just sent it to you," Steele snapped, already ahead of her. "Execute at maximum acceleration."

"Aye, sir." Hale's hands were steady as he keyed in the new vector. *Ranger* began to pivot, the gravitic drive blossoming and roaring to life as the ship pushed hard against inertia.

"She's launched!" Ishida called. "Twenty-two missiles inbound. Time to impact: twenty seconds."

"Point-defense system—engage!" Steele ordered, before looking back at Ishida. He'd just had an idea... the book in his office, *Command Decisions* and the chapter he'd read a few days back—the one on Captain Jabob Thomas's stand. "Guns, what's the charge on the maser cannons?"

"Fifty-nine percent, sir, and climbing," Ishida replied, her focus sharp.

"Target those incoming missiles with the main batteries," Steele said.

"With the maser cannons?" Ishida sounded incredulous, her head jerking toward him.

"Those missiles are too close for advanced evasive maneuvers. If we're lucky, we might take one or two out with a lucky shot. Now bloody well do it! That's an order!"

"Targeting now," Ishida said.

"PDS firing!" Quinn called. The bridge filled with the low rumble of automated turrets and the bright hissing of energy discharges as the point-defense system went active. *Ranger's* defenses lit up, throwing kinetic slugs and energy pulses into the rapidly closing missile swarm.

Steele's eyes flicked between the incoming projectiles and the plot, tension coiling in his gut. The *Starfish* wasn't giving them any room to breathe and there was certainly no time for any evasive maneuvers.

"I don't think anyone's ever used main batteries as PDS before," Chase muttered, her voice strained.

"They have," Steele said. "I've read about it."

"You read about it?" Chase cast him a skeptical look.

"I did."

"Main batteries firing!" Ishida announced. On the HTD, bright beams of energy lanced out, slashing through the blackness toward the incoming missile swarm. Steele's unconventional strategy had turned *Ranger* into a deadly porcupine, bristling with defenses, throwing everything she had at the *Starfish*'s attack.

Steele's stomach twisted into a tight knot as the enemy ship-killer missiles streaked toward *Ranger*, their bright, ominous trails burning on the tactical plot. The grouping was unnervingly precise. He barely dared to blink, his fingers gripping the armrests of his command chair as death sped rapidly their way.

The missiles closed the last few thousand kilometers in a blur, the distance shrinking alarmingly fast. Then, almost as one, they vanished from the plot in a series of brilliant flashes.

"Good hits!" Ishida called out. "All missiles are down... no, wait... one missile still inbound."

"Quinn!" Chase snapped, her voice cutting through the tension like a whip. "Hit that missile!"

"Targeting it with all PDS batteries!" Quinn barked back. There was a long, agonizing pause as the PDS turrets recalibrated, the hum of rapid-fire kinetic and energy discharges filling the bridge.

"Good hit," Quinn announced, her voice breaking the silence. "Missile is down."

A collective sigh rippled through the bridge. Steele exhaled, then leaned forward, his gaze snapping back to the HTD. "Guns! TOT attack, maximum two volleys. Are missiles loaded and ready?"

"They are ready, sir," Ishida confirmed, her tone steady despite the adrenaline. "Ready to kill them dead, sir."

"Fire," Steele commanded.

"Firing!" Ishida reported sharply. "Missiles away."

On the plot, Steele watched as *Ranger's* two missile pods flushed, releasing twenty missiles into the void in quick succession. But instead of streaking directly toward the *Starfish*, they arced outward, spreading like predatory birds circling their prey.

"Twenty good launches," Ishida reported with satisfaction, her eyes on her screens. "Reloading... forty-five seconds until the next volley."

Steele's eyes remained glued to the plot as they waited for the second wave to be launched. He watched the missiles fan out into space, their trajectories adjusting dynamically. Each missile was a hunter, its AI systems calculating the best approach vector to bypass the *Starfish's* defenses. The enemy ship loomed on the HTD, her shield profile bright, powerful, and unmistakable.

"What's the charge on the maser cannons?" Steele asked.

"Just shy of twenty percent," Ishida reported.

Steele considered their options for a fraction of a second. "Target the *Starfish* and fire. I know it's extreme range, but let's remind them we're here and they can be hurt."

"Firing," Ishida confirmed. The hum of the maser batteries releasing reverberated faintly through the ship, a low and menacing growl. Moments later, a streak of energy surged outward from *Ranger*, slicing through the darkness of space.

"Sir," Quinn interrupted, "I've got two new contacts. Both frigates. They've dropped stealth, raised shields, and are under power. Adding them to the board now."

Steele's gaze darted to the HTD as two new markers flared to life, their identifiers plain against the expanse of space. He scrolled out to get a wider view and spotted the frigates' positions. One was slightly over two hundred thousand kilometers distant, the other at four hundred thousand—far enough to pose no immediate threat.

"At this range, neither will influence the outcome of our engagement with the *Starfish*," Steele observed.

"It looks like the LDF set up a screen." Chase glanced at the governor, who stood silently with Miller and Zeldin near the edge of the bridge. Both men seemed transfixed by the tactical plot.

"A screen?" Zeldin asked, his brow furrowing. "What do you mean?"

"To catch the governor if she came out of the Reach," Chase explained.

Steele gave a curt nod. "Unfortunate for us, then."

"Hits confirmed on the *Starfish*," Ishida said. "Her shields flared but held steady. No significant degradation to speak of, sir."

"Recharge the cannons," Steele ordered. *Ranger* was already pushing 20g and still accelerating, her gravitic drive humming as it worked to its limits. On the plot, the enemy battlecruiser loomed, her acceleration far slower at only 10g. It didn't matter —*Ranger* was well within her engagement envelope, and Steele knew it. "Prepare to intercept and fire on any incoming volley."

"Cannons recharging," Ishida reported.

"Do we have an estimated reload time for the *Starfish*?" Chase asked, leaning forward. "What's in the records?"

"Seventy-two seconds between missile volleys, ma'am," Ishida replied.

"Very good," Steele said, his attention shifting back to the tactical plot. He studied the positioning of *Starfish* and the two incoming frigates. The closest frigate was maneuvering into a firing arc, slowly creeping into a position where she could bring her missile batteries to bear on *Ranger*. Steele's mind raced, calculating their options.

"Guns," Steele said, "after this next missile volley at *Starfish*, load long lances and target the closest frigate."

"That's a long shot, sir," Chase said, casting him a doubtful glance. "They'll have plenty of time to react."

"I know," Steele replied. "I want another TOT attack on them. Let them think we've got more to throw at them than we actually do."

"But, sir," Ishida said hesitantly, "we only have ten Mark Sevens left in the magazine."

"They don't know that," Steele said, his voice hard. "Just do it."

"Aye, sir," Ishida replied, and her hands moved over her controls with renewed purpose. "Second volley up. Firing at *Starfish*."

On the plot, *Ranger*'s two missile pods flushed, spitting out twenty missiles that streaked into the void, their drives flaring brightly.

"Twenty good launches on *Starfish*," Ishida reported. "Reloading with long lances now."

Steele's gaze shifted to the HTD, where the missile launches were displayed in sharp clarity. The second volley streaked toward the incoming battlecruiser. Meanwhile, the first volley had altered course, their drives now burning bright as they accelerated hard toward the *Starfish*. It was a time on target maneuver. *Ranger*'s broadside—twenty missiles—now effectively became forty, both volleys timed to arrive in one near-simultaneous barrage. This tactic gave the smaller ship the firepower of a much larger vessel, at least for a moment. Steele hoped it would give him the edge in this knife fight.

"Thirty-five seconds to impact," Ishida reported. "Reloading missile pod one to fire on the frigate. Sir, what do you want done with the second pod?"

"Reload standards and retarget the *Starfish* with the other ten," Steele said without hesitation. "Send them my love."

"Yes, sir," Ishida replied, then paused. "Incoming! *Starfish* has launched another volley. Twenty-two missiles inbound. Thirty-eight seconds until impact."

Steele's gut clenched at her words, but he kept his voice calm and steady. "Quinn," he said, glancing at his electronic warfare officer, "work your magic."

"Aye, aye, sir," Quinn replied, already engaged at her station. The holographic interface around him flickered with data streams as she activated jamming frequencies and coordinated the ship's point-defense systems.

"*Starfish* has a capacity for thirty missile launches," Chase said, her voice tense but thoughtful. "Why only twenty-two?"

Steele glanced at her, his mind racing even as he analyzed the HTD. "*Starfish* is an older ship, well past her prime. There's no telling what systems are still functional—or if they've been cannibalized for parts."

Chase nodded in understanding, her gaze returning to her own displays.

"EW active," Quinn reported, his voice tight with focus. "Jamming initiated. PDS batteries are online and firing."

On the HTD, *Ranger*'s defensive systems came alive, thundering outward at the incoming missile volley. Automated kinetic rounds and energy discharges filled the space behind them, creating a deadly net designed to intercept the incoming missiles. On the HTD, the glowing contrails of the enemy projectiles burned toward the ship, closing the distance with terrifying speed. Every second stretched into an eternity as the bridge crew worked with cold efficiency.

Steele's knuckles whitened as he gripped the armrests of his command chair, his gaze locked on the HTD. The unfolding battle played out in detached, clinical precision, with data tags and icons dancing across the screen. Yet, despite the sterile nature of it all, the reality was raw and deeply personal. They meant to kill him, his crew, and to break his ship, to destroy *Ranger*. His mission, his ship—everything—hung in the balance.

In return, he aimed to do the same to them. It didn't get more personal than this.

"Enemy countermeasures and PDS fire detected," Ishida reported. "Wow... she's throwing up a wall of fire."

Steele's eyes narrowed at the plot, where *Ranger*'s volley of missiles was streaking toward the *Starfish* and on final approach. The battlecruiser's defenses were formidable, her PDS churning out rapid bursts of energy and kinetic fire to intercept the incoming ordnance. On the display, missile after missile winked out, consumed by the blinding flashes of her countermeasures. Still, the remaining projectiles pressed on, fighting the storm to breach her defenses.

At that moment, Steele felt the weight of the comparison between the two ships. The reality of what he was facing hammered home. The *Starfish* was nearly as large as a battle-ship, bristling with heavy guns and powerful defenses. *Ranger*—despite being state-of-the-art—was a mere destroyer, much smaller in size and power. The thought of it alone brought home the reality of the odds they faced.

"Guns?" Chase's voice broke the tension of the moment. "Do we have torpedoes ready to go? Can they make the turn if we fire now?"

Steele's eyes flicked back to the display. Five of *Ranger*'s missiles disappeared in rapid succession, obliterated by the *Starfish*'s PDS fire. Then another two were struck down as the volley closed the gap.

"They can make the turn, ma'am," Ishida replied with urgency, "just barely, given our speed, but they can do it. That said, they'll be highly vulnerable to the enemy's PDS once in the open."

Steele didn't hesitate. "Fire the torpedoes, Guns. Let them bloody have it."

"Firing," Ishida reported, her fingers dancing over her

console. "Two good launches. Torpedoes away. Torpedoes away!"

On the HTD, the pair of torpedoes appeared, their icons blinking to life as they raced away from *Ranger*. They moved like predators, their guidance systems already locked onto the *Starfish*. Fired from the bow of the ship, the path the torpedoes took was not direct, curving to arc widely back toward the enemy ship.

"Sixty-five seconds to torpedo impact," Ishida added.

Steele's gaze stayed locked on the HTD, the swirling chaos of data and icons reflecting the deadly ballet of combat. He didn't bother looking at the others—his focus was on the volley he'd launched at the *Starfish*, the one in final approach. The battlecruiser's defenses were carving through the missile wave like a butcher with a cleaver.

Ten of his missiles were obliterated in rapid succession, their signals vanishing from the plot. A few seconds later, another five winked out, followed swiftly by two more.

"Come on," Steele muttered under his breath. The remaining missiles were weaving and juking, their advanced guidance systems doing their best to outmaneuver the *Starfish*'s countermeasures and reach the target. Burning in at velocities between 100 and 150g—speeds and stresses no living being could endure—the missiles were pushing the limits of their maneuverability. They zigged and zagged, fighting to avoid the torrents of fire aimed at them.

Then, they struck.

The icons representing the remaining missiles merged with the *Starfish* on the HTD. A brilliant, searing flash of energy flared across the display, momentarily distorting the feed. Steele felt a fierce surge of satisfaction. He had hit the *Starfish*—and hit her hard.

But how hard?

"Firing main batteries at incoming missiles," Ishida said.

Steele's gaze snapped back to the new threat: the *Starfish's* retaliatory broadside was still inbound. A swarm of missiles streaked toward *Ranger* at lethal speed, their energy signatures glowing ominously on the plot. His stomach tightened into a knot as he watched the deadly dance unfold.

Ranger was desperately fighting back with everything she had. Her point-defense systems were spitting kinetic projectiles and concentrated energy bursts outward, while electronic warfare systems scrambled to spoof, confuse, and misdirect the enemy's incoming ordnance. A few missiles wavered, veering off course before detonating harmlessly. Then, one by one, more missiles began disappearing from the plot as the point-defense began to take a toll.

"Two down..." Ishida murmured. "Five more gone."

The barrage was thinning, but not fast enough. Steele could feel it in his gut. They were about to be hurt. He clenched his jaw as the remaining missiles closed in on their final approach, their trails streaking through the last few thousand kilometers with terrifying rapidity.

"Shit," Chase breathed, her knuckles whitening as she gripped the edge of her console. "Brace! Braaa—"

Ranger rocked violently, her entire frame groaning under the force of the impact. Steele's head snapped back against the headrest as a deafening roar filled the bridge. A brilliant flare of light washed across the room, momentarily blinding him, followed by an intense wave of heat that prickled against his skin.

The lights flickered wildly, casting chaotic shadows across the walls, and then plunged the bridge into darkness. For a brief, terrifying moment, the only sound was the creaking and groaning of the hull, snapping and popping loudly, followed by the distant rumble of secondary explosions. Then, with a metallic *clunk*, the emergency lighting snapped on, bathing the bridge in dim red hues.

Steele's chest heaved as he tried to steady his breathing. His automatic restraints had engaged, locking him firmly into his station. He winced as he became aware of a sharp, metallic taste in his mouth. Blood. His tongue throbbed painfully—he must have bitten it.

The consoles at his station sputtered as they attempted to reboot, the displays flashing error messages and resetting slowly. A faint but acrid smell of smoke reached his nostrils, mingled with the sharper tang of scorched circuitry and something worse: burned flesh. He could hear the distant hiss of the air scrubbers struggling to clear the contaminants from the atmosphere.

"Report," Steele demanded, his voice cutting through the smoke-filled air.

"My station is still resetting," Ishida said. Sparks sputtered from nearby wiring and cabling that dangled from the overhead, casting erratic flashes in the dim red emergency lighting.

"Quinn's down!" Chase's voice was sharp, tinged with alarm. Steele snapped his gaze over to see Quinn sprawled on the deck, her right cheek and side an angry, blistering red. She'd been badly burned. A jagged piece of the wall above her station had been blown inward, leaving a blackened hole surrounded by warped metal. Steele's stomach twisted at the sight.

"Atheena," Chase called. "Medical to the bridge!"

"Notifying medical," the ship's construct replied instantly, her calm, measured tones contrasting sharply with the chaos around them.

Steele gripped the armrest of his chair, glancing at his screens, which were still rebooting, their systems sluggishly coming back online. His jaw tightened; the delay told him all he needed to know. *Ranger* had taken a serious hit. His ship was hurt.

"Atheena," he barked. "Damage report."

"Captain, I am still assessing damage. However, I can report the ship has sustained multiple impacts," Atheena responded smoothly, though the weight of her words made his chest tighten. "Damage is moderate to serious. I am detecting several hull breaches across multiple decks. Emergency bulkheads are sealing affected sections. There are two fires that have yet to be contained and there are also reports of casualties throughout the ship. Shields are currently in a nonfunctional state."

"What about the gravitic drive?"

"The gravitic drive remains operational. We are maintaining thrust. The ship is currently accelerating at 32gs and climbing."

Steele allowed himself a moment of grim relief at that last bit of news.

"Thank you for small miracles," Chase muttered, her voice low but audible. She hadn't taken her eyes off Quinn, whose chest was faintly rising and falling—a sign she was still alive.

Steele forced his attention back to the bridge as his main display finally flickered to life, displaying a battered but still-functioning status readout. "Ishida, the moment your station is up, I need targeting back online."

Just then, the rest of the screens at Steele's station flickered back to life with a series of sharp beeps. He leaned forward, his eyes narrowing as he studied the ship's plot. *Ranger* was a degree off course—barely noticeable, but enough to tell him how hard the blast had rocked them. Despite the deviation, they were still moving in the general direction plotted before the hit.

His gaze shifted to the status board. Red and amber lights dominated the display, each representing a system that was damaged or nonfunctional. Precious few lights gleamed green, speaking to just how badly *Ranger* had been hit. Even the gravitic drive was showing an amber warning light.

"Still moving... and in one piece," Steele muttered under his breath, his jaw tightening. His gaze flicked to the *Starfish* on the plot. The battlecruiser was still there, too, lumbering through space, but her readings were incomplete. Sensor systems were sluggishly gathering data, likely hindered by the interference from residual energy discharges.

He knew they had hit her... but how hard?

"Guns, what's the status of our weapons?" Steele demanded.

Ishida's reply came slowly, her words slurring slightly. "Missile pods are functional... but half our masers are offline."

Steele glanced over his shoulder. Ishida was still at her station, blood trickling down her cheek and streaming from her forehead. She looked dazed but determined as she continued working.

Miller and Zeldin were crouched beside Quinn. A medical pack lay open between them, its contents scattered across the deck. Zeldin was carefully applying a burn salve to the angry red wound on Quinn's face, while Miller worked to stabilize her vitals.

Governor Tancrest, who had been thrown to the deck during the blast, was now pulling herself upright using the back of a nearby chair. Her movements were slow and deliberate. A dark bruise marred her cheekbone, evidence of the impact she'd taken. She caught Steele's eye and gave a small, tight nod, brushing dust from her borrowed ship's suit.

"Governor, are you all right?" Steele asked, glancing at her briefly before turning his attention back to the HTD.

"I've had better days." Her eyes flicked to the screens, clearly trying to assess the situation. "But I'm still standing. What about the ship?"

Steele didn't answer immediately. His focus was on the *Starfish*'s hazy readings. "We're still in the fight," he finally said with determination. "But we're going to need every trick we've got to stay that way."

As if to punctuate his words, a status alert flashed across his screen. Another subsystem had failed, life support on deck three. Steele ignored it for now—priorities had to be managed. He glanced back at Ishida and saw her pressing a rag against her temple and forehead as she wiped away blood, still working despite her injuries. Smoke lingered in the air, illuminated by the red emergency lights that cast a hellish glow over the scene.

"Tancrest," Steele said sharply, his gaze locking onto the governor. "Kindly take over at EW."

"What?" Tancrest glanced between Steele and the blood-spattered console, as though unsure she'd heard him correctly.

"You were a serving officer in the navy. You can man that console, and I need someone there before *Starfish* shoots at us again. Atheena, grant the governor full access."

"Access granted, Captain," the ship's construct replied coolly.

Tancrest hesitated, her eyes lingering on the console. The screens flickered steadily, displaying the status of the electronic warfare systems and the pulsing readouts of the PDS arrays. The sight of Quinn's blood staining the surface seemed to root her in place. "But it's been ten years," she said, her voice softer now, tinged with doubt.

"It hasn't changed all that much since the last war." Steele's gaze was unrelenting as he leaned forward in his chair. He pointed at Quinn's empty station. "Someone operating PDS is better than no one. I have no doubt you can figure it out. Now, bloody do it!"

For a moment, Tancrest stood frozen, visibly grappling with her uncertainty. Then, with a curt nod, she straightened her back and squared her shoulders.

"Yes, sir," she said, her voice steadying.

She stepped forward and slid into the chair, visibly wincing as her hand brushed against the slick surface of the bloodstained console. Clearly pushing the discomfort aside, she tapped at the controls. The station came alive beneath her fingers, the inter-face responding.

"Atheena," Tancrest said, growing more confident, "display current jamming parameters."

"Displayed, Governor," the construct replied, the screens shifting to show the intricate web of active and passive jamming systems.

Tancrest scanned the information rapidly, her military training kicking in. "All right," she muttered, mostly to herself. "PDS array is active... targeting sequences are running. Jamming intensity set to auto-adaptive mode. I can work with this."

"That's the spirit," Steele said, a hint of approval in his tone. "Keep our defenses up and coordinate with Ishida. This isn't over yet."

"Understood, sir," Tancrest said.

"Sir," Ishida said. "Missiles are up. Do you still want the long lances targeted at the frigate, with our volley split?"

"I do. Fire when ready," Steele replied without hesitation. He turned his attention to Hale. "Helm, do you have control yet?"

"Flushing pods," Ishida reported. "Eighteen good launches, two misfires."

Hale was working at his console, his brow furrowed in concentration. "I do, sir. Just running diagnostics on the maneu-vering pods. Several are offline. I've reported them to damage control teams."

"Good. Get us back on course as soon as you can," Steele ordered.

"Aye, sir," Hale acknowledged.

Steele's gaze shifted to the HTD, the tactical display updating in real time. On the plot, the missiles streaked away, splitting into two groups. One volley angled toward the crippled *Starfish*, while the long lances adjusted their trajectory to the distant frigate and burned outward at a slower rate.

"Do we have an update on *Starfish*?" Steele asked.

Chase glanced up from her station. "I've been analyzing the data. It looks like we hit her harder than she hit us. Her shields are down. I repeat, *Starfish*'s shields are down."

Steele leaned forward, his attention narrowing. "And her status?"

"She's still on course and at speed, but her gravitic drive appears to be offline. We're rapidly pulling ahead. I'm also seeing power fluctuations—could be issues with her reactors."

"Could she still fire on us?" Steele asked.

"It's possible. But with no gravitic drive, she can't maneuver effectively, and those power fluctuations suggest she's struggling just to maintain systems. If her reactors fail outright, she's dead in the water."

Steele's gaze lingered on the HTD, where *Starfish*'s icon flickered faintly, surrounded by damage markers.

"Missile launch," Ishida announced. "Five inbound from *Starfish*. Impact in forty-seven seconds."

"EW," Steele snapped, turning his gaze to Tancrest, who was now manning Quinn's station. Her brow was furrowed in concentration as her fingers flew across the controls.

"PDS firing," Tancrest reported, her voice edged with strain. "EW systems are showing active, but they're actually nonfunctional. Damn it, I don't even know how many PDS cannons are operational."

Steele clenched his jaw. They were under immense pressure, but there was no time to dwell on the breakdowns. "Guns," he barked, "use the maser cannons again."

"Firing," Ishida replied. The hum of the cannons releasing reverberated faintly through the deck as they discharged.

"Helm," Steele ordered, "evasive maneuvers. Get us out of their firing solution."

"I'll do what I can, sir," Hale responded, calm despite the chaos. The ship shuddered as it banked, pushing the gravitic drive to its limits to evade the incoming missiles. "I am going to use the gravitic drive to shift our course at the last moment, if I can." He paused and glanced back at Steele. "I think *Ranger* can take it."

"Very good." Steele's eyes remained fixed on the plot, his stomach churning as the enemy missiles streaked closer. Each glowing icon represented a harbinger of death, and the grim reality of their situation pressed down on him like a weight. Was this it? Had everything they'd done—all the risks, all the sacrifices—been for nothing?

Then, one of the missiles winked out of existence on the plot, quickly followed by another. Relief flickered briefly, but the threat wasn't over. Two missiles remained, now on final approach. Steele's gut tightened further. They were seconds from impact.

"Hale," Steele barked, "do something. Do it now!"

Before the words fully left his mouth, *Ranger* lurched violently. The gravitic drive roared, gripping the very fabric of space-time and wrenching the ship into a desperate evasive maneuver to port. The sudden shift was something the ship was neither designed for nor meant to endure, especially at such high speeds.

Alarms blared throughout the bridge, shrill and deafening, as the inertial compensators fought valiantly to keep up with the abrupt and unnatural motion. The warp bubble surrounding the ship strained to its limits, the systems maintaining it teetering on the brink of collapse and catastrophic failure. Despite the restraints holding him in place, Steele was slammed hard against the left side of his command station, the impact nearly knocking the breath from his lungs. Someone cried out behind him, a sharp sound lost amidst the cacophony of noise.

Ranger groaned deeply, a sound like the anguished protest of a wounded beast, her frame shuddering under the tremendous strain. The deck beneath Steele's feet quaked, and for a fleeting moment, it felt as though the entire ship might tear herself apart.

The bridge lights flickered ominously before stabilizing, casting eerie shadows across the tense faces of the crew. Steele's station remained active this time, the glowing screens flickering but holding steady. Then everything went still, the trembling and shuddering settling down.

"Two misses!" Ishida called out, her voice strained, somewhat slurred, but triumphant. "One of the missiles detonated five hundred meters off our starboard side. The armored hull took some heat, but damage appears minimal. That last-minute trick using the gravitic drive may not have been good for the ship, but it saved us."

Steele exhaled sharply, the adrenaline pounding in his veins. "Good job, Hale!" he shouted. "Excellent work."

Hale glanced back from his station, grinning. "Thank you, sir. I thought we were screwed anyway, so I figured—why not risk a little?"

"Risk a little, gain a lot." Steele allowed himself a dry chuckle, then sobered. He understood just how close *Ranger* had come to suffering a catastrophic failure. "Just make sure you don't pull a stunt like that again, not anytime soon. I don't think the coils can take any more of that abuse, at least not today."

"What about our chief engineer?" Chase asked. "Hale, I am sure you just gave him a coronary." She paused and looked over at Steele. "Heck, the coils may need to be replaced after that..."

"Maybe even his shorts, ma'am," Hale replied.

Steele glanced over at Chase. Their eyes met and he nodded. The coils had clearly been stressed beyond reasonable limits and would likely need to be replaced. It was something else for the admiralty to be unhappy about. But that was a concern for later.

"Seriously, sir," Chase said, "our coils are bound to have

micro fracturing. Until they can be properly inspected, we're going to have to go easy on them."

"Helm, the XO's right, keep it steady from here on out," Steele said. "I want the coils to last until we're out of the system. I don't need the drive failing, not after everything we've been through, not now. Understand me?"

Hale's grin widened, though his eyes betrayed his worry. "Yes, sir. In the future, I'll try to keep the heart attacks to a minimum."

Steele let go a breath and turned toward Tancrest next. "Governor, if you can't find a job after this, there's a place for you in Fleet, on my bridge, if you want it."

Tancrest looked up briefly and gave him a weary nod. "Thank you, sir. I might just take you up on that..."

A groan drew Steele's attention toward the back of the bridge. Miller was helping Zeldin to his feet. The man's face was pale, and he was cradling his arm, which was bent at an unnatural angle.

"We've hit *Starfish* again," Chase reported. "At least three of our missiles scored direct hits."

Steele's gaze snapped to the HTD. The *Starfish*'s icon flickered as sensor data updated in real time. Her gravitic drive remained inert, and two of her reactors were offline, their signatures completely gone, likely an emergency shutdown event. The battlecruiser's power readings were faint, but even a crippled ship could still fire and Steele had no idea how much more *Ranger* could take. "What's her real status? Can she still shoot?"

Before Chase could answer, two brilliant flashes erupted on the HTD as both torpedoes struck home simultaneously, slamming into *Starfish* amidships. The armor-penetrating torpedoes, each equipped with miniaturized gravitic drives, burrowed deep into the battlecruiser's heart before detonating with a ferocity designed to gut ships her size.

The HTD feed distorted momentarily as two new suns

formed within the heart of *Starfish*. When it cleared, *Starfish* was gone—ripped completely apart. Steele watched, feeling grim satisfaction as the battlecruiser broke in two. Secondary explosions rippled through the wreckage, and then her final reactor lost containment. The resulting blast was catastrophic, vaporizing what remained of the vessel and taking every soul aboard with her into the next life, leaving only an expanding cloud of debris and gas behind to mark her passing.

The bridge fell into a stunned silence, broken only by the faint crackle of static from damaged systems. Steele felt the tension in his chest ease, replaced by an almost surreal sense of finality.

"Scratch one battlecruiser," Chase said softly, her voice barely above a whisper.

"We've killed them dead, sir," Ishida said.

"That we did, Guns." Steele sucked in a deep breath, steadying himself. It wasn't over yet—not by a long shot. The frigate was still out there, closing the gap and poised to enter engagement range. The battle hadn't been won yet.

"Guns," Steele said sharply. "How's that reload coming on the missiles?"

"Just about ready, sir," Ishida replied, her speech still slurred from her injuries. Blood streaked her cheek, running down her neck and onto her chest. Her hands were trembling almost violently. The rag she clutched was now thick with blood. "But she's too far out for the Mark Fours. Only the long lances will reach."

"I know," Steele said, nodding. "They saw what we just did to *Starfish*. Let's make the TOT attack look convincing. Fire when ready."

"Firing," Ishida said. "Fourteen good launches. The rest are hung up."

The second volley of missiles streaked outward. The weapons shot straight before angling sharply to join the first wave of long lances, which had been burning at a slower rate. The long lances immediately ramped up their speed as the coordinated salvo came together, aiming and converging on the frigate now angling toward *Ranger* and inching toward her own engagement range.

"Four minutes to target," Ishida reported.

Steele glanced at Chase, who was watching the display with an intensity that matched his own. "After what we just did to *Starfish*, I'm hoping her captain is reevaluating his life choices about now."

Chase smirked, though her expression carried a hint of exhaustion. "He should be. Since they started this fight, we've been a wrecking crew for the LDF."

Steele allowed himself a low, grim chuckle. "We have been, haven't we?"

"Four enemy combatants and an entire planetary defense grid gone," Chase said, leaning slightly forward at her station. "Not bad for a single destroyer."

"Not bad at all," Steele agreed.

Ranger might be the hammer that struck, but he was the one who wielded it.

Steele glanced over at Chase and frowned, pointing at her arm. "You're bleeding."

She followed his gaze, clearly noticing for the first time the tear in her sleeve and the ragged line of blood seeping down her forearm. "Huh... I didn't even feel it." She probed the wound lightly with her fingers, her expression calm, almost detached. "Looks like a minor laceration. Nothing to worry about. I'll patch it up later."

Steele studied her for a moment, then gave a short nod. "Don't let it wait too long."

The hatch hissed open, drawing Steele's attention. Three marines entered, one carrying a collapsible stretcher. Without hesitation, they moved to Quinn's side, where Miller was still kneeling. Quinn's quiet groans filled the otherwise tense air, her burned face contorted in pure pain.

Steele turned his focus back to the plot, watching intently as the missiles streaked toward the LDF frigate. He briefly considered ordering a course change for *Ranger*, his mind racing through the calculations... but any shift in trajectory would only save them a fraction of time in the engagement window, and *Ranger* was already picking up real steam now. The gravitic drive pulsed through the deck, a subtle but reassuring vibration. No matter what he did, the frigate would still manage to get one volley off on him.

"42g and climbing," Hale reported, his voice steady.

"Two minutes, twenty seconds," Ishida added calmly, her focus locked on her station.

Steele met Chase's gaze, both of them sharing an unspoken understanding. The balance of survival hung by a thread. *Ranger* did not have much left, and in her current state, a single hit could easily disable them. She gave him a slight nod, her composure as steady as his.

"Shields are coming back online," Tancrest reported from the EW station. "They'll be at twenty percent, maybe less, but it's better than nothing."

"That's good news," Steele replied, his voice steady even as his thoughts churned. He caught movement behind him as the bridge hatch slid open with a soft hiss. Steele turned and saw the marines entering the lift, carrying Quinn carefully on the stretcher. Zeldin followed close behind, his injured arm cradled by the other.

Miller remained, his attention fixed on the HTD at the front of the bridge. His face was grim, his usual stoicism replaced with a quiet intensity. The marines exited, the hatch sealing behind them.

Steele turned back to the plot. *Ranger* had been battered, her systems straining to keep up, but it was the human cost that gnawed at him. The reports flashing on the status board painted a grim picture as to the damage she'd suffered—hull breaches, offline systems, and more than a few red tags.

Thinking back to his earlier conversation with Voss... After all this, a full reskin would be the least of *Ranger*'s issues when they returned. There would be names to account for, lives to grieve. He forced himself to push the thought aside. There would be time for mourning later, but for now, the survival of those still living was all that mattered.

"She's braking!" Ishida's voice cracked with excitement. "The frigate is braking hard and turning away. She's disengaging, sir! There's no way she's going to catch us now, let alone enter engagement range."

The bridge erupted in a mix of cheers and relieved exclamations. The tension that had gripped the crew broke like a wave, and for a moment, Steele allowed himself to share in their elation. He let out a heavy breath, feeling the weight on his shoulders ease as he sagged slightly into his chair. They had done it—they would live to fight another day.

His eyes returned to the HTD, where *Ranger*'s final volley of missiles still streaked toward the retreating frigate. Though the ship had turned away, the engagement wasn't quite over, not from his perspective.

As he watched, the older missiles in the volley began to falter, their drives cutting off as reactors burned out. Their warp bubbles destabilized, leaving them to tear apart under the relentless strain of their high-speed trajectory and sudden temporal irregularities caused by the failure of the bubble. One after another, they disappeared from the plot, their fiery ends marked by faint ripples of energy.

But the long lances... they held steady and continued onward doggedly to the target.

"PDS fire detected," Ishida reported, her tone more measured now, but still charged with focus.

The frigate's PDS lit up on the plot, energy bursts and kinetic rounds lancing out toward the incoming ordnance. Steele leaned forward, his gaze fixed. One by one, the enemy's defenses picked his missiles off. Flashes marked the destruction of each as they closed the gap—until only one remained.

The HTD flashed brilliantly.

"One got through," Ishida said. "One good hit!"

On the plot, the surviving missile struck home, detonating against the frigate's shields. A pulse of light briefly flared, followed by ripples of energy across the frigate's defensive barrier. The shield didn't collapse, but the hit was undeniable, and it had to have damaged that ship.

Steele allowed himself a grim smile, his gaze still on the plot. "A parting gift. Something to remember us by."

Steele closed his eyes for a moment and breathed out, letting the tension of the battle go with it. He felt wrung out, like an old dishrag that had been twisted far too many times. There may be hard questions from the admiralty concerning his actions in Illidran, but Steele understood without a doubt he had proven himself in battle, along with his right to command *Ranger*. Whatever happened later, he was personally satisfied with his actions. He would hold his head high, for he had done his duty. He opened his eyes and lifted his gaze.

"Helm," he said, his voice steadier than he felt. "How long until we reach the Fringe?"

Hale glanced at his console, hesitating briefly as he calculated. "Approximately fifty-nine hours and twenty-two minutes, sir."

"Very good." Steele shifted his focus to his executive officer. "Chase, go get that arm looked at. I'll hold down the fort and start picking up the pieces here. I want you back as soon as Yates certifies you are good to return to duty. We have a lot to do to get *Ranger* shipshape before we jump from this system and enter Slipstream space."

"Yes, sir," Chase replied. She unhooked herself from the emergency restraints with a wince, her injured arm cradled protectively at her side. It was clear the wound was worse than she'd let on. Rising, she gave him a curt nod before making her way to the lift.

Steele's attention turned next to Ishida. "That goes for you too, Guns. Get yourself patched up."

Ishida gave a weary but affirmative nod. "Yes, sir."

As Chase stepped into the lift with Ishida, Steele scanned the bridge, his gaze sweeping over the remaining crew. "Is anyone else injured? Check yourselves. Do it now."

A moment of silence followed as everyone quickly assessed their condition. No one spoke up.

"Good," Steele said, turning toward Calder. "Is the transmitter array functional?"

Calder tapped her controls, her brow furrowed as she reviewed the system status. After a few moments, she gave a sharp nod. "It's operational, sir."

"Open a transmission, broadband," Steele ordered. "Put me on. I have something to say to the entire Illidran Star System."

"Aye, sir," Calder said. A moment later, she turned toward him. "You're live, Captain."

Steele drew in a steadying breath, then leaned forward, his voice ringing out across the comms with a deliberate, unyielding tone.

"This is Captain Steele of the UNS *Ranger*, broadcasting to the Valkorian Hegemony in-system, the LDF, and any other traitorous bastards listening." He paused for effect, letting the weight of his words settle before continuing. "We, the Union, will be back."

A LETTER FROM MARC

I want to say a huge thank you for choosing to read *Forged in Battle*. If you did enjoy it, and want to keep up to date with all my latest releases, just sign up at the following link. Your email address will never be shared and you can unsubscribe at any time.

www.secondskybooks.com/marc-alan-edelheit

I hope you loved *Forged in Battle* and if you did I would be very grateful if you could write a review. Reviews keep me motivated and help to drive sales. I make a point to read each and every one, so please continue to post them.

Again, I hope you enjoy this book and would like to offer a sincere thank you for your purchase and support.

Best regards,

Marc Alan Edelheit

KEEP IN TOUCH WITH MARC

www.maenovels.com

facebook.com/MAENovels

x.com/MarcEdelheit

instagram.com/marcedelheitauthor

amazon.com/stores/Marc-Alan-Edelheit/author/B00WN-MAX2S

patreon.com/marcalanedelheit

APPENDIX

Please find some additional information on the universe and *Ranger*.

Note: Intra-System Travel

Note to the Reader:

The following is a detailed explanation of both intra-star-system and interstellar travel, including how speed and acceleration function and are measured in this universe. If you enjoy exploring the mechanics of futuristic travel and the science behind it, feel free to dive in.

The Gravitic or Gravity Drive

The gravity drive is an advanced propulsion system that moves a starship through space by generating a stable gravitational field around it. This field creates a warp bubble—a localized area of stable space-time—that allows the ship to carry a portion of space and time with it. This technique enables the ship to travel at high speeds without experiencing relativistic effects, such as time dilation. By manipulating the properties of the gravitational field, the gravity drive maintains a set speed rather than accelerating indefinitely, redefining "1g" in this context as a specific speed rather than a measure of gravitational acceleration.

How the Gravity Drive Works

In this context "1g" is a set speed, specifically **2.24 km/s**. Unlike traditional acceleration, where "1g" refers to an increasing force, here it represents a fixed speed. The gravity drive can hold this set speed, scaling up through 2g, 3g, and so on, with each "g" increment marking a consistent increase in velocity.

To reach "1g speed" (or "cruising speed"), the gravity drive must create a stable warp bubble around the ship, insulating it from the relativistic effects that would otherwise distort time and space at high velocities. This bubble effectively isolates the ship's internal space-time, allowing the crew to experience time at a normal rate. This safeguard enables high-speed travel without experiencing the effects of time dilation.

Calculating Distance Traveled at Constant Speed

If we treat "1g speed" as a set rate, calculating the distance traveled becomes straightforward. At a constant speed:

$$\text{distance (d)} = \text{velocity (v)} \times \text{time (t)}$$

where:

d is the distance traveled

v is the velocity, determined by the "g" setting of the gravity drive, and

t is the time in seconds

For example, at "1g speed" over the course of one day (86,400 seconds), the ship would travel:

$$d = v \times 86{,}400 = 2.24 \text{ km/s} \times 86{,}400 = 193{,}536 \text{ km}$$

As the "g" settings increase, the distance covered increases proportionally. For instance, at 10g, the ship would cover ten times the distance in the same period.

Why Travel above 55g Is Inadvisable

Ranger can reach speeds up to 55g, which represents its maximum warp bubble stability threshold. Beyond 55g, the gravitational field required to maintain the drive becomes so intense that the warp bubble risks destabilization. This instability poses significant hazards, including uneven temporal effects within the bubble, as well as potential physical harm to the ship and crew. If the bubble were to destabilize, the ship would be exposed to relativistic time dilation and extreme forces, making speeds above 55g highly dangerous.

In summary, the gravity drive allows *Ranger* to traverse space at controlled, high-speed intervals defined by "g" settings. The warp bubble provides protection from relativistic travel complications, though the technology requires careful management at higher speeds. The 55g limit serves as a practical safety measure, balancing speed and stability.

Speed Table for Gravity Drive Settings

Speed (km/s)

1g

2.24 km/s

2g

4.48 km/s

3g

6.72 km/s

4g

8.96 km/s

5g

11.2 km/s

10g

22.4 km/s

15g

33.6 km/s

20g

44.8 km/s

25g

56.0 km/s

30g

67.2 km/s

35g

78.4 km/s

40g

89.6 km/s

45g

100.8 km/s

50g

110 km/s

55g

123.2 km/s

Light Speed and the Gravity Drive

To understand the impracticality of achieving light speed with the gravity drive, consider that the speed of light is approximately 299,792 km/s. With 1g equal to 2.24 km/s, reaching light speed would require approximately:

$$\text{gs for light speed} = 299{,}792 \text{ km/s} \div 2.24 \text{ km/s} \approx 133{,}836g$$

This calculation demonstrates why traveling at light speed far exceeds the gravity drive's 55g stability threshold, making such travel impractical with current technology.

Example Calculation: How Long Would It Take to Travel from Earth to Mars at 55g?

To calculate the time it would take to travel from Earth to Mars at the maximum speed of 55g, we use the average distance and the given speed.

1. **Determine the Distance from Earth to Mars**
2. The average Earth–Mars distance is approximately 225 million kilometers (225,000,000 km).
3. **Calculate Speed at 55g**
4. Given that 1g equals 2.24 km/s, then:

$$55g = 55 \times 2.24 \text{ km/s} = 123.2 \text{ km/s}$$

5. **Calculate Travel Time**

$$\text{time} = \text{distance} \div \text{speed} = 225{,}000{,}000 \text{ km} \div 123.2 \text{ km/s} \approx$$
$$1{,}826{,}298.7 \text{ seconds}$$

6. **Convert Time to Days**

$$\text{time in days} = 86{,}400\,1{,}826{,}049 \approx 21.1 \text{ days}$$

Answer:

At a speed of 55g (or 123.2 km/s), it would take approximately 21 days to travel from Earth's high orbit to Mars's high orbit when distance between the planets is at its average.

Light Speed Comparison

For reference, light takes about 12.5 minutes to travel the average distance from Earth to Mars (225 million kilometers):

1. **Calculate Light Travel Time**

$$\text{time} = \text{Distance} \div \text{Speed} = 225{,}000{,}000 \text{ km} \div 299{,}792 \text{ km/s} \approx 750 \text{ seconds}$$

2. **Convert to Time to Minutes**

$$\text{time in minutes} = 750 \div 60 = 12.5 \text{ minutes}$$

Answer:

It takes light approximately 12.5 minutes to travel the average distance from Earth to Mars, highlighting the significant difference between even the highest gravity drive settings and light-speed travel.

Interstellar Travel: Explanation of the Jump Drive, Fringe Zone, and Slipstream Travel

The jump drive is humanity's primary means of interstellar travel, enabling ships to traverse the immense distances between star systems far faster than any conventional propulsion system. It functions by transitioning a ship into Slipstream, an alternate dimension of space-time that allows travel at speeds vastly exceeding those achievable by the gravitic drive. Here's how it works:

How the Jump Drive Works

The jump drive leverages the physics of Slipstream, a higher-dimensional layer of reality where distances between points in normal space are compressed. To enter Slipstream, a ship must generate:

1. **A Warp Bubble**: This protects the vessel and its occupants from the relativistic effects of high-speed travel. The warp bubble carries a portion of normal space-time with it, ensuring time dilation and other relativistic phenomena are neutralized.
2. **A Transition Pulse**: Using the jump drive, the ship emits a high-energy pulse that tears a localized rift between normal space and Slipstream. This requires escaping the star system's gravity well (explained below).
3. **Slipstream Navigation**: Once in Slipstream, the ship uses advanced navigation systems to steer through this compressed dimension of space-time, avoiding disturbances or anomalies that could destabilize the journey.

The Fringe Zone

Before initiating a jump, a ship must reach the **Fringe Zone**— a location well outside the significant gravitational influence of any star or planet. Gravitational fields disrupt the formation of the Slipstream transition, so ships typically travel at high speeds using their gravitic drives to reach this zone. Once there, the ship transitions into Slipstream.

Slipstream Travel and Speed

While in Slipstream, ships travel far faster than light relative to normal space. However, movement in Slipstream still takes time because the compression of space-time is not infinite. The jump drive operates at a speed that is roughly **2,760 times faster than the gravity drive operating at 55g**.

For reference:

The gravity drive at 55g achieves a speed of **123.2 km/s** (or **0.000411 AU/hour**).

In Slipstream, the jump drive achieves **548 AU/hour**.

This enhanced Slipstream speed ensures practical interstellar travel times. For example:

Travel Example: Sol to Alpha Centauri

The distance between Sol and Alpha Centauri is approximately **4.37 light years**, or **276,364 AU**.

To calculate the travel time:

Determine the Slipstream Speed

speed = 548 AU/hour

Calculate Travel Time

time = distance ÷ speed = 276,364 AU ÷ 548 AU/hour ≈ 504 hours

Convert Time to Days

time in days = 504 ÷ 24 ≈ 21 days

Result: Using Slipstream travel, the journey from Sol to Alpha Centauri takes **approximately 21 days**.

Limitations and Dangers

1. **Gravitational Interference**: Ships cannot jump within a star system due to the destabilizing effects of gravity on Slipstream transitions.
2. **Slipstream Anomalies**: This alternate dimension is not uniform; turbulence and anomalies can increase travel time or damage a ship.
3. **Energy Demands**: Transitioning into Slipstream requires enormous energy. Overusing the jump drive can strain a ship's systems.

Why the Jump Drive Matters

The jump drive revolutionized interstellar travel by enabling humanity to traverse cosmic distances in weeks rather than years. Though it isn't instantaneous, the ability to move between star systems at **548 AU/hour** makes it indispensable for trade, exploration, and warfare. Together with the Fringe Zone and Slipstream's unique mechanics, the jump drive ensures humanity can explore, trade, and defend across the galaxy.

The Union of Free Stars

Executive Title: Chancellor. As the head of state and commander-in-chief of the military, the prime executor has both political and military authority.

With the **Union of Free Stars** governed by the chancellor, the executive has the power to veto legislation, direct foreign policy, and oversee military operations, while the Assembly retains influence over domestic matters and resource allocation. This system creates a balance between centralized leadership and regional autonomy.

The twelve star systems within the **Union of Free Stars**:

1. **Auraxis System**
   - **Capital: Navaar**
   - A hub of commerce and diplomacy, Navaar is known for its sprawling trade stations and the grand central plaza, where the chancellor's palace is located.
2. **Veridion System**
   - **Capital: Elysara**
   - Famous for its lush, terraformed world and advanced agricultural production, Elysara serves as a primary food supplier for the Union.
3. **Talassa System**
   - **Capital: Aventis**
   - A mining and industrial center, Aventis is built into the cliffs of a high-gravity planet rich in valuable minerals.
4. **Myridorn System**
   - **Capital: Kalendra**

- A strategic military hub, Kalendra is heavily fortified and serves as the main base for the Union's fleet operations.
5. **Nyvera System**
   - **Capital: Thalium**
   - Known for its shipyards, Thalium is where the Union's starships are constructed and repaired. The system has a strong focus on technological innovation.
6. **Veldros System**
   - **Capital: Galenia**
   - A cultural center, Galenia is famed for its art, music, and higher education institutions, making it a haven for artists and intellectuals.
7. **Drakos System**
   - **Capital: Damarus**
   - A harsh, rugged system with a reputation for producing the Union's toughest soldiers, Damarus is located on a planet known for its extreme environments.
8. **Seren System**
   - **Capital: Islaire**
   - A system with beautiful natural landscapes and tourist destinations, Islaire is considered a retreat for the wealthy and influential.
9. **Kessar System**
   - **Capital: Nemoris**
   - Home to advanced research and development facilities, Nemoris is where the Union's most ambitious scientific projects take place.
10. **Rethan System**
    - **Capital: Prythos**
    - A frontier system known for exploration and

settlement efforts, Prythos attracts pioneers and those seeking new opportunities.

11. **Lantheon System**
    - **Capital: Sevastia**
    - Specializes in bioengineering and medical research. Sevastia is famous for its cutting-edge hospitals and healing facilities.

12. **Zypheron System**
    - **Capital: Vestra Prime**
    - Known for its strategic position near the border of hostile territories, Vestra Prime serves as a key defense outpost.

The Protectorate

Protectorate Star Systems

1. **Calethar System**
   - **Capital: Yarith**
   - Known for its industrial capabilities, Calethar produces valuable resources for the Union's military. It has a strong Union presence, with outposts and patrols to deter any external threats.
2. **Illidran System**
   - **Capital: Torvell**
   - A strategically significant system due to its proximity to trade routes. Torvell is a fortified city on a desert planet, serving as a forward defense point and logistical hub for Union forces.
3. **Vossir System**
   - **Capital: Erevale**
   - Features lush, habitable worlds that were once thriving trade centers for the previous nation. Erevale has become an administrative center where the Union governs Protectorate affairs.
4. **Brelak System**
   - **Capital: Fethis**
   - A frontier system with a rugged population of settlers and mercenaries. Fethis is on a cold, mountainous world, which the Union uses as a training ground for special operations forces.

Valkorian Hegemony

Valkorian Hegemony

- The Valkorian Hegemony is an expansionist, militaristic state known for its strict hierarchy and autocratic rule. The war with the Union occurred when the Hegemony attempted to annex border territories, sparking a conflict that resulted in the Union's capture of the four systems. The Hegemony still considers the Protectorate as occupied territory and remains a significant threat, constantly probing the border for weaknesses.
- The Protectorate serves as a crucial buffer zone for the Union, balancing the interests of keeping the Valkorian Hegemony at bay while ensuring the local systems remain relatively autonomous to avoid inciting unrest.

UNS *Ranger*

Ship Overview:

- **Class:** Ranger Class Destroyer
- **Length:** 185 meters
- **Crew Complement:** Fifty-four personnel
- **Operational Range:** Six months without resupply
- **Max Speed:** 55g
- **Jump Capability:** Equipped with a Slipstream jump drive, requiring a twenty-four-hour cooldown period between jumps

Key Systems and Capabilities:

1. **Stealth Capabilities:**
   - **Adaptive Hull Coating:** *Ranger*'s exterior features a dynamic, adaptive coating that can alter its surface temperature and light reflection properties to blend in with background radiation, making it hard to detect using thermal or optical sensors.
   - **Gravitic Nullifier:** Uses a low-level gravitic field to reduce the ship's gravitational signature, making it difficult for enemy sensors to lock onto.
   - **Emission Masking:** The ship is capable of minimizing its heat signature and radio emissions by redirecting waste heat into specialized sinks.
2. **Weapon Systems:**
   - **Maser Batteries:** High-energy microwave beams used to target enemy ships and fighters.

Ranger has four primary maser turrets, two mounted dorsally and two ventrally, with a 360-degree firing arc.

- ○ **Missile Launchers:** Two ship-to-ship missile pods capable of launching a variety of ordnance, including anti-ship warheads, EMP payloads, and decoys. Each pod has ten tubes, with a reload time of forty-five seconds between volleys.
- ○ **Torpedo Tubes:** Two forward-facing tubes designed for long-range engagements and penetration of hardened targets. Torpedoes can be equipped with fusion warheads, kinetic impactors, or nanite payloads for specific mission objectives.
- ○ **Orbital Darts:** Specialized kinetic projectiles used for planetary bombardment. Can be deployed from orbit to target surface installations with extreme precision. *Ranger* carries twenty orbital darts, each with an adjustable payload.

3. **Defensive Systems:**
   - ○ **Point-Defense Systems:** Includes rapid-fire maser turrets and autocannons for intercepting incoming missiles, torpedoes, and fighters. The ship can maintain 360-degree coverage through automated tracking software.
   - ○ **Electronic Warfare Suite:** Capable of jamming enemy sensors, spoofing targeting systems, and deploying decoy drones to mislead attackers. The suite has an effective range of 50,000 kilometers.
   - ○ **Defensive Screens:** Utilizes localized gravitic distortion fields to deflect physical

projectiles and lessen the impact of energy weapons. The screens can absorb up to sixty percent of a direct energy hit. This is also dependent upon ship velocity at the time of the impact.

- ○ **Energy Shielding:** A high-energy barrier designed to absorb directed energy attacks and minor collisions. It requires significant power, making it more effective in short bursts rather than continuous use.

4. **Support Systems:**
   - ○ **Slipstream Jump Drive:** The jump drive allows travel through the Slipstream, with a jump cooldown of twenty-four hours to dissipate built-up energy. Navigational accuracy is crucial to avoid arriving too close to massive objects.
   - ○ **Automated Damage Control:** The ship's nanite-based repair systems can seal hull breaches and restore critical systems, allowing *Ranger* to remain operational even after sustaining significant damage. This process is managed by the ship's construct (limited artificial intelligence).
   - ○ **Life Support:** *Ranger*'s life support is rated for eighty-five personnel in emergency situations. Environmental control systems can maintain habitable conditions in all compartments even if damaged.

Ranger is a sleek and formidable Destroyer Class starship, designed for both combat and stealth operations. Its exterior appearance reflects its cutting-edge technology and multi-role capabilities, combining aggressive lines with advanced stealth features.

Exterior Description:

- **Overall Shape:** *Ranger* has a narrow, elongated hull, with a length of about 185 meters. Her silhouette is sleek and angular, optimized for speed and maneuverability. The ship's design features a low profile, minimizing its radar/sensor cross-section to enhance stealth capabilities.
- **Hull Plating:** The hull is coated with adaptive stealth plating, which has a matte black finish with subtle, dark gray accents. The plating is designed to absorb sensor scans and distort light, making the ship difficult to detect. The surface is slightly textured, with overlapping armor plates that form a scaled appearance, providing both protection and stealth.
- **Bridge and Command Section:** The bridge module is located near the forward upper section of the ship, integrated into the hull to avoid protruding surfaces.
- **Engine Configuration:** *Ranger* has four main engine thrusters at the rear, arranged in a rectangular pattern. These engines emit a deep blue glow when the gravitic drive is engaged. The thrusters are recessed, partially concealed within the hull to reduce the ship's thermal signature. Smaller propellant-driven maneuvering thrusters are placed along the sides and underside, enabling rapid changes in direction.
- **Weapon Systems:**

- The primary maser batteries are located along the spinal axis, integrated into the hull with retractable ports that conceal them when not in use.
- Missile and torpedo launcher pods are embedded in the sides of the hull, covered by armored hatches that open during deployment.
- Point-defense turrets are positioned in strategic locations around the ship, with smaller, retractable guns emerging from panels in the hull. These turrets are mounted on elevated platforms that can rotate 360 degrees for maximum coverage.
- Orbital dart launchers, used for planetary bombardment, are installed along the underside of the ship. These launchers are covered by stealth panels when not in use.

- **Sensor and Electronic Warfare Arrays:** The ship's sensor arrays are mostly internalized, with only minimal external features, such as retractable antennae and small protruding nodes that can extend for high-sensitivity scans. The electronic warfare systems are concealed behind stealth panels.
- **Defensive Systems:** *Ranger* features a combination of energy shielding and defensive screens, which shimmer faintly when active, creating a subtle glow along the hull's edges. The adaptive stealth plating can also slightly alter its surface color to blend with stellar backgrounds or appear invisible against the blackness of space.
- **Hull Markings:** *Ranger* has minimal exterior markings, consistent with its stealth profile. The ship's name and designation (UNS *Ranger*) are

inscribed in a muted gray font near the forward section of the hull, barely visible except at close range. Small indicator lights along the hull can activate during docking or emergency situations, otherwise remaining off.

Additional Features:

- **Hangar Bay:** The hangar entrance is located on the ventral side, toward the rear. The hatches are well-armored and fit seamlessly into the hull when closed, maintaining the ship's smooth appearance.
- **Armor Paneling:** The outer hull is lined with advanced composite armor, including sections with reactive plating that can shift to absorb impact, providing increased resistance to direct hits.

Illidran Star System

Star: Illidra Prime

- **Type:** G-type main-sequence star (yellow dwarf) nearing the end of its life
- **Age:** Ten billion years
- **Description: Illidra Prime** is an old and failing star that has begun to exhibit signs of instability. The star's energy output has become erratic, with a gradual dimming and cooling over centuries. This instability affects the entire system, creating a pressing need for the **Solar Rejuvenation Initiative**—an ambitious project involving **energy injectors**, **gravitic stabilizers**, and **solar mirrors** designed to restore the star's stability and reignite consistent fusion reactions.

Planets, Moons, and Habitats:

1. Illidra I (Forgeheart)

- **Type:** Rocky planet (inner system)
- **Distance from Illidra Prime:** 0.4 AU
- **Surface Conditions:** Extreme temperature fluctuations, with cycles of intense heat during solar flare-ups and cooler periods when Illidra Prime dims. The atmosphere is thin, with minimal shielding against solar radiation, requiring most activities to occur underground or in heavily shielded environments.
- **Moons:** None

- **Habitats:** Underground colonies and orbital mining platforms.
- **Points of Interest:**
  - **Stellar Shield Array:** A network of solar shields in orbit to protect mining operations from solar radiation spikes.
  - **Magma Foundry Station:** Processes metals and refractory elements mined from the planet, playing a key role in producing materials for the Solar Rejuvenation Initiative.
- **Industry:** Heavy mining and metal refining, providing materials essential for starship construction and the rejuvenation project.

2. Illidra II (Gildarra)

- **Type:** Terrestrial planet (habitable zone)
- **Distance from Illidra Prime:** 1 AU
- **Surface Conditions:** Cooler temperatures and changing weather patterns due to the failing star. Climate control stations and thermal energy collectors are widely used to stabilize local environments, especially for agriculture.
- **Moons:** Three
  - **Thalmar:** The largest moon, with agricultural colonies and orbital solar reflectors to redirect sunlight onto Gildarra.
  - **Voss:** Hosts mining and processing facilities for fusion materials.
  - **Irith:** Features luxury resorts and research centers focused on biomedical technology.
- **Habitats:** A mix of surface cities, floating ocean platforms, and orbital habitats.
- **Points of Interest:**

- ○ **Torvell (Capital City):** The system's administrative hub and the headquarters for the Solar Rejuvenation Initiative.
  - ○ **Azure Expanse Platform:** A major oceanic research and agricultural facility, specializing in aquaculture and solar energy collection.
- **Industry:** Agriculture, tourism, biomedicine, and solar energy collection. Gildarra is a critical food supplier for the Illidran System and the Union.

3. Illidra III (Silicara)

- **Type:** Rocky planet (outer system)
- **Distance from Illidra Prime:** 2.5 AU
- **Surface Conditions:** Cold and arid, with a silicon-rich crust and a thin atmosphere. The planet experiences extreme temperature variations due to its distance from the cooling star.
- **Moons:** Five
  - ○ **Obra:** The largest moon, with automated manufacturing facilities for gravitic engineering components.
  - ○ **Shalor:** A mining hub for rare minerals and precious metals.
  - ○ **Tannis, Quen, Idris:** Smaller moons with scientific outposts and storage facilities.
- **Habitats:** Mainly subsurface industrial complexes and orbital fabrication platforms.
- **Points of Interest:**
  - ○ **Obra Automated Manufactorum:** Produces robotics and components for the solar rejuvenation infrastructure.
  - ○ **Silicara Orbital Fabricator:**

Manufactures precision materials for high-tech applications.

- **Industry:** Focused on manufacturing, mining, and gravitic technology for the system's infrastructure needs.

4. Asteroid Belts

- **Inner Belt (the Shattered Reach):** Located between 3 AU and 4 AU, the belt is rich in metallic asteroids, with dense clusters of iron, nickel, and platinum.
  - **Points of Interest:**
    - **Freehold Station:** A large industrial habitat that serves as a hub for independent miners and ore processing.
    - **Vaskin Refinery:** Processes raw asteroid materials into refined metals for use throughout the system.
    - **The Exclusion Zone:** Known colloquially as *the Graveyard*, the Exclusion Zone is a somber and deadly section of the Reach. It is a dense cluster of debris, wreckage, and derelict ships—the remains of one of the last and bloodiest battles of the great war. The zone is steeped in electromagnetic interference, making navigation and sensor operations highly unreliable. Many ships avoid the area altogether due to the lingering radiation and occasional gravitational anomalies caused by wrecked capital ships and other debris. However, it remains a focal point of intrigue, rumored to conceal forgotten

technologies and dangerous secrets from the war.

- **Illegal Habitats and Black Sites**
- Hidden within the asteroids are unregistered habitats and covert stations. These range from isolated miners seeking anonymity to off-the-books facilities conducting illicit operations, such as smuggling or experimental research.

- **Outer Belt (the Fringe):** Positioned between 8 AU and 10 AU, the belt contains ice-rich bodies and volatile materials, suitable for water and fusion fuel extraction.
  - **Points of Interest:**
    - **Rimehold Station:** A refueling and water extraction outpost supplying the system's fusion reactors.
    - **The Drift:** A network of asteroid-based habitats for mining crews and transient workers.

5. Illidra IV (Glaciera)

- **Type:** Ice giant
- **Distance from Illidra Prime:** 6 AU
- **Surface Conditions:** A frozen atmosphere dominated by methane, ammonia, and water vapor, with temperatures reaching extremely low levels.
- **Moons:** Twelve
  - **Crython:** The largest moon, featuring subsurface oceans that are mined for helium-3 and deuterium.
  - **Nevalis:** Hosts laboratories focused on cryogenic research and extremophile life.

- **Habitats:** Orbiting fuel-processing stations and moon-based mining outposts.
- **Points of Interest:**
  - **Glaciera Fuel Refinery:** A major helium-3 processing facility for fusion reactors across the system.
  - **Nevalis Cryo-Laboratories:** Conducts research on cryogenic materials and advanced life support technologies.
- **Industry:** Focuses on fusion fuel production, cryogenic research, and deep-space exploration support.

6. Illidra V (Tenebris)

- **Type:** Dwarf planet
- **Distance from Illidra Prime:** 15 AU
- **Surface Conditions:** Dark, cold, and rocky, with extensive methane and nitrogen ice deposits. Receives very little sunlight, even when Illidra Prime is more active.
- **Moons:** Three
  - **Umbra:** Features deep mining for exotic elements.
  - **Shade:** A research outpost dedicated to studying outer-system gravitational anomalies.
  - **Nyxis:** Home to a dark matter observatory.
- **Habitats:** Predominantly underground mining facilities on Umbra and orbiting research stations.
- **Points of Interest:**
  - **Umbra Deep Mining Station:** Extracts transuranic isotopes and exotic materials.
  - **Nyxis Observatory:** Monitors dark energy fluctuations and cosmic radiation.

- **Industry:** Centers on exotic material extraction, dark matter research, and advanced scientific exploration.

7. New Asteroid Belt: The Periphery

- **Location:** Positioned between 18 AU and 20 AU, resembling a Kuiper Belt-like region.
- **Composition:** Contains primarily icy bodies, comet-like objects, and a few metal-rich asteroids.
- **Points of Interest:**
  - **Vanguard Station:** A remote deep-space research and refueling outpost, also serving as an early warning station.
  - **Helios Extraction Facility:** Specializes in helium-3 harvesting from icy bodies, supplementing the system's fusion fuel.
  - **The Abyssal Field:** A region known for high cosmic radiation, used for radiation shielding tests and extremophile durability research.

System-Wide Infrastructure:

- **Solar Rejuvenation Network:** A comprehensive system of orbital energy injectors, gravitic stabilizers, and solar mirrors, aimed at reigniting consistent fusion in Illidra Prime.
- **Energy Redistribution Grid:** A network that transfers power from various energy collection points to support the solar rejuvenation efforts.
- **Outer System Defense Network:** An array of monitoring stations, defense platforms, and early warning systems located throughout the outer

reaches to protect against potential interstellar threats.

Key Industries:

1. **Solar Rejuvenation:** The primary industry, involving stellar engineering and gravitic manipulation.
2. **Fusion Fuel Production:** Located around Glaciera, the Fringe, and the Periphery, essential for the system's power needs.
3. **Dark Matter and Cryogenic Research:** Conducted on Tenebris, Glaciera, and in the Periphery.
4. **Mining and Manufacturing:** Provides raw materials and high-tech products to sustain the system and support the rejuvenation infrastructure.

ACKNOWLEDGMENTS

Writing *Forged in Battle* has been a labor of love and an absolute joy. It is my sincere hope that you love it as much as I do.

I want to take a moment to thank you for reading and for keeping me employed as a full-time writer. Your support means everything. For those of you who reach out to me on social media or by email, I simply cannot express how humbling it is to have my work so appreciated and loved. From the bottom of my heart—thank you.

I wish to thank my agent, Andrea Hurst, for her invaluable support and assistance.

I would also like to thank my beta readers, who suffered through several early drafts. My betas: Paul Klebaur, James Doak, David Cheever, Sheldon Levy, Walker Graham, Bill Schnippert, Jimmy McAfee, Joel M. Rainey, Ed Speight, James H. Bjorum, Marshall Clowers, Brian Thomas, Adrian Lee, Lance Dahl, Dragos Ramniceanu, Steven Dye, Kieran Maisonet, Michael Brown, Dominick Maino, Nathan Hildebrand, Tom Moore, Steve Koratsky. I would also like to take a moment to thank my loving wife, who sacrificed many an evening and weekend to allow me to work on my writing.

A special thanks to my amazing editor at Second Sky, Jack Renninson, whose keen eye and insight helped shape this book into what it is. Your guidance, support, and dedication to bringing quality stories to life is truly appreciated.

Editing Assistance by: Hannah Streetman, Audrey Mackaman, Brandon Purcell

Cover Art and Design by: Tom Edwards

Agented by: Andrea Hurst & Associates, LLC

Marketing
Alex Crow
Melanie Price
Occy Carr
Cíara Rosney
Martyna Młynarska

Operations and distribution
Marina Valles
Stephanie Straub
Joe Morris

Production
Hannah Snetsinger
Mandy Kullar
Ria Clare
Nadia Michael

Publicity
Kim Nash
Noelle Holten
Jess Readett
Sarah Hardy

Rights and contracts
Peta Nightingale
Richard King
Saidah Graham